Praise for Karen Whiddon

"I love how this book is a sweet romance but also manages to be an action-packed story that…keeps you on the edge of your seat."
—*Aussie Bookworm* on *The Wolf Siren*

"A nice backstory and exciting plot make this a must-read. Whiddon's talent for pacing is apparent in the skill with which Lilly conquers her fear and learns to live again. The author's flair for character development is clear as Kane develops into a perfectly sexy hero."
—*RT Book Reviews* on *The Wolf Siren* (4.5 star review)

"*The Lost Wolf's Destiny* is action-packed with a lot of twists and turns that lead the reader on an amazing ride."
—*Fresh Fiction*

Praise for Linda Thomas-Sundstrom

"Linda Thomas-Sundstrom makes her Vampire Moons series constantly entertaining, and *Immortal Obsession* is a compelling romance with intriguing scenarios."
—*Cataromance*

"Linda Thomas-Sundstrom's well-written, action-packed novel will keep readers entertained from start to finish."
—*RT Book Reviews* on *Guardian of the Night*

"*Golden Vampire* will wrap you into a story that you will not want to put down."
—*Night Owl Reviews* (Top Pick)

Karen Whiddon started weaving fanciful tales for her younger brothers at the age of eleven. Amid the Catskill Mountains of New York, then the Rocky Mountains of Colorado, she fueled her imagination with the natural beauty that surrounded her. Karen now lives in north Texas, where she shares her life with her very own hero of a husband and three doting dogs. Also an entrepreneur, she divides her time between the business she started and writing. You can email Karen at KWhiddon1@aol.com or write to her at PO Box 820807, Fort Worth, TX 76182. Fans of her writing can also check out her website, karenwhiddon.com.

Karen Whiddon
and
Linda Thomas-Sundstrom

SHADES
OF THE WOLF

and

WOLF BORN

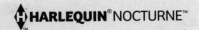
HARLEQUIN® NOCTURNE™

Recycling programs for this product may not exist in your area.

ISBN-13: 978-0-373-60124-0

Shades of the Wolf and Wolf Born

Copyright © 2015 by Harlequin Books S.A.

The publisher acknowledges the copyright holders of the individual works as follows:

Shades of the Wolf
Copyright © 2015 by Karen Whiddon

Wolf Born
Copyright © 2015 by Linda Thomas-Sundstrom

Printed in U.S.A.

HARLEQUIN®
www.Harlequin.com

CONTENTS

SHADES OF THE WOLF

Karen Whiddon

Once again, to my husband. I can never thank him enough for loving me and supporting me. He is a special man and I love him very much.

Chapter 1

The man appeared in her peripheral vision, just like all the others who had come before. A hazy shape, flickering into mist before solidifying somewhat. Her black cat, Leroy, hissed his usual back-arched warning. Anabel Lee clenched her teeth and ignored the apparition, willing the ghost's ethereal form to dissipate so she wouldn't have to look at him.

Or worse, hear him try to speak to her. Mentally, she cringed. The voices were what bothered her the most. Whispers and muffled laughter. Wisps of conversation drifting on the breeze.

And pleas for help. Almost always cries for help. She had come to realize ghosts never appeared unless they wanted something. For whatever reason, they all seemed to think she could give it to them. Instead she steeled herself and sent them away.

This wasn't the first time one had appeared inside her home either. They were prone to popping up in all kinds of places, everywhere. Some wailed; some screamed. Others simply glared at her with burning eyes, as if she could read whatever was left of their mind. And most asked—begged, actually. Until she ordered them gone. Doing so cut off the voices.

Since there seemed to be a method to her madness, she simply closed her eyes. "Go away," she ordered, speaking slowly and loud. "I don't want you here."

Having spoken, she counted silently to ten, quite confident that when she opened her eyes again the apparition would be gone. They always went, once she ordered them gone.

Only he wasn't. Instead it seemed he'd moved closer. Her eyes widened. Dimly, she registered he was—or had been—a beautiful man. Tall and broad-shouldered, with a narrow waist and capable, long-fingered hands. He wore his dark hair unfashionably long, which she also appreciated, since she too made a practice of skirting the edge of current style. This hair did not go with his camouflaged military fatigues and combat boots.

Leroy hissed again, then gave an indignant yowl and stalked away, his yellow cat's eyes flashing.

"What do you want?" she asked rudely, pretty sure she already knew the answer. And she got ready to strain to hear the whisper or brace herself for the shriek, since ghosts apparently couldn't speak in a normal tone.

"I need your help," he said, his deep voice strong and edged with velvet. Such a sexy voice, she felt the impact all the way to her toes.

Stunned, she stared at him. "I didn't expect that."

One corner of his well-shaped mouth quirked. Damned if she didn't feel a little electric tingle deep inside.

"What, that I'd need your assistance?"

"No, not that." She waved him away. "All the ghosts want some kind of help. But you're different. You can talk. Not whisper, but speak. That's unusual."

"Is it?" Appearing unconcerned, he shrugged. To her consternation, he appeared to be solidifying the longer she looked at him. Handsome, sexy and getting more real by the second. Maybe she finally *had* lost her mind.

"I've been sent back here for a reason," he continued. "And your energy is strong. It directed me to you."

This was new. Of course, she'd never gotten this far with a specter before. This ghost was different. For one thing, he was massive. And ruggedly handsome. His self-confidence was even sexy, making her feel something she hadn't since David's death. Things she definitely shouldn't be feeling.

Resolutely, Anabel ignored him. Eventually, he'd disappear. He had to. He had no reason to hang around haunting her. She'd brought her vegetables in from her garden for dinner. She planned to roast summer squash, zucchini, tomatoes and onions. Not only did she love the fresh taste, but the bright colors made eating feel like artwork. This, along with some quinoa, had become one of her favorite meals ever since she'd decided to give vegetarianism a try.

Which had given the townspeople of Leaning Tree even more to talk about. After all, who'd ever heard of a shape-shifter who didn't eat meat?

Anabel didn't care. At least that was what she told herself—ever since David had been killed and she'd lost her mind, she'd long ago stopped caring about what other people thought of her.

"Earth to Anabel." The ghost snapped his fingers. At her. And she could actually hear them. "Shutting me out won't make me go away."

Ignoring him should have worked. Sometimes she'd found she could actually *will* them away, as if she had magical power over ghosts or something. Closing her eyes, she wished him gone.

"Hello? I know you can hear me. This is really important. Otherwise I wouldn't have come."

Him again. Still here. Worse, he actually knew her name. None of the other ghosts had called her anything but *lady*, or *ma'am*, or even *Ms*.

"Fine." Sighing, she crossed her arms and faced him. "I'm listening. Go ahead and tell me what you want."

She expected him to immediately start listing his demands. If they followed along with the other spirits who'd visited her, they'd be along the lines of *find so-and-so, my wife, my mother, my father, and tell them I love them and that I'm at peace.* Which she absolutely refused to do. Mostly since she knew no one would believe her. She already had a reputation as a nut job anyway.

So she waited for him to begin his laundry list of demands before she could shoot him down.

Instead he cocked his head and studied her. Anabel realized she'd never seen eyes that hazel, in either a live man or a ghost. Especially a ghost.

"You miss him, don't you?" he asked, his deep voice kind. "Your husband, that is."

She started, only the slightest twitch, but she thought he noticed it anyway. "If you're here to tell me he's all right, that he's not in pain and that he's happy, don't."

Even though she tried to keep the misery out of her tone, she knew she'd failed. "After all," she continued, "if he really wanted me to know, he'd have told me himself."

"I'm sure he couldn't." Again the flash of a smile, far too radiant for an apparition. "It seems to be some kind of rule or something, prohibiting us from appearing to those who loved us the most."

Which made sense. Though it didn't lessen the hurt. "I see ghosts. Not everyone can do that. I would appreciate just a short visit, or even a message..." She broke off, squinting at him and not bothering to hide her suspicion. "And don't take that as a good excuse to hand me some syrupy fake message. I'll see right through you. David and I had our own form of code. He'd definitely use it to prove to me that any communication actually was from him."

As she wound down, she noticed how his mouth quirked upward in amusement. He had a ruggedness and vital power she found very attractive. Which felt not only weird—he was a ghost, after all—but entirely unwelcome.

"I don't have a message from anyone," he said, not sounding the slightest bit regretful. "I'm sorry."

"Don't be." Irritated, embarrassed and more than a little bit flustered, she waved his words away. "Just tell me what you want so I can get on with the rest of my day."

"What I want..." His expression stilled and grew serious. "I need you to help find my sister. Somehow she managed to reach out to me. She's in danger."

This was a new one. "But you're a...ghost. You should be able to find her yourself."

"I have tried." He sounded frustrated. "And all I can tell is she's in some dark, windowless place. Underground, maybe. No matter how long I search, her exact location is blocked. She's still alive, though her light is beginning to fade. She is running out of time. The man who has her will kill her soon."

Her heart skipped a beat. "The man who has her? Are you talking about a serial killer? Or just some sort of psycho?"

"I don't know." His lips thinned as his expression turned inward. "He's probably killed more than once, because when I'm around my sister, I can also feel the whispers of other lost souls."

A shiver snaked up her spine. This just kept getting stranger. Not only did a ghost too good-looking to be real show up, but now he was spouting stuff about serial killers? She really, really needed him to go away.

Crossing her arms, she studied him. His massive shoulders filled out army camouflage. Her stomach swooped. The combat uniform had been exactly what David was wearing when he was killed. Coincidence? She thought not.

Steeling herself, she took a deep breath. "I have to ask. Why me? I don't even know you. Did someone else, some other *ghost*, send you to me?"

"No." His quick answer crushed all her hopes. "Your energy drew me to you. I need someone with your power. Not only that, but you live in the same town as I used to. My sister still lives here." He frowned. "Don't you ever wonder why you can hear the voices of the dead?"

"Not really. Mostly I only hear whispers."

"You can hear me. And the energy you send out directs the spirits to you."

Pain stabbed her. "Funny thing, that. You're right. I do attract a lot of departed spirits. All of them want something from me. But the one voice I most want to hear has never come to me."

"Your husband, of course…" Gaze intense, he frowned. "Maybe I can help with that."

"I received word David was killed in Afghanistan eighteen months ago. I just knew he'd come to me, at least to say goodbye. But he never did."

His frown deepened. "I cannot appear physically to my sister, even though she's in danger."

"That's nonsense." The words burst from her, practically vibrating with hurt. "I hear all the time of people seeing the shade of someone close to them. I don't understand why…" Tears pricking at the backs of her eyes, she couldn't finish the sentence.

He dipped his chin, as if he understood. "All I can say is I'm sorry."

"So am I." Though for once, she'd been able to say David's name without her voice cracking. "It's been really tough. David and I were mates. That's why I just don't understand."

"Mates. Interesting. During my time on earth, I never had the privilege of meeting my mate."

"Not everyone does. I got lucky. And I don't think it's too much to ask that he contact me. Or, if there's a rule to prevent that, he could reach out to someone else and send a message to me." It dawned on her that was what all the other spirits she'd sent away had been trying to do and for all she knew, David might have had the same luck if he'd made the attempt.

"Sometimes, when a soul has suffered a traumatic injury, he is taken away and given positive, healing energy," the handsome ghost continued. "Time passes differently there. Your David may not even be aware eighteen months has passed since his death. For him, it may feel merely like minutes."

His words felt like a soothing salve poured on a festering wound. They helped, even if she didn't really understand the logic behind what he'd said. The connection between mates should have transcended both space and time.

This ghost simply didn't understand. She felt bad for him; she really did. And she felt worse for his poor sister. Being held prisoner in a dark place sounded like her worst nightmare come to life. Add in serial killer, and it went way beyond the realm of terrifying. So much so that she knew she didn't want to have anything to do with it.

Now to convince him of that. She swallowed hard, lifted her chin and boldly met his gaze.

"Your eyes are the color of burnished copper," he said.

Nonplussed, she completely lost her train of thought. "Uh. Thanks. I guess."

The quick flash of a devastating smile further derailed her. "You're welcome. And I should thank you, for agreeing to help."

That snapped her out of whatever twilight land she'd gone to. "That's just it. I haven't agreed to anything. Look, I understand that I can hear you. But I'm just one person, a widow who, quite frankly, isn't well regarded in this town. Serial killers scare the heck out of me too. So what do you think I can do to find your sister?"

"More than I can," he shot back, his smile vanishing. "You have a physical presence. You can talk to people and be heard. You can ignite a fire under law enforcement. And you are able to research and hunt down the clues that occasionally flash into my consciousness. Once you and I figure out who this man is, we can have him arrested."

Still, she considered. Lately, she'd made a career out of avoiding just about everyone in town. For all she knew, they'd laugh at her if she started asking questions about a missing girl.

"How did you die?" she asked, feeling as if she needed to know.

"In Afghanistan," he said, his voice curt. Clearly, he didn't like discussing his death. "Like your husband and a lot of others. For me, it was a suicide bomber at a roadside checkpoint."

A chill snaked over her. This ghost and David had both lost their lives in a similar fashion. It couldn't be a coincidence, even if she wasn't sure how she felt about that.

"I'll find your husband," he offered. "And try to bring him to you. If I can't, I'll bring back to you exactly what he'd like you to know. But time is of the essence. The longer Dena—my sister—is in that place, the weaker she becomes."

Again the image. A poor woman, curled up on the cold concrete floor, hoping to ward off blows—or worse. That could be any woman, even Anabel. She had to try to save her. Just like that, she decided.

"If I help you find your sister," she said, pretending she still didn't know, "you say you'll make sure David comes to me."

"Yes." A muscle worked in his jaw. "But not just find. *Save* my sister. And not *if*, but *when*."

"Fine." She cleared her throat. "I promise you, when I commit to something, I go all out. I will devote every spare second I have—when I'm not working, that is." These days, unlike the job she'd had as an executive secretary when she was married to David, she worked as a cook in the back of the diner, which suited her perfectly.

It was easier spending her time interacting with food rather than people.

He continued watching her, his hazel eyes both intelligent and insolent. "I'll need your word."

Of course he did. She decided not to tell him that her word wasn't worth anything around this town. "Then I give you my word. I will do whatever I'm permitted to do."

Gliding closer, in that disconcerting way of all ghosts, he held out his hand. It looked remarkably solid. Even though she knew it wasn't. For a second, she pictured how such sensual fingers would feel on her skin.

Seriously. She gave herself a mental shake. What on earth had gotten into her?

"Tyler Rogers," he said, the velvet murmur of his voice filling her with longing.

Damn.

"You do know I won't be able to shake that," she said, hoping he didn't notice how breathless she sounded.

For half a second, he appeared abashed. And then he grinned, an irresistible, devastating grin that made her knees go weak and her entire body tingle. "You're right," he said, lowering his hand.

"I'll do some checking," they both said at the same time. Anabel found herself smiling, something she didn't do very often. It felt good. And wrong. Again she wondered if she'd finally lost what was left of her mind.

"I'll make sure no other ghosts bother you," he told her, apparently not noticing her inner struggle.

As distractions went, his statement was pretty good. Intrigued, she tilted her head. "How will you do that?"

"Simple. I'll ask my spirit guide to put a circle of protection around you."

"What?" she started to ask. But he was gone. Just like a candle flame snuffed out by a gust of wind.

Alone again, she sighed. Maybe she'd dreamed all this up. It was entirely possible the eighteen months of celibacy since David's death had made her come completely unhinged.

Except for one thing. Why would she even think about serial killers and sisters in need of rescue?

Whichever Tyler Rogers turned out to be, a genuine ghost or a figment of her lonely imagination, she'd do what she could to find out information on his sister. Dena, he'd said. Surely it wouldn't be too difficult to find someone named Dena Rogers in a town the size of Leaning Tree.

That night, when she turned out the light, she went to sleep in blissful silence. No ghostly specters haunted her, not in her house or in her dreams.

The next morning, she opened her eyes and sat up in bed, feeling completely rested and refreshed. Outside, bright sunshine hinted at the heat to come, but since it was only seven in the morning, she knew it would still be comfortable outside.

In the time since David had died, she'd gradually changed her bedroom, adding little feminine touches here and there. David had hated flowers, though Anabel loved them. A new comforter—floral—and some artwork that she loved had made the room totally hers. She'd told herself she might as well like it, since she'd be spending the rest of her life alone.

Stretching, she thought of her ghostly visitor. Today was her day off. Originally she'd planned to spend it puttering in her garden and hanging out with her cat, Leroy.

He was big and fluffy and black and the laziest cat she'd ever known. She loved him so much it hurt.

Instead she guessed she'd better get busy seeing what she could find out about missing girls from Leaning Tree and the surrounding area.

"Good morning," a sexy male voice said behind her, making her jump. "I trust you slept well."

Gasping, she spun around so fast she nearly fell. "Rule number one. You can't just pop in and out of here whenever you feel like it."

Boldly handsome, he stood between her bed and her window. The sunlight made copper highlights in his brown hair.

"Why not?" He sounded genuinely puzzled. "It's what I do."

"Well, stop it. And rule number two, no reading my mind." She stomped off toward her bathroom, shooting him a warning look. "And stay out here until after I've showered and dressed."

Once she'd closed the door, she looked at herself in the mirror and grimaced. She'd braided her long hair before bed, to keep it from tangling. That, combined with the oversize (and to be honest, ratty) T-shirt she slept in, made her look a little witchy. Since half the people in Leaning Tree thought she was a witch, she guessed it didn't matter.

Shaking her head at her weird and out-of-place vanity, she turned the shower on hot, pulled off her T-shirt and jumped in.

Though she normally rushed through her morning preparations, since she usually had to be at the diner to cook for the breakfast crowd, this morning she took her time and enjoyed the peace and quiet. No ghostly images swirled in the steamy mirror as she blow-dried her hair. No voices cried out their muted torment while she dressed. She hadn't realized how much she appreciated the silence until now. Maybe she wasn't going crazy after all.

Finally, she emerged to find Tyler reclining on her sofa, long, muscular legs spread out in front of him. Today she saw he again wore a soldier's combat uniform, camouflaged desert colors, and boots. She froze, flashing back to the last time she'd seen David, wearing the exact same thing as she'd taken him to the airport to make the long flight back to Afghanistan.

"Are you okay?" Peering closely at her, her ghostly visitor seemed a bit more solid than he had the day before.

"Don't you know?" she asked crossly, turning away so she wouldn't have to look at him.

"You asked me not to read your mind."

"Oh. Right." Crossing into the kitchen, she made herself a cup of coffee. "Thank you. And also thanks for the protection-circle thing or whatever you said. It worked. I didn't have a single ghost last night."

The fragrant smell of coffee made her mouth water. She poured herself a cup, adding a spoonful of powdered creamer and a packet of sweetener.

When she turned, she caught him eyeing her mug with a wistful expression.

"I miss that," he rumbled. "Among other things."

Heat flashed through her, so intense she nearly staggered. Not good, especially if Tyler could intuitively guess how she felt.

Deciding to let that comment go, she scowled at him. "Why are you here?"

One dark eyebrow arched. Sexy, again. "You didn't

really think I'd retreat into the ether and wait for you to summon me, did you? We're working together on this."

She shrugged, pretending not to care. "Fine. I'm going to do some research on the internet first. I need to find any news stories about missing girls. I also want to do a search for Dena Rogers."

"Plus, I can tell you where she works and lives," he offered. "We might even go there."

"Of course." Rummaging in the refrigerator, she grabbed the roll of bagels, sprayed each side with vegetable oil, popped them in the toaster and, when they were done, spread a generous dollop of peanut butter on each one.

Tyler watched, his hazel eyes glittering, as she retrieved her breakfast and sat down to eat it.

"What?" she finally asked. "Have you never seen anyone cook breakfast before?"

"Cook?" he snorted. "I don't call that cooking."

She rolled her eyes in response. Since her mouth was full, she didn't deign to reply. Protein and carbs, and tasty too. When she'd finished, she got up, rinsed the plate off and placed it in the dishwasher. Taking a deep sip of her coffee, she padded to the room she used as an office and booted up her ancient desktop. She sensed Tyler right behind her, her awareness of him a prickling along her spine.

"You don't have a laptop?" Tyler asked, the astonished tone in his voice making it clear he thought she lived in the Dark Ages. The mischievous look in his eyes filled her with unwanted longing. To cover, she shook her head.

"Ghosts don't get to be picky," she pointed out, sitting back in her chair while she waited for the computer to finish booting up. If she didn't look at him, maybe she could manage to avoid all these unwanted feelings. "And yes, I had a laptop. David took it with him to Afghanistan. It never made it back, so I'm guessing someone from his unit kept it."

Finishing her coffee, she got up to make another cup, walking right past his still surprisingly solid form, her heart pounding, without him commenting.

When she returned, she checked on her computer, which appeared to be ready, and clicked on the icon for Google Chrome.

"Doesn't that drive you crazy?" he asked. "Computers aren't that expensive anymore. I'd think it'd be worth it to spring for a new one."

"Maybe." Concentrating on the screen, she searched for the local newspaper. "But not today." Once she had the paper up, she searched the archives, using keywords *missing* and *lost* and even *runaway*.

"I'll be—"

Suddenly, he materialized right next to her, practically on top of her, making her jump and bump her knee on the bottom of her desk. "What?" he asked. "Let me see."

"Don't. Do. That." Rubbing at her knee, she glared at him, though he didn't even notice as he was busy reading the on-screen text.

"There *are* more missing women," he breathed. "Four, including Dena. And they're all from different towns in Ulster County."

Immediately, she began reading too. "Your sister's the only one from Leaning Tree." Hitting the print icon, she eyed him. "But it doesn't appear the police are even considering them to be linked in any way."

"That's where you come in." He stretched, causing the material of his shirt to expand over his muscular arms.

Suddenly, she realized he'd changed and no longer wore the camo. Instead he had on civilian clothes, a tight black T-shirt and faded, well-worn jeans, though he still wore his combat boots.

For a ghost, he looked virile as hell. Tantalizing. Captivating.

No. This had to stop. Time to shut this ridiculous and unwanted attraction down. She no longer thought about sex, or at least she tried not to. Her mate was gone and she didn't want anyone else. Ever.

Chapter 2

Now that Anabel had settled the matter, she felt better. Straightening her shoulders, she knew she was strong enough to resist Tyler Rogers's ghostly allure.

"Let's go talk to the police," he said, flickering in and out, his form alternating between solid and ethereal. She figured this was probably due to the enthusiasm vibrating in his husky voice.

Maybe she'd do better if she treated him like a brother. At least that way, his nearness would no longer be so overwhelming.

"You know, for a ghost, you sure look concrete sometimes," she commented, clicking her computer to sleep before getting up from her chair.

"Thanks," he said, flashing that devastating smile that sent a bolt of heat straight to her stomach—and elsewhere.

Brother, she reminded herself. "Come on." Snatching up her car keys, she headed for the garage. "And whatever you do, don't speak to me while I'm talking to the police. Everyone around here already thinks I'm crazy. If I start answering you back, it'll just make it worse."

She didn't look to see if he followed as she opened the garage door and got in her car. The little red Fiat had been a gift from David the first year they were married. She loved everything about it, from the tan leather-trimmed seats to the upgraded radio.

"This?" Tyler said, the disbelief in his voice making her smile. "You expect me to ride in this? There's not enough room."

"You'll manage," she replied. "If not, then I guess you can wait here." As she slid behind the wheel, he materialized in the passenger seat, legs folded almost up to his chest. She nearly laughed out loud.

Instead she masked her amusement with irritation. "Quit doing that too," she ordered. "When you're with me, you don't need to act so ghostly."

"Ghostly?" His rich laugh struck a chord low in her belly. "I am a ghost. That's what we do. But for your sake, I promise to try and pretend I'm human."

She shuddered at the word. "You never were just human, I can tell. Before you died, you were Pack. Like me."

Regarding her curiously as she backed out of her driveway, he finally nodded. "How did you know? I'm told the dead no longer have the aura."

Anabel couldn't keep from snorting out loud. "Maybe not to each other. But you do to me. I can see it just as clearly as the aura from any living shifter."

And then she turned up the radio to discourage further discussion.

The winding, tree-lined roads were beautiful in summer and in autumn. Right now, with the leaves beginning to turn, she felt as if she lived in a postcard. She knew other people who'd lived here all of their lives as she had became so used to the natural beauty that they rarely even noticed it. Not Anabel. She appreciated and marveled at her surroundings every day.

As she drove to downtown Leaning Tree, she tried to think how to best approach this. Turning the radio down slightly, she glanced at him. "Any ideas on what I should say? I mean, I can't just walk into the police station and demand information on the search for the missing girls. That would make them really suspicious."

"I see what you mean," he replied, frowning. "You'd become an immediate suspect, especially since you believe everyone considers you off your rocker anyway."

His words stung. "Hey," she protested. "It's fine for me to say stuff like that. Not so much for you."

Again the deep-throated laugh. "Of course," he said, shaking his head in mock chagrin. "I should have understood."

Shocked, she realized he was teasing her. No one had joked with her in any way since David died. Probably because everyone at first felt bad for her and then later, after her breakdown, most folks acted afraid of her.

This used to hurt and baffle her, before she'd given in and decided to embrace her own semiscary weirdness. She'd started dressing in black after David was killed anyway. With a little embellishment using Stevie Nicks for inspiration, she'd taken black to a whole new level. And the funny thing was, she loved wearing one of her flowing outfits and seeing the way everyone eyed her. She thought she looked pretty. Who cared if everyone else disagreed?

Another sideways look at her ghostly companion, steeling herself against his masculine beauty, confirmed her suspicion.

"For someone who's worried about his sister, you're a bit of a jokester, aren't you?"

Just like that, his half smile vanished, replaced by a steely expression. Instantly, she regretted her comment.

"Are you always so serious?" he asked, faint mockery in his voice.

She decided to answer honestly. "Yes. Especially when dealing with something like this. I don't find serial killers or women being held prisoner amusing."

"Neither do I," he shot back. "But I have found making a joke or two can help relieve some of the pressure."

Since she didn't have a response for that, she kept quiet.

"I do have a question." Clearing his throat, he eyed her. "Exactly how powerful are you?"

So intent had she been on focusing on thinking of him like a brother, the question didn't immediately register. She blinked, frowning, as she met his gaze. "I'm sorry—what?"

"How much power do you have?"

"That's what I thought you said. I don't understand what you mean. If you're talking about firepower, yes, I do own a gun. I've even taken classes to learn how to handle it. For my own protection, of course."

Now he frowned. "I'm not talking about a weapon, though that may come in handy, and I think you know it. I'm asking about your powers. You know, your magic. How strong is it?"

"Magic?" Then she remembered she was talking to a ghost. "Tyler, the only magic I possess is the ability to see and hear spirits. Most times it's more like a curse than magic."

His gaze slid over her, the assessing look in his eyes saying he wasn't sure if she was serious. And then he grimaced and shook his head. "I understand. Good one. You've proved your point. I shouldn't have accused you of being too serious."

"But—"

He waved away her protests. "You almost had me fooled for a moment. You must be a very powerful witch indeed, if you're trying to hide it."

More oddness. A powerful witch, huh? Maybe he thought she dressed like this because she had magic. Or something. Who knew? Every second she spent with him kept getting weirder and weirder. "I'm just a regular person who happens to see ghosts." And had already had one mental breakdown. She fervently hoped this wasn't another. "I thought you ghostly beings knew everything."

One dark eyebrow arched, his face showing an uncanny awareness of how uneasy she was becoming.

"What makes you think that? If we knew everything, I'd know exactly where to find my sister." He turned away, staring out at the road ahead of them. "And I wouldn't need you."

Good point. Somewhat relieved, she decided to keep on trying to help. "Let's head to the police station. I'll figure out something to say that won't get me thrown in jail." She hoped.

* * *

Tyler rode in the passenger seat of her car as if he were alive, just because he wanted to study this Anabel Lee a bit more closely. When he'd received Dena's frantic pleas for help, he'd searched for the most powerful witch he could find. He'd been drawn to the energy radiated from Anabel, just like all the other ghosts, apparently. He'd immediately realized he'd made the right choice when she not only looked at him, but could hear him when he spoke.

One thing that had taken him by surprise was her beauty. Tall and graceful, slender and shapely, and her delicate features left him momentarily speechless. Her midnight hair tumbled carelessly down her back, adding to her attraction. But her copper eyes fringed in long, sooty lashes had done him in. He'd never seen anything like her. Exquisite, enchanting and sexy as hell. The instant he'd met her, he'd felt the impact of her femininity like a sucker punch to the gut.

Which pissed him off royally. After all, he'd come back as a ghost to save his sister, not fight an overwhelming attraction to a witch. Which, despite Anabel's claims to the contrary, she most definitely was.

He didn't understand why she insisted on lying about her magical ability. Maybe if he told her they were most likely dealing with not only a serial-killer psychopath, but a powerful warlock, she'd come clean. Because everyone knew to fight magic with magic, didn't they?

Or maybe, maybe she just didn't know.

The instant that idea occurred to him, he discounted it. How could she radiate power and not understand who and what she was?

For now, he decided to let that topic rest.

"So," she asked, shooting him a sidelong glance that told him she felt nervous, "in the afterlife, do you still shift into a wolf?"

"Of course," he answered, playing along. "We are what we are. Dying doesn't change that." He thought for a moment and then completed his statement. "At least, until we're reborn into a new body."

"Of course." And she laughed, as if he'd made a joke. "Reincarnation too? Why not."

Not sure what to think about this, he decided not to pursue this topic either. Things were confusing enough, what with warlocks and serial killers and ghosts. What choice did he have but to let it go? For all he knew, powerful witches thought differently from everyone else.

And, he reminded himself, Anabel Lee had to be a witch with very strong powers. She had to be, if they were to have a prayer in defeating the man who'd captured and enslaved his sister. If it turned out she wasn't, then he'd chosen wrong and Dena would die.

Contenting himself with looking out the window, though Leaning Tree looked exactly as he remembered, he was struck anew by the rustic beauty. Right now the green leaves flirted with shades of yellow, red and orange. In a few weeks, they'd blaze with color, as soon as the first crispness started to creep into the air. Autumn had always been his favorite time of year.

A moment later, they pulled up at the police station. The one-story, redbrick building looked the same. Again, memories surfaced. He'd spent a fair amount of time here as a kid, when his father was arrested for whaling on his mother.

"Wait here," she ordered, shooting him a stern look as she got out of her car.

"Right." He did exactly as she said, for maybe ten seconds. And then he materialized inside the station, waiting for her by the battle-scarred counter of the front desk as she walked in.

The dirty look she gave him made him smile.

"Anabel Lee." The frizzy-haired woman behind the counter sounded less than thrilled. "What do you want?"

To her credit, Anabel didn't react to the overt hostility in the receptionist's tone. "I'd like to see Captain Harper, please."

The other woman, whose name tag read Brenda Winder, appeared unmoved, squinting at Anabel through thick glasses. "Of course you would. Why don't you tell me what it is you need, and I'll see if I can find someone to help you? Since I am, you know, the dispatcher. That's what we do." Her unkind smile had Tyler clenching his fists.

He glanced at Anabel, to see what she would do. To his surprise, she'd assumed a deferential posture. "I'd prefer to discuss it with him, thanks."

Pursing her mouth, the other woman glared at her. "Have a seat. I'll let him know you're here."

Without commenting, Anabel found a metal folding chair and lowered herself into it.

Enraged, he went to her. "What was that? Why do you let that person talk to you that way?"

Her sigh sounded more weary than exasperated. She kept her voice down, since to anyone else it would appear she was carrying on a one-sided conversation with herself. "I tried to tell you. Most of the people around this town consider me crazy, an unwelcome nuisance at best. No one in Leaning Tree wants to have anything to do with me, never mind talk to me."

"Because of your power?"

She moved her hand in a chopping motion. "Enough about the power. I don't have any, so stop pretending I do."

Before he could respond, Anabel looked up. Her entire body stiffened. "Now look what you made me do," she hissed, her porcelain skin turning tomato red.

Brenda Winder stood back behind the desk, staring at Anabel with a horrified and smug expression on her meaty face. "Talking to yourself again?" she drawled. "Crazy is as crazy does."

Stone-faced, Anabel kept staring straight ahead and didn't bother to reply. Finally, Brenda tired of tormenting someone who wouldn't respond and went back to reading something on her computer.

A few minutes later, a stocky man with wide shoulders and an even wider belly stomped into the room. His bushy gray eyebrows lowered in a frown, and he eyed Anabel as if he expected her to present him with something disgusting and distasteful. "You wanted to talk to me?" he asked, sounding anything but accommodating.

"I did." Smiling, Anabel got to her feet gracefully. "Good to see you, Captain Harper. Could we please talk in your office?"

"Out here will do just fine."

"No." Anabel straightened her shoulders, her smile fading and her gaze direct. "It won't. I need a little privacy, please."

The captain sighed, stopping just short of rolling his eyes. "Sure. Why not? Come on back. I'm sure you know the way."

Another puzzle. Resolving to try to find out from Anabel what all this meant, Tyler glided along after them as they walked through the crowded open area buzzing with activity. They passed several uniformed officers, a few criminals or complainants, and not a single person acknowledged or greeted Anabel. She made a beeline toward a small office in the back corner.

Most of the police officers were busy, which might excuse them. Some were on the phone, others talking to people sitting in their desk chairs. Suspects? Tyler looked for handcuffs, noting two people at opposite ends of the room who wore them.

Despite that, the instant they realized who had just walked into the room, every single person stopped what he or she was doing and stared.

Tyler would have liked to believe this was due respect for her power, but some of the officers seemed disgusted. A few others exchanged glances with their coworkers, even going so far as to shake their heads or roll their eyes.

Not respect, then. Eyeing Anabel's slender form as she marched across the room, head held high, ignoring them all, for the first time he wondered what her story might be.

Truth be told, until now he hadn't wondered about her story. He'd gone to her simply because he'd heard she could see and hear him and she'd radiated amazingly great power. They'd come to an arrangement. He'd help her get what she wanted if she'd help him save his baby sister.

End of story. Except it wasn't.

Even though he'd been a shape-shifter, able to change into a ferocious wolf, wizards, warlocks and witches generally creeped him out. Any shifter with a lick of sense tended to avoid magical beings, since they were powerless against them. Even the vampires were careful to avoid them.

But now one had Dena. And if Tyler wanted to save her, he had no choice but to take on a warlock. At least he had a powerful witch at his side.

Once again he eyed Anabel, who'd finally reached the captain's office and had taken a seat, crossing her gorgeous long legs and tilting her head as she waited for the captain to work himself down into his own chair and work his enormous stomach behind his desk.

Finally, he grunted and got himself settled. "All right, Anabel. Since Lilly and all the rest of the McGraws refused to press charges against you, I'm guessing you haven't come here to talk about any of that."

Anabel shook her head rapidly, sending her long, dark hair whipping around her face. Tyler caught himself aching to wrap a strand of it around his finger and pull her to him.

"Of course not," she said. "That's history. They've moved forward, as have I."

"Then what can I do for you?"

She took a deep breath, her jaw tightening. "A friend of David's wrote me from Afghanistan. He wanted me to check on his sister. She lives here in Leaning Tree. According to him, she's gone missing."

Brilliant. Tyler wanted to hug her. He restrained himself, not wanting to startle her. Besides, without a corporeal body, she wouldn't be able to feel it.

"Really?" The captain's gaze sharpened. "What's her name?"

"Dena Rogers," Anabel answered. "Her brother, Tyler, is really worried."

"Let me see what I can find out." Using his computer,

Captain Harper tapped in some information. "Ah, yes. Here we are. Two weeks ago one of her coworkers asked us to do a welfare check when Ms. Rogers didn't show up for her shift at the junior-college cafeteria. We checked but found nothing. Her house was empty, but there were no signs she'd met with foul play or anything. My officer determined she must have left willingly."

"I don't think so—" Anabel began.

"Ms. Lee." Speaking sternly, Captain Harper interrupted. "It's entirely possible she went on vacation."

"Not without telling her brother," Anabel shot back, her spine straight. "That's why he got in touch with me."

"I see." Steepling his fingers, the older man sighed. "Then why don't you tell me what it is you want me to do?"

"Find out what happened to her. Her brother told me she'd been talking about several other missing girls. Has anyone in your office put together information linking them?"

To give him credit, Captain Harper's expression remained unchanged. Except for his eyes. Those appeared about to bug out of his head. "I don't have any idea what you're talking about."

"That's sad."

The captain narrowed his eyes but didn't respond.

"I would appreciate it if you would look into it," Anabel continued with a quiet dignity. "As soon as possible. It's not enough that Tyler Rogers is over there serving our country. I don't want him worrying needlessly about his sister."

"I'm sure there's no need to worry. She'll turn up eventually. Young people frequently disappear on some crazy adventure."

The man's patronizing tone set Tyler's teeth on edge. "If you won't at least do your job—" Anabel stood, the movement graceful "—I'm going to have to investigate on my own."

To Tyler's disbelief, the police captain winced. "No need to do anything rash."

"Twenty-four hours." Anabel looked him right in the eye. "I want you to investigate the disappearance of several young women in the area around Leaning Tree over the past few months. I'd like to know what you've learned by this time tomorrow. If I don't hear from you, I'll consider that notice that you want me to take matters into my own hands."

From the tight set of Captain Harper's jaw, he wasn't happy at all about her proclamation, but he nodded. "I'll see what I can find out."

"You do that." With that, she turned to go.

Following her out the door, Tyler marveled at the powerful energy radiating from her. How was it possible she didn't realize her own strength? It wasn't. Therefore, he had to believe she simply didn't want him to know.

She sailed through the outer room and past the startled receptionist without a word. Outside, she rushed over to her little car, opening the door and climbing inside.

Only once she was there did Tyler realize her hands were shaking too hard to fit the key in the ignition.

"Deep breaths," he told her as he folded himself up into the small passenger seat. He wasn't sure what he could do to help. "Do you want to talk about it?" In his admittedly limited experience, most women welcomed the opportunity to discuss their feelings.

But Anabel was not most women. "No," she said,

averting her profile. "I'm fine." A moment later, she managed to start the car and put it in Drive.

"What was that, back there?"

Not looking at him, she lifted one delicate shoulder in a shrug. "I already told you, people in this town think I'm crazy."

"But you didn't tell me why."

She shot him a sideways glance, her eyes shuttered. "Does it really matter?"

"I guess not. But I'd still like to know."

"I talk to ghosts. Think about it."

He couldn't help laughing at the sour note in her voice. "They see you walking around talking to air. Is that what you're telling me?"

"Exactly. And I dress the part. Plus, I did something I shouldn't have and almost cost a really sweet woman her life. I don't think anyone will ever forgive me for that."

Thus the captain's reference to the McGraws. He, like just about everyone in Leaning Tree, knew the family. Since they'd declined to press charges, whatever Anabel had done couldn't have been too bad. Tyler wondered if he should ask, but the raw agony in her expression made him decide not to. Whatever she'd done, it seemed clear she felt bad about that now.

Neither spoke as she drove slowly down Main Street. He took his time admiring the huge leafy oak and maple trees, the restored old buildings and the bustling shops. "It still looks the same," he mused. "I see the small Dutch Reform church is now fully restored. And the shops and restaurants appear to be doing a booming business."

"We get a lot more tourists than we used to," she grudgingly admitted. "It's really busy in the fall when all the city people take drives to see the foliage." Again she looked sideways at him, almost as if it hurt her eyes to meet his gaze dead-on.

"I remember," he said.

"How long have you been gone from here, anyway?"

"That's a good question." He tried to calculate, failing miserably.

"A reply like that means you aren't really going to answer."

He laughed. "Give me a minute. I'm trying. Like I said, time passes differently in the hereafter."

"What's the last year you remember? Let's start with your last tour of duty in Afghanistan."

Flashes of light, an explosion, red and yellow and orange. Screams of pain. Wincing, he tried to block the random sights and sounds from his memory.

When he finally found his voice again, he sounded hoarse. "Not there. Too intense. Let's start with something better, more pleasant."

"Okay. When did you graduate from high school?"

Now, that he could answer. "Nineteen ninety-seven." Thinking about that, he couldn't help smiling. "Leaning Tree High. Did you go there?"

"I did, but I graduated in 2001. I was just starting high school the year you finished."

"Which would explain why we never met," he said.

"How do you know we didn't?" Though her question was casual, for some reason it sent a chill up his spine.

He decided to keep his answer light. "Because I'd remember." The rest of it, what he didn't say, was that she, with her long midnight hair and exotic bronze eyes, was the loveliest woman he'd ever seen. He had to believe his younger self would have recognized that too, even back then.

Chapter 3

Apparently oblivious of his chaotic thoughts, Anabel continued to question him. "And then after high school, what did you do? Did you enlist right away?"

His head had begun to hurt. "My turn. I get to ask you something next."

"Really? I had no idea we were playing some sort of game." Since her dry tone contained a thread of amusement, he decided to take that as encouragement.

"What did you do after high school?" he asked.

"I went to college. Columbia, to be exact. Three months in, I loved life and the city. Then I met David Lee. From Tennessee. He was in New York on leave."

Though he hated the dark sadness that crept over her lovely face, he wanted to know more. Before he could speak, she forestalled him by making a chopping motion with her hand.

"My turn," she said, earning a reluctant smile from him.

"Go ahead."

"Remember, we're trying to get a rough idea of how long you've been a ghost," she said.

Though he didn't know why that mattered, he decided to play along. "Okay."

"When did you enlist?"

He sighed. "About two months after graduating from high school."

"No college?"

"Nope. Not only did I not have the money or the grades, but I didn't have the inclination. I was working a dead-end job, learning how to do bodywork at a Chevy dealership. I woke up one morning, decided I wanted to be a soldier and drove to the army recruiter's office."

"And then—"

"My turn." He softened his tone to lessen the sting. "How long were you married?"

"Nope," she said, turning away, but not before he saw the hurt flash across her face. "My marriage is off-limits. Ask something else."

Thinking quickly, he spoke. "What about friends? Surely you must have some friends in this town."

She gave him a look designed to stop a charging leopard in its tracks. "You're going to keep pushing this, are you?"

"I'm just trying to figure out what makes you tick, that's all."

"Well, don't. There's not a reason in the world you would need to know."

"Actually, there is." He gave her what he hoped was an unguarded smile. "If we're going to be working together, I should at least learn a few things about you."

"I talk to ghosts," she said, her voice curt. "Isn't that enough?"

"Not really." Equally blunt, he rubbed the back of his neck. One thing that always startled him was how he occasionally still had human aches and pains and itches, even in ethereal form.

"What?" Staring at him, she frowned. "Explain yourself."

"You talk to ghosts. I get that. It's great, and that particular talent is what enabled me to get you to see and hear me. But how is the ability to view spirits going to assist you in freeing my sister?"

She looked thoroughly annoyed. "Maybe I should remind you that you asked me to help you with this, not the other way around."

"I did. But I was under the impression you had some form of magical ability, as well."

Now. Now he expected she would finally admit the truth.

"Well, you were wrong."

His heart sank. "It's more likely you just don't know your own powers."

"Really?" Shaking her head, she snorted. "I know myself better than you think. And to answer your other question, I do have a few friends. They're all sort of fringe people like me."

"Fringe people?"

"Yeah." Expression carefully blank, she smiled at him. "As a matter of fact, you need to meet one of them. My friend Juliet. She owns the yoga studio and metaphysical bookstore downtown and calls herself a medium."

"And you don't believe her?"

"I have no opinion either way. She's my friend and

whatever she wants to accept as true is fine with me."
A hint of mischief sparked in her amazing eyes as she
widened her smile, which made him catch his breath.
"That's why I want you to meet her. I'm curious to see
if she senses your presence."

"Has she ever sensed one of your other ghostly visitors?"

"No, but I've never brought one into her studio. I usually get rid of them as soon as they appear."

Curious, he nodded. "Do they appear often?"

Instantly, her smile vanished. "Too much," she said
grimly. "There are an awful lot of dead people trying to
communicate with the living."

"You know, you could make money if you had a TV
show and traveled around the country like the *Long
Island Medium*. Why don't you?"

Clearly, his attempt at a joke fell flat. She looked at
him as if he'd grown two ghostly heads. "That's not
for me. All I want is for the specters to leave me alone.
Which, thanks to you, they are."

When he was in the afterlife, Anabel's energy had
pulled him to her. He'd been seeking, and then the blaze
of energy she gave off shone like a beacon, cutting
through gray. The fact that she'd been able to see and
hear him had been a welcome bonus.

"You draw them to you," he said slowly.

"How? And why? Surely there must be a way to turn
it off."

He debated the best way to tell her. Finally, he decided
to just say it. "Anabel, I believe you have magic inside
you. Untapped, but powerful. We're going to need to figure out how to bring it to the surface."

"Bring it to…" They stopped at a red light and she

turned to face him. "Why would I want to do something like that?"

If her crossed arms were any indication, she definitely wasn't going to like what he had to say next. "Because whoever has my sister is a warlock. And you're going to need your magic to defeat him."

"A warlock?" Repeating Tyler's words, Anabel sucked in her breath. As a shape-shifter, she knew there were all kinds of other supernatural beings out there, like vampires and mer-people, but as far as she knew, no one had any special powers, except for the fae. Even as a child in school, when they'd learned the history of the Pack along with all the other supernatural, witches and warlocks had never been mentioned. Not once.

While she—and others of her kind—could change form, as far as she knew, no one could fly. Or start fires with a look or a wave of their hand. Magic didn't exist.

Yet Tyler talked as if it did. There were certainly insane living people; therefore, it followed that there could be crazy dead people, as well. "Look, Tyler. I agreed to help try and find your sister. You didn't say anything about having to defeat some sort of magical being."

"I believed—believe you have magic too."

She waited, in case there was more, but he didn't elaborate.

"Well, if you need somebody who can fight magic with magic, you've picked the wrong person," she said. "I'll assist in every way I can, but you'll need to find another witch or warlock to help get her out once we find her."

"Deal," he said promptly, which sort of annoyed her. "Do you know any witches?"

Fine. He wanted a witch, she'd get him one. "My

friend the yoga instructor is not only a medium but a witch." Okay, technically Juliet was Wiccan, but Tyler was a ghost and Juliet wouldn't be able to see him.

Tyler's ghostly form briefly solidified, which she was beginning to realize meant excitement. "Do you think she'll help us?"

Immediately, she regretted saying anything. "Tyler, she's Wiccan. She runs a yoga studio and metaphysical bookstore, like I said. If she practices any magic, which I doubt, it's not powerful."

"How do you know?" His husky voice vibrated with enthusiasm. "She might hide it from you. Most magical beings don't go around advertising their power, you know."

"No, I don't know." Apparently, he was serious. She sighed. Maybe new insights into the world were learned in the afterlife.

"When can we meet her?" Tyler asked, his hazel eyes glowing.

Fine. She gave in. "How about now? We're already in town."

Again his form appeared solid. "Sounds great."

Mentally shaking her head, she took the next left onto Third Street. Juliet's bright green VW bug was parked in front of the small white-frame corner building, with a bookstore on one side and a yoga studio on the other.

"You're in luck. She's here."

Pulling up next to her friend's car, Anabel parked and got out. As she headed toward the yoga-studio door, she glanced at Tyler's strikingly handsome form, floating a few feet off the ground. "Remember, Juliet won't be able to see you."

"You never know," he said agreeably. "She might have

a few secrets from you, the same way you keep things from her."

Resisting the urge to grumble under her breath, she inhaled deeply and opened the door. The set of tiny bells chirped and chimed their usual muted happy sound. The air smelled like spearmint and rosemary. This never failed to make Anabel smile.

At the sound, Juliet glided from the back room, her unlined face serene. "Anabel!" Moving forward, she hugged Anabel and kissed her cheek. "Class was over an hour ago."

"I know. We came because..." Crap. Not only had she said *we*, as in plural, but she really didn't have a good reason for being there.

"We?" Juliet's perfectly arched eyebrows rose. She peered behind Anabel. "Is someone else with you?"

"No. Sorry." Ignoring Tyler, who now hovered over Anabel with a look of intense concentration on his face, she swallowed.

"What's wrong?" Juliet placed a soothing hand on Anabel's shoulder. "Something is troubling you. I can sense it."

"Aha!" Tyler crowed. "See? She has powers. I knew it."

Anabel could have sworn Juliet glanced at Tyler, though she didn't acknowledge his presence. Of course she didn't. She wasn't crazy, like Anabel.

Doing her best to ignore Tyler's outburst, Anabel nodded. "Do you have a moment to talk?"

"Of course." Turning, Juliet pushed through the row of beads making a curtain in the doorway and led the way back to her office.

Once inside, Anabel took the second chair, since Tyler had materialized in the first one.

"Now tell me what's bothering you." Juliet's dulcet tones were, as far as Anabel was concerned, one of her best assets.

"Um, okay." Might as well just blurt it out. "I hope I'm not being offensive, but as a Wiccan, do you happen to practice...magic?"

To Anabel's relief, Juliet smiled. "We do practice some small, white magic." She leaned closer. "Anabel, have you come because of your power?"

Stunned, Anabel gaped at her friend and tried to ignore Tyler's smug smile. "Power?"

"Yes. You have an aura of power surrounding you. More than just your shifter aura. I thought perhaps something had happened to make you realize this, so you'd come to me for help."

"Power." Aware she was repeating the word yet again, Anabel shook her head. "You do realize my life is already strange enough, don't you?"

Smile widening, Juliet leaned over and patted her arm. "No rush. When the time is right and you have questions, please come to me. I'm not an expert by any means, but I can enlist the help of my coven to teach you. It's far better to use such power for light rather than dark."

Despite herself, Anabel shivered. "Dark magic." Her throat felt dry. "You're telling me that such a thing is real?"

"Unfortunately, very real." And then, while Anabel was trying to digest all this, she swore her friend cut her eyes and looked right at Tyler. As if she too could see him.

"I think she can see me," Tyler said, confirming her thought.

"I can," Juliet admitted, making Anabel gasp. "And hear you too. However, I only see a blaze of energy, not a physical body. Is that what you see, Anabel?"

"No." Still in shock, Anabel looked from Juliet to Tyler and back again. "I see him like he must have looked when he was alive."

Tyler flashed a cocky grin. "Of course you do," he said. "You have way more power than she does."

"I need to go home." Anabel stood, suppressing a flash of panic. "I need to go home right now."

Knowing her friend would understand, Anabel rushed outside and got into her car. She managed to get the key in the ignition, start the engine and put the car in Drive before she realized Tyler wasn't there.

Fine. He was a ghost. He'd show up eventually. Right now she needed to be alone.

Tyler remained seated, though with every fiber of his being he wanted to rush after Anabel. Instead he studied Anabel's friend, taking comfort in the aura of peace and tranquility radiating from her.

"Why are you here?" Juliet asked, apparently having no issues with conversing with a ghost. "Many others have tried to contact her and she's sent every single entity away. What's different about you?"

"I don't know. Maybe it's because I really need Anabel's help," he answered. "I was drawn to her, by her power."

"A lot of spirits are. I get the odd few myself, every now and then, but not nearly as many as she." She leaned forward, her faded blue eyes twinkling. "She thinks I don't know."

"Why?" he asked. "What is it about her? Is she a witch? How is it possible she isn't aware of her power?"

"Anabel is descended from a long line of powerful witches. Unfortunately, her mother died when she was young. There was no one else to teach her. My coven and I have been waiting for the right time." Cocking her head, she studied him. "It would appear your arrival has signaled that the time has come."

"Why wouldn't you have taught her before now? It seems to me she could have used an advantage."

The other woman shook her head. "Anabel has been very unsettled since losing her husband. There were instances when she might have chosen to use her power for bad rather than good."

"How do you know all this?"

"I've been tasked with helping guide her. My coven has long been aware of her and her family, and we watch to make certain she continues to walk within the light." Juliet looked pensive. "Of course, she's given me a few scares a couple of times. Like when she almost caused that poor girl, Lilly McGraw, to get recaptured by that cult. You might know the McGraws, if you're from around here. They own and operate Wolf Hollow Motor Court Resort."

"I know the McGraws, but I don't know Lilly."

Juliet nodded. "Lilly was here with Kane McGraw. She'd been held captive by some crazy cult, and they were hunting her down even after she was freed," she continued. "For whatever reason, Anabel helped this cult. Maybe out of jealousy, as she apparently once had a thing for Kane."

"Helped them?" Tyler wasn't sure he understood. "Anabel helped cult members locate Lilly?"

"Yes. She led Lilly into a trap. Both Lilly and Anabel almost lost their lives with that one."

"Why? Why would she do such a thing?"

"She was confused." Juliet sighed. "And hurting. After David died, Anabel became convinced that Kane Mc-Graw was her mate. She wrote him letters. He never responded. When Anabel learned Kane and Lilly were true mates, she went a little...crazy."

Now everything fell into place. "That explains the way everyone at the—" about to say *police station*, he caught himself "—in town treated her. Like she was dirt."

Expression sad, Juliet nodded. "Folks have long memories around here."

He shook his head. "I'm sure she had her reasons. Anabel's energy shows she's a good person. Did she say why?"

"Maybe if you ask her, she'll tell you," Juliet said gently. "It's her story to share or not. Meanwhile, I'd like to know what you need someone with power for."

Eyeing her, he made a split-second decision and decided to trust her. "A powerful warlock has taken my sister—and maybe a couple of others—captive. I need power to locate them."

"And fight him," she finished. "I see. I'm not sure Anabel is your best bet. She's powerful but completely untrained."

"What about you?" he asked.

But the older woman had already begun shaking her head. "I am not nearly powerful enough. In fact, Anabel is the most powerful witch I've ever known. It's in her blood."

"Then I have no choice," he said. "Maybe you can train her, if you can do it quickly. There's not a lot of time. My sister's life is in danger."

She blinked up at him. "You're a ghost. You should be able to find your sister."

"Yes, that would be true. If a powerful warlock wasn't shielding himself and her."

"Oh." Juliet still sounded stunned. Shell-shocked, even. "Do you know who this warlock is?"

"No." Tyler glided toward the doorway. "Thank you for visiting with me," he said.

"You're welcome." Her wide smile attested to the truth of her words. "If there's anything I can do to help you and Anabel, let me know."

"I will." And he winked out, reappearing in Anabel's living room. She hadn't arrived home yet, which was probably a good thing. She'd seemed pretty freaked out, and the last thing he needed was for her to make a panic-fueled decision to try to send him away again.

Her cat hissed and puffed up his fur immediately upon seeing Tyler. The long-haired black beast had been enjoying a sunny spot on the carpet near the front window. As cats went, this one was large and appeared powerful.

"It's okay, cat," Tyler said, lowering his voice and trying to sound friendly. "I'm not here to do any harm."

Apparently, the feline believed him, as he settled back down, turning his head and pretending to ignore Tyler while grooming his fur and stretching, all at the same time.

Tyler guessed this was a good thing. He'd never had much to do with cats, like most shifters. The two species—wolf and feline—were natural enemies. Tyler supposed it was a measure of Anabel's uniqueness—or maybe her power—that she had a cat as a pet.

The sound of a car pulling into the driveway heralded Anabel's arrival. She slammed into the house, looking around wildly until she saw him.

"You are trouble. Nothing but trouble," she cried. "My life was already messed up before you arrived, but you're making it even worse."

He grimaced. "I'm sorry. I have no choice."

"How?" she demanded. "How do you even know your sister's in danger? You're dead. How the heck would she be able to contact you?"

"Her energy reached out to me. She asked me to save her from him. She's pretty desperate. Who wouldn't be, in her situation?"

"I want no part of it. I'm done." Straightening, she waved her hand, giving him a flat, cold stare. "I want you to leave."

Though he knew she couldn't see it, her power flared, radiating from the edges of her fingertips as she pointed at him.

This time, he had no choice but to do as she commanded. As the compulsion filled him, he felt himself being pulled away, as if a giant vortex had opened to suck him right back out of this world.

"Wait," he shouted, desperation fueling his words. "You can't let my sister die. This is your chance to atone for what you did to that Lilly girl."

Instantly, the energy sending him away faltered and then dissipated. Relieved, he wiped his hands down the front of his pants.

Anabel sighed, looking down before meeting his gaze. "Juliet told you about that?"

Glad now that he'd stayed and talked to the other woman, Tyler nodded. "She did." Impulsively, he moved forward and put his hand on her shoulder. Of course, she couldn't feel his ghostly touch—heck, he could see through his own fingers—but the gesture made him feel better. "My sister is only twenty-five years old. She doesn't deserve to suffer like this."

After a moment, she nodded. "I'll try my best. I can promise you that. As to this mysterious power I supposedly have, I don't know what to tell you about that."

He took a deep breath, deciding to bulldoze ahead since he really had no choice. "Juliet said she could train you."

Her beautiful bronze eyes narrowed. "Oh, she did, did she?"

Might as well tell her the rest of it. "She told me you're descended from a long line of powerful witches. Your mother died before she could train you."

"Or even tell me." Moving away from him, she sighed. "My mom was killed in a fire when I was three. My dad got me out and went back for her. He died too."

"I'm sorry." He considered and then decided, why not? "If you'd like, when this is over, I can try to find their spirits too."

"We'll see." Spinning around, sending her gauzy black skirt flaring out around her like a flamenco dancer's, she headed into the kitchen. "I'm starving. It's long past the time I normally eat lunch. I hope you don't mind if I eat."

"Why would I mind?" he asked, genuinely curious.

"I guess I assumed eating was something you missed," she said, flashing a tentative smile. The power of that smile almost brought him to his knees.

Stunned, chest tight, he wondered if all the men in

Leaning Tree were blind. Anabel was the most beautiful woman he'd ever met. And eighteen months of being a widow was long enough for every red-blooded man to make a move. How was it that they weren't beating a path to her door? That was something he'd never understand.

If he'd been alive… As soon as he had the thought, he pushed it away. He wasn't alive, hadn't been for a long time. No point in tormenting himself with what-might-have-beens.

Oblivious, she'd turned away and had already started sautéing something in a cast-iron skillet. Curious, he moved closer, frowning slightly when he realized the thing was full of vegetables.

"Where's the meat?" he asked. "That's the one thing I do miss. As a carnivore, I liked a nice rare steak."

"Eww." She actually shuddered. "I'm a vegetarian." Then she watched him, apparently waiting for him to react to her joke.

Laughing, he obliged her. "Good one."

She shook her head, turning back to the skillet. "I'm serious. When I need protein, I turn to other sources like beans, nuts, soy and grains."

Horrified, he eyed her. "It's a wonder you're not sick. Shifters need meat. End of story."

"Really? You're entitled to your opinion, but I haven't had meat in over a year. And I've never felt better."

Her black cat leaped up onto the counter, eyeing the sizzling food. Anabel shooed him off. "Get down, Leroy."

Immediately, the feline obeyed, twining around her ankles and mewing.

"He's hungry," she said. "Just a minute, baby."

Eyeing the cat, Tyler shook his head. "Please tell me he's not a vegetarian too."

"Of course not. He eats high-quality dry cat food. Tuna flavored, I think."

Finished cooking, she turned off the burner and transferred her meal to a plate. Then she went to the cabinet and poured her pet a bowl full of kibble, placing it on the floor for him to eat.

She carried her plate to the table, sat and dug in. Even watching her eat was an act of sensuality. "Now, if we're done discussing my diet, let's get back to our plan of action. I was thinking about talking to some of your sister's friends."

"Since the police won't?"

"Have they? Do you even know?"

"Since they've been treating her disappearance like she left voluntarily, I'm guessing no."

She finished chewing before responding. He watched as she blotted one corner of her full mouth with a napkin, aching to put his tongue there instead. "I'll find out. I'll need a bit more information, like where she worked and lived. How about we start this afternoon?"

Gratified, he nodded. "I like that you don't waste time."

"Might as well do it on my day off. I have to go back to work tomorrow. On workdays, my time is limited."

"Work?" He said the word as if it were foreign. "What do you do, exactly?"

"I used to be an executive secretary to the president of Leaning Tree Bank. I was well regarded and made good money. Best of all, I was respected, the competent wife of a military man. But that had been in another life, before David died and my entire world had been turned apart."

Heart aching for her, he instinctively realized the last

thing she'd want would be his pity. "What do you do now?"

"I cook," she answered, lifting her chin. "In the diner. I'm on the morning shift. I have to be there at six a.m. I work until two." She didn't mention that the pay was minimal. If not for the life-insurance policy that David had taken out when they were first married, she'd have had to take a second job.

"Leaving your afternoons free."

She shook her head. "I do have errands to run too, you know. But I'll work on your sister's case each day."

"Each day?" Horrified, he stared. "Don't you understand? She doesn't have that much time. We need to find her now."

Chapter 4

*N*ow. If only she really did possess some magical power that would enable her to help him. Anabel hated the idea of a young girl, trapped in some dark place, subject to the whims of a cruel and probably psychotic man.

"Tell me how," she entreated. "I'll do whatever I can. But I don't know what else to do."

"Find the warlock."

"Okay." She waited for him to say more, but apparently he thought that was enough. "And how do I do that?" she finally asked. "And don't say 'use your power,' because I have no idea how."

And furthermore, she wasn't entirely sure she even had power to begin with. And if by some miracle she succeeded in finding the warlock, then what? Call the police? She doubted they'd even help. They'd already made it clear they regarded her as a dangerous eccentric.

He thought for a moment. "Maybe Juliet can give you a crash course in magic. She did offer."

"Maybe. Though I have a feeling something like what you're talking about isn't simple."

"Probably not." He straightened, meeting and holding her gaze. "But we're talking about my sister's life. I'd hope you'd do whatever it takes to save her. We're about out of time."

Telling him she'd think about it, she finished eating her meal, concentrating on the food while trying to puzzle out some sort of solution. She wanted to help him find his sister; she really did. She just had no idea how.

When she looked up, her ghostly visitor had vanished. Blinking, she looked around. Tyler was gone.

He didn't reappear that afternoon, though when her phone rang shortly before five and it was her boss, Jeb, calling to tell her she wasn't needed tomorrow and, in fact, could have a few more days off, she knew somehow Tyler had been working behind the scenes to clear the time she needed to help him.

Though she wouldn't like the lost wages, she thanked Jeb and agreed, promising to be back by the end of the week. She hoped she wasn't losing her job. While Jeb had never seemed to mind what the townspeople thought of Anabel, especially since she'd worked out of sight in the kitchen, she wouldn't put it past some uptight haters to try to cause her to lose her employment. There were a few small-minded people mean enough to do something like that.

She kept waiting for Tyler to reappear, though she knew she should have been relieved at his absence. He fascinated her, though, and she was honest enough with herself to know part of that was because he was so ruggedly masculine. If he hadn't been a spirit, she imagined her skin would sizzle if he were to touch her. Even the thought sent a bolt of heat through her.

Pushing the thought away, she occupied herself with weeding her garden and trying to gather up the nerve to call Juliet and ask her to help. But she couldn't even imagine the conversation. How did you ask someone, even your best friend, to teach you how to use your magic like a witch?

At dinnertime, she took to the internet and tried to find information about magic. But the general weirdness put her off, and she stopped before she felt too alienated from herself. If the townspeople thought she was strange now, imagine if they learned she supposedly was a witch with magical abilities.

For a few minutes, she sat in her living-room chair, eyes closed, trying to concentrate. "Magic," she whispered, feeling slightly foolish but going ahead anyway. "If you're there, help me out. Show me where to find Tyler's sister."

But nothing happened. To be honest, she wasn't sure how she would have reacted if something had.

Absurdly lonely—odd because she'd gotten used to being by herself—and sort of missing Tyler, she puttered around the house until her normal bedtime.

Since she didn't have to be up at four thirty, she didn't have to turn in early. But old habits died hard and Anabel had always taken comfort in a routine. So she got herself ready to turn in.

Tyler didn't return, not even when she turned out the lights and climbed into bed. Counting her blessings, she closed her eyes with a smile on her face, waiting to fall asleep.

That night, he invaded her dreams. The instant Anabel realized it was his arms holding her close rather than David's, she struggled, trying to wake herself up. But sleep gripped her tightly, refusing to release her. So she settled for pushing Tyler away.

But her body, so long untouched and alone, craved his, and every touch brought a thrill of electric longing pulsing through her. And truthfully, when she pretended to twist away, and he came in for the kiss, molten fire seared her lips as his mouth claimed hers.

Deep within her, desire flared, tugging at her, turning her inside and out. But she'd pledged herself to one mate and had sworn not to ever betray him. Not even in death.

"No." Meaning it, she broke the embrace and pushed Tyler away. The hurt look on his handsome face gave her pause. But then, it was her dream and she had the right to control it.

Except…a little voice whispered in her mind. It *was* only a dream. And more than eighteen months had passed since she'd allowed her body to experience the thrum of physical need, the heady thrill of desire. Only a dream. Not really betrayal.

So she let herself flow forward, back into his strong arms. In her dream, Tyler was no longer ghostly. No, he was a man and had substance. She ran her fingers over corded muscle, her breathing hitching, while her lips ached to kiss him again.

And so they did. Kissing and touching, nothing more. No sin, this. Her clothes stayed on, even if it seemed the heat blazing through her veins might melt them off. And so it went, endless in the way of dreams. Until she woke and the dream vanished like a puff of smoke.

The guilt struck her the instant she opened her eyes.

Unreasonable, unfathomable, but there nonetheless. The tangled sheets looked as though someone had actually been there, and her body ached with a heaviness that had nothing to do with reality.

She told herself it had been only a dream, that she hadn't really been unfaithful to David, as if you could be with a ghost anyway.

Still, first thing after getting up, she reached into the nightstand drawer and pulled out the photo of her deceased husband she'd always kept there. Once, she'd kept it right beside her bed so it would be the first thing she saw in the morning and the last at night. A year after his death, she'd finally put it away, finding the pain still too unbearable. Now she needed to gaze at David's beloved face, as if doing so could erase her memory of her sinfully sensual dream.

"Is that a picture of your husband?" Tyler's deep voice made her jump. And blush, instantly hot all over, as if he might somehow know about her nighttime subconsciously lustful thoughts.

"Yes." Short answer, while she stared at the photograph and waited for the familiar grief and agony to consume her. When it didn't immediately slam into her, she nearly panicked.

"I miss him so much," she whispered. And then, with the words, came the familiar throat ache. "We loved each other, you know. He was a great husband."

"Let me see."

Heaven help her, she started again. While she'd been intent on her former husband's face, Tyler had glided so close he was looking over her shoulder.

Wordlessly, she held up the frame. "This was right before he left for his last tour."

Tyler swore, shocking her. "I know that guy. Or knew him, I should say."

"What?" Not sure she'd heard correctly, Anabel spun around to face him. She felt numb, except for the slow, insistent beat of her heart in her chest. "You knew David? Are you sure?"

"Let me see the picture again."

Slowly, she turned the frame around. "Where were you stationed?" Her voice seemed to come from a distance.

"That's classified." Grimacing, he shook his head at what had apparently been an automatic response. "Sorry. It doesn't matter now, of course. I was stationed at Tangi Valley, Maidan Wardak Province. As was your husband."

"Eighty klicks from Kabul. He told me that, even if he couldn't tell me the exact name of the place." Hearing the defeat in her tone, she sighed. "David said the troops called it Death Valley."

"It wasn't a pleasant area. Lots of Taliban." He winced, as if the memory was unpleasant. "It's where I died."

"David too."

"Roadside bomb?" He sighed, not waiting for an answer. "We dealt with that a lot. Our presence has always been a bone of contention among the locals."

She nodded, unable to think past one thing. He'd known David. Finally. Someone who could speak of her husband as a living, breathing person rather than a mere statistic. Desperate to hear more, she sat down on the edge of her bed, still clutching the frame. "How well did you know my husband?"

"Dave?" He scratched his head. "Not all that well. We were on different shifts, so I didn't see him all that often. But we played cards a couple of times."

"He didn't like being called that," she said. "Dave. He always made everyone use his full name, David."

"Really?" He shrugged. "Out there in hell, formality and civility die with every explosion. We called him Dave. Everyone did. Heck, my name is Tyler and everyone referred to me as Ty."

That made sense. "I wish you'd known him better. In the last month or so before he died, I hardly heard from him. What few letters he was able to get out didn't even arrive until after he'd been killed." She swallowed to get past the lump in her throat. "I'd love it if you could share some stories about him."

"I'm sorry. I wish I could too."

Almost afraid to ask, she did anyway. For months she'd been plagued by nightmares, picturing various scenarios in which her mate had been killed. "Were you there when he…died?" Her voice came out a whisper. "All I know was that it was a bomb. They—the military—told me there was nothing left of his body to send back. So I didn't even have that."

For once, Tyler went silent. She watched him, praying with every fiber of her being that he would be able to tell her something. Anything. When she'd pressed for more information, all the military did was give her their apparently standard line: "killed in the line of duty."

"No," Tyler finally answered, crushing her hopes. "I was not there when he died. At least, not that I know of. When I try to reflect on my last memory of that place, I'm pretty sure he was still alive. So I must have died before him. How long did you say he's been gone?"

"A little over eighteen months." Which meant Tyler had been dead longer than that.

"I see." He nodded. "Again, I'm sorry I can't tell you

more. From what I knew of him, he seemed like a nice guy."

"Thank you for that." She put the photograph back inside the drawer. Though it wasn't much, actually hearing something, anything, about David, helped ease the edge of the constant ache she always carried inside her. Lately, though, she'd noticed it had lessened. There were actually larger and larger patches of time when she didn't think about David at all. Guilt stabbed her as she realized this. She'd promised herself never to forget him.

Looking up, she met Tyler's gaze. Something in his tortured expression made her stomach lurch. For a ghost, his features were really well-defined. "What is it? You're not telling me everything, are you?"

With a shrug, he nodded. "Nothing bad, so don't worry. Just something else I remembered. I think I know how I died."

She waited, bracing herself.

"There had been a few of the guys, including me and your David, who'd skirted the edge of danger working to help some of the locals, most particularly the children," he continued. "Our superiors had reprimanded us once, turning a blind eye after that."

"That's good, isn't it?"

"Yes. Of course. But dangerous."

"Yet you and David still did it," she marveled.

"It was impossible not to. The locals were starving. We smuggled rations to the women, brought the children trinkets and treats sent from home and did our best to ease the damage."

She waited, aware there were often two sides to every story.

"The Taliban sympathizers hated this. That's how I was killed."

Though she detected a tinge of shame in his voice, she saw none in his expression.

"They watched and the next time we snuck out to deliver goodies, they'd set up a trap."

Bracing herself, she nodded. When he didn't speak again, she sighed. "Let me guess. The suicide bomb you'd mentioned before?"

"Yes. Took out at least two of us, and some women and children too." Rugged features expressionless, he stared off into the distance, as if remembering the sound of the gunfire and explosions, the screaming and shouting. All the pain.

His next words confirmed this. "Anabel, they didn't even care that they'd killed themselves or their own people."

Aching, she wished she knew a way to comfort him. "I'm sorry," she said, aware her words couldn't possibly be adequate. Then, because he was a ghost and she really wanted to know, she went ahead and asked. "What was it like to die?"

Lost in his thoughts, he didn't at first respond. When he raised his head to look at her, all emotion had been erased from his handsome face. "A sharp flash of pain. And then…nothing."

"Nothing?" She frowned. "I was hoping for something more inspiring. Like you could say you found yourself in a tunnel, moving toward a bright light, all that. You know?"

"I do know."

Was he laughing at her? She squinted at him, not sure.

"And?" she finally prodded. "Are you going to tell me what it's like?"

"It was liberating," he said. "Once I'd shed that ruined body, joy filled me. I went to another place. Another plane. I knew I'd come home."

Nothing but contentment and happiness filled his voice now. "But because of the violent manner of my death, my spirit went into shock. It was all too traumatic, and they took me to a healing place."

"A healing place?"

He waved his ghostly hand, about to say more, and then didn't. "That's all I can tell you."

"But…why are you here? Why didn't you move on?"

"Because somehow I heard my sister's cries. Her prayers for help. So instead of moving forward as I should have, I was allowed to remain tethered to earth."

"I'm not sure I understand. You're a ghost."

"Yes." He smiled, and the beauty of him struck her deep inside her heart. "I was permitted to come back as an ethereal being in the hopes of saving my sister. She's being tortured, and while death would be a release from the pain, it's not her time to die. Still, I fear he will kill her. And if he doesn't, her suffering is terrible. We've got to get her out of there."

"We'll figure out a way," she promised, reacting to the sheer desperation in his voice.

Apparently overcome, he turned away. For a moment, his ghostly form flickered and vanished, before solidifying once more.

"Thank you." When he met her gaze, his hazel eyes glowed with determination. "Meanwhile, have I answered all your questions?"

She thought of her dead husband, the man she'd

mourned for so long. "Since you said David was still alive when you died, I take it he wasn't with you that night?"

"I don't actually know. If he was there, I don't remember him. But I'm guessing he was killed doing something similar."

Miraculously, this helped ease her heart more than anything she'd heard or read about the troops in Afghanistan. "He died helping women and children," she whispered, marveling again that war hadn't changed her husband's generous heart.

"Most likely." Tyler shrugged. "Though I wasn't there, so I can't know for sure."

"I do. I know inside me." Turning, she headed toward her bathroom. "I'll be out in a little while. You can wait in the kitchen, if you'd like."

His wry grimace made her smile. "Sure. I'll go in there and inhale the aroma of the coffee brewing. I used to enjoy my first cup in the morning." With that, he drifted away, his broad shoulders and narrow waist drawing her eye until she could no longer see him.

Shutting the door, she couldn't help feeling sorry for him. He'd died a noble death too. Had he no one to mourn him? She realized she'd never asked about his family. Surely he must have had parents, maybe even other siblings, someone to mark his passing. She'd ask him later.

She knew only of the one sister, Dena, who'd surely mourned her brother. So much so that she'd cried out to his spirit in her pain and terror. Their tie had been so great that he'd come back from wherever he'd been to try to save her from a fate worse than death.

Again, a noble man. One with a generous spirit, like David.

She glanced at herself in the mirror and paused. A

woman of purpose stared back at her, brown eyes blazing, expression resolute and determined. And resilient. Somehow, after all she'd been through, she realized she'd emerged stronger for it.

Fine. Decision made, she turned the shower on and, as soon as the water got hot, stepped inside. If she had magic power inside her, she'd learn how to use it to locate Tyler's sister. As for doing battle with the warlock person, well, she'd have to deal with that when it happened.

As Tyler drifted into the colorful kitchen, he took in the green cabinets, orange walls and colorful paintings. More of Anabel's personality. How strange that it happened that the woman he'd sought help from had been married to one of the guys in his former unit. He was pretty sure it wasn't a fluke. One thing life after death had taught him was that there were very few real coincidences. Things happened for a purpose, and while he might temporarily be blinded to what that might be, he knew to keep an eye out.

While he and Dena were growing up with a drug-addicted father, his mother had shielded them as best she could. Older by ten years, Tyler had tried to be the man in the family, but as a kid, he hadn't fully realized that his father might kill him rather than hurt him. His mother had, always stepping in front of the blows, taking the brunt of his father's drug-fueled wrath.

Desperately wanting to defend his mother, despite her strict orders not to intervene, Tyler had helped in every way he could besides beating the man to a bloody pulp, which he fully planned to do once he was older and stronger. In the meantime, he'd taken care of his mother when her bruises and broken bones incapacitated her.

He'd cooked and done laundry and watched after his baby sister. He'd learned to change her diapers and mix her formula, sleeping on the floor by her crib in case his doped-up father got any stupid ideas. When his mother had found out about this, she'd put a stop to it, promising Tyler she'd make sure nothing happened to the baby.

And she had. She'd always made sure to be in the way of her husband's fists and vitriolic bile. Despite her petite stature, she'd displayed enormous courage, though Tyler had never understood why she wouldn't leave. All she'd say when he asked was that he was too young to understand. Eventually, he'd figured out that his father had sworn to hunt her down and kill her and his children should she ever try to run.

Finally, their father had disappeared. Tyler had heard the man now lived on the streets, a slave to his own demons. Periodically, he'd show up at the house, but only to take money, which he used to buy more drugs.

Tyler had never understood why his mother gave the man anything at all.

As soon as he'd graduated from high school, Tyler had enlisted in the army. For him, the military was not only an escape, but a chance to make something of himself, to make sure he didn't end up like his father.

Their father had overdosed when Dena was seventeen. Tyler had been stationed at Fort Bliss in El Paso, Texas. He'd been granted leave and had hurried home to help out.

He hadn't been sure what to expect. A celebration, perhaps? Instead he found his mother insensible with grief and his baby sister angry at the woman who'd raised them.

"What's wrong with her?" Dena had asked. "He spent his life making her miserable, and all she can do is cry."

"I don't understand either," he said, putting his arm around her shoulders. "But I do know Mom needs us. Let her grieve, and be there for her, the way she always was for us."

"She should have left him" had been Dena's response. Since Tyler tended to agree, he didn't reply.

After the funeral, he'd gone back to base and kept in touch with his sister. He'd celebrated with her long-distance when she got a job at the junior college. Sure, it was in the cafeteria, but she'd had plans, she told him. She wanted to take some classes, with an eye on earning her degree. He'd been proud.

What Dena hadn't told him was that their mother had started using the very same drugs that had killed their father. Heroin, mostly. Sometimes meth. Their mom had died right after Tyler was sent to Afghanistan, though he hadn't learned about it for two weeks. He'd raged and grieved and worried that his sister might follow this horrible family pattern. Dena had assured him that she wouldn't. He'd believed her. Neither of them had wanted anything to do with that lifestyle.

After that, he and his sister had been on their own. And then Tyler had gone and gotten himself killed. And Dena had gotten into a bigger mess than he ever would have thought possible. If he didn't get her out, she was going to die too young, just as he had. Even though it wasn't her time to go.

Anabel had to help him save her. She had to. He would accept nothing else, even if it cost him his own movement into eternity.

Being a ghost felt more like being alive than he'd expected. Sure, he couldn't eat or drink, didn't have to eliminate bodily waste or sleep, but he felt all the same human emotions he'd experienced when he was alive.

Including desire. That one had surprised the hell out of him. Every time he got close to Anabel, his entire body tightened in places that shouldn't have been possible for a ghost. At first, he'd tried to keep telling himself that it was due to her beauty and the power that radiated from her.

But after the first night, when he'd found himself watching her sleep, aching with the kind of physical need he couldn't possibly satisfy without a flesh-and-blood body, he'd known it was more. Much, much more.

He wanted her. Desired her. In all the ways a man wanted a woman. Except he wasn't a man. He was a ghost.

This had to be his own personal form of hell. Because there was absolutely nothing he could do to ease the craving.

When Anabel finally emerged from her morning preparations, showered and dressed in a pair of faded black jeans that hugged her curves, with her dark hair in a jaunty ponytail, he couldn't make himself stop staring. She was the sexiest woman he'd ever seen, bar none. Again, that lust stabbed through what once had been his body.

"You look…glowing," he said. He really sucked at compliments.

"Thank you. I guess." Her smile made her aura illuminate even brighter, making a glowing halo around her head.

For whatever reason, he felt the need to elaborate. "I don't just mean your aura, though yours is spectacular. But your human form is beautiful."

Her smile widened, making her whiskey eyes sparkle. "Wow. Thanks. You kind of made my day."

He found himself smiling back. Maybe he wasn't so bad at this complimenting thing after all.

He let his gaze drink her up, his entire body burning. Funny how he still felt as if he had a body, even though he didn't. Even when she turned away, completely unaware of his desire, he tracked her with his gaze.

Focus, he reminded himself. He'd come back for a reason—to save Dena, not ache for a woman he could never have.

Pouring herself a cup of coffee, she added cream and sugar before taking a deep sip. "Ah," she sighed. "That's good."

"Torturing me now?"

For an instant, she looked stricken, and then she shrugged. "Not my intention at all. But I apologize nonetheless."

He gave a quick dip of his head to show the apology had been accepted. "What's on the agenda for today?"

"I'm going up to the college where your sister works. I want to talk to some of her friends."

"Sounds good." Action, finally. He approved. "What about?"

She gave him a long look, clearly debating what she had to say. "I need to find out about her boyfriend."

"I can save you some time on that. Dena didn't have one," he answered, confident.

One eyebrow raised, she nodded. "Okay, then I need to find out about anyone she might have dated or slept with."

"No need." He shook his head. "Between work and school, she didn't have time. She would have told me if there was anyone special."

Making an exasperated sound, she grimaced. "Tyler, I hate to be the one to break it to you, but I'm pretty sure your sister isn't a saint. This man who has her had to have met her somehow. I'm going to try and gather information to see if we can figure out who he is."

Chapter 5

Tyler started to speak, then thought better of it. No doubt she was right. Not only was she pretty and socially active, but Dena was a healthy twenty-five-year-old. He shouldn't be acting like the overprotective big brother, not now. Not only had he managed to get himself killed and leave her without any family, but clearly he hadn't succeeded in teaching her to be careful.

Unless, as Anabel said, the man who'd grabbed her had been someone she'd trusted.

"You're right," he admitted. "But you have to consider that it could be a teacher, or a janitor, or even one of her coworkers."

"Or some guy she'd dated," Anabel pointed out. "There are a lot of crazies masquerading as normal in the dating scene, let me tell you."

He cocked his head. "You've been dating?"

"I tried. Once or twice—that was it. Just a month ago. I thought it might help me to, you know, get over David. After that, I gave up and deleted my profile from all the dating sites."

Jealousy stabbed him, completely unwarranted.

"Good for you for trying," he said, aware of the lie and feeling like a fool. "I think after eighteen months, Dave would approve of you getting back out there."

"No," she said softly, her expression shutting down. "He wouldn't. David was my mate. You were Pack. You know what that means. He's the only one I will ever love."

Slowly, he nodded. "I do, though I'm not sure I believe in that particular myth."

"Myth?"

"Yes. I honestly don't know anyone who actually met their mate."

She pointed to her chest. "Now you do. Me."

Ignoring the emotions swirling inside him, he eyed her. "How did you know? I mean, we all have people we're attracted to, even people we love. What made you think Dave was actually your mate?"

"I didn't just think it. I knew, the instant he kissed me."

He thought of what he'd learned from Juliet. "And Kane McGraw? Did you also *know* he was your mate?"

At his words, her eyes filled with tears. "I had a breakdown, Tyler. I wasn't myself." Holding herself stiffly, she turned away from him.

Clearly, he'd gone too far. He'd realized it the instant he finished speaking. "I'm sorry," he said. "I just wanted to point out to you that it was possible for you to find love again."

Like with me. More foolishness, as he was nothing

but a shade of a man. He waited for Anabel to shoot him down.

But she didn't respond. Instead she hurried away. A minute later, he heard the sound of her bedroom door closing.

Though initially she'd been hurt by Tyler's words, the more she considered them, the more Anabel understood his thought process. Of course he'd doubt her conviction once he learned she'd erroneously dubbed a second man her true mate. As if she'd ever been unsure about David, or he about her.

No, she'd been lonely, stumbling around close to the end of a ledge, and when she learned Kane McGraw had come back to town, she'd sought a way to end the dark cloud of loneliness. Back in school, she'd always had a crush on Kane, even dated him a few times despite his being several years older than her, and with the twisted logic of depression, she'd managed to convince herself that the impossible was real.

When he rejected her, saying he loved another, it had been the final shove and she'd gone under. Her bewildered pain and her burning desire for vengeance had blinded her to the truth and to the light. In a moment of weakness, she'd let the darkness in and had nearly caused a good woman to lose her life. Worse, she'd later learned that Lilly Gideon, the woman Kane loved, had spent fifteen years imprisoned by her own father and his religious cult. She shuddered to think she'd nearly sent Lilly back to that awful life.

After that, she'd lain low. Gradually recovering, aware no one in town would ever look at her the same way again.

She'd made several clumsy attempts to make it up to Lilly McGraw, until finally the other woman had hugged her and told her to stop, that she forgave her. For that, Anabel had been grateful.

Now, for the first time in a long while, Anabel had hope. Never once had she imagined she'd be given the chance to atone by saving Dena Rogers.

While she didn't personally know Tyler's sister, she could only imagine what kind of hell the younger woman now faced. Similar, she thought, to what Lilly Gideon had once faced. The parallels of the two women's predicaments didn't escape her.

Once she freed Dena, she would have wiped her own slate clean once more.

And Tyler could… She couldn't help wondering what would happen to Tyler once they'd succeeded in freeing his sister. He'd go back into wherever ghosts went when it came time to move on. The light, she assumed. At least she hoped so. The alternative would be very bleak.

Glancing at her watch, she saw it was nearly nine. If she wanted to get her day started, she couldn't hide out in her bedroom forever. One thing she'd learned since her meltdown was she had a lot more inner strength than she'd ever suspected. Magic would be a definite bonus.

So she straightened her shoulders, took a deep breath and opened the door. When she walked back into the kitchen, Tyler's ghostly form hovered exactly where she'd left him.

Again struck by his large, masculine frame, she sucked in a breath. How he, even though a ghost, could practically radiate virility stunned her. Though this time, she noticed an air of isolation around his tall, broad-shouldered figure.

The question in his hazel eyes made her heart skip a beat.

"I'll do it," she said, not giving him a chance to speak. "I need to see if I can take a crash course in learning how to access my magic. Once I have some sort of grip on that, I can seriously hunt for whoever abducted your sister."

He bowed his head, a swath of dark hair falling onto his forehead. "Thank you."

Uncomfortable with her visceral reaction to so much male beauty, she nodded. Keeping busy would be the best distraction from those kinds of crazy thoughts. "Let's go." Snatching up her car keys, she headed toward the door. "We'll stop and talk to Juliet. I think her first yoga class of the day just finished up. I'm hoping she'll have some pointers for me."

Trying not to smile as Tyler crammed his long legs in the passenger seat of her Fiat, she sang along to the radio during the short drive downtown.

As it turned out, Juliet had a lot more than pointers to help Anabel. "You'll need to read these," she said, grabbing a short stack of books from a bookcase behind her desk. "This will be a good starting place. Once you have, come back to me with questions."

Anabel glanced at the books, then at Tyler, who gave an almost imperceptible shake of his head. "Juliet, I'd love to read them—and I will, eventually—but right now I'm short on time. Tyler's sister's life is in danger, and I'm afraid I'm going to need a crash course in magic in order to save her."

Appearing nonplussed, Juliet swallowed and slowly put the books down on top of her desk. "It's not that simple," she began.

"Make it as simple as possible, please." Though she hated to interrupt her kind friend, Anabel knew every second must be an eternity to the poor woman being held prisoner.

Eyeing her, Juliet appeared to consider. "All right," she finally said. "But you need to know, magic can be dangerous without knowledge. Extremely dangerous."

Anabel locked eyes with her friend. With her smooth face and long gray braid, Juliet always radiated peace and tranquility. And strength, Anabel thought. "Teach me how to protect myself."

"I'll do my best. But understand, you could still be killed. I don't know how powerful this warlock is."

Tyler began to flicker, his form wavering in and out of view. Anabel glanced once at him, bracing herself for the swooping of her stomach as she did. Their gazes locked and held as he slowly solidified. *I'm okay,* he mouthed.

Once she knew he was all right, she refocused all her attention on Juliet. "Teach me as much as you can in as short a time as possible."

Juliet nodded. "How long do I have?"

"A woman's life is at stake, so I don't have long." Anabel glanced again at Tyler. "A day?"

Frowning, he shook his head.

"How about twelve hours?"

This time, Tyler reluctantly nodded.

"Twelve hours?" Eyebrows raised, Juliet glanced at her wrist even though she wasn't wearing a watch. "Sorry. What time is it now?"

"Nine thirty. That gives us until tonight."

"It'll have to do, I guess." Juliet sighed, her soft blue eyes sharpening. "It's not nearly long enough, but let's get started on some basics."

After a quick explanation of what magic was—not so much an external thing, but part of Anabel's inner spirit—Juliet told her it was time to see if Anabel could feel her power deep inside herself.

Anabel didn't even have to think. "No."

"Well, then we're going to try and feel it."

"I already tried last night. Nothing happened."

"We'll try again."

"How?"

"Take a deep breath," Juliet advised. "First, you need to slow down your pulse. Your heart is beating so fast I can see the fluttering in the hollow of your throat."

Self-consciously, Anabel raised her hand to her neck. "Sorry. I'm a little nervous."

"Deep breath."

Obediently, Anabel inhaled. "I can't help it," she said, fidgeting in her chair. "This is all very odd."

"Then we'll wait until you're tranquil." Rising, Juliet lit a candle, moving it over so the scent was close to Anabel. "We may have to do some yoga if this doesn't help. Breathe. It's eucalyptus. Very calming."

Desperate, Anabel inhaled the scent, trying to think calming thoughts, using the same mantra she used when meditating. A moment or two later, she blinked. Darned if she didn't feel better. More confident and stronger.

"Now we'll talk about power," Juliet said, smiling slightly as if she knew Anabel's thoughts. "Everyone has a spark of magic inside. Some just have more than others."

Anabel nodded, the fear trying to creep back in. She couldn't really explain her intense nervousness, but for some reason the entire idea of having magical powers scared her.

If Tyler's sister hadn't needed her help, Anabel figured she would just have let the so-called magic stay locked up inside her. If she'd even ever learned of its existence, that was.

"That you are able to see ghosts as more than energy speaks to your level of power. That's one of the ways it manifests itself." Juliet grinned. "And the fact that your ability to see and hear spirits didn't make you go stark, raving crazy is another testament to your strength."

Strength. "I rarely feel strong, though I've realized what I've been through and overcome has given me strength. But that doesn't matter. Tell me what else I should be able to do. Most important, I need the ability to track this creep who has Dena."

"And fight him," Tyler chimed in, making Juliet jump.

"I forgot about you," Juliet said, shooting a stern glance in his general direction. "Fighting won't be possible, not without a lot of practice. But I can teach Anabel to protect herself."

"That will have to do," Anabel said grimly. "As long as I can hold him off long enough to get his captive—or captives—out."

"And then what?" Juliet asked, her sharp voice telling Anabel what she thought of that idea. "He'll likely be furious. You won't be able to hold him off forever."

Again Anabel and Tyler exchanged a glance. Again, her heart turned over in response. Tearing her gaze away, she focused on Juliet. "Then you'd better do your best to teach me as much as you can. It's not like I even have a choice."

Tyler didn't know what it was about Anabel—other than her beauty—but every time their eyes met, he found himself entranced. His fascination deepened the more time he spent with her, which was not only impossible, but an unnecessary distraction. He'd come back to the earthly plane with one objective—to save his sister—and he couldn't let this compelling attraction detour him.

So he decided to leave the two women alone. There wasn't much he could do anyway, other than be a disruption. Anabel had asked Juliet for twelve hours—an eternity for his sister, trapped and tortured. But this was only the second day since he'd appeared and begged Anabel for help. She needed to learn how to tap into her power if she wanted to have a prayer of finding Dena. He had to allow himself to trust and to hope.

He left the human plane and went to the gray area he privately thought of as the in-between place. Not earth, but not the afterlife either. Once there, he made himself still and then sent himself out. Seeking, searching, for the spark of life force that belonged to his sister.

There. Faint, but still burning. He zoomed to it, passing through nothing and everything, clouds and earth and night sky. When he reached her, in that damp, dank place where she was being held, he once again tried to communicate with her and comfort her.

But Dena had no power and couldn't sense his presence. In fact, he realized she'd sunk into a state of consciousness where she couldn't sense much of anything at all.

Horrified, he took stock of her condition. Her once slender body had become emaciated, and even though she lay curled in a corner in the fetal position, he could see the sharpness of her bones. Her labored breathing attested to her general state of unhealthiness, as did her lank and tangled hair. Even her aura had changed, becoming speckled with brown and black, as if a rotting poison festered inside her system.

She didn't have much longer. Tyler wanted to weep. And rage and storm. Most of all, he wished he had substance, so he could free her from the metal shackles tethering her bony ankles to the concrete wall.

As his emotions roiled inside his spirit, he felt the approaching force of a heavy blackness descending on him. On them. Not just dark, but…evil.

Which meant the warlock had sensed his presence. Magic, reaching even into the realm of spirit. Dangerous. Deadly, even.

Tyler tried to retreat but found he could not. Invisible chains bound him, as surely as if a giant arm had reached out and held him against the concrete.

Shocked, horrified, he made his form as ethereal as he could. Still, he could not escape the grip of the other. How powerful was this man, that he could not only sense a ghost, but also hold him down without saying a word?

Magic. Something inside him stirred in response.

Again, he eyed Dena, aching at the palpable pain radiating from her. Even in her comatose state, his sister must have sensed the presence, as well. She began to shake, making faint sounds—protests or pleas for help.

Tyler concentrated on her. With every bit of energy he possessed, he willed her to lift her head, to realize he'd come in answer to her entreaties. From the light, bringing a small illumination to the shadows.

The instant the thought occurred to him, the dark energy coalesced into a black flame of energy. And laughed, a chilling sound that echoed in the concrete chamber. Whatever part of the warlock that held Tyler became a fist. And the fist began to squeeze.

Despite the fact that none of this should have been able to happen, Tyler felt the tightening grip crush the spark out of him. He stifled panic, struggling to fight. Another few seconds, and he didn't doubt it would be snuffed out permanently.

How was it possible for someone—anyone—to have this much dark power?

Anabel. He called out her name with every fiber of his being, hoping against hope that she'd somehow hear him. And that she'd be able to save him.

Tired, Anabel once again allowed Juliet to put her through the paces. "Focus, concentrate and expand," she chanted obediently, trying like heck to send her energy outward. She felt extremely foolish that after three hours of trying, she still had not succeeded even once.

This time, she did. Something pulled her, tugged at the edges of her consciousness, and she allowed herself to follow the shining threat tethering her to him. To Tyler. Shocked, she realized he was in some sort of trouble.

The instant she reached him, she understood. She felt the dark oppression of the other's magic like a heavy weight on her physical chest, even though her actual body still sat in a chair in Juliet's office.

With her heart beating a rapid tattoo, she tried to do as Juliet had instructed. Focus and concentrate. Tyler was a ghost. While it shouldn't be possible to trap an ethereal spirit, the other had done so, using magic.

Therefore, it followed that Anabel could use her magic to free him. "Come to me, Tyler," she ordered. "Come to me now."

Air whooshed—physical or otherwise—and Tyler came to her. All at once, she found herself back in her body in Juliet's office. The impact of what she'd done knocked her from the chair to the floor. She felt dizzy and weak, as though her legs might not be able to stand. Taking a shaky breath, she held on to the back of her chair as she slowly climbed to her feet.

"Are you all right?" Juliet rushed around the desk to help her up.

Anabel waved her away, searching for Tyler. "I'm fine."

"What happened?"

Spotting Tyler, nearly incandescent, in the doorway, Anabel smiled. "I just freed Tyler, my ghostly friend. It looks like the warlock had trapped his spirit. Such a thing shouldn't be possible, should it?"

"No." Juliet gaped at her, her faded blue eyes wide. "You seriously went up against this evil psycho and won?"

Dropping into the chair, Anabel put her head between her knees, willing the vertigo to stop. "Whatever I did seriously zapped my strength."

"But you succeeded?"

"Apparently so." Anabel gestured at Tyler. "Maybe I do have a prayer of saving your sister after all."

"Maybe so." Tyler drifted closer, flickering in and out of existence. Even so, the maddening hint of arrogance about him made Anabel smile.

Rather than smile back, Tyler shook his head. "We need to be careful. He wasn't aware of us before. Now he most certainly is."

Then, before Anabel could react or respond, Tyler vanished in a tendril of smoke.

"Ask him what happened," Juliet urged. "How'd the warlock get him?"

"He's gone." Anabel rubbed her aching temples, missing Tyler more than she should. "I'll ask him later, when I see him again. In the meantime, let's work some more. If that warlock does come looking for me, I want to be as prepared to face him as I possibly can be."

Eyes bright, Juliet nodded.

They practiced drills over and over until Anabel could barely see straight. Eventually, she was able to focus her concentration enough to light a wadded-up piece of paper on fire. Juliet clapped. "Very good!"

"That's something, right?" Anabel asked, desperately in need of an encouraging word. "I'd hate to think we've spent all this time for nothing."

"It is something," Juliet responded, her smile slowly fading. "And that shows your potential. But if you really want to win against a warlock, it's not nearly enough."

Anabel groaned. "I'm exhausted. I think I'm finished for today. I have no more energy. Let me sleep on this tonight and I'll practice in the morning."

Something in her tone made Juliet lean closer, concern in her eyes. "Practice what? Promise me you only mean to try these simple exercises like we've been working on."

Anabel didn't even have to think. "I need to do more. And to do it better. The clock is ticking and I must find where Tyler's sister is being held. First thing in the morning, I'm going to try to locate her."

"How?"

"I'm not sure. But if Tyler could use her energy to find her, surely I can do the same. And since I'm alive and can't float through the air, I'm hoping I can trace her that way."

"It's not much of a plan." Arms crossed, Juliet sighed.

"And since the bad guy now knows someone with magic is looking for him, it could put you at risk, as well."

Frustrated, Anabel pushed to her feet, stumbling slightly. "If you have a better idea, please let me know."

"I don't," Juliet admitted. "But still..."

Anabel hugged her friend. "I know you're worried, but I'll be fine. I've got to pick up the pace. Tomorrow will be the third day since Tyler came to me asking for help. That's entirely unacceptable. His sister has been held prisoner for way too long."

Juliet opened and then closed her mouth. Looking nearly as exhausted as Anabel felt, she nodded. "Fine. Practice. Read the books. And call me if you have any questions."

Driving home, Anabel kept expecting Tyler to pop into her car. When he didn't, the disappointment felt way deeper than it should have. After all, he'd been in her life for only two days. Had she really gotten used to having him around that quickly? If so, her loneliness had made her more vulnerable than she'd realized.

Despite giving herself a stern talking-to all the way home, she felt a sense of urgency in her need to see him. When she got home, it was all she could do not to run into her house, looking for him.

But he wasn't there. Stopping short of calling his name, she felt the emptiness of the place in a way she hadn't since David's death. Just great. Despite her self-imposed isolation and her confidence that she'd become self-reliant, put a sexy man in her path for a few days and she'd already become—not dependent, but intertwined with him somehow. Not fair. She of all people didn't deserve the ache of missing someone again. Especially someone she barely knew. Who happened to be a ghost.

Putting him from her mind, she fixed herself a bowl of cereal for her dinner and then got ready for bed.

After crawling beneath the covers, she must have fallen instantly asleep. Because when she came awake again, startled, her nightstand clock showed it was almost three in the morning.

What had awakened her? Sitting up, she peered around the pitch-dark room, trying to get her bearings. Had Tyler returned?

But no, she saw no ghostly presence, no shimmer of energy either. Since the sun hadn't yet risen, she assumed that he'd retreated to whatever place ghosts came from.

Something else, then. Something inside her...

The urge came upon her suddenly, like a match lit to dry timber. She needed to shape-shift. More than a need—a visceral command that she do so immediately. Right now. The instant she realized, she tried to think back, to remember when she'd last changed into wolf.

Too long. More than a month, actually. Which explained the fierceness of her urgency to comply this instant.

Which was good, since shape-shifters who didn't change walked a slippery slope into madness. Again, she found herself wishing for Tyler. It would be exhilarating to have another wolf to run with. That was, if he could still change. Even though her kind was meant to run in packs, lately Anabel had done all her shape-shifting alone. She liked it that way, really. She'd told herself that so often that she almost believed it.

Slipping from the house into the cool, predawn breeze, she let the light of the three-quarter moon pull her toward the woods. Since she wore only the large T-shirt she slept in, as soon as she'd stepped into lush undergrowth below the towering oaks and pines, she pulled it over her head and draped it across a stack of large rocks. She always used them for the same purpose when she changed.

Then she smiled and turned around in a complete circle, lifting her arms high to the forest and the night sky. This ritual wasn't necessary, of course, but it made her happy, so she always did it.

Beneath her skin, her wolf rippled with impatience, wanting out. For a moment, she held her inner beast at bay and then dropped to all fours to begin the process.

Chapter 6

As Anabel initiated the change, the shifting tore through her, swift and vicious, almost as if the beast feared she'd change her mind. Pain mingled with pleasure, a peculiar combination. And then she was wolf.

Lifting her head, she sniffed the air, amazed as always by how different the wolf viewed the world. Her beast used smell first, then sight and sound.

And tonight, as usual, the forest was a feast for the senses. She tried to start off at a walk, but the joy to be wolf filled her and made her run. She crashed through the underbrush, feet drumming into fertile earth, rustling through long-fallen leaves.

Smaller animals bolted ahead, terrified by her passage. Even though they were prey, she wasn't hunting. At least not yet.

When she burst upon a clearing, she slowed to a trot,

then a walk. Finally, she stopped and inhaled deeply. The human part of her regretted that she'd gone so long without letting her wolf run free. As wolf, she lived in the here and now, without worries or guilt or stress. In the days after David had been killed, she'd taken to spending days as wolf, the sorrow too deep to face as human.

Of course, like all shifters, she'd had no choice but to eventually change back to her human form.

Now, though, as wolf, she refused to think of those things any further. At this moment, she thrilled to the power in her muscular, lean form.

A flash of movement to the right caught her eyes. Sniffing, she smelled nothing, no other animal's telltale scent. Which wasn't good. At all.

Dropping into a hunting crouch, she began to approach the area where she'd seen the movement. Her nighttime vision was good, and as wolf, she never imagined things that weren't real.

A moment later, she had her answer. There, near the dense underbrush near a towering oak, sat another wolf. One whose form shimmered in and out of existence with each wisp of wind and who bore no scent. Like Tyler.

A ghost wolf? Mystified, she continued to study the other animal. Previously, all her ghostly encounters had been as human. She'd never before seen the specter of a wolf. Like Tyler, this one was big and gave off the aura of a male.

And then, as she drew closer, the other wolf cocked his head. Something in the glimmer of his eyes gave her the answer.

It was Tyler! Her ghostly companion must have finally shown up at her house and found her gone. So he'd followed her wolf, wearing the form of his own beast.

She hadn't known ghosts could do that.

She also hadn't known how happy she'd be to see him once more. Especially now, since she was running without a pack.

Heart singing with joy, she panted at him. And then, because she was wolf, she spun and took off running again. Delight pulsed through her with the pounding of every paw on the earth.

Wolf Tyler kept pace, his shimmering ghostly form beautiful. He ran full out, making her think he had difficulty matching her pace, which only had her increasing her effort to see if she could outrun him.

Tongue lolling, grinning a wolf's grin, she ran and ran until she could run no more. Even a lope or a jog failed her. Sides heaving, she let herself crash to the ground. Lying there, panting and trying to catch her breath, she refused to even glance at the shade of her visitor.

Because she knew what came next. Shifters always became aroused when they changed back to human. Most times, unless they were with an agreeable party, they ignored it. Usually when a male and female shape-shifted alone, consent and desire were implied.

Shock rippled through her as she realized what she wanted. She wondered if he felt the same. But if he did, how would that even work with a ghost?

There, on the rock where she'd left it, her nightshirt. She'd run full circle. The time had come.

With a groan, she initiated the change back to human. This time, the shift went slowly, as her beast felt reluctant to relinquish the form. It hurt. A lot. Yet even so, her body tingled with pleasure.

And desire.

Foolish, foolish girl. Always wanting something she

couldn't have. And even if she somehow, miraculously, could, doing so would be too dangerous.

Ignoring Tyler for her own peace of mind, not wanting to see if he'd remained wolf or changed back too, she got up slowly, wincing at her sore muscles and aching bones. Snagging her oversize T-shirt off the rock, she dropped it over her head. The soft material rubbed against her pebbled nipples, making her bite her lip.

Despite her exhaustion, her entire body buzzed with want. She knew if she turned and faced him, she'd lose what little control she had and make a fool of herself.

Frustrated, she kept her eyes straight ahead, praying he didn't decide to materialize in front of her, and plodded back to the house. Once inside, she headed straight back to her bedroom. A quick glance at the clock showed she still had over an hour until sunrise, so she crawled beneath the sheets and hoped for sleep.

Instead she lay there burning.

At some point, she must have drifted off. When she next opened her eyes, yellow sunlight streamed through her window. A quick glance around her bedroom revealed she was alone, so she stretched and smiled. She'd done it. Resisted temptation and spent time in her lupine shape.

Being wolf had been good for her. More than that. Freeing her wolf brought perspective to the craziness that had been her life for the past two—now three—days since Tyler had shown up.

Now she felt as though she could accomplish anything. She could do this. Not only that, but she would succeed.

As if thinking of him had summoned him, Tyler appeared in the doorway. Still as wolf, his ghostly fur shimmering in the lemonade light of morning.

Studying him, she realized he was beautiful. Large

and strong and powerful, his silver fur gleaming. He padded closer, and she noted his eyes still looked the same, shining with intelligence and humor. Awed, her chest tight, she thought he might have been the most beautiful wolf she'd ever seen, bar none.

At the thought, guilt hit her hard. She shouldn't think that, couldn't. David also had been a striking wolf, with his glossy black pelt and compact, muscular body. David should always have been the perfect wolf to her. Not Tyler, a man she barely knew.

While she watched, the ghostly wolf shimmered and faded away. A second later, a man stood in its place. A naked man, fully aroused.

Heat shot through her. She dragged her gaze away, but not before she noticed the size of his massive arousal. She'd only thought she'd faced temptation the night before. Desire consumed her. She felt it coursing through her blood like an electrifying drug. Her harsh, uneven breathing testified to how turned on he made her. One look from his smoldering eyes, and she nearly came. As she bit back a groan, her body tingled in response.

So did her guilt. Again. She shouldn't be fighting the urge to climb all over him, but she was. Worse, she could barely restrain herself from taking the hard length of him into her— No.

"Put some clothes on," she barked, her voice raspy and wobbly. "You're a ghost, so make some materialize. Now."

He knew, damn him. He raked his eyes over her, slowly, seductively, making her clench. Then, as she continued to glare at him, he slanted a look at her, part mischief, part smoldering, before waving his hands. A second later and he was back in his military fatigues. Still as handsome, still as sexy, but no longer naked.

Damned if she didn't feel a twinge of regret. Though she could still see the bulge from his still-aroused body.

"What was all that?" she lashed out, furious with herself as much as or more than him. "Didn't I ask you to stop just appearing? You don't have to shadow me every step of the way."

Was that hurt flashing across his chiseled features?

As he drifted closer, she saw the way his hands were clenched into fists.

"Anabel," he said, the hoarse tone almost a plea. When he reached for her, she didn't try to dodge him, well aware a ghost couldn't connect by touch.

But somehow Tyler did. Not a ghost, but a man, strong and solid, pulled her against his muscular chest. A shudder of raw desire immobilized her. Shocked, she froze. Unable to resist or move.

Tyler was real. She could feel his uneven breathing, as rough as hers, and his heart pounding under his skin. While she tried to process this, he cupped her face in his large hands and covered her mouth with his.

The strong hardness of the kiss burned her like fire, searing her to the core. This…wasn't real, couldn't be real, and yet as pleasure made waves inside her, she realized she could no longer fight. As his mouth ravished hers and she felt his arousal swell against her, a hot ache grew inside her, making her dizzy. Her body throbbed with passion, with desire, disbelief, a potent combination of wonder and lust.

Heart hammering foolishly, and an undeniable web of attraction building between them, she knew this couldn't be happening. If it did, she might have finally crossed the line between reality and insanity.

Finally, that realization gave her the strength to resist, despite her inner protests. "No," she said. Throat aching, she pushed against him, both with her physical body and her inner strength.

This time, her hands went right through him, exactly as they should.

She gaped at him, once again a ghost. "How did you...?" she asked faintly.

To his credit, he appeared as stunned as she. "I don't know." His hazel eyes smoldered and blazed, pinning her. The rasp in his voice matched hers. "That shouldn't have been possible. Unless..."

"Unless what?" But she knew. Somehow she knew. She'd wanted him so badly she'd willed him to change from ghost to man.

"Unless your magic made it happen." As if he'd read her mind.

"I didn't do anything." Defensive, she shook her head. Conflicting emotions roiled inside her. Longing—yes, still that—and amazement, mingled with a healthy dose of terror.

What had almost just occurred? She didn't understand and, apparently, neither did Tyler.

Even worse, her entire body still sang with desire for him. She craved him. Someone who not only definitely was not David, but was a ghost.

Body still throbbing, she took a minute to try to gather up her shredded composure. "You're here to save your sister," she reminded him firmly.

"Yes."

"Nothing more."

"No." He sounded certain.

"Good." They could do this. If she simply didn't think about how Tyler made her feel, she could focus. Dena Rogers was in big trouble. And the evil warlock who had her had become aware of both Tyler's and Anabel's presence.

Tyler stayed in the other room as Anabel hurried through her morning rituals. She needed to learn, to cram as much information into her brain as she could by studying the books Juliet had given her to read.

After a quick shower, she blow-dried her hair and pulled on jeans and a T-shirt before heading to the kitchen, again forgoing her normal witchy attire. The irony wasn't lost on her either, though for now she figured it would be best to dress like everyone else if she wanted to roam around unobtrusively and ask questions.

Tyler waited at the kitchen table, appearing as his usual ghostly self. He watched as she approached, unsmiling, a serious look in his hazel eyes.

Her cat, Leroy, groomed himself on the counter behind the ghost, appearing completely at ease while waiting to be fed. Contrary to his past behavior, which had involved arching his back, whipping his tail and a lot of hissing and snarling, he no longer appeared bothered by Tyler's ghostly presence. Great. Even her own cat had become a traitor.

Leroy blinked at her, meowing once, asking for his morning meal. Which she gave him, filling his bowl with tuna-shaped kibble before turning to attend to her own breakfast.

A bowl of cereal, a mug of coffee and she settled in to scan through the first book while she ate. She flipped through the pages rapidly, seeing more of what Juliet had told her. *Focus, focus, focus.* A lot of practice exercises involving the inner self and chanting, and more talk about focus.

Finally, bored and feeling a bit cranky, she closed the book and eyed Tyler. "Today, I'm definitely going over to the college since we never made it there yesterday. I need to talk to as many people as possible who might have been friends with your sister. Someone has to know something."

This time, Tyler didn't speak. Nodding, he simply hovered a few feet off her floor, looking more ruggedly masculine than any ghost had a right to.

She ignored her body's twinging and aching and forced an impersonal smile. "Go ahead," she said. "Ask. Whatever it is, let's get it out of the way so we can start the day."

"Okay. First question. Do you always shift alone?" Tyler asked her.

Whatever she'd expected him to say, that hadn't been even close. "Yes. Oh, I didn't used to. Back when David was alive, I did like everyone else and changed in a big pack of shifters. No one minded. But these days, they've made it clear I'm not welcome."

"Who?" He sounded outraged, making her smile.

"It doesn't matter." Carrying her bowl to the sink, she rinsed it and placed it inside the dishwasher. "I'm running late. If you're coming with me, since it's my turn to ask a question, I'll want an explanation of where you disappeared to yesterday after I pulled you from the darkness."

As they buzzed along the road in the impossibly tiny car, while sitting next to the most beautiful woman he'd ever met—alive or dead—Tyler wished she would mention the kiss. The soul-shattering, gut-wrenching, incredibly arousing, *real* kiss. Impossible as that sounded. Anabel must have a great deal more magic than anyone realized to do something like that.

"Well?" she demanded, barely a moment after backing out of her driveway. "Where'd you go?"

Deliberating, he sighed. There were things he could talk about and others he wasn't allowed to. If he even tried to put voice to the something forbidden, he knew from experience that he'd find himself unable to speak.

Where he'd retreated yesterday was one of those sacred and thus secret things.

"I can't," he finally said. "Maybe it's enough to say I went back to rejuvenate my energy."

She shot him a look from under her lashes, her bronze-colored eyes gleaming. "Like a heavenly spa?"

Throat as tight as his chest, he gathered himself enough to respond to her deliberately light tone. "Sort of."

"That warlock who tried to crush you. I don't suppose you happened to get a look at his face, did you?"

"No. He was pure energy. Black, oppressive darkness. And very powerful."

Her sigh echoed his feelings. "I gathered as much."

Once they exited the main road, as they pulled onto the college campus, he directed her to the area where his sister had always parked when she went to work. "It's close to the cafeteria," he explained, pointing at the neatly landscaped beige brick building. "All the buildings with red roofs are part of the college."

"Good to know." Pulling the key from the ignition, she dropped it in her purse. "I need to remind you again to do me a favor. Please don't talk to me when I'm asking other people questions. Not only is it confusing, but if I forget and speak to you, everyone thinks I'm nuts."

"I promise," he said, meaning it. Not for anything would he cause her the kind of hurt she'd suffered the last time they went to town. At least he didn't think anyone in this part of town knew much about her. This area had a younger demographic, and the kids rarely went to the older part of downtown, preferring to hang out in the immediate area.

Or at least that was what he'd gathered from the few times he'd visited Dena when he was home on leave.

With a nod, Anabel got out of the car and began to walk briskly up the sidewalk toward the building. Her jeans fit her well and she looked young enough to be a student here. He followed, unable to keep from admiring the utterly feminine sway of her hips and the perfect heart shape of her rear.

Pulling open one side of the heavy metal door, she glanced at him quickly before stepping inside.

The smells were a powerful combination of wonderful and confusing. He thought he could identify bacon and toast (mouthwatering) and cleaning detergent and cigarettes (nauseating).

The interior of the cafeteria appeared pretty much deserted. Of course, they were too late for breakfast and just a bit early for them to start serving lunch. Most of the kids inside were either studying or hanging out, waiting for the workers to put the food out.

Anabel eyed the room and then apparently made a decision. She went to the clean and empty counter and stood. "Excuse me."

Busy cooking or preparing or talking, most of the people working in the back ignored her. Only one person, a slender girl with straight dark hair and huge brown eye-glasses, looked up.

"I'm sorry. We're not open yet," she said, smiling politely at Anabel.

"I understand." Anabel smiled back. "I'm looking for Dena Rogers."

That brought the girl over. "I'm sorry. She quit. Or something. It was really unlike her, to just not show up for work like that. We were friends, but she won't answer her phone." She shrugged, her expressive face unable to hide her hurt. "I'm hoping she's all right."

"Well, that explains that," Anabel muttered, managing to sound both shocked and disappointed. "I wanted to surprise her. I am—or was—a good friend of her brother's. Before he died, he asked me to give her something of his."

"Oh no." Brushing her hair away from her face, the younger woman grimaced. "She loved her brother. She was devastated when he was killed. I think that's why she joined that church."

Church? Tyler barely restrained himself from demanding Anabel get more info. His sister had never been all that interested in religion.

"Do you know the name of the church?" Anabel asked, smiling sweetly. "Maybe they'll know how I can find her."

"Sure." Turning, the girl grabbed a receipt book and a pen. "It's called Everlasting Faith. It's a nondenominational church in the old shopping center by the train tracks." Handing the paper to Anabel, she pushed her glasses back up on her nose. "Do me a favor, will you? When you find Dena, ask her to call Lola. Tell her I've been worried about her."

"I will." Anabel folded the paper and put it in her purse. "Thank you so much."

Once they were back outside, Tyler could barely contain himself. "She has to be wrong. Anabel wasn't the type to go to church."

"Maybe not. But maybe after you died… Grief makes people act in strange ways," she said, sounding unperturbed. "Let's go check this place out and see if we can learn anything more."

A few minutes later, they pulled up in front of a shopping center that had been converted into a church. The sandstone-colored brick gave the place a mellow appearance, though if not for the sign out front, Tyler would have no idea it had become a house of worship.

"I swear this used to be a grocery store," he said, following Anabel as she headed to the smudged glass front door.

"Shhh." Finger to her lips, she glared at him. "Remember, no talking to me once I'm in there."

Inside, the place appeared deserted. It had been sparsely decorated, an inexpensive oak table with a vase, a mirror and a few chairs. A vibrant blue area rug was the only color in the monochrome room. Tyler supposed that since it wasn't a Sunday, the church ran on a skeleton crew, but the pastor should be around here somewhere.

"Can I help you?" A pleasant-faced, older woman with curly gray hair approached. She wore what looked like a seventies housedress and white Keds.

"Yes, ma'am." Anabel's pleasant smile didn't reach her eyes. "I'm looking for the pastor."

The older woman drew herself up, narrowing her eyes as she studied Anabel. "Don't I know you? Weren't you on the news? You're the one—"

"Is the pastor here or not?" Anabel cut her off.

"He's here." Still staring at Anabel as if she'd brought the plague into the sanctuary, the woman—apparently the church secretary—spun around to go and then stopped. "His schedule is pretty busy, so I'm not sure he'll be able to see you," she said. "You might need to make an appointment and come back another time."

Clearly, the place wasn't exactly a beehive of activity.

From the rigid line of Anabel's back, Tyler knew she had to be biting her tongue. "Tell him it's an urgent matter concerning one of his church members and her deceased brother."

Deceased. Tyler suddenly realized he despised that word.

Though she had to have heard, the secretary hurried off without responding.

"Nice, wasn't she?" Tyler commented. "So much for treating others like one wants to be treated."

"Shhh." Anabel shot him a quelling look before turning to eye the hallway.

A moment later, a tall, barrel-chested man with wire-rimmed glasses and a shiny bald head appeared.

"Hello," he said, his voice friendly as he held out his hand. "I'm Pastor Tom Jones. And you are?"

"Anabel Lee."

He laughed as he shook her hand. "It's great to finally meet someone who's been burdened with a name as famous as mine. Do you get a lot of people mentioning the raven saying 'Nevermore' to you?"

She grinned back. "Probably as often as you get people singing songs their grandmothers danced to, like 'Delilah.'"

"I'm surprised you know it." He looked thoughtful.

"Though you're right. A lot of our mothers and their mothers loved that guy. Me, not so much."

Still smiling, she nodded. "I can imagine."

"Now, what can I do for you?" he asked.

Her expression stilled and grew serious. "I'm trying to locate Dena Rogers. I went by the college cafeteria and was told she'd quit. Someone mentioned she regularly attended this church. I'm hoping you know where I can find her."

The pastor studied her, his expression unchanging. "Do you mind telling me what this is about? Lola—the young lady you talked to earlier in the cafeteria—called me. She said you'd brought Dena something from her deceased brother?"

"Yes." Anabel nodded. "I did. But that, I'm afraid, is private, for Dena only. Can you tell me where I might find her? Or, if you can't do that, could you call her and ask her to meet me here?"

Appearing lost in thought, he finally dipped his chin. "I would if I could, but Dena hasn't been to church at all the last few Sundays. I can call the number I have on file for her, if you'd like."

"Yes, please. If you don't mind, that would be very helpful."

"Wait here," he said. "I'll just be a moment."

The instant Pastor Tom left the room, Tyler crossed over to stand in front of Anabel. "All we've been able to establish is that Dena's disappeared. We already knew that."

"Give it a minute," she hissed back. "The more people we talk to, the more information we might learn about where she went. I do find it interesting that Lola found it necessary to phone the pastor warning him we might come by."

Giving a slow shake of his head, Tyler crossed his arms and moved away to wait. A moment later, the pastor returned. "I called." He grimaced and spread his hands. "The call went straight to voice mail, like she had her cell turned off. I'm sorry I couldn't be more helpful."

Tyler didn't think he sounded all that sorry. He reached out, trying to unobtrusively test the limits of the man's power. The pastor must have sensed something, because he swatted at the air near his face, as though a mosquito or fly circled him.

"I'm really sorry," he repeated.

Anabel made a sound of disappointment. "That's too bad. It's not often I get to deliver something to someone from a relative who died serving our country."

"Ouch." He grimaced again. Glancing at Anabel, he then looked past her. Tyler could have sworn the other man stared directly at him.

Could Pastor Tom have magical ability? And if he did, could he be the man who'd captured Dena and even now held her hostage?

Chapter 7

Trying not to show her frustration, Anabel gave the pastor her number in case anything else turned up, and they left the church. Once in the car, she followed Tyler's directions and drove to the apartment complex where Dena had lived. Her ghostly companion had gone oddly silent, probably because he found this painful.

The apartment building, though older, appeared well taken care of. The brick had been painted a bright white, and the blue trim gave it a cheerful appearance. There were two floors, with all the doorways on the outside, and a set of steps at each end. In addition, each unit had one floor-to-ceiling window next to the blue front door.

"Not too bad," Anabel said out loud.

"Yeah, if you don't mind the lack of landscaping."

After Tyler's comment, she realized he was right. There were a few scraggly shrubs and no trees until the edge of the half-dead grassy area. Just parking lot and building. "I wonder what happened."

He shrugged. "As far as I can remember, it's been like this ever since the place was built."

As they crossed the parking lot on the way to the stairs, Anabel stopped. An icy chill spread over her, originating in her solar plexus and radiating from there to the tips of her fingers. It wasn't painful, more like uncomfortable. "Wow." Placing her hand on her stomach, she took a deep breath. "Do you feel that?"

Tyler frowned. From the perplexed look on his face, he didn't. "Feel what?"

She shook her head, unable to articulate. They continued on, and she'd just about begun to wonder if she'd imagined things when she felt it again. "There," she gasped. This time, the cold felt like a fist aimed at her stomach. She nearly doubled over, trying not to panic. Dimly, she knew she needed to remember to breathe.

"Anabel!" Tyler's voice, sharp and decisive. The sound of him caught her, pulling her back from whatever edge she'd been about to tumble from.

"That's not good," she said, her breath coming shallow and fast.

"Do you think it's the warlock?" Fist clenched, he appeared ready to do battle.

"I don't know." She inhaled, forcing out the breath. "It could be. Probably is. But why here? You don't think he's keeping her prisoner in her own apartment?"

"No. I've checked the place out thoroughly." Tyler floated ahead of her. "Come on. It's this way, up the stairs."

The energy's icy grip on her dissipated after she reached the top of the concrete stairs. Following Tyler to unit 205, she paused in front of the door and tentatively reached out, using the method she'd been taught by Juliet. *Focus, focus, focus.*

And nothing.

Relieved, she exhaled. "Whatever it was, it's gone now."

Unable to tell if Tyler appeared disappointed or glad, she raised her fist and knocked on the door.

A moment later, she knocked again. "Well, that was a waste of time. But then, since we both knew she wasn't here—"

She cut off as the door opened. A tall, slender girl with long, blond hair and heavily mascaraed eyelashes peered out at her. "Can I help you?"

Stunned, Anabel closed her mouth. "Yes. I'm looking for Dena Rogers."

Affecting a bored look, the young lady began to close the door. "She's not here."

Anabel thought quickly and stuck her foot in to keep the door from closing. "And you are?"

After a yawn, which she didn't bother to cover with her hand, the girl sighed. "Tammy. Dena's friend. Roommate, even. She's been letting me crash here."

"For how long?" Tyler demanded, forgetting she couldn't hear him.

Anabel glared at him. "Really?" Directing her attention back to Tammy, she narrowed her eyes. "How long has it been since you even saw Dena?"

Tammy shrugged. "I don't know. A week. Two weeks. It's been a while."

"Did she tell you where she was going?"

"No. I'm not her mother." Scrunching up her freckled face, she grimaced. Despite this, she still managed to look pretty, fresh and innocent. An all-American girl next door, heavily made up. "Are you a cop or something?"

"No. I'm—I was—a friend of Dena's brother. He sent something to me and asked me to give it to her."

Interest flickered in Tammy's bright blue eyes for the first time. "The guy who was killed in Afghanistan? I saw pictures of him. He was pretty hot."

Unable to help it, Anabel glanced up at Tyler to catch his reaction. To her surprise, he appeared unamused and unimpressed, still eyeing Tammy with apparent distrust.

"Ask her how she knows my sister," he demanded.

"Did you work with Dena?" Anabel asked.

"No. We both go to the same church."

"Everlasting Faith?"

Surprise registered on Tammy's face. "Yes."

"We just spoke to Pastor Tom before coming here. He didn't seem to know where Dena was either."

"Look." Tammy shifted her weight from foot to foot, clearly done with the conversation. "I don't know what you want. I can't help you." Then, nudging Anabel's foot out of the way with her own, Tammy closed the door. A second later, they could hear the sound of the dead bolt turning.

Anabel sighed. "Another dead end."

"For you," Tyler said. "Wait here." And he swirled into mist, through the door and into the apartment.

Great. Damned if she was going to lurk outside some-one else's apartment door while he did who knew what inside. Anabel headed back toward the stairs, bracing herself in case the chill came on. But she made it all the way to her car without reexperiencing anything and she got inside to wait for Tyler.

A moment later, she shook her head. Tyler was a ghost.

He could appear wherever he wanted. Since there clearly wasn't any danger, he could just meet her at the house.

She drove away. Still, misgivings plagued her. What had been that negative energy back at the apartment? Should she have waited, just in case whatever it had been attacked Tyler?

Considering, she almost went back. But her misgivings also directed her to study her own house.

Everything seemed exactly the same as when she'd left earlier. No open doors, broken windows or signs of forced entry. Outside her own entrance, she stopped, using the focusing techniques she'd learned to see if she could sense any dark energy.

Nothing came up and hit her in the face.

Relieved, yet still hesitant, she unlocked the door and went inside. The instant she stepped into her foyer, Anabel knew something was wrong. Off. Her first clue was the way Leroy stood, backed into a corner of her living room, all puffed up and hissing. At nothing.

In the past, this had meant they had a ghostly visitor, which Anabel could always see, just as well as her cat.

Not this time. She squinted, peering around the room. Nothing. She could feel the faint tingle of some sort of leftover energy, residue but nothing more.

Most perplexing. But hopefully not dangerous. Whatever or whoever had been must have gone.

"It's all right," she told her cat, going to comfort him. Leroy was having none of that. He yowled and hissed and took off as if the hounds of hell were nipping at his heels. Anabel stared after him, debating if she should catch him, put him in his carrier and go somewhere else.

But surely if she were in danger, she'd sense something.

Leroy reappeared, leaping sideways, the way he did when he'd indulged in too much catnip. Keeping close to the wall, he moved right behind Anabel, still eyeing something only he could see.

A heartbeat later, Tyler appeared. Anabel glanced at her cat, who continued to stare in a completely different direction.

"I thought I asked you to wait," he began. "I checked out the apartment and—"

"Not now." She gestured toward Leroy. "Look at him. I don't see anything, but clearly he does. Can you tell if there's another ghost here?"

Frowning, Tyler drifted around the room, sniffing as if he wore his wolf form. Finally, he looked at her and shrugged. "I've got nothing. The protective circle is still in place."

Leroy didn't think so. Back arched and black fur fluffed up so much he looked as if he'd touched a live electrical wire, the cat hissed again and jumped sideways. He took off running, disappearing down the hall.

"Leroy thinks differently."

Lazily appraising her with his gaze, Tyler shrugged. "I don't know. You're the one with all the power. Did you sense anything?"

"I tried. I found nothing." She took a shaky breath, frustrated at the way his nearness got her all hot and bothered. "I'll try again." And once more, she followed the same steps she'd used to find Tyler before and pull him free. *Focus. Focus. Focus.* Fully expecting to find absolutely nothing.

This time, she felt a rush of darkness, as deadly icy as the feeling that had stabbed her earlier. But as quickly as she felt it, the dark energy cut off, like an iron wall slamming down, blocking Anabel.

Dizzy, she opened her eyes. "I felt the same thing earlier, at Dena's apartment. Dark and heavy, just like the force that had you trapped." Suddenly, she realized what she'd said. "He was here," she gasped. "I felt the lingering traces of his magic."

Hurrying over to the coffee table, she grabbed one of the books and began flipping through it. "I know I read something about the tracks magic leaves in the atmosphere. Here it is."

Looking up at Tyler, she read the passage out loud. "Both good and bad magic leave trails of pure energy for an adept to read. They are easily distinguishable." The rest went on to describe something similar to what she'd experienced. Icy cold and pain for dark magic, and warmth and goodwill for bright.

"That's all very interesting." Tyler sounded frustrated. "But yet another day is nearly over and we're no closer to finding my sister than we were before."

"Yes, we are," Anabel insisted. "At least now we have some suspects. There's Pastor Tom and that Tammy person, who's taken over Dena's apartment." She couldn't quite keep her dislike from her voice. She couldn't pinpoint exactly why, but Tammy had gotten on her last nerve. That in itself could be a clue.

"True, but I think you can scratch Tammy from your list. Whoever has Dena is clearly male."

"Really?" Tilting her head, she regarded him. Every time she looked at him, she ached for his touch. "And you know this how?"

"I saw him when my sister first reached out to me.

And her voice, calling out to me to save her from him. Him."

"Okay." Anabel dropped into a chair. "Though I'm still not willing to give up on Tammy yet. She could be a helper or something."

He shrugged. Eyeing him, sexy as hell, even standing at attention with his entire posture ramrod straight, she wondered why he never let himself be off duty and relax. Maybe even wear something else besides the uniform, especially since it made him look even more ruggedly virile. Each time she saw him, the pull grew stronger.

Maybe the uniform and military posture were his way of dealing with that tug. It was entirely possible he was having the same problems dealing with this attraction as she was. Heat shot through her at the thought.

Focus, she reminded herself, deliberately shutting out any awareness of him. They needed to work together to find Tyler's sister. "Do you think there's any possibility it could be the preacher?"

His look felt so galvanizing that her mouth went dry. "It could be. But I thought you could sense the darkness. Did you get anything like that from him?"

"No," she admitted. "Though if he is the warlock and really is that powerful, maybe he can cloak it."

"Maybe." He narrowed his eyes. "One thing I could tell about Tammy is that she's not powerful at all."

His insistence on defending Dena's roommate gave her pause. But for now, she decided to give him the benefit of the doubt.

"Okay, so we can probably cross Tammy off our list, then." She couldn't explain her reluctance to admit this. "Even though my gut instinct says she knows more than she admits."

"Well, leave her on our short list, then," he said, one corner of his mouth curling up in a slight smile. "Though personally, I think this church has something to do with Dena's disappearance. Something about that pastor rubbed me the wrong way."

She couldn't help smiling back. "Not religious, are you?"

"Not particularly. I've never been one for organized religion. I always had my own relationship with the divine, though."

Gaze locked on his, she admired the certainty in his voice. Of course he was certain—he'd actually died.

"You know, I've talked to a lot of ghosts since David died. But I never had an in-depth conversation with one."

One eyebrow arched, he gave a slow nod.

"Do you mind if I ask you a few questions?"

"Go ahead." He sounded resigned.

"After you, um, passed, did you know everything right away? Was it really like coming home?"

Moving closer, he continued to hold her gaze, making her pulse speed up. "It was," he said. "And that's about all I can tell you right now."

Slightly disappointed, she nodded. The message was loud and clear. No more questions about the afterlife.

Unwilling to let him see how his closeness affected her, she stood her ground. "Okay, then. Back to the church. If you really think they were involved with Dena's disappearance, you must have some theories as to why."

Was it her imagination, or did he seem relieved?

"There could be any number of reasons. Power, sex and money usually are involved somewhere. For all we know, Pastor Jones could be a power-hungry, sex-crazed megalomaniac."

Though she nodded, because, after all, anything was possible, she seriously doubted it. "I didn't get that vibe from him at all."

"So maybe I'm wrong." Tyler sounded glum. "Because if he was sex-crazed, he definitely would have reacted to a woman as beautiful as you."

Beautiful? Stunned, she froze. Even David, who'd loved her, had called her only pretty. She'd never in her life been told she was beautiful. Even though she knew she wasn't, she felt a flush of pleasure that Tyler found her so.

Focus, she reminded herself. She couldn't keep letting her ultraconsciousness of his appeal distract her.

"Do you think he's the one who grabbed your sister?" Though she didn't like to consider the idea, it certainly wasn't beyond the realm of possibility. It wouldn't be the first time that a so-called man of God had hidden behind his religion to do awful things.

"I don't know," he admitted.

Her stomach growled, reminding her she needed to make something to eat. Wishing she could get herself to think of Tyler as a buddy or a brother or something, she bustled around the kitchen and put together a quick evening meal.

The doorbell rang just as Anabel finished making her dinner salad. With a sigh, she looked at Tyler, who shrugged.

"Make sure you check through the peephole," he cautioned her, sounding unruffled.

"Of course," she responded, slightly miffed that her meal had been interrupted.

When she looked out to her doorstep and saw who was standing there, she gasped. "It's Pastor Jones."

Instantly, Tyler dropped his carefree attitude. "Don't let him in. The fact that he came here proves I was right about him."

"He could have a valid reason to pay me a visit," she pointed out, whispering. "Maybe he has some new information about your sister."

Finally, Tyler nodded. "Fine. I hope he does."

Taking a deep breath, she squared her shoulders, opened the door slightly and stared at the preacher.

"Good evening, Ms. Lee." His smile seemed friendly enough.

Still, she continued to stand in the doorway, blocking entrance into her house. "Pastor Jones. I have to say, I'm surprised to see you here. How'd you find out where I live?"

"My dear, it's very easy to look anyone up on the internet," he gently pointed out.

Since he had a point, she nodded. His appearance still felt wrong, a bit like stalking. "You could have called. Especially since I gave you my number."

He lifted one shoulder. "I wanted to have a face-to-face conversation."

This was kind of creepy. She tried not to show her unease. "All right, then. What can I do for you?"

Looking pointedly past her, he pushed his glasses up on his nose and sighed. "May I come in?"

"I'd rather talk out here."

This surprised him. Appearing slightly hurt, he cocked his shiny bald head. "You don't trust me."

"I don't know you," she countered. "And I'm not in the

habit of letting strange men into my house. Once again, why are you here?"

"You said to contact you if I had any news of Dena Rogers." Pushing his glasses up his nose again, he appeared frustrated. "I am the pastor of a very respectable church. I can assure you, I have no ill designs on your well-being."

She had to give him props for effort, even if his overly white smile reminded her of a television preacher, which increased her nervousness. Still, he *was* a pastor and she didn't have any bad vibes from him.

Finally, she went ahead and stepped aside. "I'm sorry. Please. Come on in."

His barrel chest led the way as he entered. "What a lovely home you have," he said, his tone gentle and respectful. She supposed he often visited with shut-ins or members of his congregation. Which would explain why he believed he was so good at making people feel at ease.

Except he wasn't. Not with her, at least. She wasn't worried or stressed, just watchful. Something about the man got her hackles up, but she also supposed that might be due to her past negative experiences with zealously religious people.

Meanwhile, Tyler stood in the entrance to the kitchen, massive arms crossed, shaking his head. She was actually glad the preacher couldn't see him.

"What did you find out?" she asked, turning back to Pastor Jones. His blank look made her instantly suspicious. "About Dena," she clarified.

"Oh yes." His self-depreciating laugh made her want to cross her own arms. "I don't actually have anything concrete to report. But when I put the email request out for any information about her disappearance, one of her girlfriends contacted me."

Now, this could be helpful. Anabel kept her expression blank, not wanting to show too much eagerness. "And?"

Instead of answering, he looked pointedly at her couch. "May I sit?"

Pushy, wasn't he? Hating to be rude, Anabel neverthe-less shook her head. "I'd rather stand. I was just about to eat my dinner when you rang my bell."

Of course, he apologized profusely.

Waving this away, she finally did cross her arms. "Are you going to tell me what Dena's friend told you?"

"Oh yes." Yet he didn't say anything else.

One of her books on magic was open on the coffee table. The pastor wandered over to it and began flipping through the pages. The instant he realized what kind of book it was, he recoiled.

"Magic?" Frowning, he glared at her. "Are you a devil worshipper?"

Though she wanted to laugh, Anabel knew to do so might be dangerous, so she shook her head instead. "Not at all. I'm doing some research. Now seriously, I'm hun-gry and I'd like to get back to my meal. Do you have some information to give me or not?"

If the older man took umbrage at her rudeness, he didn't react. Instead he studied her intensely, making her feel as if she were under a microscope. This was getting stranger and stranger. She actually began to think Tyler might have been right. The pastor might have been the one to abduct Dena.

Which would mean she'd just placed herself in grave danger by letting him into her house.

Tyler moved closer, standing by her side as though he

considered himself reinforcement. Even though only she could see him, she gathered strength from his presence.

The pastor continued to study her, his expression kindly. "Do you attend church?" he finally asked, managing to sound both sad and confrontational all at once.

"Not that it's any of your business, but no. I don't. Now please, Pastor Jones. What did Dena's friend tell you?"

Still eyeing her as if he expected horns to pop out of her head at any moment, he finally sighed. "She came to tell me she thought Dena's new boyfriend must have done something to her. Since I never met the young man, and can't vouch for him either way, I thought I'd simply pass the information on to you."

Finally. A real, live, genuine clue. Careful not to show her eagerness, Anabel nodded. "May I have her name and number so we can contact her?"

"We?" His puzzled frown and the way he peered around her, as though trying to see someone else in the room, made her wonder if the pastor could actually see Tyler but wasn't letting on.

Cursing her careless slip of the tongue, Anabel gave him a sheepish smile. Tempted to pass it off as a joke and say she'd used the royal "we," she wondered if the pastor would even get it. "Sorry. I meant so I can contact her, not we."

Which she supposed was better than some lame nonexplanation. Or the truth, which would make her sound even crazier. She could picture Pastor Jones's reaction if she told him she'd meant herself and a ghost, who happened to be present in the room at that very second. No, that wouldn't go over well at all.

The older man's face grew troubled. "I don't have her phone number on me, though I can check the church directory when I get back. I know she's attended services in the past, several times with Dena. The two of them used to hang around together a lot."

Anabel nodded, unable to resist glancing at Tyler. "Can you describe her?" Maybe if they got a description, Tyler might recognize her.

"Sure. She's tall, slender and blonde. She does wear too much makeup. Cute girl."

A sneaking suspicion made Anabel ask, "Does she have freckles and blue eyes? And look like she could be a cheerleader for a professional football team or something?"

The pastor's face relaxed. "Yes, that's her," he said happily. "Tamara, I think her name is."

Tammy. The girl who'd been staying in Dena's apartment. She'd made no mention of Dena having a boyfriend.

"Thank you so much, Pastor Jones," Anabel said, crossing to the door and reaching for the handle. "I really appreciate you stopping by." Which she did, sort of. Mostly she still felt a bit creeped out, as if he might be a potential stalker.

"It's my pleasure. Please call me Tom," he said, apparently not getting the hint as he made no move to leave. Clearly, he was too well mannered to simply take a chair since she hadn't invited him to sit. She supposed she ought to be grateful for the small blessing.

"Uh, okay. Well, thanks again for coming by." Maybe if she actually opened the door?

Still oblivious, he nodded. "You're welcome. Since I'm already here, how about we talk about you paying a visit to one of our services? We have four on Sundays, starting at eight in the morning."

"No, thank you," she said, as politely as she could while reining in her impatience. "Now if you don't mind, I've got to eat since I have somewhere I need to be. If I don't leave soon, I'm going to be really late. And hungry." Behind her back, she childishly crossed her fingers at the tiny white lie.

Finally, he got the not-so-subtle hint. He nodded. "All right, I understand. Please, if you change your mind, just stop by. Anytime, all right?"

As she opened the door, she nodded and forced a smile. All she could think of was how badly she needed to jump in her car and drive over to the apartment to confront Tammy.

As he passed her, the pastor stopped and bent down, giving her a fatherly kiss on the top of her head. So help her, she was so startled she jumped, bumping his wire-rimmed glasses and sending them flying from his head.

"I'm s-so sorry," she stammered, reaching to pick up the glasses before something worse happened.

Unfortunately, Pastor Jones reached for them at the same time, nearly causing them to bump heads. With his face mere inches from hers, he mouthed two words. *Be careful.*

Chapter 8

Stunned, Anabel handed the pastor his glasses and got to her feet. He left in a hurry, without saying anything else. Immediately, she rushed over and closed and locked her front door, heart racing.

"Dena didn't have a boyfriend," Tyler said, clearly having missed the last exchange. "If Tammy is saying so, then she's lying."

"Um, Pastor Jones just told me to be careful." She scratched the back of her head. "A second ago, when we were face-to-face."

Moving closer, Tyler stared. "What? When? I didn't hear him."

"Right when we were both trying to retrieve his eyeglasses. He mouthed it at me, almost as if he thought someone might be listening."

Their gazes locked. Once again, she felt that irresistible lure of him. She thought he must have felt it too, as he broke eye contact. "That's weird. I wonder what he's not telling us."

"Exactly."

He began to pace the room, looking more like a man and less like a ghost. His long-legged stride captivated her. "Of course, we already know to be careful. We're dealing with a warlock, after all. I'm more worried about what this Tammy is trying to do."

"Good point. Let's go ask her right now." Anabel reached for her car keys.

"Let's not," Tyler countered, surprising her. "How about we just call her instead? Since she and my sister still have a house phone, I have the number memorized."

Disappointed, Anabel considered. "I really want to see her face when we ask her why she didn't mention her worry about Dena's boyfriend."

"Maybe because you had a ten-second conversation with her. You were a total stranger, showing up at her front door and demanding to know about her friend. Of course she got defensive. She was so worried she went to talk to her pastor instead."

Anabel eyed him. "Why are you defending her? Again?"

Something flickered in his hazel eyes. "I'm not. I'm just saying it's logical that she'd say more to the leader of her church than to a random stranger."

He had a point. Mulling this over, Anabel finally decided he was right. "Fine. Let's give her a call."

Dialing the numbers as he gave them to her, Anabel listened to the phone ring on the other end, aware her name would display if the other woman had caller ID.

When Tammy finally picked up, Anabel was so surprised she almost couldn't speak.

After she'd identified herself and told Tammy why she was calling, Tammy murmured her okay. At first, she didn't say anything, and Anabel got a sinking feeling as she wondered if this call had been a colossal waste of time. Anabel reiterated that the pastor had told her about Tammy's concern, hoping this would reassure the other woman.

"I'm worried about Dena," Tammy finally said, her voice shaky. "We both go to the same church, and I'm afraid her disappearance has something to do with them."

"Not her boyfriend?"

"Boyfriend?" Tammy's shock didn't sound contrived. "Dena didn't have a boyfriend. At least not that I know of."

Anabel's stomach lurched. "That's really strange," she said. "Pastor Jones just left here. He told us you'd come to him to discuss how worried you were about Anabel and how concerned you were that her boyfriend had done something to her."

"He did?" Tammy sounded shocked. "But that's a complete and outright lie. I did talk to Pastor Tom—I called him—but I never said any of that. Not that I'm not worried about Dena, because I am. But I've never discussed anything about boyfriends with the pastor."

At a loss for words, Anabel looked back at Tyler, wondering if he could hear the other side of the conversation. Apparently not, as his impatient expression told her he was waiting for her to finish the call.

"Is there anything else you might be able to tell me, Tammy?" Anabel said, hoping against hope that Dena's roommate would trust her enough to share.

"Yes, there is." Voice stronger, Tammy sounded determined. "I'm concerned about the church. Everlasting Faith. I think there's something weird going on with them, and Pastor Tom is in the middle of it."

Anabel opened her mouth to reply, but Tammy hadn't finished. "My suggestion to you, if you're really investigating Dena's disappearance, is that you should investigate that church. I've quit going. Being around those people is not a safe place to be."

With that, Tammy muttered a quick goodbye and hung up.

"Wow." Speaking fast, Anabel repeated everything to Tyler.

"One of them is clearly lying," Tyler mused. "But who?"

"And why?" While Anabel didn't entirely trust the pastor, she trusted Tammy even less. "One of those two knows something about why your sister is missing. We need to figure out which one, and maybe that will help us find her."

Leroy yowled from the kitchen, reminding her it was past his mealtime.

"I need to feed my cat. And…" She eyed her salad longingly. "…eat my own meal."

As she headed to get the cat food, Tyler followed, studying her pet. "I wish there was a way to talk to him."

Startled, she looked up at him. "Talk to who? Leroy?"

"Yes. Obviously he sensed something when we did not."

Reaching for the container of cat food, she shrugged. "Cats are sort of known for stuff like that. And I did feel something, though it was just a slight tingle of energy."

The instant she spoke, she felt it again. Even worse,

Leroy, who'd never missed a meal in his life, let out a screeching yowl and turned tail and ran.

One minute Tyler had been standing there talking to Anabel, eyeing her cat in order to refrain from admiring Anabel's lush body, and the next, he found himself surrounded by complete and utter darkness.

Meanwhile, he had no idea what might have happened to Anabel.

Tyler swore. He might be dead, he might be a ghost, but he had been a soldier. And he was damn tired of getting pushed around.

"Show yourself," he shouted, clenching his teeth as he spun in the mind-numbing absence of light. "If you're so all-fired powerful, why are you afraid to show yourself?"

Lightning struck, a maelstrom of overbright flashes, painful even to ghostly eyes. And then nothing. Not even a rumble of thunder.

"The hell with you," he shouted, beyond caring if anyone even heard him. He was sick of being powerless and having to rely on someone else to do things he wanted to do himself.

A thought occurred to him. While he knew nothing about the man who'd imprisoned Dena—other than the fact that he was a warlock—he knew men. Most men could not resist a challenge.

"You know, I don't think you're so powerful," he shouted into the void. "You have to pick on weak, defenseless young women. Why don't you take on someone your own size, someone like me? I think I know why. It's because you're afraid."

Nothing. Tyler's heart sank. For all he knew, the warlock had already departed, leaving nothing but his dark magic behind.

A yowl had him spinning around. A second later, he relaxed, realizing that it sounded like Leroy. Which meant, despite the inability to see, he might actually have remained in Anabel's kitchen. This also might have something to do with the warlock's refusal to show himself.

For whatever reason, apparently the warlock didn't want Anabel to see his face.

Right now Tyler had had enough of being blind and powerless. Even though he knew he'd never had Anabel's kind of magic, he gathered his frustration, his rage and his worry for Dena, gathered all of it into a roiling mass of emotion. And then, opening his arms wide, he flung it into the universe. With a grunt and a heartfelt desire that the warlock would take the brunt of it like a fist to the stomach.

Instantly, the darkness vanished, as though Tyler had simply snapped his fingers and made it disappear.

And, as he'd suspected, he'd remained in Anabel's kitchen. "How about that?" he marveled, turning to see Anabel minus her cat, still standing exactly where she'd been. As if time had stopped, freezing her in place.

"Anabel?" While he stared, Anabel blinked and slowly came back to life. Leroy sauntered into the room and began grooming himself.

Tyler felt a flash of fear.

"What just happened?" Anabel asked quietly, her amber eyes wide with fear, her expression puzzled. "I couldn't see you, but yet I felt your presence."

"What about him? Could you tell the warlock was here?"

Her frown told him she couldn't, even before she gave a slow shake of her head.

"He's learned how to shield himself from you or something," he said.

"Maybe." She eyed him. "But what I want to know is, how did you send him away? You had to have used magic. Why didn't you tell me you had magical ability?"

"I don't. At least, not that I'm aware of." He paused, collecting his thoughts.

"Well, if that wasn't magic, I don't know what it was."

She had a point.

"Tell me exactly what you did," she ordered, pushing a strand of her midnight hair behind her ear and then putting the bowl of cat food in front of Leroy. Keeping her gaze on him, she then reached for her salad and began eating.

He wondered if she could see the sensual light that passed between them.

"Tyler?"

Collecting himself, he nodded. "I gathered my emotions and sent them out like a bullet toward the darkness. And bam. Just like that, everything went back to normal."

"That's magic. Of course, my understanding is a bit limited. I'm learning, though, and what you just described sounds a lot like what Juliet told me to do. Focus, concentrate and then…magic."

The idea that he, a ghost, had any magic should have been laughable. But the desperate need to save his sister had Tyler grasping at straws. "Maybe we need to talk to Juliet. I'm thinking if I do have magic, and you and I put ours together, we might be invincible."

Anabel nodded, clearly not convinced. She continued

eating, clearly trying to get her salad down before something else happened.

"It's worth a shot," he persisted. "Call her and ask her."

"Fine." She glanced at her watch. "But it'll have to wait. Her next yoga class just started."

Antsy, Tyler nodded. What had happened earlier with him and the dark magic felt as though it had energized him. While Anabel finished her dinner, he left her house, floating high above the neighborhood, heading downtown and gazing down at the town where he'd grown up. Leaning Tree, New York.

He'd missed it while stationed in Afghanistan. But places and things were transitory. People were not. Most of all, he'd missed his baby sister. Knowing she was in trouble and being powerless to help her was awful, as bad as or even worse than dying.

Thinking back to the way he'd been able to gather up energy, he wondered. Maybe he wasn't nearly as powerless as he'd thought. And if he and Anabel put their resources together, they might have a shot at beating this warlock.

By the time he returned to Anabel, night had fallen. In the middle of her bedtime preparations, she greeted him with a sleepy smile. "I wasn't able to reach Juliet," she said. "But I left her a message. I'm sure she'll call me in the morning."

Stunned, his chest tight, he managed to nod back, even though he had his heart in his throat. He wondered how she could be so unaware that her smile was a thing of great beauty. "Sleep well," he murmured. "I'll catch you in the morning."

With a casual wave, he drifted into the other room. He knew she'd think he'd left, retreating to whatever place

spirits went. Instead he waited, knowing she'd drift off
in a few minutes. Then he'd go into her room and spend
the night guarding over her.

He found he enjoyed watching her sleep, taking care
that she didn't know. The instant her breathing would
change, indicating she'd soon wake, he'd retreat, taking
himself into another room. She would have been horrified to find him there, no doubt citing her sleep-ruffled
hair and drowsy eyes. Again, he marveled how it could
be possible she had no idea how beautiful she was. Or
how sexy and full of life.

Thinking back to his too-short life, he knew if he'd
met Anabel while he was alive, he'd never have let her
go. No wonder Dave had married her. He actually found
himself jealous of the other man.

Dave had been one lucky guy. Tyler couldn't believe
they'd been in the same unit. While he was thinking of
that, one small thing in the back of Tyler's memory had
been bothering him. At base, it had been common practice for the men to flash photos of their girlfriends or
wives and family. Tyler couldn't remember one single
instance of Dave ever doing this.

Heck, Tyler would have been showing Anabel's picture to anyone who'd look at it.

Which, when he thought about it, sort of blew his
mind. Why on earth any man, married to a woman as
special as Anabel, wouldn't want to show her off was
beyond him.

Anabel stirred, drawing his attention back to her.
Watching her like this felt like torture, an addictive combination of pleasure and pain. He burned for her, the
irony of that longing striking him as retribution. Before
his tour in Afghanistan, he'd never been a monk. In fact,

he'd been far from it. His friends had always joked about that, claiming he'd dated 75 percent of the women in the county. And while he'd never made promises, he was under no illusions that he might have broken a heart or two. Maybe this was payback.

Throw in his worry over his sister, and he might as well have entered the first or second layer of hell.

Dena no longer called out to him or even tried to reach him. He could no longer even detect the slightest spark, which made his stomach turn and his chest hurt. He could only hope the bastard hadn't killed her. Surely not. Not in the short number of hours that had passed since Tyler saw her, huddled in that dank and foul room.

"A dragon," Anabel said clearly, startling him as he realized she'd come awake suddenly, without any warning.

She sat up in bed, her dark hair cascading wildly over her alabaster shoulders, her bronze eyes gleaming in the shadowy room. The pull of attraction was so strong he had to clench his hands into fists to keep from reaching for her.

"What?" he managed to say, swallowing hard as he fought to remain unaffected by her lush beauty.

She blinked as she realized he was there. "How did you— Never mind. It's not important. I saw him. The man who has your sister."

Stunned, he stared. "You saw him? You saw his face?"

"No. Not that." Rubbing her eyes, she winced. "But I came up on him from behind. And then he shape-shifted, right before I reached him." She began speaking faster, her words all running together, almost as if she feared he wouldn't believe her. "And when he changed, he wasn't a wolf."

Tyler waited. The Pack wasn't the only shape-shifting

species. There were bears and leopards too. Such a thing wasn't that unusual. "What did he become?" he finally asked, when she didn't continue.

"A dragon. Like the ones in medieval tapestries or myths. The beast was huge, with iridescent scales and wings twice as long as a man."

He relaxed. Not that he didn't believe her, but clearly what she thought she'd seen had been only a dream. "Dragons are the stuff of ancient legends," he said carefully, admiring her imagination. "Maybe since it was only a dream, you should consider the possibility that it wasn't reality."

Those marvelous eyes sparked defiance. "Oh, it was real." The certainty in her voice still didn't sway him. "I went there, followed him to his lair. It's underground, like a tornado shelter or bunker. In the woods, like maybe a remote part of the Catskill Forest Preserve or something."

Taking a deep breath, she rushed on. "I saw Dena, as well. She's still alive. Barely, but her heart still beats and she still breathes."

Relief flooded him, even though he still wasn't sure whether or not to believe her. "That's good. I haven't been able to feel her at all."

"He's cloaked her. And himself, which is why I couldn't sense his presence here."

He thought about it for a moment and then decided he had to ask. "Are you sure?"

She didn't even hesitate. "Yes. This was not a dream."

Right then he knew he had to choose. "I believe you," he finally said.

Excitement made her copper eyes shine. "We finally know what we're dealing with. Now we just need to make a plan and free your sister."

A plan. Dealing with a mythical beast no one thought still lived. "How do you know all this? You're just learning about magic."

A quizzical smile spread over her face. "Good point. I don't know. I just do. I've never been more certain of anything in my life."

"A dragon, huh?" Still trying to process the idea.

"Yes." Her voice went dreamy. "He was beautiful, in a frightening sort of way. All glistening scales, blue and green, the colors of a stormy sea. And when he unfurled his wings and launched himself into the sky, I ran after him. I don't think he ever saw me."

From what he remembered reading about dragons, she was lucky the beast hadn't noticed her.

"Even better," Anabel continued, "when he took off and I ran after him, I couldn't help checking out the surrounding area. I saw a few landmarks that might give us some indication of where he's keeping your sister."

Now, *this* was progress. "Tell me," he ordered. "I know this area like the back of my hand."

Jumping up from her bed, she crossed to the dresser, her long legs flashing ivory. She grabbed a pad of paper and a pen and began to make notes. "I have to get this down before I forget," she explained. "I'll let you look at them once I'm finished."

Too impatient to wait, he drifted slightly above her and watched as she sketched out what she'd seen. To his dismay and disbelief, he didn't recognize a single landmark. "What's this? A windmill?"

"Yes," she said, putting the finishing touches on her sketch. "One of those decorative ones, though larger than normal. Something like this should be unusual enough that even if you don't know where it is, someone will."

He nodded. "What about this?" She'd drawn something that looked like the shell of a concrete building, without windows or doors, except for a single metal door in the middle. "A bomb shelter?"

"Maybe." With a sheepish expression, she shrugged. "I have no idea what it is, but that's where the dragon lives and where he's keeping Dena. I drew it exactly like I saw it. I take it you don't know either?"

"No. Sorry." At her crestfallen expression, he actually reached for her, wincing as his hand passed right through her shoulder and then hoping she hadn't noticed. "It's okay. These landmarks are better than nothing. If we start asking around, maybe we can locate them."

Exhaling, she nodded. "Now what do we do?"

A quick glance at the clock revealed it was just after 4:00 a.m. "I think you should try and go back to sleep. We can work on this again in the morning."

"Sleep?" She sounded affronted. "There's no way I can sleep now."

"Well, you can't call Juliet," he said. "Can you?"

She laughed. "Not at this hour of the morning. How about I look in these books for now?" she said in a reasonable tone of voice. "And see what I can find out about dragons. Maybe there'll be some mention of this sort of thing in there."

"Okay."

She dragged her hand through her hair. "Give me a minute." She padded into the bathroom, closing the door behind her.

He decided to wait in the living room.

A minute later, she reappeared, pushing back strands of midnight hair from her heart-shaped face. Her delicately carved face turned pink with excitement. As he let his gaze rove over her, he saw she'd slipped on a bra and a pair of denim shorts, though she still wore the clingy oversize T-shirt.

A bolt of pure lust rendered him unable to speak. Fortunately for him, Anabel had focused her attention on books.

"Let me see." Eyeing the stack of books, she grabbed the largest one. It had an ornate leather-looking cover, embossed with scrolls and medieval-type writing. "This one seems the oldest."

Carrying it into the kitchen, she pulled out a chair and sat down at the table. She began flipping through the pages.

As soon as he regained his composure, he sat down beside her and read over her shoulder.

They both saw the section on dragons at the same time. "The Drakkor," Anabel breathed. "A breed of shape-shifter so rare it's now believed to be a myth." Raising her head, she met Tyler's eyes. "Except they're not."

"I don't believe this," Tyler said, eyeing the illustration. "Does that look like what you saw?"

"Yes. Exactly, except in real life the colors are much more vibrant."

Crud. Forcing his gaze back to the page, he continued reading out loud. "'Drakkors were considered the most powerful of all shape-shifters. In addition to their ability to change into a fearsome, fire-breathing beast with the gift of flight, they also have magical talent. It was this same magic that brought about their downfall.'"

Anabel picked up where he left off. "'In medieval times, the Drakkors were as numerous as the Pack. But struggles for power led to war. Two sides were formed—

the Drakkor of the Light and the Dark Drakkor. Battles raged, wiping out legions of the beasts. Those few that remained went into hiding. Over the centuries, they began to die out. A sickness attacking only the Drakkors further thinned their numbers.'"

Tyler shook his head. "Wow."

"I know." Eyes glowing like polished bronze, she practically vibrated with excitement. "This is like reading a fairy tale."

"Except for one thing," Tyler pointed out. "If your dream was correct, apparently the warlock is not only a Drakkor, but a dark one. And he has my sister. How do we fight against something like that?"

Once they'd flipped through all the other books, finding only one other reference to the Drakkor, Anabel yawned. Tyler hid a smile. A quick glance at the clock on the microwave revealed that only half an hour had passed.

"You know what?" she said, rubbing her eyes. "I think I am going to go back to bed. Even though I usually get up at four or four thirty when I have to be at work, I've been sleeping until six thirty."

He nodded, wishing more than anything that he could crawl into bed with her.

When she stood, she started to turn to leave and then froze. Wrapping her arms around herself, she tilted her head to look up at Tyler. "I wish you could hold me until I go to sleep," she said, surprising him. "I confess I'm a bit worried I'll be seeing dragons in my sleep."

The image that came to his mind had nothing to do with sleep. He burned, wondering how even as a ghost, he could still ache with desire and need.

"I can try," he said, remembering the kiss and how he'd managed to become solid that one time. And then, as if he thought she could read his mind, he had to avert his gaze, afraid she'd read the yearning in his eyes.

"Would you?" And because she sounded so damn grateful, he knew he would, even if lying next to her unable to touch her would be akin to lying on hot coals.

Chapter 9

Though she'd worried at first she wouldn't be able to keep her apparently sex-crazed libido from acting up, Anabel felt comforted having Tyler lying in bed with her. Just having him there was nice, even if she couldn't feel the weight of his body on the mattress. When he draped his ghostly arm over hers, she sighed, closing her eyes and pretending to snuggle against him. Aside from a few twinges of lust battling with her exhaustion, she felt better having him close.

Amazingly, she drifted off to sleep.

When she opened her eyes, the nightstand clock said 7:10, which meant she'd overslept slightly. Her heart skipped a beat as she contemplated what would happen if she turned and gave Tyler a good-morning kiss. But rolling over, she realized he'd already vacated the room. Her immediate sense of loss made her chest feel heavy, but she shook it off. If she'd had any dreams, she didn't remember them and woke up remarkably rested.

More than that, actually. Stretching as she got out of bed, she took note of the exhilaration zinging through her veins and glanced at herself in the mirror, unable to keep from smiling. Finally, she had a lead on Tyler's sister. He might not recognize the landmarks she'd sketched, but someone, somewhere, would. The dragon—or Drakkor—had thrown an unexpected wrench in things, but for some reason she felt confident they'd figure out a solution.

Juliet called a few minutes after Anabel finished her breakfast. "I'm so glad you called," Anabel began. "I've got something I need to ask you—"

"First, tell me this," Juliet interrupted. "Who did you piss off now?" She sounded worried and a bit scared.

"No one that I know of. Why?"

"Do you know a Doug Polacek?"

Anabel thought for a minute. "No. I don't. Why do you ask?"

"Think," Juliet insisted, still not answering. "Maybe he was a customer at the diner and didn't like something you cooked?"

"Maybe." Still not too concerned, Anabel sighed. "Those people—who are few and far between, by the way—deal with the waitstaff or the manager. They never make it back to the cook. You still haven't told me what's going on."

"This Doug Polacek has been talking about you, all around town. He's a big guy, at least six-four and three hundred pounds. Pretty intimidating. Even so, he claims you're harassing him. He's hinting you went psycho on him from a love affair gone bad."

Stunned, Anabel gasped. "That's—"

But Juliet hadn't finished. "There's more. From what I hear, he's even gone to the police to get a restraining order against you."

Dumbfounded, Anabel couldn't respond at first. When she did find her voice, a few heartbeats later, it came out shaky. "I don't understand. I don't even know this person."

"Well, for whatever reason, he's got the entire town stirred up about you again. Almost as bad as last time."

Anabel groaned, her stomach roiling. She remembered how that had been. She'd ended up having to head to the next town over to do her shopping. Between the way everyone had either stared her down without speaking or crossed the street to avoid being near her, she'd felt like a pariah in her own town.

When the harassment started—the eggs on her house and car, the burning bag of poop on her doorstep, her doorbell ringing at all hours of the night and rocks shattering her windows—she'd gotten no help from the police. Though they hadn't come out and actually said so, she'd gotten the impression that they felt as if she deserved such treatment, kind of like making restitution for her sins.

And now some guy whose name she didn't even recognize was starting things up again.

Closing her eyes, she took a deep breath, trying to push away the confusion and fear. *Focus.* When she opened them again, she felt calmer and more centered, as well as resolute. "Juliet, I have no idea why this total stranger has it in for me, but I have enough on my plate. I don't have time to deal with him right now."

Juliet started to argue, but Anabel cut her off. "Listen,"

she said. "This is way more important. I have a question for you. What do you know about the Drakkors?"

Clearly, she'd stunned her friend into silence.

"The...what? Drakkors, as in mythical dragons?" Juliet's tone made it clear she was worried Anabel had finally stepped off the deep end.

"Not so mythical, as it turns out," Anabel said. "The warlock who has Tyler's sister is a Drakkor."

"Not possible."

The instant denial made Anabel smile. "It is, actually."

"And you know this how?" At least Juliet sounded willing to hear her out.

"I saw the warlock shape-shift. Instead of a wolf, he became a dragon. A huge, monstrous, fire-breathing thing."

"You *saw*?" Juliet practically shouted. "When? Where?"

Now came the hard part. "In a dream."

Silence. When Juliet spoke again, she sounded much calmer. Relieved, even. Clearly, she chose her words carefully. "Hon, you are aware dreams aren't real, right?"

"It's funny how you and Tyler say the same things," Anabel responded. "And both of you know better. Of course I am. But this wasn't an ordinary dream. The warlock had been here. He tried to grab Tyler. Leroy—my cat—sensed him. I think he used a cloaking spell on me."

Another silence.

"You've been reading the books I gave you, haven't you?"

"Studying them," Anabel confirmed. "Believe me. Please. If you learn anything about the Drakkors—anything at all—let me know. I—we—need all the help we can get."

"Wow. I'll see what I can find out. But you also need

to deal with this Polacek guy. He's trying really hard to make your life miserable for no reason I can tell. Oh." Juliet's voice changed. "My last morning class is here. I'll talk to you later, okay?" And she ended the call.

Puzzled, Anabel relayed the information about Doug Polacek to Tyler. "I have no idea who he is or why he's trying to turn the town against me." She took a shaky breath. "I'm pretty sure this has something to do with that warlock. I wonder if he's just revealed his identity."

"It wouldn't be that easy."

"Maybe not. Or he might be upping the stakes."

"I hadn't considered that." As the realization dawned on him, horror spread across his face. "You're saying you think it's all a game to him? He's having fun?"

She thought of her dream and the way the warlock had thrown himself into the air after he changed. "Of course he's enjoying himself. What other reason would he have for doing this?"

Ignoring Tyler's frown, she took a deep breath, aware he wouldn't like the next question, but knowing she had to ask it anyway. "Yesterday, I think you showed you have some latent magic ability. Is there any possibility that your sister might have some, as well?"

He frowned, his form once again flickering in and out. "I honestly couldn't tell you that. I'm still trying to figure out if that's really what happened with me. The only thing I can say is if she did she never told me about it. Why?"

"A theory I'm beginning to have. Remember the legends about dragons? They feed off energy. And magic generates a lot of energy."

Hazel eyes dark, he stared at her, so handsome it almost hurt her to look at him. She pushed that thought away, reminding herself that she had to focus if she wanted to continue to learn and grow.

"So you're saying…?"

"He captures those with untapped magic, in order to feed off them."

Expression like a stone mask, he considered. "I don't know. That's a bit far-fetched, don't you think?"

"Maybe. Maybe not."

"If he's capturing people with untapped magic," he said, the concern in his voice telling her he'd realized what this could mean, "then you're also at risk from him."

"True." She knew she sounded unconcerned, but all she could think about was she might have finally found a way to locate his sister. "Think about it, though. If I can draw him to me, I can reach your sister before it's too late."

"No." Clearly horrified, he began to flicker in and out more rapidly, the way he always did when agitated. His eyes flashed. "That's too dangerous. I don't want you to risk your own life. Then where would we be? Dena would still be his prisoner, and you'd be there along with her. There's no one else I can communicate with except Juliet. I couldn't assist you."

"Juliet knows people who could. She belongs to a pretty tight-knit coven."

He spread his hands. "What does that even mean? How could she—they—help?"

With a shrug, she tried to downplay his concern. "I'm not sure. But surely they could."

"Well, if they can—and we don't have to put you in danger—let's enlist their aid right now."

Though for some reason all her nervousness threatened to come back and grip her, she managed a smile.

"She's teaching a yoga class now. I'll call her later. I wish I'd thought of it sooner."

"Me too." He paused, his expression going serious as his form became more solid. "Though I have to say, if Juliet and her coven really can assist us, why didn't Juliet herself mention it sooner?"

He had her there.

"We might not have to stress about that anyway. I can't help feeling as if he's going to continue to attack us to keep us off balance."

Looking decidedly not ghostly, with his muscular legs spread in a warrior's stance, Tyler considered her statement. "He'd only do that if he considered us dangerous."

Though just looking at him made her mouth go dry, she managed a nod. "You know, I think we just might be. And though I'm just learning, it doesn't seem to matter on the magic thing that you're a ghost and I'm not."

Something flickered in his eyes, reminding her of the amazingly real kiss they'd shared. Her entire body heated at the memory.

It was when she caught herself actually swaying toward him that she snapped out of it. Rushing over to the stack of books, she grabbed one randomly and carried it over to the table. "I don't know about you, but I'm going to try and learn more. Knowledge is power."

To his credit, he met her dramatic—and rather prim, if she did say so herself—proclamation with only a nod.

"While you do that," he said, "I'm going back to the world of the spirit to see what I can find out about the Drakkors."

"Good idea," she began, but he had already gone.

"Whew." Leaning back in the chair, she closed her eyes. Battling an attraction to a ghost. She swore she could feel the sexual magnetism rolling off him in waves—intense and compelling, at times confusing. She didn't understand how she could want him so much.

She stood, alone in her house once more, turning a slow circle. Finally, alone. Even with the urgency of the need to find his sister hanging over her, right now she should have been relishing her time alone. This was how she'd always lived, by herself. At least since David had been deployed. While she'd missed him, especially at night when lying in her empty bed, she was used to it and appreciated the space and the knowledge she could do whatever she wanted, eat whatever she liked and make her own schedule.

Over time, even her bed had come to feel less empty. She'd become accustomed to widowhood. Yes, she often found herself lonely, but she mostly dealt with it by keeping busy. This had worked pretty well. Until now.

Now she missed Tyler. *Tyler.* A man—no, a *ghost*—she'd known only a few days. Not such a long time in the scale of things. Yet she ached for him, craved him as though he were a drug and she an addict. She took comfort in the fact that he didn't know about her constant battle to keep from touching him, caressing him, kissing him. Which, when you considered that their bodies wouldn't be able to actually make contact, felt pretty darn nutty.

Had loneliness driven her to this? Maybe, since his presence was like a bright beacon in thick gray fog, she'd been more lonesome than she'd realized.

Once all this was done, she knew he'd be gone. He couldn't stay. But what he'd given her seemed immeasurable. In a way, a ghost had brought her back to life. Because of him, she now had a purpose. Saving his sister, whose plight had become all too real. Freeing Dena would be more than a way to make retribution to the universe for what she'd almost done to Lilly McGraw. She wanted to save her because no one deserved to suffer like that.

The warlock had to be stopped. She might be new at this magic stuff, but even a novice could sense the breadth of the darkness that consumed this man. Or correction—this dragon.

Her naturally curious mind couldn't help wondering if there were more of his kind out there somewhere. He couldn't be the last one, could he? Maybe there were other Drakkors who'd pledged themselves to the light, who could use their magic to counteract the evil darkness of his. Allies.

As for this Doug Polacek, whoever he was, Anabel decided she had much more important things to do than worry about him and whatever mischief he was trying to cause, though she still needed to investigate whether or not he had any potential ties to the warlock/Drakkor.

Juliet phoned back thirty minutes later, which must have been a few minutes after she got her last client out the door.

"I've called an emergency meeting of my coven," Juliet said, sounding breathless from excitement.

Her coven. For a second, Anabel had forgotten that Juliet was Wiccan. "Do you think they can help?"

"Everyone has magic. Some just have more than others," Juliet said, her positive energy practically crackling across the phone line. "At this point, we might as well try. What have we got to lose?"

"Good point." Anabel sighed. "I hate that I supposedly have so much magic, yet I haven't been able to do much to find Tyler's sister."

"I'm hopeful we can help you with that. We're meeting in the woods near the hill with the changing tree. I'd really like it if you and Tyler could come."

The changing tree. The place where the Pack often met to shape-shift and hunt in small groups. Anabel hadn't been there since David died. Too many memories.

She took a deep breath, pushing away her thoughts. "I don't know. We're not changing or anything, right?"

"No, no. Just meeting." Juliet paused. "Maybe a ritual or two, if it's needed."

"Then why there?"

"It's a place of power and we need all the help we can get. Will you come?"

Willing her heartbeat to slow, Anabel considered. Eighteen months had passed. She'd been gradually trying to move on, to let go of the past. Maybe seeing the changing tree would be another step.

"I can do that," Anabel finally agreed. "We can, I mean. But will the others be able to interact with Tyler like you and I do?"

"I don't know. We'll find out soon enough. I've asked everyone to be there in thirty minutes or so. See you there." Juliet rang off.

Thirty minutes? Juliet wasn't wasting time. Anabel turned to tell Tyler and then realized he was gone. Not only that, but she had no idea how to summon him back, or even if that was possible.

All she could do was try. If that didn't work, she'd have to go meet Juliet and the coven by herself.

Taking a deep breath, she sat cross-legged in the middle of her floor. Then she closed her eyes, chanting the single word that had become a new mantra of sorts.

Focus. She pulled inward, shutting down each and every stray thought the instant it occurred.

Finally, she reached that place she considered to be the center of her being, the spot where all her energy lived. Now she must gather and weave, sending tendrils outward, hopefully crossing the barrier between the land of the living and the land of the spirit. To wherever Tyler resided.

She wasn't sure this was the way to do this, nor had she seen anything in any of the books on how to contact a ghost. Just in case, she tried calling his name, raising her volume with each cry.

Tyler. Inhale. Exhale. *Tyler.* Again. And once more. *Tyler.*

Nothing. She didn't sense him or feel him or, when she opened her eyes, see him. It was as if he'd gone so completely into that other dimension that he'd severed all ties to earth and her.

Crud. Disappointment made her throat ache. She got up, dusted her hands off on her jeans. He'd show up when he was ready to. There wasn't a whole lot she could do about that.

"Tyler," she said out loud, speaking to an empty room. "If you can hear me, I'm leaving in a minute to meet with Juliet's coven. They're going to try and help. Juliet said she'd really like it if you could be there."

Again, nothing but silence answered her. She even felt slightly foolish, aware of the fact that if anyone from town were to have seen what she just did, they'd consider her certifiable. Of course, even if Tyler had actually been here, as far as the casual observer would have been concerned, she'd have appeared to be conversing with empty air.

Forget them. She was tired of their condemnation without proof. And the fact that some total stranger had them believing his pack of lies, without them even asking her, made her aware that she needed to take a stand.

Once she saved Tyler's sister, that was. Then she'd deal with the small stuff.

Grabbing her car keys from the counter, she called Tyler once more and then scribbled a quick note before she headed for her car. The changing tree was about fifteen minutes away, but she figured she'd be a few minutes early so she'd have time to collect her thoughts.

And deal with the memories.

She considered those as she drove to the out-of-the-way spot. When she and David had first started dating, they often participated in pack hunts. They both found the mating ritual for wolves much more exciting—and fun—than the long, drawn-out courtship humans endured.

They'd run and played, nipping each other playfully in their wolf form. He'd often brought her his first kill, a particularly juicy rabbit most times. And how great she'd felt the time she beat him and had been the one to gift him with her own small game.

Together as wolves, they'd been quite the hunters. She firmly believed this had strengthened their human relationship.

And the changing tree was where they'd made love for the first time. Where she'd secretly hoped to conceive their baby. Though it hadn't happened, more than ever she wished they'd had a child together. One way to keep a part of him with her always.

David had also proposed here. Right there, kneeling close to one of the giant roots. Anabel had accepted, and once he slipped the ring on her finger, they'd made love in the shade of the old oak.

Sorrow stabbed her. No wonder she'd avoided this place.

As she pulled up in front of the massive oak tree and parked, she closed her eyes. The tree looked exactly the same, just the way the image of it had been burned into her memory. Throat tight, she eyed the twisted branches, the weathered bark and the lush canopy of vibrant green leaves. Juliet was right. It was a place of power. This was the reason the Pack had changed her, going as far back as when the town of Leaning Tree had been established in the 1700s.

Glad hers was the only car in the small parking lot, she got out, last year's dead leaves cracking underfoot as she walked slowly down the winding path toward the huge and ancient tree.

Now that she'd become slightly more attuned to such things, the power radiating from the tree made her skin tingle.

"Wow," a voice said from behind her. "The changing tree. It's been so long, I forgot how much I'd missed this place."

Tyler. Relieved, Anabel turned. "I tried to contact you before I left. I wasn't able to. So I left you a note."

"I'm sorry," he said, his deep voice both soothing and sexy. "I didn't go by the house. I just searched for your energy and came and found you. Why are you here?"

She explained about Juliet and the coven. "They should be here in a few minutes."

Turning back to the tree, she made a slow circle around the massive trunk. With a reverent touch, she laid her hand on the rough bark, feeling the life energy radiating from the oak. "It's so old," she said, her eyes unexpectedly stinging. "I can only imagine what kind of life it's seen."

Tyler watched her rather than the tree, his gaze shuttered. Something in his haunted expression made her shiver. "The Pack has made sure this tree has been taken care of over the years."

She nodded, stopping at the exact spot where David had knelt in the leaves. To her surprise, while she felt the sorrow of an old, precious memory now gone, the crushing pain seemed to have faded.

Life moved on. She'd begun to finally make that journey toward healing.

Another vehicle pulled into the parking lot. Juliet's green Volkswagen. Anabel waved, just as two more cars drove around the corner and parked next to Juliet.

Juliet and another woman got out of the car. Anabel didn't recognize the tall, silver-haired woman, though she admired her grace and the smoothness of her dusky complexion.

Including Anabel, there were seven women in attendance. Most of them wore their hair long. There were only two older women, Juliet and her companion. Anabel waited silently, a bit tense, as they all convened on the changing tree.

"Hello," she ventured, when they were close. "Juliet, I had no idea there would be so many of you."

"Our entire coven," Juliet said, beaming. "Let me introduce you. Everyone, this is Anabel Lee. She's the one I told you about, the one who can talk to ghosts."

Everyone stared at her. Anabel waited for the familiar distrust to cloud the others' expressions. Instead they all murmured serene greetings, dipping their chins as Juliet said each of their names, still smiling. None of them appeared offended by her presence. In fact, they gave off a completely welcoming—even sisterly—vibe.

Stunned, Anabel tried not to show her shock. As she'd realized earlier, she'd grown far too complacent about letting the townspeople of Leaning Tree treat her poorly. Luckily, she didn't have that problem with these women.

"Blessed be," several said at once. Anabel wasn't quite sure how to respond to that, so she simply nodded.

She didn't know what she'd expected with meeting a coven of witches. A group of calm and centered, mostly middle-aged ladies hadn't been exactly the first thing that came to mind.

Granted, she had no experience with this type of thing. Her perceptions were based on what she'd seen on television and in movies or read in books.

Knowing that according to Juliet, Anabel herself was descended from a line of powerful witches didn't help. Actually, she thought, eyeing them as they held their hands out to her so they could make a circle around the tree, she was glad for the complete lack of drama. And if there was one thing she'd come to despise in her life, drama would rank right up there on top.

Still, she mused. They were witches and there was magic involved. She supposed she expected something.

Sliding her hand into Juliet's cool one, she reached out to connect with the woman waiting patiently on her other side.

Chapter 10

A flash of movement caught her attention. Tyler. His set face, clamped mouth and tight jaw showed his irritation at being left out of the circle. She wished he could be included. But then, Anabel didn't think any of the others could see him, except for Juliet.

"An orb," the dusky-skinned woman breathed, pointing directly at Tyler. "I think we're being visited by a spirit."

She sounded so delighted and excited that Anabel couldn't help grinning.

"Didn't you tell them?" she asked Juliet.

"No. Not yet. All in good time," Juliet said, one corner of her mouth lifting as if she tried to hide a smile.

One of the women—Anabel couldn't remember her name but judged her to be the oldest one there—cleared her throat loudly. "Are you ready?" she asked.

A silence fell. One by one, they nodded. Again, the overall mood felt solemn and respectful.

Except for Tyler, glowering at her. Clearly, he hated not being able to participate.

Giving in to impulse, she broke contact with the woman on her right and held out her hand to Tyler. "Come join us," she said, smiling.

One of the women gasped, to be shushed immediately by Juliet. Needing no second urging, Tyler came to stand beside Anabel, gripping her hand with his.

This time, his fingers didn't go through hers. Once again, Anabel could actually feel his touch. As if he were solid. As if he were alive. Just like when he'd kissed her. A thrill ran through her at the notion.

Just as instantly, she squashed it. "Is everyone ready?" she asked, looking pointedly at the woman on her right, who needed to be holding Tyler's other hand.

This woman—called Mary, if Anabel remembered correctly—gave her a perplexed look. "Will you take my hand again?" she asked. Clearly, she could not see or sense Tyler at all.

"Tyler, can you hold her hand?" Anabel wasn't sure how this worked. Was she the only one to whom he could appear solid?

"I can try." Confidence rang in his voice. He reached for Mary's fingers. And his hand went right through hers.

"I feel a chill." Eyes wide, Mary shivered. "Is that orb you guys claimed you could see near me?"

"Tyler is not an orb," Juliet told them, her voice firm. "He's a spirit and he's here with us right now."

Mary gasped, her gaze darting left and then right. "What…what does he want?"

"He needs our help to find his missing sister," Juliet

continued. "He is, in fact, the reason we're here. Now please push your fear away and see if you and he can complete the circle. Take his hand."

"You want me to touch a...a ghost?" Mary sounded terrified.

"He won't hurt you, I promise." Anabel gave her a reassuring smile. "I'm holding his hand right now. Won't you please at least try?"

Grimacing, the woman glanced at her friends, maybe hoping for support, maybe for encouragement. No one else spoke, though the other women appeared to wait with an air of calm reassurance.

Finally, Mary took a deep breath and held out her hand. "Go ahead," she said, gazing up at empty air. "Take it." She glanced at Anabel. "Will I be able to feel— Oh!"

Anabel smiled. Apparently, Tyler's strange ability to ground himself more in this world temporarily enabled the other woman to feel his touch, as well.

"Are we ready now?" Juliet asked. Her voice sounded richer and more confident than Anabel had ever heard her. The voice of a woman of power.

Murmurs of assent came from the group. They'd barely died out when Juliet began chanting. The other women picked up the chant with her, making Anabel wonder if they'd memorized the words.

Only Anabel and Tyler remained silent. Beside her, Tyler still felt disturbingly solid, as if she could lean over and lick the corded muscles of his neck.

Shocked, she nearly jerked her hand free. Where had that thought come from? No matter. She had more important things to think about than her totally unrealistic attraction to a ghost.

Focus. Even as she thought the word, Anabel saw

the power begin to coalesce in the air. Sparkling, like a braided rope made from lightning, it coiled around the circle of women and then from there, around the massive base of the tree.

Her very skin felt electrified. Sizzling. She fought the urge to break contact with the others, somehow aware if she did, this—whatever this was—would disappear.

Yet while she felt its power, she had no idea of its purpose. Surely Juliet or someone knew. Maybe they'd clue her in soon.

All of the energy vibrating in the air made her dizzy and she briefly closed her eyes. When she did, instead of the blessed cool darkness, the face of the dragon appeared. And his obsidian eyes were fixed directly on her.

She supposed she screamed. At least, she tried to. But when she opened her mouth, no sound came out. Something wrapped around her throat, crushing her breath. Dragon claws, huge filthy talons, tearing into her skin and making her bleed, even as she choked.

Struggling, she tried to fight. As her vision grayed, the notion flashed at her that she was not fighting with her physical self when the attack was in another realm entirely.

Help. She needed help. Yet she couldn't even open her eyes. Tyler still held one hand, one of the witches the other. What was wrong with them? Could they not see she was in trouble?

Focus.

The single word gave clarity to her panicked thoughts. *Focus.* Yet how could she when she could barely breathe?

Power shot through her, almost as if she'd been struck by lightning. She jolted up, conscious that she must not, no matter what, break the circle.

The power sent the Drakkor backward, breaking his death grip on her. She gasped, sucking in air, shaky and grateful and so damn full of energy she thought that if she were to launch herself into the air after her enemy, she could fly.

Who knew? Maybe she could.

The Drakkor roared, a sound of frustration and fury. Any moment she expected fire to shoot from his mouth.

As he retreated, she knew that if she was ever going to locate Tyler's sister, she needed to follow him, somehow.

Taking a leap of faith, she jerked her hands free and jumped into the air. To her relief, she lifted, flying steady and straight, almost as if she had wings or a jet pack on her back.

Ahead of her, the Drakkor flew like lightning. She increased her speed enough to be able to keep him in sight, but not so much that she grew close enough for him to notice. And then what? Once she found his lair—or perfectly ordinary house, which might very well be the case—what did she plan to do?

The safest thing might be to note the location.

Even as she had this thought, the beast turned. Terrible jaws open in a furious roar, it headed straight at her.

Anabel had no weapon with which to fight. Acting on instinct, she stifled a scream and threw up her hands in defense.

Energy whiplashed from her palms, like some fantastical movie special effects. Directing it on her attacker, she bared her teeth. She slammed her power into him, hoping, praying this—whatever this was—would work. And stop him.

Apparently, it did. The Drakkor struggled, roaring in

defiance, unable to reach her. Unable, that was, as long as her power held.

Suddenly, she noticed what a drain this took on her energy. The vitality leached from her, more and more with every second that passed. If the Drakkor realized this, all he'd have to do would be to wait her out.

And then what? Most likely she would die here, wherever she was. Alone, taking Dena's last chance at salvation with her.

Decision made, she knew she had to flee, to get back to the safety of the coven, to find Tyler and Juliet and the others.

But how to beat a retreat while holding her enemy at bay?

The Drakkor roared again, launching himself at her. She could feel herself growing weak and knew she wouldn't be able to hold him off too much longer.

She thought of the others, hands linked in a circle around the ancient oak tree. Willed herself there, with every fiber of untapped power that might be left inside of her.

And just like that, she hurtled through space, so quickly even the stars became a blur. Until she found herself lying on the soft earth at the base of the tree, dead leaves crackling under her.

Tyler had sensed something might be wrong with Anabel when her small hand jerked in his. He glanced at her, finding her utterly still, with her eyes closed. Just like, he thought, glancing around the circle, all the others.

He wondered if the others could see the power shimmering like a golden rope made of sparks. As he watched, fascinated, it circled the tree and them. The hair on the women's heads danced with an electrical beat, and their skin seemed to sizzle. Apparently, this didn't hurt. Not one person moved. Yet despite all the stillness, he sensed Anabel had gone a different kind of quiet.

It was dangerous to break the circle. He dared not let go. His own ethereal body appeared unaffected.

The chant ended. Still the women stood, silent and still as statues. Anabel swayed, her mouth opening as if she meant to speak, but no sound came out.

Concerned, he watched her. He felt as if, more than ever, the importance of not breaking the circle overrode everything else.

She began to thrash, side to side, swaying like a hammock between the hands holding on to hers. Tyler remained solid—this was the longest he'd ever been able to do this, which he figured was due to the power generated by their circle and the tree.

Anabel cried out, making his heart leap in his throat. He looked at her friend Juliet, to see what she thought, but she remained standing, eyes still closed.

No one else seemed perturbed. He told himself to relax, that Anabel was right there, her hand securely in his, and nothing could happen to her anyway while she stayed surrounded by all this power.

But he remembered how the Drakkor had taken him unaware and nearly crushed him. Again he eyed Anabel, wondering if she'd give him a sign if she needed some sort of help. She tightened her grip on his hand, which reassured him. As long as her chest continued to rise and fall with her breathing, and she didn't appear threatened, he waited.

Just as he reached this decision, Anabel let out a powerful scream. Jerking her hands free, she jumped forward. And fell, as surely as if struck by a giant, invisible hand.

He ran to her, reaching to cradle her in his arms. But he'd gone back to his ghostly, unsubstantial form, and his hands passed right through her. This made him want to lift his head to the sky and howl with frustration.

The others rushed over, making soft sounds of distress. Juliet and her friend, who appeared to be the leader, gathered Anabel up.

Rage filled Tyler. He hated being a ghost, despised the lack of the ability to help both Anabel and his baby sister. Once again, he was sick and tired of being insubstantial. Why even allow him to be contacted, if he couldn't even help protect the ones he loved?

Loved.

This should have shocked him, but his anger and frustration eclipsed everything else. That and his concern for Anabel, who hadn't stirred at all since she'd fallen to the ground.

Juliet and her friend were speaking. He moved closer so he could pick up the words.

"Her physical body is fine. The attack was on the other plane."

He shook his head, but no one noticed him. Of course they hadn't. He'd managed to briefly forget that he was a ghost and thus invisible to most of them.

Anabel groaned, her eyelids fluttering. She sat up, moaned in pain and looked around. "What just happened?"

"We don't know," Juliet said. "We were gathering the power, and you just collapsed."

"No." Anabel met Tyler's gaze. "The Drakkor found me."

Several of the women gasped. Juliet, however, remained as calm and coolly collected as ever. "Us," she gently corrected her. "The Drakkor found us."

Anabel nodded, clearly unwilling to battle over semantics.

"And then what happened?" Tyler prodded.

"He attacked me. Wrapped his claws around my throat." Her hand went up, gingerly probing her neck. "He was trying to choke me. His talons tore into my skin and made me bleed."

Tyler nodded, despite the fact that her throat appeared untouched.

"I fought him off," Anabel continued. "And when he flew away, I followed."

Another collective gasp. Only Juliet and the older woman remained silent, their blue eyes watchful.

Anabel kept her gaze locked on Tyler. "I wanted to follow him, to learn where he might be keeping your sister. But this time, I saw nothing I recognized, no landmarks to help guide us." She grimaced. "Maybe because he noticed me after him."

If Tyler had been alive, he would have been holding his breath. "And then what happened?" he asked quietly.

"He came for me." Briefly, she closed her eyes. When she opened them again, they shone like polished copper. "And I fought him off, this time using some sort of magic or energy."

"How?" Juliet asked, sounding unsurprised and intently curious. "What precisely did you do?"

"I used my palms. I'm not sure how exactly, but energy came from them and stopped the Drakkor. I was able to hold him motionless and keep him from reaching me."

Then she told them all how she'd simply decided she needed to come back and she had.

When Anabel finished speaking, the assembled group remained silent. Anabel began shaking, and Tyler once again tried to go to her and offer comfort. But he was not permitted such luxuries. The ache in his chest became a stone.

"Let's go home," he said. "I think we've had enough excitement for one day."

She nodded, saying her goodbyes to the women. Initially, a few of them protested, wanting her to stay longer, but a single look from Juliet quelled their requests.

As she walked to the car, her gait seemed odd, as though her entire body felt sore. Once she unlocked it and got inside, she took a deep breath and grabbed the steering wheel, dropping her head on her hands. "I'm exhausted," she said, her voice husky with weariness. "Even though I didn't physically fight that dragon, my body feels like it did and got its ass kicked."

He waited until she'd started the engine and put the car in Drive before speaking. "We're running out of time," he said. "If we don't get to her soon, my sister will die. I don't know how I know this, but I feel it in my heart."

Straightening, she nodded. "I'm doing the best I can. If you can think of anything else I should try, I'm willing to give it a shot."

Since he had nothing else to offer, he managed a smile and thanked her. Neither spoke for the rest of the short ride home.

As soon as they reached the house, Anabel headed for her bedroom. "I need to sleep," she said, the exhaustion plain on her beautiful face. "Just a couple of hours, and then I'll get up and make myself something to eat."

"Okay," he replied, trying not to sound too worried. "You definitely need to keep up your strength."

The ghost of a smile hovering at the edges of her mouth called him out. Still, he couldn't help smiling back. "I'll wait for you."

The words sounded oddly prophetic.

Tyler checked on Anabel several times during the night. Her even breathing and lack of restlessness told him she slept deeply, healing her body and her spirit. Though he wanted to stay with her while she slept, his attraction had grown so strong it interfered with his thinking. The more distance he maintained between them, the better.

Finally, as the sun began to rise, he retreated to his own corner of the living room and tried again to contact Dena.

The instant he stilled himself, for the first time in far too long, he was able to feel his sister reaching out to him. This time, he could barely feel the feeble spark of her energy, it had grown so weak.

Unlike before, she didn't speak or even plead for help. He doubted that she could. Nothing but misery and pain radiated from her. Stomach sinking, horrified and afraid, he knew then that they were running out of time to find her. If they didn't locate her soon, the next time he'd see her would be in the misty world of spirit.

He tried to comfort her as much as he could, but he wasn't sure if she even felt his presence. Nevertheless, he remained, trying to transfer some of his energy to her, surrounding her with vibes of healing and strength.

To his relief, some of it must have reached her. She quieted and appeared to breathe better.

Damn, he cursed himself. Here he battled a foolish attraction to a woman he couldn't have when he should have been focusing all his energy on Dena.

The urgency of her situation had never seemed clearer. Now that morning had arrived, it had been five days since he first made contact with Anabel. They had to locate and rescue Dena within the next day or two or she'd die.

They'd learned so much—but not enough.

Having done all he could, he retreated. Back in Anabel's living room, when he came out of his trance, he saw at least an hour had passed, judging by the angle of sun streaming in the window. Great. More time wasted. Exactly what he—and more important, Dena—didn't need.

Anabel had dreamed of landmarks. They needed to go comb the woods, drive around the more remote wooded areas and try to see if they could locate any of the markers she'd seen in her dream.

Fired up, he hurried to find Anabel, figuring she'd still be sleeping. Instead her bed was empty. He rushed past it and found her in her bathroom. She'd just stepped out of the shower. Reaching for a towel, she glanced up and saw him, water drops glistening on her white satin skin. Naked, she was even more alluring, an unwelcome attraction he certainly did not need.

Looking away, he knew the image would forever be burned into his retinas. He clenched his jaw so tightly it hurt. He needed to focus on rescuing his sister, not his mounting attraction for this enigmatic woman.

Eyes wide, Anabel hurriedly wrapped herself in the towel. "Why are you in here?" Her voice came out high and breathless. "What's going on?"

"I need your help," he rasped. "Dena's fading fast."

"I know. We've got to find her." She pointed at the doorway. "But a few minutes isn't going to change anything. Out. Go wait for me in the kitchen. I'll join you once I'm dried off and dressed."

As he backed out of the room, Tyler kept his gaze averted. It was safer that way.

The instant Tyler disappeared, Anabel let out the breath she'd been holding. When he'd walked in on her naked, she'd known an instant's thrill of pleasure. For a moment, she'd wished he wasn't a ghost, but a real, live man, the way he'd been earlier in the circle around the changing tree.

The constant aching of desire never left her. Even when she pushed it away so she could focus, it remained, humming along just under her skin. How ridiculous was that? Bad enough she craved another man's embrace, but how ironic the man wasn't even alive.

Sighing, she toweled herself off and hurried through her normal morning routine. Dressed, she gave a quick glance at herself in her mirror, shaking her head at the woman who stared right back at her. Sometimes she didn't even recognize herself.

Heading to the kitchen, where Tyler waited, she went straight to the coffeemaker and made herself a large mug of coffee. A couple of sips in, she finally felt ready to face her ghostly visitor.

"I'm trying my best to help your sister, Tyler." She let some of her frustration show. "But I don't know what else to do."

"Try again to locate the Drakkor," he said immediately. "He's the only one who knows."

Remorse stabbed her. "I can't," she said. "I'm sorry, but I don't have enough energy still. I need more rest before I try any more magic."

A shadow crossed his face, though he nodded. "How

about we take a drive in the countryside? Somewhere in the Catskill Forest Preserve."

She stared at him. "We can do that," she said slowly. "But you do realize that's 287,000 acres and goes through Ulster, Greene, Delaware and Sullivan counties? Where do you propose we start?"

Burying his face in his hands, he cursed. "Damn it. I hate being so freaking powerless."

Stunned, she didn't know what to say. When she finally found the words, she hoped they did her thoughts justice. "Powerless? You are dead, Tyler. Yet somehow you managed to come back as a ghost and do everything you can to help your sister. That sounds pretty damn powerful to me."

He raised his face, staring at her. A spark of some indefinable emotion glowed in his eyes. "Thank you for that," he said quietly.

"You've just got to remember we're doing all we can. I get frustrated too. I hate the thought of her at the mercy of that Drakkor."

"Me too."

"What I don't understand is why." Anabel rubbed her aching temples. "Nothing I've read about these Drakkors mentions them capturing young women and holding them hostage."

Tyler's grim expression told her he thought he knew the answer. "Well, there's your feeding-off-magic theory."

"I can't find any information to support that. There's got to be another reason."

Mouth twisting bitterly, he looked away. "Sexual deviants aren't particular to any one species."

Though his answer made her feel sick, she kept her voice professional. "True, but I can't help feeling there's more to it than that." She reached for the stack of ever-present books she'd placed on the table and tapped on one particularly thick book. "I keep reading and hoping I'll find it."

Though he appeared skeptical, she chose to believe she saw a glimmer of hope.

"No matter what, fighting that Drakkor almost did me in. I've got to rest up," she said. "I plan to spend that time learning as much as I can about our enemy. I think that's the key. If we can find out why he does what he does, we can figure out a way to beat him."

"Maybe." Tyler didn't sound optimistic. "I can only hope it doesn't take too long, or we'll be too late for my sister."

"You can fly," she pointed out. "While I study, why don't you go and search as much of the preserve as you can, starting with the areas closest to town? You never know—you might see one of the landmarks."

"I think I will."

Though she only nodded, inside she seethed with frustration. Talk about feeling powerless. Supposedly she had been blessed with great magical ability, but because of her lack of training, she had no idea how to utilize it. She'd give anything to be able to zoom to Dena Rogers's side, zap the stupid Drakkor and bring Tyler's sister to safety.

Now she was too darn weak to do anything but rest.

After making some soft-boiled eggs for breakfast, Anabel spent the morning poring over the books. Though Tyler had left, he returned shortly before lunch, brooding and silent, his rugged profile dark and somber. When she asked him if he'd had any luck, he only shook his head, gesturing that she should go back to her reading.

Finally, she closed her book and rubbed her eyes. "I need a break," she announced. "I'll make a quick lunch and then get back to it."

Just as she spoke, she heard the sound of the postal truck delivering the day's mail. "This is really getting to be a habit," she said, half laughing at her own foolishness. "I'll be right back."

Two sales catalogs, one air-conditioning-repair brochure and a letter from a company inviting her to take a competitive look at her home insurance. At least there were no bills.

On her way back in, she realized a piece of paper had been taped to the front door. Curious, she pulled it down and opened it. The black-and-white flyer had been printed on regular paper rather than glossy, so the photograph in the middle looked dull, as if dimmed by the passage of time.

The two faces smiling at the camera made her gasp. The woman, with her long mass of dark hair and exotically tilted eyes, was Dena Rogers in better times, according to the caption. The other, a man with his arms draped casually around her shoulders, was Dena's older brother, Tyler.

Chapter 11

Dumbstruck, she studied the picture, uncomfortably aware that Tyler had not only been alive in this photo, but much more carefree. His ghost self rarely flashed that kind of confident smile, though when he did she felt its impact all the way from her heart to her feet.

Handsome, sexy, masculine—all those adjectives came to mind. How she wished she'd known him then, before she'd met David. Shocked at the wayward thought, she shook her head. What on earth was wrong with her? She'd loved her husband and he'd loved her. They'd been mates, hadn't they?

If so, then why did she feel such an overwhelming attraction to another man? Even worse, to another man's ghost. Mates were just that—one male, one female, for life. Once David had died, she wasn't supposed to ever be able to love another man.

Still she couldn't look away. When she realized she'd been mooning at the photograph long enough, she shook her head at her own foolishness and read the text. And then, disbelieving, read it again to be sure while walking back inside.

"Wow." The sound of his deep voice behind her made her start. Heat flooded her entire body as she met his gaze. Hurriedly, she looked back at the photo, hoping she hadn't inadvertently revealed how he affected her.

"Where did you get that?" he asked, his voice thick with pain.

"It was on my front door. Evidently, Everlasting Faith Church is holding a candlelight prayer vigil for your sister." Composed again, she faced him. "That's pretty awesome, don't you think?"

"Yes," he said thoughtfully, his focus still on the picture. "I find it hard to believe that anybody who can do something so caring could possibly have anything to do with her disappearance."

"Unless that's exactly what they want you to think," she felt compelled to point out.

"Maybe so." When he finally looked up from the flyer, he gave a slow shake of his head. "I haven't seen that photo in a long time."

"When was it taken?"

Glancing quickly at her, he flashed a distracted smile. "Two years ago, when I was home on leave. We'd just come back from a night out eating pizza. We were both so happy to be together again. Family is—was—everything to both of us."

Her throat ached for him. In that moment, she would have given just about anything if she could give him back both his sister and his life.

Of course, she couldn't do the latter, so she'd have to settle for getting Dena free.

"Are you going to go?" He jerked his head at the flyer. "To the candlelight vigil."

Though she hadn't intended to, she gave the idea some serious thought. "Do you think it would help if I did?"

"Maybe. Who knows? But if whoever did this to my sister is there, he might do something to reveal where he's holding her."

"True. I have read that people like that often try to insinuate themselves into the investigation."

He nodded, his chiseled features expressionless. "Then you'll go?"

"Will you come with me?"

The smile that spread across his face had his eyes crinkling and made her catch her breath. "Yes."

Since the candlelight vigil was that night, she wondered if anyone from the church had managed to notify the media. "Media coverage would really help," she mused out loud. "I'm going to call Pastor Tom and see if he's taken care of that."

She had her phone locate and dial the number for her. Pastor Jones sounded surprised to hear from her. When she outlined the reason for her call, he chuckled. "Great minds apparently think alike. I've sent a press release to the local NBC, ABC, CBS and Fox affiliates. Several reporters have already contacted me with requests for interviews at the vigil. So we should have more than adequate media coverage."

"Great." Feeling a bit self-conscious, she glanced at Tyler, who gave her the thumbs-up sign.

"Thanks for checking, Ms. Lee. Are you going to be in attendance, as well?"

Glad she and Tyler had just discussed this, she answered in the affirmative.

"Fantastic." The warmth in his voice made her smile. "I look forward to seeing you there." And he hung up.

Feeling slightly dazed, she put her phone back in her pocket. "I am beginning to see how he has such a high rate of conversions to his church. That man has serious charisma."

Tyler studied her. She didn't know if it was her imagination or not, but he seemed a bit sad. "I think he likes you," he said.

She had to laugh. "No. He merely sees another poor soul whom he hopes to save."

Tyler nodded. "About the vigil. When we're there, try to continually scan the crowd. Look for anyone who seems out of place. I'll do the same."

"Okay." She nodded. "Of course, you have the added benefit of being invisible."

He gave her a fleeting smile. "Fingers crossed we learn something useful."

Though they arrived ten minutes before the scheduled start time, the church parking lot was already packed. "Surely not all of these are members of the congregation?"

Tyler shook his head. "No, I don't think so. This event has been pretty heavily promoted, between the flyers and the TV news and even the newspaper. I bet they did something online too. I'm sure there are a lot of outsiders here, as well."

She thought she could look into his eyes forever. Grimacing at the thought, she parked. "Are you ready?"

"Definitely."

She took a deep breath. "Then let's do this."

One thing Anabel didn't tell Tyler was that she'd always hated crowds. More than that, too many people around her made her feel the panicked urge to flee.

She'd told herself too many times to count not only that such an irrational fear was ridiculous, but that she couldn't allow such a foolish weakness to get in the way of her search for Tyler's sister. Better to endure the sweaty press of people milling around in the early-evening heat than be held prisoner, trapped in some dark hole.

Thus fortified, she made her way through the crowd, most of them already holding their Dixie cups and candles, though unlit.

She saw Juliet and a few of the other women from the coven. Even her former best friend, Denise Jarvis, had come, waving at her from her position next to her mother and several older women who had to be her mother's friends. Though Anabel hadn't seen Denise in years, she waved back.

Pastor Jones stepped up on a smallish raised platform. A woman seated below him at a small electric keyboard hit a series of notes, and all around, the talking and other noise quieted.

"Let us bow our heads in prayer," the pastor said. All around, everyone did exactly that. Anabel too, though she kept her eyes open and continued to scan the crowd through her lashes. While she didn't know the majority of the people attending, she really didn't see anyone who looked out of place.

Maybe she needed to use more than just her eyes.

As the pastor continued to pray, Anabel focused her attention inward, gathering up her scattered thoughts and silencing them one by one.

Until inside she went quiet.

And then she sent her essence outward, touching the others quietly, seeking what, she wasn't sure. An odd vibration, maybe unquiet tension.

She couldn't read their minds—she wasn't a psychic. But she could feel what kind of heart beat within. Many of the people in attendance were focused on the pastor's words and then on the hymn they'd all begun to sing.

As her essence drifted through the crowd, she found lust and anger, jealousy and irritability. Normal human emotions—nothing on the scale of what she searched for. Nothing like the furious rage consuming the Drakkor.

Finally, the sound of clapping made her blink. Instantly back in her own body, she looked around. Everyone had begun to move, talking to each other.

Juliet made a beeline over. "That was very nice. Did you learn anything?"

"No." With a disappointed—and tired—sigh, Anabel shook her head. "Unfortunately not. If he was here, he's really good at cloaking himself."

"I wouldn't be surprised," Juliet said. "Did you bring your friend?"

"My friend?" Mind blank, Anabel didn't understand at first what the other woman meant. When she realized, she nodded. "You mean Tyler? Yes, he's around here somewhere."

"Good. I talked briefly to Pastor Jones. He seems like a good-hearted man. He's doing everything he can think of to help."

Anabel nodded. "I have to say, I'm sort of surprised to see you here."

"Because we're Wiccan?" Not waiting for Anabel's response, Juliet looked around and shrugged. "There's good energy being generated here. Prayers have power, no matter what religion. This is more like what we do than you realize."

Worried she'd offended her friend, Anabel tried to apologize. Juliet instantly waved her words away. "No worries, hon." She gave Anabel an impulsive hug. "I'm going to run now. If you hear of anything or have any questions, give me a call."

After promising she would, Anabel turned to look for Tyler. As she did, she saw Pastor Jones purposely making his way toward her. Though the last thing she wanted to do was speak with him, she wanted to thank him for putting on the vigil.

Unfortunately, the poor man kept getting sidetracked by members of his own congregation. At this rate, Anabel figured it'd be at least twenty or thirty minutes before he reached her.

Taking matters into her own hands, she expertly weaved through the crowd until she reached his side. "Excuse me," she said, interrupting the ongoing conversation. "Pastor, I just wanted to thank you for putting on this prayer vigil. It was very much appreciated."

"Thank you."

She could tell he wanted to say more but because of his attentive audience, couldn't.

"Time to go," Tyler said, his deep voice so close to her ear she jumped. Which made the pastor and his circle of friends eye her.

"Bug bite," she said, hiding a smile. Then, thanking him again, she took off.

On the drive home, she wondered at the restless feeling making her jittery. Recognizing it, she pushed away the anger. It had been a long time since she'd craved a man this much. Correction—a ghost. All day, the craving had been building inside her, until she felt as if she might explode.

If she'd been a runner, she might have taken off and tried to outrun it. As things stood, she'd simply have to let her desire simmer inside her until it hopefully burned itself out.

Unless… She gasped out loud as a thought occurred to her. A frightening, yet delightful thought. One that energized her more than a hundred naps. Her heart began pounding as she contemplated whether or not she'd have enough courage to carry it through. Or if such a thing would even work.

Once, just once, she wanted—no, *needed*—to allow herself to feel again. Her husband had died, she was alone and her actions would hurt no one but herself.

"You're in a strange mood," Tyler commented as they pulled up in her driveway.

"Maybe," she allowed, parking and turning off the engine. Now or nothing. "I have a question for you. About that trick you did once before and again during the circle at the changing tree?"

"Trick?"

"Yes," she said, trying to sound casual as she got out of the car and headed toward her front door, despite the fact that she'd begun trembling. "Becoming solid. Any idea how you did that?"

As she put her key in the lock, Tyler materialized next to her. Eyeing her as he followed her inside, he cocked his head. "That? I have no idea how that happened."

Tossing her purse onto the counter, she faced him. Her heart now beat so fast she wondered if he could see it in the hollow of her throat.

"Are you all right?" he asked, eyeing her warily,

clearly not understanding. "Why do you want to know how I became solid? All I know is one minute I was a ghost and the next I wasn't. It didn't last long, though."

Again, she wondered if together they could make it last long enough.

"It seems like a form of magic," she prompted. "Surely you must have some idea how you made it happen. Think about it, please. It's important."

Some of the pent-up heat in her tone must have reached him. He eyed her, his gaze going dark. "No, not really. I just was."

"Did you think about it first? Like I have to make myself focus, the way Juliet taught me?"

"Focus." He considered. "Maybe. Part of me wanted it, so I decided to be. And I became flesh, for a short while."

Decided to be. Though she could barely catch her breath, she still tried to sound calm. "I have a question for you. Do you think you can do it again?"

He shrugged. Was he playing with her? Or did he truly not get her feeble innuendo?

"Maybe. Probably. Why?"

Her face heated. She'd always had this unfortunate blushing issue, despite her dark hair. Her pale complexion went from milky white to the color of a ripe tomato.

"I, uh." Deep breath, swallow. Lifting her gaze to his, she managed to push out the words. "I wanted you to be solid because I wondered if you could kiss me again." Even though she ached for more, she'd settle for a kiss. Or so she told herself.

There. She'd said it. She had no idea what she'd do if he said no. Deal with it and move on, as she did with everything else.

In the silence that followed, Anabel panicked. Maybe

she'd just made a horrible, awful mistake. Or worse, she didn't want him to think he had to or to feel obligated out of pity. Oh no. "Of course, it's up to you," she began. "Though I think it might somehow help give me back some of my missing energy."

Where had that come from? Maybe it was true. What on earth was the *matter* with her?

"Shhh." Suddenly, Tyler was right there. Eyes glowing, a few inches in front of her, looking handsome and manly and oh so alive.

He kissed her then, before she could even exhale. His mouth—solid and very unghostlike—slanted over hers, making her go weak at the knees.

Tongue mating with his, she deepened the kiss. She knew she shouldn't have, but she had been widowed for so long, and she wanted him with every fiber of her being.

Wanted more than a kiss. Much, much more.

This so shocked her she attempted to back away. But her arms were locked around his neck, her hips molding to his in an invitation that was anything but tentative.

When he kissed her again, she forgot about her hesitation. Heck, she forgot her own name or the fact that he was a ghost. All she could think about was how badly she wanted him inside her.

Energy blazed through her. Whether his or hers or a combination of the two, she had no idea. He moved his mouth from her lips to the hollow of her throat, making her shiver.

"Anabel?" He whispered the question, his breath tickling the edge of her ear. She knew what he asked, without him having to say anything but her name.

Should she? Could she? Throwing out logic and refusing to debate, she took the plunge. "Yes," she said, giving herself permission to let her hands explore. "Definitely yes."

In that moment, and the ones that followed, Tyler ceased to be a ghost. He became real, and Anabel let herself delight in touching every corded muscle, thrilling at his body's response as she skimmed her fingers against his flat stomach.

When she went to tug at his clothes, it occurred to her to simply will them away, and she did. They vanished just like that. Allowing her to feast her eyes on his massive arousal.

"What about yours?" he demanded, his voice like smoke and whiskey. "I want to see you. Every inch of you."

What the heck—why not? Smiling seductively, she blinked and her own clothing vanished. "Here you go," she murmured, groaning as he fastened his mouth over one erect nipple.

"You're absolutely beautiful," he said gruffly.

"So are you," she replied, meaning it. Each touch, every caress and kiss and sigh made her body turn to liquid and fire. When he entered her, she gasped with stunned pleasure as the sheer breadth of him filled her completely.

"Oh," she cried. And then again as he began to move.

Never before had lovemaking felt like this. Carnal and primitive, yet tender and full of emotion. Of love.

No. Shoving that random thought out of her head, she gave herself over to the pleasure building with each thrust of his body.

In a white-hot supernova, she let herself explode. Pulses of pleasure, rocking her body, her world and, ultimately, him.

Tyler followed her into release just as her spasms began to slow down. The brilliant flare of energy, of magic, settled into a steady glow.

As she lay in the circle of his arms, marveling, refusing to feel guilty, she sort of expected him to go all ethereal on her again, back to his ghostly form. But he remained solid, his sweat-slickened body cooling with hers. Nothing had felt as sweet as his embrace, at least not in a long time.

Now what? Deciding to worry about that another time, she let herself relax. To her amazement, she fell asleep.

Leroy's furious yowls woke her. Sitting up, alone once more, she glanced at the clock. She'd managed to sleep past her pet's dinnertime.

Not only that, but Tyler was nowhere in sight. If not for her soreness and the small black-and-blue bite mark just above her boob, she might have thought she'd once again dreamed the entire thing.

Except she felt blissfully, vibrantly, happy. Everything about her—from her skin to her heart to her senses—felt enhanced somehow. She recognized the feeling. After all, she'd felt it once before when she fell for David.

No. She wasn't that stupid. She couldn't be emotionally involved with a man who wasn't even alive.

When her phone rang just as she'd gotten calmed down, Anabel glanced at the caller ID. "Denise Jarvis?" She wasn't sure she wanted to answer. Denise had been her best friend in high school. After Anabel married David, Denise had taken off for parts unknown. She'd always wanted to travel, so Anabel had assumed her former friend let her wanderlust carry her wherever she wanted to go. They'd grown apart organically, leading such different lives.

She'd often wondered why Denise had never tried to keep in touch, and then had put it down to the definite possibility that she'd heard about Anabel's actions from family members still in town and wanted nothing to do with the kind of person everyone believed Anabel had become.

So why call her now?

Deciding she'd welcome the distraction—any distraction—Anabel pressed the button to take the call. "Denise," she said cautiously. "Long time, no see. How on earth are you?"

"I'm okay. Sorry I haven't gotten in touch, but I've been traveling again. I just got back in town a couple of days ago." Denise cleared her throat. "Anyway, I wondered if you wanted to have lunch with me. I'm kind of worried about you."

Resisting the urge to respond truthfully, Anabel sighed. "I promise you, I'm fine. I know you've heard about some of my actions a couple of months past, but I'm trying to move past that."

"Are you?" Denise sounded desperate to believe her. "How do you feel?"

"I'm healing," Anabel said, wondering if she really was. Part of her couldn't help wondering, since apparently she'd become fixated on a dead man, one who was just barely more accessible than her deceased husband.

"I'm glad," Denise said. "Really, really glad. But I've been hearing an awful lot of talk about you and this guy Doug Polacek. Mostly, I'd been putting it down to gossip, but I got a chance to meet him the other day. He's really angry with you. What exactly did you do to him?"

Him again. First Juliet had mentioned him and now Denise. "That's just it. I've never even met him."

Silence. Anabel figured Denise was trying to decide whether or not to believe her. "Look, Denise. I really don't care whether or not you think I'm telling the truth. I don't know Doug Polacek and I have absolutely no idea why he's trying to discredit me."

"Wow." Denise sounded shocked. "Maybe we'd better do some digging and see what we can find out."

Surprised by the *we*, Anabel didn't respond at first.

"How about we get together? We can discuss this at lunch," Denise continued. "Are you free tomorrow?"

Though the idea of meeting an old friend for lunch in a public place made Anabel nervous, she found herself agreeing. Who knew? Maybe it would do her good to get out and get away from Tyler. And she needed to try to find out what this Doug Polacek's problem might be. It might even be tied in to the thing with Tyler's sister.

After lunch, as long as she was in town, she could stop by the police station and see if Captain Harper had dug up any other information.

They decided to meet at Cow Burgers, which had become the carnivorous townspeople of Leaning Tree's favorite burger joint. Anabel's mouth started to water at the thought of one of those thick, juicy hamburger patties, but since she'd given up meat, she'd opt for a vegetarian entrée.

Once she ended the call, she turned to see Tyler watching her, his form much less substantial than usual.

What had she just done? Trying not to panic, she managed a smile. "Are you all right?"

"I think so." His shuttered expression made her wonder if he too was full of regret. Oddly enough, thinking he might be helped. "All that physical manifesting apparently has drained my energy. It's taking every bit of strength I can dredge up to remain here with you."

Now would be the perfect time to tell him to take himself off and get healed, but she couldn't make herself say the words. She both wanted him to leave and wanted him to stay.

Good night, she'd become even more of a mess.

"I'm sorry," she said softly. A quick glance at his still-flickering form revealed he was studying her, a hungry look on his rugged face.

Her stomach lurched. *No, no, no.*

It'd be so much easier if he'd simply pretend nothing had happened, wouldn't it? Or would that hurt even worse?

She no longer knew which end was up. "I'm meeting a friend in town tomorrow. While I'm there, I thought I'd stop at the police station and see if the captain took me seriously."

"Good idea."

"I thought so." She settled on deliberately cheerful, even though her insides were churning.

"I used to love a Triple Cow Burger," he said, still watching her. "Ghosts don't get hungry and we sure don't have to eat, but I'd give a lot if I could just taste a single bite of one right now."

"I haven't been in a long time," she said. "But if I could figure out a way to make you solid again, I'd bring one home for you."

As soon as the words left her mouth, she realized what she'd said. Her entire body blushed. "I mean, so you could eat. But since you can't, I'll just have to enjoy a burger for you—though a veggie burger."

"Oh, I'm going with you." His tone left no room for

argument. "There's no way I'm letting you try and face that crazy Doug guy without a little ghostly help."

Still in shock from the sudden onslaught of feelings, she glared at him. Panicked, she wanted to push him away, make him leave, give her time to regain her bearings. "Not this time, okay? I think you should go back out in the forest and search some more. Actually, I need a bit of a break from all this."

Tyler had gone awfully still. "How is confronting Doug Polacek taking a break?"

"It's time," she said firmly. "I don't know what his problem is, nor do I care. But he needs to stop. Besides, if he confronts me, what are you going to do, anyway?"

Tyler's furious expression told her she might have gone a bit too far. "You know what? You're right. I'm nothing more than a spirit, a specter, a shade. I'm absolutely powerless to do anything without your help. And I should let you know how seriously pissed off that makes me feel."

Though she almost reacted in kind, with anger, she reined herself in again. For an instant she wondered if she should say more, like how terrified their burgeoning—and impossible—relationship made her feel. In the end, she decided to simply repeat her earlier apology. "I'm really, really sorry."

"It's not your fault," he said tightly. "Nor mine. Someone up there is playing a giant, cosmic joke on me. All I wanted to do was try and save my sister, not get tangled up emotionally with you."

Before she could even think of a way to reply to that, he winked out and disappeared.

Leaving her aching and confused when she should have been relieved. His words haunted her. Tangled up emotionally? Really? Clearly, she wasn't the only one having feelings she shouldn't be having.

People in town already believed her crazy. Well, she definitely would be if she allowed herself to fall for a ghost.

Tyler had stated the facts very well. They needed to work together to save his sister. Once that had been accomplished, Anabel could go back to her empty, lonely life. And Tyler could return to being…dead.

Chapter 12

Cow Burgers had just begun to fill up when Anabel arrived the next day. It had just turned eleven thirty, so the die-hard lunch rush wouldn't start for another half hour.

Head held high, ignoring the few people who cast her looks, censuring or otherwise, Anabel searched the interior. Hopefully, Denise would already be seated so Anabel could simply slide into a booth and hide behind a menu if she wanted.

Except she didn't. She'd actually begun to grow weary of always hiding. Since she didn't see Denise yet, she approached the front desk and asked for a table for two.

The teenage girl nodded her pink-tipped head, clearly not recognizing her. Laughing at herself—did she really think she was such a celebrity that everyone in town knew her name?—Anabel followed the hostess to a table, rather than a booth. She pulled out her chair, taking a seat facing the entrance. She decided to wait on looking at the menu until her friend had arrived. Since she worked as a cook, she didn't go out to eat much and she decided to enjoy this rare treat.

Instead of hiding away, she kept her head up and gazed around the room. Several people openly stared, though they looked away when she met their gaze. She refused to let them ruin her day. Heart light, she smiled and waved as Denise walked in.

Her friend looked exactly as she had the last time Anabel had seen her. Tall, with an angular prettiness and close-cropped blond hair, the crinkles around her bright blue eyes a testament to her ready smile.

Anabel jumped up and they hugged. Denise still wore the same perfume, a fragrance that smelled faintly of roses. "You look fantastic!" Anabel exclaimed.

Studying her, Denise grinned. "So do you. I can't believe it's been so long since I've seen you."

After they'd taken their seats, Denise pushed the menu away, still smiling. "I don't even have to look. I always get the Fiery Cow Burger. It has pepper jack cheese, guacamole and jalapeño peppers."

Anabel winced. "Ouch. But you know what? That sounds perfect, except I'll have a veggie burger with the same toppings."

When the waiter came, they both ordered. Once he'd left, Anabel leaned forward. "It's really great to see you," she said softly.

"Same here." Denise glanced around. "I have to tell you, I've heard so much bizarre gossip about you, I got concerned. Actually, you're partly the reason for my stop in Leaning Tree. I decided to take a minivacation here and make sure you were okay."

Touched, Anabel swallowed. She didn't want to tell her old best friend how alone she'd felt after David's death. She knew Denise had been busy with her career as a journalist, traveling all over the world reporting for a prestigious magazine.

"I thought of you often," she finally said. "I even bought a subscription to your magazine, just so I could follow your stories."

Pleasure flashed in Denise's eyes. "Thank you," she said softly.

"Was it exciting?" Anabel asked. "Living the kind of life you did?"

Before Denise could answer, the waiter brought their diet colas.

"Sometimes." Denise took a sip from her straw. "I've been all through Europe and most of Asia. Next I'm being sent to check out Australia and New Zealand."

"I used to always want to travel," Anabel admitted. "In fact, until David was killed, we kept a list of places we wanted to go."

"I'm so sorry." Denise covered Anabel's hand. "I wish I could have met him. I couldn't believe it when my mother told me he was killed in Afghanistan."

In the past, Anabel had found discussing David too painful to bear, so she'd always changed the subject. This time, she felt a slight twinge of grief, but nothing she couldn't handle.

"Thank you. After eighteen months, I guess I've gotten used to being a widow," Anabel said, realizing it was true. "At first, it was hard and I briefly came unhinged. I actually believed Kane McGraw and I were meant to be together."

Denise winced. "I heard about that. I take it you're all better now?"

"Yes. I am." And she was. She reached into her purse and pulled out her wallet. "Since you never met my husband, here's a picture of him right before his last tour."

Studying the snapshot, Denise beamed. "Wow. I can see why you fell for him. He looks good in a uniform." She passed the photo back.

Completely relaxed and feeling more confident than she had felt in months, Anabel nearly told her about Tyler. The second she realized her mistake, she closed her mouth. She could imagine how that conversation would go. *And he's a ghost but looks sexy as hell in his uniform...* No. She'd have to let that pass, thank you very much.

Instead Denise started discussing an area in Thailand where she'd spent six months, and the conversation moved on to other things.

Their burgers arrived and they both dug in. "Every bite tastes as good as I remembered it," Denise gushed, rolling her eyes in bliss.

Mouth full, Anabel nodded. Neither woman spoke again until they'd both finished their burgers and half their fries.

"I'm stuffed," Anabel groaned.

"Me too. But there's one other thing I've been missing from this place and I swear I'm going to make room."

As if he'd heard, the waiter appeared and asked about dessert. Anabel and Denise shared a quick look and then both said "cheesecake" at the same time. Just like in the old days. "One slice, two forks," Anabel clarified.

Once the waiter left, Anabel sighed and leaned forward. "Okay, even though I've thoroughly enjoyed this lunch, I think we've beat around the bush long enough. Now tell me, who *is* this Doug Polacek guy, anyway?"

Denise gave her a shocked look. "You really don't know?"

Taking a deep breath while wishing for patience, Anabel shook her head. "I told you, I don't even know him. I couldn't pick him out in a line of men."

"Wow. I thought you were kidding."

"Nope. Not about something like this."

"Ah." Denise gave her the secret smile that—back in high school—Anabel had called her *gossip grin*. "Where do I start? Doug Polacek is single, a lawyer, relatively new in town. He's very handsome—like he could be a TV star. Women are all over him. From what I hear, he's cut a wide swath through most of the women under forty in town."

"Under forty?" Anabel grimaced. "Exactly how old is this guy, anyway?"

"I don't know. My best guess would be right around forty."

Then and there, as the waiter brought out their shared dessert, Anabel knew what she would do. "I want you to take me to meet him," she said, stabbing the cheesecake with her fork. "Right after we finish here."

Denise stared, her fork in hand. "You what?"

Chewing, Anabel swallowed. "That's really delicious. Try it."

"I will. But first I need to know what you've got planned."

"Planned." A second bite met the same fate as the first. War on cheesecake. "I think I've got the right to actually confront the man who's going around town accusing me of everything under the sun."

Denise had finally gotten her own forkful. She chewed it as if it were made of ashes. "Um, I think he might have gotten a restraining order on you. I don't think you can actually meet him."

"Really?" Anabel whipped out her phone. "Let me call the police department and find out."

Since she had the number stored in her contact list, this took only a few seconds. Brenda Winder answered on the second ring.

"Leaning Tree Police Department," she sang cheerily into the phone. However, as soon as Anabel identified herself, Brenda's pleasant tone changed.

"I'm sorry—he's in a meeting," she said in response to Anabel's request to speak with Captain Harper.

"Fine, then let me speak to someone else. I don't care who, as long as it's someone wearing a badge."

Brenda stuck her on hold without another word. For whatever reason, Barry Manilow played on hold. Halfway through "Copacabana," someone who identified himself as Officer Pitts came on.

"How may I help you?" he drawled. Something in his voice told her Brenda had used the time Anabel had been on hold to fill him in on the nutcase he was about to speak with.

For that reason, and that reason alone, Anabel resisted the urge to make a joke about his name. As in, police work must be the pits for him. She knew he probably got jokes all the time and no doubt didn't appreciate them.

And right now she needed him as much on her side as she could get.

"I need to find out if there's a restraining order against me," she said.

"We don't handle restraining orders, ma'am."

Stunned, she wondered if he might be messing with her, then dismissed the notion. He had no reason to lie. "If you don't, then who does?"

"That would be the court. You'll need to contact Judge McCurdy."

Just perfect. Judge McCurdy wasn't one of Anabel's admirers, to say the least. He'd sat in when the McGraws had debated filing charges against her for what she'd done to Lilly, Kane McGraw's true mate. Lilly herself had talked them out of it. Bad memories from what seemed like another lifetime. Anabel politely thanked the police officer and ended the call.

"Well?" Denise asked. "What did you find out? Do you have a restraining order or not?"

"I don't know. I have to call the judge." Instead of doing so, she put the phone down on the table. "But if he got a restraining order, wouldn't the court have to serve me notice?"

Denise shrugged. "Maybe. I don't know. I have no experience with that sort of thing."

Anabel did a quick search of the internet using her phone. "According to this, he could have gotten an emergency, temporary order if he truly felt his life was in danger." She snorted. "I don't think he could have proved that. For a regular restraining order, the judge has to hold a hearing and both parties have the right to attend and present evidence or offer testimony. And bring witnesses. After all that, the judge has to determine if there really is a threat."

She looked up and grinned at her friend. "So I'm thinking it's safe to say that there is no restraining order against me."

Expression fascinated, Denise nodded. "Well, that's

good, then." Her eyes widened as Anabel grabbed the check, glanced at it and then dropped a twenty and a five on the table.

"Lunch is on me," Anabel said. "Now take me to where this Doug Polacek guy works. I need to ask him what his problem is."

Though Denise offered a few token protests, Anabel could tell she was more curious about what might happen than worried.

"His office is downtown," Denise said. "Off Main."

They located the two-story stucco-and-glass building easily. The new construction stood out like a sore thumb.

"Let me guess," Anabel said. "The architect was from California or New Mexico."

"Arizona, I think." Denise grinned. "It's a pretty building, though it's out of place here in upstate New York."

Parking, Anabel shrugged. "I agree," she said. "Are you ready? Let's go."

Denise hung back, her smile fading. "Are you sure we can't get into trouble? The one thing I do know from my job is you don't mess with lawyers. They can sue you."

"For what? He can't sue me for asking him where he gets off dragging my name through the mud. Come on."

Denise groaned, but she got out of the car.

Righteous indignation propelled Anabel through the lobby, where she looked on the signboard to figure out which office housed Polacek. "There. Smith, Howard and Polacek. I guess he's a partner. They're on the second floor."

Denise punched the elevator button, but Anabel decided to take the stairs. "It's only one floor up," she said, sprinting up. Denise followed a bit more slowly.

At the door housing the law firm, Anabel didn't hesitate. She pushed the door open, smiled pleasantly at the young, blonde receptionist. "We're here to see Doug Polacek," she announced.

The young woman tilted her head. "Do you have an appointment?"

"No." Moving closer, Anabel kept her smile in place. "But give him my name. I know he'll want to see me."

When she spoke her name, the receptionist's blue eyes widened. "J-j-just one moment," she stammered. Instead of using the phone to let her boss know of his visitor, she got up and headed back to deliver the news personally.

"I bet they kick us out," Denise pronounced in a gloomy voice. "Or call the police."

"They won't. And they can't call the police. We've done nothing wrong. Since Doug Polacek has gone through such lengths to get my attention, he's going to see me. Just wait and see."

And wait they did. Five minutes, ten. Watching the second hand move on the clock, Anabel refused to fidget. She didn't know why or how she knew, but she had a good idea there might be some sort of concealed camera in the reception area. No doubt this Doug Polacek watched them, hoping for signs of discomfort.

Well, she wouldn't be giving him that much satisfaction. She made poor Denise discuss current fashions and when she'd exhausted that, sports. Denise had begun to eye her as if wondering if she'd lost her mind.

Finally, after they'd been waiting nearly twenty minutes, a tall, muscular man with longish dark hair sauntered into the room. An overabundance of confidence came with him.

"Anabel," he exclaimed, arms opened wide for a hug, as though he already knew her and they were long-lost friends. "You didn't tell me you were coming to see me today. What on earth are you doing here?"

"Cut the crap," Anabel said sternly, ignoring Denise's shocked gasp. "I don't know you and you've never met me. Not even once. So I want to know why you're spreading nonsense about me all around town."

Flashing her a dazzling white smile, he held out his hand. "Why don't you come with me to my office? We need to discuss this privately, don't you think?"

Ignoring his outstretched hand, Anabel nodded. Every single instinct she possessed had gone on high alert.

"Come on, Denise," she said, feeling as if she could use all the help she could get.

"No." He uttered the single word with authority. "You come alone, or I have nothing to discuss with you."

"I'll wait here," Denise piped up, sounding both thrilled and utterly terrified. "Take your time. I'm sure you two have a lot to talk about."

Since she now had no choice, Anabel straightened her spine and nodded. Head held high, she followed Doug Polacek down the hall.

"Here we are." Stepping aside, he gestured toward a large corner office. "Have a seat, please."

Obstinately, she shook her head. "Thanks, but I'd rather stand."

He cocked his head quizzically, then finally nodded and closed the door. When he went around to sit behind his massive mahogany desk, she found herself moving away, instinctively careful not to have her back to the door.

While part of her scoffed at this—what did she really think would happen?—the careful, watchful part of her wholeheartedly approved.

"Well?" she finally asked, since after Doug took a seat in his fancy leather chair, he only placed his hands on the top of his desk and looked at her. "What do you have to say for yourself?"

"I'm not sure I take your meaning." He spoke the lie with a calm casualness that infuriated her.

"I've been told by several people that you've been going around saying horrible things about me. Accusing me of stalking you, when in fact we've never even met. Why are you doing this to me? I don't even know you."

"That's where you're wrong," he replied, his voice changing somehow, from oily pleasantry to sharp, ruthless steel. "We have met and you have been stalking me. I had to go public, in hopes of getting you to confront me."

Dumbfounded, wondering if he was insane, she stared at him, at a complete loss for words. Then, as her gaze locked on his, she realized he spoke the truth. Her heart froze in her chest.

"You," she whispered, realizing where she'd seen that particular glinting gaze before. "You're the Drakkor."

"I am. I should tell you, it wasn't very difficult for me to learn your identity once you followed me and then paid me that little visit. And now you, my dear, have walked right into my trap."

One of the supernatural abilities Tyler had as a ghost was the ability to make himself invisible. All he had to do was increase his vibratory frequency. Most people couldn't see him anyway, but since Anabel and a few others could, he knew he could keep this ability in reserve.

And today, since his energy level was at an all-time low and Anabel had ordered him to stay away, he knew he'd need to use it. In fact, the instant he'd heard Anabel agree to meet a friend in town for lunch, he had a gut feeling he'd need to watch out for her. Especially since she'd mentioned Doug Polacek.

Not wanting to be a complete stalker, he'd followed her to the restaurant, hovering just far enough away to give her privacy, but close enough that he could zip over if she needed him. The irony of his lack of physical ability to help her didn't escape him.

Still, he knew he'd try whatever he could should the need arise. Even magic.

When she and her friend left the restaurant and headed downtown, he rode along in the car, aware he might need to know where they were going.

The instant he heard Anabel say the name Doug Polacek, he stifled a groan. On the one hand, he admired Anabel for refusing to put up with that guy's verbal abuse any longer; on the other, he thought this might be the worst possible time to stir things up. His sister needed to be Anabel's primary focus right now. This was day six, and he didn't know how much longer Dena could make it.

Still, Tyler knew he had to trust Anabel's instincts. If she thought confronting this Polacek guy was important, then maybe it was.

Hidden, he waited in the reception area with Anabel and her friend, felt a shock of recognition when the attorney presented himself. Recognition, but from where? If he'd met Doug Polacek while in the physical form, he sure as hell didn't remember.

Was it possible they'd met in the realm of the spirit? Not unless the lawyer had the capability to move between worlds, which seemed highly unlikely.

And then Tyler had gone along to the other man's office, where he'd heard words he'd begun to despair of ever hearing.

"You're the Drakkor," Anabel said, sounding completely unafraid.

The instant Doug confirmed it, Tyler let himself become visible.

Anabel's eyes widened slightly as she saw him, but she made no comment.

The Drakkor looked directly at Tyler and smiled. "A bit late to the party, aren't we?"

Tyler could barely contain himself. He lifted his lip and snarled at the man. "Release my sister," he ordered.

"You know, I just might," Doug said pleasantly. "She turned out to be worthless. She's of no use to me now. Of course, I definitely will want something in return."

"I don't have a lot of money," Anabel put in.

"Oh, I do." Doug continued to smile that shark's smile, his obsidian eyes revealing only a hint of how dangerous he was. "I don't need your money, dear."

"Then what do you want?" Anabel shifted her weight from foot to foot, almost as if she felt the need to assume a fighting stance. Tyler felt that might be a wise instinct on her part.

"Why, I would have thought that was obvious." Doug chuckled, then stood up and stretched, his muscular arms showing his physical prowess. "I want you, Anabel Lee. With your magic and shape-shifting ability, I believe you and I can forge a powerful destiny."

Shocked, Tyler eyed Anabel to see her reaction. Aside from a quickening of her breath, she gave no hint of what surely must be churning around inside her mind.

"Why?" she finally asked. "And you'd better tell me the honest truth."

"A life is at stake," Doug reminded her, appearing amused. "Yet you want to discuss trivialities?"

Anabel remained calm and appeared unimpressed. "I understand a life is at stake. First off, I don't even have proof that Dena is still alive. Second, since you're basically asking me to turn myself over to you, I need to know what you intend to do."

The attorney towered over Anabel, his expression thunderous. For a split second Tyler feared he might strike her. Instead he strode to the door and yanked it open.

"You have forty-eight hours to decide. If I don't hear from you by then, I will kill the girl and be done with it."

Standing straight and tall, Anabel continued to face him down. "I want proof of life. Before I can even begin to consider your proposal, I need to know she is still alive."

"Very well." Ice coating every word, Doug swallowed. Spinning, he fixed his dark glare on Tyler. "You. Contact your sister tonight. I will not interfere. Then you can tell Anabel that Dena is not dead. Yet."

Tyler nodded, hoping Anabel would see the wisdom of making a quick exit right away. Because maybe, just maybe, if he were permitted to interact with his sister, they could figure out a way to learn where she was being held.

Denise still waited in the lobby, apparently enthralled by a television show in which people rushed to fix up a dilapidated old house. She blinked when Anabel appeared, before going back to staring at the TV. Anabel wondered if the Drakkor had placed her under some kind of a spell.

"Hey." Anabel touched her friend's arm, making Denise jump. "Are you ready to leave?"

"I...uh... Yes." Moving as if she had just woken from a deep sleep, Denise shuffled toward the office door. This time, Anabel thought it might be prudent to take the elevator.

"This way." Taking her friend's arm, Anabel helped her outside and into her car. Tyler had materialized again and sat silently watching from the backseat.

As each minute passed, Denise seemed to come more and more awake. Anabel felt relieved and grateful. She'd worried Doug had done something to her friend that she wouldn't be able to reverse.

After she'd dropped Denise back at the restaurant to retrieve her own car, she glanced at Tyler. "You might as well reappear up here in the front," she said. "We've got a lot to discuss."

Instantly, he was wedged in the front passenger seat, looking both angry and worried. "I'm wondering if we can use this situation to our advantage," he said. "Since he's promised to back out when I contact Dena, I'm thinking maybe we could figure out where she is being held."

Anabel nodded. "I was thinking along those lines myself. If we could free her, then I wouldn't have to even worry about trading myself for her."

"You're not going to think about that, no matter what," Tyler ordered. "I refuse to even consider such a thing."

"You're not in control of me," Anabel pointed out, as gently as possible. "Your sister is young. She has much to live for. Me, I've lost my mate. No one around here likes or respects me. This would be a good trade."

Tyler shook his head. "I thought you were done with feeling sorry for yourself."

Stunned—and a tiny bit hurt—Anabel swallowed. "I'm just being realistic."

"No. You're not. When I came to you for help, you trading your life for hers was never on the table."

"Really? Why not? I already see and hear ghosts. Maybe I'd like to be one." And then she also could find David.

"This is about your husband." As usual, Tyler intuitively understood her thoughts. "I already promised you that I'd find him and bring him to see you."

She bit her lip. "What if that's not enough?" she whispered.

Pain, stark and deep, flashed across his handsome face. "It's not your time."

Wondering at the desperation in his husky voice, she sighed. "Maybe not. Either way, I can't just sit by and let him kill your sister."

"You don't have to." Fierce determination rang in his tone. "We will get her out of there. Before the forty-eight hours are up. But first, I'm going to contact her and make sure she's still alive."

Chapter 13

Once upon a time, Anabel Lee had believed in fairy tales. She'd known love and happiness and had greeted every new day with delight. She'd also known sorrow, lost her confidence and had a mental breakdown. Picking herself back up from the ashes, she'd learned self-reliance. More than that, she knew she could never count on others.

Part of her still believed this. But the few days she'd spent hanging around with a ruggedly handsome ghost had shown her otherwise. Tyler and Juliet had both been essential to her learning her way around her newfound abilities.

But Tyler had taught her something else. How to feel again. He'd plucked her up from the pit of self-pity, depression and despair and forced her to care about someone other than herself. For that, she would be forever grateful.

When the sun set this evening, six days would have passed since Tyler had appeared begging for her help. Six long days while a young woman suffered, hovering at the edge of death.

If she could do one thing right in her life, Anabel knew she had to figure out a way to save her.

Leroy meowed, his standard warning, before leaping in her lap. She caught him easily, taking comfort in the strong vibration of his purr. Holding him, she suddenly remembered the old wives' tales about witches and their familiars. Was that what Leroy was meant to be, her familiar? Was she truly a witch?

Thinking along these lines, she grabbed the phone to call Juliet and fill her in on what she'd learned. Before she could even look up the contact, her phone rang. Caller ID flashed Juliet's name.

"Talk about ESP," Anabel teased. "I was just about to call you. I've learned something about the Drakkor."

"I've learned something about the Drakkor too." Juliet sounded both excited and wary. "I think I know why he's capturing Pack women. As a race, the Drakkors are slowly dying out. It seems their females are being born sterile."

Appalled, Anabel grimaced. "So they're looking for fresh breeding stock."

"Exactly. But from what I've been able to learn, their seed doesn't take root in any other races. The female, whether human or shape-shifter, sickens and eventually dies. I'm afraid that might be what's happening to your ghost's sister."

Anabel glanced around the room, looking for Tyler. For once, he didn't appear to be anywhere in sight. "Now it all makes sense," she said. "I met the Drakkor today. He wants to trade the sister for me."

Juliet gasped. "You met the… Please tell me you aren't even considering this."

"How could I not? There's a young woman slowly dying who needs my help."

"No. Let someone else save her."

Anabel couldn't believe what she was hearing. "How can you even say that?"

"Because you are the last in line of a powerful group of shape-shifter witches. You have within you magic, the kind that can change the world. If you let this Drakkor sink his claws in you, not only will your line die out, but there's a very real chance he will be able to breed with you. If he does, any child born of such a union will be horribly deformed, both physically and mentally. You cannot allow such a thing to happen."

Again, the weight of the world had come to rest on Anabel's slender shoulders. On the one hand, she couldn't let Dena die. On the other, what if Juliet spoke the truth? Would she be doing her own kind a horrible disservice by trying to help Tyler's sister?

"Is there an alternative?" Anabel asked.

"Of course there is." Juliet's voice rang with certainty. "Learn to use your power and vanquish the Drakkor once and for all."

"And I'll help," Tyler said, startling her. "For whatever reason, it seems when I'm with you, your power is stronger."

She had to admit he was right. After relaying this to Juliet, she waited while the other woman considered.

"I'm not so sure about that," Juliet finally said. "But

either way, it couldn't hurt. You say you've met the Drakkor. Who is he?"

"Doug Polacek."

Juliet cursed, something she never did, which startled
Anabel. "I should have known," Juliet said. "I've only met
him twice, but I got a bad feeling both times."

"He's a piece of work."

Juliet laughed. "Yes. Yes, he is. In the meantime, I've
located an ancient book I think you should read. There's
a lot in it about the Drakkors. I'll run it over to you in a
little while."

After hanging up, too restless to sit still, Anabel took
a quick shower, feeling the need to cleanse herself after
her brief visit with Polacek. She'd just finished drying
her hair when the doorbell rang.

Juliet stood on the doorstep, handing over the heavy
volume as if it burned her. "Sorry I can't stay and visit,"
she said, sounding breathless. "But I have errands to
run. Please, my intuition is telling me you've got to read
this book. Promise me you'll take a look at it as soon as
possible."

Mystified, Anabel promised, standing in the doorway
and watching as her friend hurried to the car and drove
off. Her cell rang, making her jump. Setting the book
on the end table, she grabbed her phone and answered.

It was Denise.

"Oh my God," Denise said, first thing after Anabel
answered the phone. "I'm guessing your little visit with
him made him angry. You are so not going to believe
what Doug Polacek is doing now."

Since Denise had no idea who or what the attorney
actually was, Anabel sighed. "Probably not. What is it?"

"He's asking for an emergency city-council meeting.

Tonight. He's telling everyone who will listen that he feels you need to be run out of town."

Stunned, Anabel didn't know how to respond at first. If she hadn't known his ulterior motive, this action would have seemed incomprehensible. But now it actually made perfect sense. Doug Polacek was merely tightening the noose. The fewer options she had available, the more likely she'd be to give in to his demands.

"Are you going?" Anabel asked. "To the city-council meeting? Are you planning to go?"

"I can." Denise sounded grimly determined. "You need someone to speak up for you, after all."

"Thank you." Relieved, Anabel took a deep breath. "What time is this meeting? I'm done hiding away while total strangers malign my character. I'm going to put in an appearance myself."

"Good for you." Denise sounded pleased rather than afraid.

Anabel wondered how much of their visit to Doug Polacek's office the other woman actually remembered.

"They're going to try and hold it at seven this evening. I'll see who else I can round up. I want you to have an entire section of supporters."

Wishing her friend luck (and meaning it), Anabel hung up. She'd consider herself lucky if Denise could find two or three others. She turned to find Tyler watching her, arms crossed. "Did you hear that? Doug Polacek is somehow pulling enough strings to make the city council hold an emergency meeting."

"He's turning up the heat." Tyler sounded as furious as she felt. "I wonder what happened to the forty-eight hours he promised you. I haven't even had time to verify she's still alive."

"You do that while I'm at the city-council meeting. As for the time, I'm going to insist I still have it. He was very specific. He didn't say he'd leave me alone for that long, just that I had forty-eight hours to make a decision. Of course, if your sister has passed—and I pray she hasn't—then all of this is moot."

Pain flashed across his features, making her heart ache. Tyler grimaced. "She has to be alive. She has to be. I'll know soon enough." He swallowed, visibly fighting his emotions. Though she knew she should look away, give him privacy, instead she waited silently, wishing she could offer him a hug or something.

Finally, he swallowed again and met her gaze. Determination now shone in his eyes. "What are you planning to do at the meeting?"

"This is the first battle of the entire war," she said, feeling very tall and strong. "It's vitally important that I win."

And then she did something that surprised even herself. She walked over to Tyler, willing him to be solid, and kissed him full on the mouth.

Stunned to the core, Tyler felt dizzy as Anabel broke off the kiss and flashed him a mischievous smile before she strolled away. She closed her bedroom door behind her, a signal telling him to stay out. Which was okay with him because he doubted he could even move at that point.

His existence had changed in so many ways in just six short days. He'd be forever grateful to the higher power who'd given him an opportunity to save his baby sister. What he hadn't imagined would happen would be that he, after having already finished his life, would meet his mate.

Tyler knew Anabel considered her former husband, David, to have been her mate. Whether she knew it or not, she was wrong. Tyler doubted any other man could love Anabel as much as he did. She'd have come to realize this too, if only Tyler hadn't been a ghost.

The bitter irony of this had to be some sort of penance he must pay. That, and the fact that he most likely would succeed in saving his sister, but to do so must sacrifice the woman he'd come to love...

He took a deep breath, trying to focus. First, though, he had to contact Dena.

Once again he reached out, praying to the Creator of all to help him. Energy zinged through him, bolstering his own limited supply. He reached out, through the river of time and place, searching for that one particular spark that belonged to his sibling.

When he finally located her, the dimness of her life force shocked and angered him. Though not much time had passed since he last saw her, the deterioration in her condition made him want to weep.

Polacek might have given Anabel forty-eight hours, but Tyler realized Dena would not make it that long. Something had to be done much more quickly.

Though it killed him, he left his sister lying there, almost a skeleton, curled into a ball on the floor. Nearly a week had passed since he first made himself manifest to Anabel, nearly seven days while Dena got weaker. He couldn't help feeling like a failure.

No longer would he remain a shade of the man he'd once been. He was a soldier, a man of action. Not some wispy, ethereal being who could do nothing but float around and watch. Dena didn't need a ghost. She needed her brother, in the flesh, to fight for her.

Tyler knew what he must do. While Anabel got ready to attend the city-hall meeting, he left the earthly plane and returned home. He planned to make his case to his spirit guide. He prayed he'd be successful, even if he was granted only a few days.

Though Anabel had always loved her flowing dresses and lacy outfits, once again she dressed in tight-fitting jeans, sneakers and a cotton, button-down blouse. She brushed her long, dark hair until it shone and then put it back in a sporty ponytail. A pair of diamond ear studs and a pretty silver watch completed what she hoped was a polished look.

When she arrived at city hall, to her surprise the place was packed. She ended up having to park a good three blocks over. Surely all these cars weren't here because of her? Her heart sank—her life had become more than a spectacle, and now she was about to learn just how greatly her neighbors feared and hated her.

Taking a deep breath, she squared her shoulders and stepped out of her car. As she walked toward city hall, she kept her gaze straight ahead, afraid of what she might see if she allowed herself to look left or right.

There were exactly thirteen stone steps leading up to the entrance of city hall. Anabel knew because she counted each one. Pushing open the double doors, she stepped into a crowded room reminiscent of a mob at a sold-out concert. Not only were there hundreds of people—had everyone in Leaning Tree turned out?—but the noise level was so loud she wondered how anyone could hear themselves speak.

Bracing herself, she murmured apologies and began the considerable task of plowing through the crowd.

Somewhere in this melee, she should be able to find Denise and Juliet, and maybe even some of the members of Juliet's coven if she was lucky, her small group of supporters.

As she maneuvered herself into a clearing, she saw the city council had assembled at a U-shaped desk up on a raised area at the front of the room. Five men and two women, they all stared out at the crowd with identical expressions of amazement.

Someone tapped on a microphone, causing most of the conversations swirling around to stop. "People, please take your seats. The meeting is about to begin."

Even though she looked everywhere, Anabel couldn't locate either of her friends, so she took a seat next to a total stranger. All around her, everyone hurried to find a chair. The room had grown so crowded that many people had to settle for standing against the back wall.

Anabel's stomach twisted. She'd been aware of the dislike and mistrust many of Leaning Tree's residents felt toward her. But to have this many people show up at a city-hall meeting? Despair flooded her, which she resolutely pushed away.

Feeling someone staring at her, she looked up and met Doug Polacek's flat black gaze. One corner of his mouth curled into a mocking smile and she realized the brilliance of his plan. This entire thing had been engineered to demoralize her and make her more prone to agree to his terms.

Not today, Drakkor, she mouthed. *Not today.*

He turned away and took his seat in the front row without responding.

When the room had become relatively silent, the mayor walked over and took the microphone from the other man. "Welcome, everyone. I must say, we usually don't get this big a crowd to a council meeting."

Several people laughed.

"We are here today to discuss many issues," he said and then cleared his throat. "But first and foremost, one of our up-and-coming citizens, attorney Douglas Polacek, has some very serious concerns he wishes to bring to our attention. He has alleged that these concerns affect all of us and can have an adverse effect on our entire town."

The murmurs started up again, growing to a roar. The mayor waited a moment for them to die down and then when they showed no sign of doing so, cleared his throat again. "People, please. We have a lot of discussion to get through."

For the first time, Anabel wondered how many of those in attendance actually knew what these so-called serious concerns were. Surely all of these people didn't really view her as a threat to their way of life, did they?

She guessed she was about to find out.

"We'll open the meeting by asking Mr. Polacek to take the mic and outline these concerns."

Smiling graciously, the Drakkor (Anabel had trouble thinking of him as anything else right now) took the stage. "Most of us here in the beautiful town of Leaning Tree are God-fearing people," he began, sounding as if he were presenting a case to a jury. "And what I've recently discovered has the possibility of shaking our town's very foundations."

Wondering what the heck he might say to follow this broad statement, Anabel caught herself leaning forward in anticipation, exactly like all the others in the audience.

"Witchcraft." The single word hung in the air, taking on a dark life of its own. "I've learned witchcraft is being practiced here within our very own city limits."

Though a few people gasped, most of the faces Anabel saw contained a healthy dose of skepticism, a few outright hostility. For the first time, she had hopes that her enemy's plan would backfire.

She actually had to put her hand over her mouth to keep from laughing out loud.

"Witchcraft?" a woman called out. "Please tell me you aren't referring to our resident Wiccans."

Polacek frowned, as if he hadn't ever heard the term. Anabel guessed maybe he hadn't bothered to bone up on the current atmosphere of tolerance and acceptance.

"I'm speaking about witches," he said, his voice booming like a television preacher. "The kind who cast dark spells."

Someone giggled. Someone else shouted out a "Get real."

"This *is* real," he countered. "Those of you who are regular churchgoers know about Satan's influence on this world."

Several people gasped. The room grew quiet.

"Demons are real," Doug continued. "As are witches. In our small, family-friendly town, there are those who are doing evil's work."

The fact that he himself was one of them made his statements infuriating. Anabel had to battle the urge to stand up and denounce him. Only the certainty that if she did so he'd publicly brand her as one of the evildoers made her remain silent. That, and the painful knowledge that most of the townspeople assembled here would believe him.

As if he'd read her mind, Doug Polacek swiveled

around, searching the crowd. The instant his gaze locked on her, her stomach sank. She knew exactly what he intended to do.

"That woman here." His arm came up, finger pointing accusingly at her. Everyone turned to stare. "She is one of the witches, using her dark magic. She has attempted to stalk me and make me do her bidding. I refuse to stand for it. Anabel Lee must be stopped. It'd be better for everyone if she were to move away from our town."

"Our town?" Anabel finally had had enough. "Not only are you talking like a crazy person, but your accusations are outright lies. I've only met you once, and this was long after you were going around inventing stories about me."

Doug laughed, the infuriating sound full of derision. "I think the good people of Leaning Tree know enough about your character to know who's telling the truth."

Anabel looked at all the faces around her and saw that he was right. Her heart sank.

"Anabel is telling the truth." A single voice came from the left side of the room. "This man, for whatever reason, has decided to target her with his hateful lies. Maybe we should think about who's really the evil one here."

Juliet. Standing tall and unafraid. Next to her, another woman stood. Denise.

"I can second this. I went with Anabel to confront Mr. Polacek and find out why he was spreading around so many lies about her. She'd never even seen him before that day."

More people stood. Not only the women from Juliet's coven, but the receptionist from Anabel's doctor's office, the dental hygienist who cleaned her teeth and the woman who worked in the library and indulged Anabel's love of a good British mystery. Each of them, calmly and rationally, offered good character references, refuting what Polacek had said about Anabel.

Tears stinging her eyes, Anabel stood and listened. Her chest and throat felt tight, but she kept her shoulders back and her head high. Today, Doug Polacek wouldn't win. Not this battle. And hopefully not the war either.

The final straw for Doug was when an elderly man stood, adding his voice to the women's. "Young man, I understand you are an attorney."

Warily, Polacek nodded.

"Then I'm sure you know all about lawsuits for slander and libel. I think you'd better ponder this before you say or write anything else about this fine young woman, who also happens to be a native of Leaning Tree."

Several people applauded. Soon, nearly the entire room had begun clapping.

Unable to stop her tears, Anabel wiped uselessly at her streaming eyes. Doug continued to stare her down, his eyes blazing.

Finally, Juliet came and took Anabel's arm, turning her away from the Drakkor's gaze. "Let's get you out of here," she said. Nodding, Anabel sniffled, trying to keep from bawling like a baby. She allowed Juliet to shepherd her outside, down the steps and into the shade of a huge, leafy oak.

"Come here." Juliet hugged her. "You are loved, my friend. More than I think you realized."

All Anabel could do was nod. Juliet handed her a tissue and she took it, using it to blot her eyes before blowing her nose. "Thank you," she said again, her heart full. And then, as she thought about what Doug Polacek had done, she let anger fill her.

"We've got to stop him," she declared. "Not only to free Dena Rogers, but to make sure he never does this again."

"I agree." Watching her carefully, Juliet glanced back toward the building. "Have you been practicing any of the exercises outlined in the books?"

"Yes. And I think I'm getting better." Or at least she hoped she was. "I need to get home and discuss this with Tyler."

"Oh, he's not here?" Juliet sounded disappointed. "Then by all mean, discuss with him and then give me a call."

"I will. We've got to go on the offensive before Doug Polacek tries something else."

Juliet nodded.

As Anabel headed toward her car, someone called her name. Denise.

"I need to tell you something." Breathless, Denise wouldn't look directly at her.

"Okay." Bracing herself for anything, Anabel waited.

"As I was leaving the meeting, Doug Polacek stopped me," Denise said, sounding worried and bemused.

Heart sinking, Anabel waited.

"The weird thing is, he was very nice. Even though he must know we're friends, he, uh, asked me out." Finally meeting her gaze, Denise blushed.

Staring at her friend, Anabel nearly choked. "Please tell me you said no."

"I can't." Denise gave an embarrassed shrug. "I know you don't like him and vice versa, but he's the first guy I've met in a long while who makes me tingle inside when I look at him."

"Yes, I get that he's good-looking," Anabel argued.

"But he's well-known for dating a lot of women. He's supposedly a master at loving them and leaving them."

"That's actually okay with me," Denise said quietly. "I'm not really looking for anything deep or serious. I'm only in town for a few weeks. I just want to have a little fun."

Ah, crud. Anabel contemplated the best way to tell her friend that Doug Polacek was not only bad news, but downright dangerous. She could only imagine why the man had contacted someone close to her. Next thing she knew, he'd be asking Juliet out too.

One difference there. Anabel knew Juliet would definitely have said no.

"Denise, come over and let's talk," she began, about to at least tell her friend that Polacek was a Drakkor.

"No, wait." Denise held up her hand, her expression pleading. "I'm going out with him. It's just a dinner date, not a wedding. Can you please be happy for me?"

Inhaling sharply, Anabel finally nodded. "I'm sorry," she said. "But at least promise me you'll be careful."

Denise only nodded in response and hurried off.

Anabel drove home in record time. Parking in her driveway, she practically ran inside, shouting Tyler's name. She needed to talk to him. Right away. While she refused to let Doug Polacek win any sort of victory, imagining what he might try next would turn her into a nervous wreck if she didn't strike first.

But when she got back inside her house, she couldn't find Tyler anywhere. She even tried summoning him, using that nifty focusing trick that Juliet had taught her, but she only succeeding in making herself dizzy.

Great. Just great. Patience had never been one of her

virtues, but it appeared she'd have no choice but to wait for him to put in an appearance.

Spotting the book Juliet had brought over earlier, she figured now might be a good time to look through it. She grabbed it and sat down on the couch, carefully opening the beautiful cover.

Judging from the brittle, discolored pages and the beautiful script, the book was very old and possibly valuable. This made her slightly nervous to handle it, but Juliet had been insistent, so she continued to read. Soon, she found herself lost in the tales. She had to skip several, as they appeared to be in another language, but the ones she did read were veritable history lessons.

Somewhere in here, she knew she would find the answer to her dilemma. She just didn't know where. And there was just so much.

As she read, she kept waiting for that one particular story to jump out at her. When it finally did, she had to read it again, and then a third time, to make sure.

Chapter 14

A knock on her front door made Anabel jump. It came again, before she even had time to head in that direction, a sharp rapping of knuckles indicating the visit might be urgent. She carefully bookmarked her place and put the book back on the coffee table.

Again the hard knocks, in rapid and impatient succession.

Thoroughly out of sorts, she yanked the door open without even using the peephole.

A man stood on her doorstep, his uncertain smile achingly familiar in his handsome rugged face. His hazel eyes blazed with emotion. At first, she could only stare, not entirely sure of what she might actually be seeing.

Was it possible? Could it be? Reaching out, she braced herself. When her hand connected with his muscular arm and warm skin, she actually gasped out loud.

"Tyler?"

"Yes." His smile spread. "It's me."

Even his voice sounded deeper. Richer. More...alive.

Still gripping his arm—his reassuringly solid arm—she tried to tear her gaze away from him. "How is this possible? You're even more real than you were when we—" Breaking off, she felt her face heat.

"I've been granted an indulgence."

Again, she couldn't seem to stop staring. "A what?"

"It's like a favor. I get to be human for as long as it takes to save my sister." His gaze locked on hers. "And to keep you safe."

Normally, she would have bristled, but seeing this, this Tyler, this *nonghostly* Tyler, was the closest to a miracle she'd ever come.

"You're alive," she said, just to make sure she understood correctly.

"Temporarily. And I've been wanting to do this for a long time." He pulled her closer.

Aching, she allowed him to. Truth be told, she helped. As his strong arms wrapped around her, she realized just how much she'd longed to feel him like this. Exactly like this.

He kissed her then. Capturing her mouth with his, demanding a response. A blaze of need roared through her, making her dizzy even as she continued to kiss him back.

Just as quickly as it began, it ended. Breathing as heavily as she, Tyler stepped back. "I swear to you, once, just once before I give up this form, we will make love."

Ducking her head, she didn't protest. Her entire body screamed assent, but she kept her mouth shut.

"Now tell me what happened in town," he said.

Speaking quickly, she told him what had transpired at

the city-council meeting. "He's trying to get people afraid of me again." And then she relayed what Denise had said.

"He's going to use her somehow." Tyler frowned. "I don't know exactly how, but he'll figure out a way to use her to get close to you."

"That's what I'm afraid of." She didn't bother to try and hide the glumness from her tone. "And worse, Denise acts like she thinks I'm jealous. Any words of caution I tried to relay, she brushed away with anger."

"You don't have a choice. Just keep an eye on things, I guess. You can't keep her from going."

He began to pace, his form solid and masculine, making her mouth go dry and her arms ache. "I wouldn't worry too much about the town. From what you've told me, he's only managed to get people thinking he's the one that's crazy."

How had she not noticed how broad his shoulders were or how narrow his waist? Clearly, he'd worked out when he was alive, judging by the toned muscles on his arms and the way his shirt strained over his chest.

She forced away her decidedly sexual thoughts and tried to concentrate on the conversation at hand.

Tyler didn't make thinking any easier. He perched on the edge of her couch and gazed at her, his hazel eyes glowing in the soft light. It took every bit of restraint she possessed not to jump his bones.

Her gaze fell on the book she'd been reading. "I found something out about the Drakkors," she said. "I think I know why Polacek is capturing women. The reason none of us have heard of them is that they're becoming extinct. I'm not sure how many actually remain—for all we know, he might be the last. I think he's trying to find someone he can mate with, someone who is strong enough to carry his child."

Tyler's tanned complexion turned ashen. "You think that's what he did to Dena?"

She didn't answer. How could she? Though she'd given him what she believed was the truth, doing so felt as if she'd ripped out her own heart.

Instead she went to him and pulled him close. Not speaking, she held him, stroking his hair and hoping her touch could offer some comfort. Amazing how good his being alive felt. She still had trouble believing it. Touching him turned her on. Aware now was the worst possible time, she made herself move away.

Deep breath. "How will this help?" she finally asked, as soon as she could think clearly. "You being human. How will it help us save your sister?"

Strolling over to her couch, he sat on the edge of one arm, looking way too ruggedly sexy for her peace of mind. "It's like this. You were right, apparently. I believe I have magic too. Even as a ghost, I could feel it. Now, in this human form, my magic will be stronger, more of a complement to yours. Together, we can use our magic to fight the warlock, who also happens to be a Drakkor."

Though she hated to ask, she knew she had to know. "And then what? Once Dena is free?"

His smile dimmed slightly, tinged with a hint of sadness.

"Then I go back where I belong. But I won't forget my promise to you. I'll make sure no ghosts ever bother you again. And I'll find Dave and make sure he goes to you."

Though hearing him say this made her want to cry, she kept her expression serene and nodded instead. "Then let's get your sister out. I have a plan."

He shook his head before she could elaborate. "If your plan involves you being some sort of sacrificial offering, then no."

"What?" She stood up straight, pulling her inner strength and that intangible something that made her magic powerful into her core. "You forget what I am. What you are. Together, we can win."

Though he crossed his arms, he nodded. "I'm listening. Tell me what you've got."

One thing Tyler had managed to forget about being human was how much more intensely people *felt* when they were alive. Sensations were everywhere. Emotions too. The instant his gaze locked on Anabel's whiskey-colored eyes, desire slammed into him. If he hadn't been prepared, the force of it would have sent him to his knees.

He managed—somehow—to continue to breathe and act normally, except for his body's violent reaction. This woman, whom he'd known just shy of a week, had rapidly become his everything. Looking at her, he knew he could drown in her gaze.

As he tried to unscramble his brain enough to formulate words, Anabel sniffed and held up her hand.

"What are you cooking?" she asked. "It smells like it's burning."

Puzzled, he frowned. "Cooking? I'm not."

"Sorry." She gave a sheepish smile. "I swear, I smell smoke. I asked out of habit. David used to love to whip up various concoctions whenever the mood struck him. He was terrible at it, and everything always burned."

Her mention of David—her deceased husband and love of her life—helped him get his thoughts back on track. Except she was right. Now he smelled it too. Acrid.

"That does smell like smoke. Something is burning." For a split second, he wondered if this was David's way of popping in from the spirit world.

"Look." She pointed. Gray smoke seeped out from under the closed door to her spare bedroom.

His heart stuttered. "Something's on fire."

"Nothing's in there but furniture. Nothing that could possibly catch on fire at least."

He hurried to the door, reached for the knob and then cursed and let go. "It's hot. Call 911, find Leroy and you wait outside."

She'd already hustled over to snatch up her cat, who'd been sleeping on the top of the couch. With her other hand, she grabbed the books Juliet had lent her and stuffed them into her tote bag. Slinging this over her shoulder while struggling with her irate cat, she punched the numbers into her phone, moving toward the front door at the same time.

Confident that she'd be safe, he headed toward the garage.

"Wait," Anabel called after him. "What are you doing?"

"Going to grab your fire extinguisher. I remember seeing one in the garage." As he reached for the knob, he didn't hear whatever she shouted in response.

Already too far into the motion, he registered the knob's heat a second too late. As he yanked the door open, a wall of flame roared at him.

Cursing, he jumped back, trying to shut the door on the orange monster.

But once given entrance, the inferno would not be denied. Flames leaped into the room, a ball of fire. Reaching out and catching hold of her drapes, he knew that soon the entire living room would be ablaze.

"Get out now," he hollered at her, still standing frozen in the hallway. "Go!" He ran toward her, even as she took off for the door.

They both made it outside before the roof caught. As it did, the fire took hold with a loud crackle. Inside, something crashed, sending up an array of sparks into the night sky.

Leroy yowled, squirming in her arms. She held on to him, almost too tightly.

"You have a death grip on that poor cat," Tyler pointed out, putting his arm around her shoulders.

"Sorry. I don't want him to escape. I should have grabbed his carrier. But it was in the garage." Which now was totally engulfed in flames.

In the distance, they could hear the siren wail as the fire engine approached. As the seconds ticked by, Tyler thought everything seemed to be moving in slow motion.

"It's going to be a total loss," Anabel moaned, standing rigid in his arms while clutching her cat. "My house. All I have left of David."

Though the words cut through him like a knife, he made sure that didn't show. Not only did he have no business feeling jealous of a dead man, but poor Anabel really had more than enough on her plate.

"You know who did this, don't you?" she said, twisting out from under his arm to face him, eyes blazing. "Doug Polacek. It's another one of his scare tactics, to force me into a decision."

"You might be right," he allowed. "Though how'd he do this so quickly?"

"He's a dragon. All he had to do was change and then open his mouth and breathe fire."

He shot her a quick look but didn't argue.

Lights flashing, the fire truck pulled up in front of the house. Right behind came an ambulance, followed by two police cars, all with lights on.

The next hour passed in a blur. Firefighters, hoses spraying water, stubborn hot spots refusing to go out. A man came up to Anabel and introduced himself as an arson investigator.

Nodding, she didn't bother to even try to act shocked. "I'm glad you're here. I happen to think this fire was deliberately set."

The man narrowed his eyes. "Are you insured, Ms. Lee?"

"Of course. What does that have to do with—"

Tyler saw the second she realized what he meant.

"I can assure you that I'm not the one who set this fire. I believe Doug Polacek did."

Stony-faced, the fire investigator stared her down. "Doug Polacek?"

"Yes. He's an attorney in town. Earlier, he accused me of being a witch."

"I see." Clearly, he didn't. Touching a finger to his forehead, he dipped his chin. "If you'll excuse me, I have work to do."

Watching him stride off, Anabel turned to face Tyler. "I didn't think of that," she said, her voice hoarse. "Of course Polacek knew people would think I did it. Almost everyone in town already thinks I'm crazy."

"Not almost everyone," he corrected her. "You said you had quite a few people stand up for you at the city-council meeting."

"True. But there are still plenty of others."

Again he put his arm around her, unable to shake the crazy thrill—even now—at actually being able to do it. "First they have to prove it. And since we both know you didn't set the fire, you don't have anything to worry about."

Leroy let out a yowl, almost as if he were trying to tell them something. "Shhh." Anabel stroked his fur with her free hand. "Don't worry, boy. We'll figure out someplace to live."

"Wolf Hollow Motor Court Resort," he said. "I used to know the McGraws. They're good people."

She winced. And then he remembered.

"I take it they haven't forgiven you."

"I don't know," she replied. "Even if they have, it would be really awkward staying with them." Expression miserable, she turned her gaze back to the smoldering ruins of her house.

He wished he could fix everything for her, make the fire and Polacek and all of her problems disappear. Since he couldn't, all he could do was distract her. "But theirs is one of the only hotels in town."

She turned her gaze back to his. "There's the Value Five Motel, out near the thruway. Muriel Redstone has always been kind to me. And I'm pretty sure she wouldn't have a problem with Leroy staying with me."

Inwardly he winced. Built in the late seventies, the Value Five was one of those cheaply constructed budget motels with no personality to speak of. The last time he'd driven by there was right after high school. He could only imagine how the place had held up over time.

"At least it's not expensive," she said, almost as if she

knew his thoughts. "Especially since I've been off work all this time with no income."

Clearly his fault. "I'm sorry." He waved at the ruins of her home. "I had no idea this would take so long. Or be so dangerous."

Now she shot him a look that clearly said she didn't believe him. "Warlocks, magic and ghosts. What could possibly be easy about that?"

She had a point.

A shout from the firefighters drew both their attention. A huge shower of sparks came to life with a roar, sending a fresh round of flames skyward as the roof collapsed.

"That's it," Anabel said. "I can't stand to watch any more. My house is gone, along with everything I own. I'm going to head over to the motel and see if I can book a room. Are you coming?"

He nodded. "Wherever you go, I go too." Though he kept his tone light, he had never been more serious.

On the way to the motel, they stopped at Walmart. She asked him if he'd mind waiting in the car with Leroy while she picked up a few things. Of course he didn't mind.

When she returned, she had a litter box, cat litter and cat food and a few items of clothing for herself. As she slid into the driver's seat, she tossed the bag in the back.

"I got underwear too," she said, then looked stricken. "I'm sorry. I didn't think about asking you if you needed anything. Would you like me to go back in and get you a few things?"

He hadn't thought of that at all. Yet the thought of Anabel selecting his underwear made him feel...weird.

Something in his expression must have clued her in.

"How about I give you some money and you can run in and buy whatever you need?" she offered.

Though he also hated taking money from her, he didn't have any other options. When she tried to hand him fifty dollars, he took only a twenty. "I don't need much," he said.

Her smile looked like a shadow of her normal self. "That's good," she said. "Because twenty bucks won't buy much."

Inside the store, he bought the most inexpensive packet of underwear he could find, a couple of T-shirts that had been marked down to three dollars and a pair of shorts. With tax, he figured the total would come in just under twenty dollars.

As he got back into the car, he tossed his bag next to hers. "Thank you. If I can ever find a way to repay you, I promise I will."

"No worries," she said, starting the engine. "Let's go take a look at my new temporary home."

The Value Five Motel looked better than he remembered it. The place had clearly undergone a renovation. "Wow," he said out loud.

"I know." Her tired smile spoke of her weariness as she parked. "Let's see what I can get. I hope it won't be too expensive. My savings are rapidly dwindling."

According to Muriel Redstone, there were only three other guests staying at the Value Five. She let Anabel have her pick of rooms, her curious gaze locked on Tyler.

He simply gave her a friendly smile back.

Once Anabel had selected a room, paid the discounted long-term monthly rate, he followed her to the one she'd chosen. It was in the back of the motel, out of sight from the road, and the window looked out onto a large field and lushly wooded expanse of forest.

"It feels a little less like a motel this way," she said, catching him gazing out into the woods.

"And an easy route to go if you needed to change."

Her dark look lightened. "That's a great idea. Let me get Leroy settled in and then we will. I think being wolf for a while will really help take my mind off things."

Once inside, he saw that the interior rooms had also been redone. "This isn't bad at all," he said.

Clearly distracted, she set Leroy down. Tail held high, the cat promptly stalked off to explore. They unpacked their meager belongings. All he could think about was running in the woods as wolf with her. The experience had been indescribable when he'd done it before as a ghost. He couldn't wait to hunt with her as a flesh-and-blood wolf.

Mate. The word echoed inside him. Sadly, he knew it was true. He and Anabel were mates, even though such a thing had become an exercise in futility. He didn't know what had happened with Dave or why she'd believed the other man to be her mate. All he knew was the truth of the here and now. By all that was right and holy, Anabel should have been his.

"Okay." Dusting her hands on her jeans, she turned to face him. "Let's get out there and hunt."

As he opened his mouth to respond, her cell phone rang.

She glanced at it, and her composure cracked. "It's Polacek." She sounded miserable.

Mentally cursing the other man, Tyler fought the urge to tell her not to answer. Instead he watched her, waiting for her to make the choice.

"I'm not in the mood to deal with him," she announced, tossing the still-ringing phone on the bed. "Come on. Let's get out in the woods before something else happens. We can start doing some exploring, looking for those landmarks. As wolves, we can cover a lot more ground much faster than as humans."

When she held out her hand, he took it. Together they ran across the field, letting the welcoming shadows of the forest envelop them.

"This time, we'll change together," she said, lifting her chin, her gaze locked with his.

Heat shimmered between them. Mouth dry, he nodded. As she pulled her T-shirt over her head and stepped out of her shorts, he couldn't breathe.

"Hurry," she urged him, a hint of amusement in her voice. Riveted, he could no more move than stop his heart from beating.

The bra came off next and then finally her panties. She stood before him, unabashed, looking like some sensual wood nymph.

He actually took a step toward her.

"I'm going to leave you behind," she warned, dropping to all fours and casting him a reproving look before initiating the change.

Hurriedly, he shed his clothes and did the same, gritting his teeth at the remembered pain.

When he opened his eyes again, he was wolf.

Alive. Narrowing his eyes, he looked for her, not seeing her. Which was okay, because as wolf, his nose told him exactly which way she'd gone.

As he raced after her, his powerful muscles working perfectly, four paws pounding the damp earth, he marveled at the joy of feeling so alive. For just this moment, he'd immerse himself in the experience. For this space in time, he'd simply live.

They ran and played, hunted and shared the rabbit he caught. Though he hesitated a moment at taking a life, since he'd been given one on borrowed time, it wasn't in the nature of wolf to let prey escape. From the laughing look in Anabel's exotic wolf eyes, he suspected she approved.

When they'd had their short recreation, the hunt was on. Even though the light was fading, they could see well enough, guided by their sense of smell.

Ranging far and wide, he felt they'd covered a lot of ground. And saw nothing like the landmarks Anabel had drawn.

He didn't know how much time had passed, but finally they turned around and made their way back to the clearing where they'd left their human clothing.

At the thought of what might happen next, his heart began pounding. All shifters knew the change from wolf back to human made the physical body aroused. Whether or not they chose to act upon it was up to the individual.

He knew what he wanted. But would Anabel want the same?

Chapter 15

Aware that once he became man, desire would over-come his body, Tyler knew watching Anabel become human would prove too much for him, so he turned away. With so much urgency driving him, he used every ounce of self-control he possessed not rushing his own change. Instead he focused on the uncomfortable sensation of wolf turning to human.

This helped, at least during the shape-shifting. But once he'd finished and pushed to his feet, stark naked and more aroused than he'd ever been, and turned to look at her, all his resolutions vanished. The raw longing on her face as she watched him gave him his answer.

She wanted him.

A part of him knew she could just need to blow off steam. That same part realized, in the end, this could only make the pain worse once he left her. But with desire pulsing through every cell in his body, he couldn't walk away.

Elation mingled with raw wanting as he slowly climbed to his feet, trying to control the dizzying current racing through him. Her gaze soft as a caress, she held out her arms. He went to her, sweeping her into his arms.

His.

He slid his hands up her arms, heart thudding a rapid tattoo. The dizzying feel of her, this woman, made his fingertips tingle as he touched her. The jolt of her hip brushing his thigh, the warmth of her body as she curved herself into him, invited more.

First, he kissed her with his eyes, his featherlight touch. And then, as his mouth covered hers hungrily, he traced the inside of her mouth with his tongue and kissed her there.

Her answering shudder told him what that did to her.

As she moaned and kissed him back, he realized he finally understood what all the books and movies said about love.

He loved this woman. Anabel, his mate. Though he knew he shouldn't, couldn't, he made a vow never to leave her. And then he sealed that vow with another deep, drugging kiss.

Naked, skin to skin, flesh to flesh. His. She belonged to him, as much as he belonged to her.

Gently, he outlined the circle of her nipple, before taking it in his mouth. He slid his hand down the silk of her belly, tangling in her womanly curls, before parting the folds between her legs and stroking the dampness there.

Her gasp was a reward of sorts, but the tremors that shook her and the rush of honey that followed nearly sent him over the edge.

Then he knelt before her and put his mouth in place of his hand, using his tongue to continue the caresses as he drank her in. Head back, body arched, she cried out as pleasure overtook her in waves and she came apart.

Again he barely restrained himself. Only the knowledge that he wanted more kept him sane. Aware he could never have enough of her—however many days he'd be granted alive would never suffice—he knew he had to sink himself deep inside her. At least once.

Finally, she shook her head and pulled him to his feet, her gaze smoldering, the sleek caress of her body a blatant invitation as she tugged him to the ground.

Wrapped around each other, his arousal pressing against her desire-slicked skin, he tried to hold back, tried to maintain some semblance of control before he entered her.

And then she pushed him onto his back and climbed onto him, taking him inside her in one smooth motion. He froze as wave after wave of pleasure engulfed him, desperate to prolong the pleasure.

But she began to move, her body wrapping around him as if she'd been made for him. He cried out, bucking her slow, deliberate motions, driven by the need to move faster, harder.

"Wait," she said, lifting herself just above him, her hands on his wrists, holding him down. "Please. Wait."

Shuddering, he managed to wrest control over his body and managed—just barely, chest heaving, heart pounding—to keep himself still.

With a seductive smile, she leaned close, claiming his mouth in a passionate kiss and writhing just out of his reach. The sleek caress of her body as she deepened the kiss made his senses reel.

"Now," she gasped, still raised up over him. "Now."

As she came down hard on his arousal, her body slick and hot and welcoming, he groaned. And then he took over, rolling so he was on top, plunging himself into her hot, wet depth.

She arched her back, meeting him thrust for thrust. He cried out in sweet agony, her voice echoing his, and power—magic—spiraled around them, through them, between them, intensifying every touch, every stroke. All at once, he could see images of what she wanted, and the instant the thought occurred to him, he did exactly that.

Pleasing her became more important than breathing, and when her body shuddered and clenched around him as she reached her climax, he used the magic to maintain an iron control on his own body.

This, he thought, was how sex should be. This was how true mates made love. And then as she began to move again under him, he didn't do much thinking at all.

When he finally let himself go, he drove into her, fiery sensations pure and explosive, and shattered into a thousand stars.

After, as he held her in his arms, both too exhausted to move, he understood the true meaning of satisfaction. More than simple bodily pleasure, more even than the give-and-take between two perfectly matched people. This.

No, what he and Anabel had just shared was a kind of vow. A promise of shared sunsets, cuddling next to each other while the snow fell, of laughter and joy, shared tears and hope and dreams. Unfortunately, sorrow filled him as he realized it was a vow he could never keep.

Stirring, Anabel kissed him lightly on the cheek as if she understood. "Come on," she said softly. "Let's go back to the motel and clean up. I don't know about you, but I'm starving."

"I am too," he said, getting to his feet and pulling her up. He spoke the truth, only he didn't say that he was starved for much more than food.

An hour later, they finished the fast food—a burger for him, a salad with fries for her—they'd picked up and brought back to their room, Leroy snoozed on the bottom of one bed and Tyler and Anabel sat together on the edge of the other.

Only then did she glance at the cell phone she'd tossed aside earlier when Polacek called. "He left a message."

"You don't have to play it back," Tyler began. "He's a bully. He gave you forty-eight hours. I don't think your time is up yet."

"It's not." She bit her lip. "What if he has something to say about your sister?"

Considering, he finally held out his hand for the phone. "Let me listen to it."

Without hesitation, she handed her cell over. "I'm going to go take a shower," she said. "I'm sure you'll tell me if he has anything to say that I need to hear."

He waited until he heard the shower start up before pressing the play button on the message.

Instead of calling to gloat, Polacek had left a simple message asking Anabel if she'd made up her mind. On impulse, Tyler pressed the callback button.

Polacek answered immediately. "Ah, so you have reached a decision," he began.

"No, she hasn't," Tyler said, trying to remain calm. "But she would like to know why you set that fire."

"Fire?" The other man sounded genuinely puzzled. "Who are you and what are you talking about?"

"Someone set Anabel's house on fire. And I'm Anabel's friend. Her *close* friend."

Polacek went silent. "I can assure you I did not do that. Now I'd like to speak to Anabel herself if you don't mind."

"I do mind. And Anabel is in the shower."

There was an even longer silence this time. "I wasn't aware she had a boyfriend."

This time, Tyler kept quiet. For effect.

"This might be a problem." Quiet fury rang in Polacek's voice. "Have you and she been intimate recently?"

Instead of answering, Tyler pressed the end-call button.

The shower went off. Getting up, he carried the phone over to the dresser and set it down.

He actually believed Polacek. From what he'd seen, if the Drakkor had set the fire, he'd have been bragging about it.

A few minutes later, Anabel emerged from the bathroom, her long hair damp. She gave him a sleepy smile. "Well, what did he have to say?"

Grimacing, he relayed the gist of the conversation. "I'm not sure what he's up to. But clearly, he's worried I might have impregnated you."

"Wow." She dropped onto the bed next to Leroy, startling the cat awake. "I didn't even think about that."

"Neither did I." Though he couldn't imagine anything more wonderful, if he were really alive, he kept that admission to himself. "We didn't use any protection."

"You're a ghost." Her indignant protest made him wince.

"I *was* a ghost," he corrected her. "Right now I'm a

man. And because of this, your getting pregnant is a very real possibility. Unless you're on birth control?"

She shook her head. "I wasn't exactly planning on this happening. However, since it has, it might work to my advantage. He'll want to wait until I have proof I didn't conceive with you. That will buy me some time."

Everything inside him quieted at her words. "What are you planning to do? Surely you're not thinking of going to that monster."

"I know you don't like the idea of me agreeing to exchange myself for Dena," Anabel said, holding up her finger the instant he started to interrupt. "But hear me out. I think if we work together on this, with a little bit of luck, we can make this work."

"I'm not a big fan of luck," he replied, his chest aching. "Still, I'm listening."

She grabbed her tote bag and pulled out one of the books she'd borrowed from Juliet. This particular volume appeared older than the others, with a well-worn, heavily embossed leather cover.

Placing it on the bed, she locked gazes with him. "You're familiar with the mythic story of Persephone? She was one of the few living beings to travel to the underworld."

"She was the daughter of a goddess. Demeter, if I remember right," he said.

"She alternates between living and dying. She dwells in the afterlife part of the year."

"It's *myth*. Not real. There is no underworld."

"Symbolism. Underworld, afterlife, it's all the same. Anyway, the story of Alcestis is what interests me most. When Alcestis traveled to the underworld to offer her own life in place of her dying husband's, Persephone sent her back and spared them both."

"Okay." He kept his tone even. "I still don't see what this has to do with our situation."

Her smile turned mysterious, fascinating him. "Well, according to this book, Alcestis was Pack."

Skeptical but intrigued, he moved closer. "Show me."

Still smiling, she flipped open the heavy book to a place she'd bookmarked. "Here. Read this."

Skimming it, he saw the author—or authors, since the tome appeared to be a compilation of ancient stories and myths from numerous races and species—claimed Alcestis had been a shape-shifter, one of the earliest members of a rudimentary pack.

"That's impressive," he said, looking up from the book. "And while I usually enjoy learning new bits of our ancestral history, how is this going to help us win against Doug Polacek?"

"When I read this, my plan occurred to me."

Though he still didn't follow, he waited.

"As far as I can tell, we have two choices. The books say dragons have two weak spots—their eyes and their unscaled belly. They can only die one of two ways—by being stabbed there or by poison. So option one is to figure out a way to kill Polacek."

When she didn't continue, he pressed. "Or?"

"Or we've got to make him think I'm dead." Finishing triumphantly, Anabel beamed at him, her copper eyes expectant.

At first, Tyler wasn't sure he'd heard correctly. "Dead? How on earth do you propose to do that?"

"I was hoping you could help."

"Oh no." Just thinking about it, he felt his gut churning. "I have no idea what you have in mind."

"Look at you." Shoulders back, she circled around him, her movements gracefully and no doubt unintentionally sexy. "You were dead and magically became alive."

He stifled a groan. "There was no magic involved in that."

"Really?" Clearly, she didn't believe him. "Then how'd you do it?"

"I asked. I'm limited as to what I can tell you of the afterlife, but there are beings with much more power than you and I."

"Magic." She flashed a triumphant smile. "If they can make you alive, then surely they can briefly make me dead."

This time, he let his frustrated groan escape. "Let's just say, hypothetically of course, that they could do this. How would you being dead help us with the Drakkor or in freeing my sister?"

"He wants me for breeding. If I'm dead, I'm of no use to him."

He admired her creativity, even if what she wanted was impossible. "And if you're dead, he has no reason to set Dena free."

"Timing," she informed him with an arch look. "Timing is everything. I won't have them make me pretend to die until after the exchange has already been made."

"You have no idea what you're saying."

"Ah, but I do." Eyes glowing with determination, she continued to pace, looking like a caged wolf.

He didn't tell her he'd never heard of such a thing, outside of ancient myths and legends, because if he did, he'd have to admit he'd never heard of a ghost being allowed to briefly return to a living body either. Actually, his very presence was proof that her idea might be possible.

But that didn't make it palatable. He knew if he tried to use emotion to convince her, she wouldn't listen. Her decision appeared to have been made with emotion. Instead he tried to sway her with logic. "What if they agree? Then what? How do you know that such a thing is not irreversible?"

She whirled and hugged him, a quick, brief, impulsive wrapping of her arms around him that made him feel as if he had been set ablaze.

"Because of you," she said. "You being here right now with me, alive and real, is all the proof I need."

It was then that he realized he'd made a horrible, awful mistake.

"I can't risk you," he said, throwing logic to the wind, his voice cracking even though he willed himself to sound steady. "Surely we can figure out another way to save Dena without placing your life at serious risk."

Her beautiful face went serious. "Look, do you want to save your sister or not? Time is running out. Unless you've come up with another plan, we've got to set mine in motion or your sister will die."

She was right—at least about part of it. Though Polacek had given them forty-eight hours, he knew better than anyone that time was running out. They had no guarantee Dena would survive too much longer.

"I want you to live," he said, his voice cracking.

"I want to live too. But I can tell you this. If I do have to trade myself for your sister, I'd rather be dead than suffer what she did at his hands."

"There's got to be an alternative."

Anabel moved closer, wrapping her arms around him

and standing chest to chest. Her scent—a musky combination of cinnamon and flowers—made him dizzy. Another part of her appeal that had been hidden to him as a spirit. "If you think of one, let me know."

Pushing away the longing and yearning, he allowed himself to hold her for the space of a heartbeat and a breath, before pulling out of her embrace. "I'll try to contact my spirit guide," he promised. "I'll tell you as soon as I hear if your proposal is even possible."

Eyeing him, she nodded. "Remember, we have a deadline. If my idea doesn't work out, I have no choice but to offer myself in place of your sister. If I don't, her death will be on my conscience. And every instinct I possess, magical or otherwise, is telling me it's not her time to die."

Tyler nodded. "I'm going to go for a walk."

Eyes wide, Anabel slowly nodded. "It's sort of weird that you can't just vanish whenever you want to."

Damned if her comment didn't feel like a knife to his chest. Apparently, when they weren't making love, she preferred him as a ghost. "One of the things about being alive," he said, keeping all his voice empty of emotion, "is that I'm limited to the earthly plane. I'll be back after a while."

To her credit, she didn't ask him to be more specific. She simply nodded and went back to studying her book. No doubt she needed some time alone with her thoughts. What they were considering was not something that could be done on a whim.

Walking out the front door, Tyler realized he hadn't felt so alone in a long time. As a spirit, he'd been constantly aware of the existence of other spirits and the shimmering chord of energy that bound all life. Human again, he could tell his awareness of this had become blunted. Though he felt his loss sharply, he knew he'd gladly give this up if he were to be permitted to remain with Anabel.

"If magic really exists," he said out loud, to no one in particular, "why can't I use it to free my sister? Why can't things be simple?"

He didn't expect an answer, so when one came, he jumped.

"You know better than that." The familiar rich voice washed over him like warm oil. He turned, eyeing the hooded figure with a mixture of reverent awe and consternation. His spirit guide, appearing as an elderly wise man. Tyler couldn't help noting the rather obvious symbolism, but that was par for Elias's sense of humor.

"I didn't expect so much pain," Tyler began and then stopped. He didn't want to complain. After all, he'd been blessed to even be allowed to return to earth as a spirit. Never mind now, as a live man.

But Elias simply smiled. "You don't have to do this all alone. You know better than that. You're never alone."

As those words sank in, all the worry and trepidation disappeared. "Everything will happen that is supposed to happen," he whispered, not as a question since he already knew the answer.

"Yes, it will. With your help." The guide's eyes sparkled, even though his voice was stern.

Taking a deep breath, Tyler outlined what Anabel wanted to do.

After Tyler left, Anabel immediately closed the book. How could she even concentrate at a time like this? She knew what she had to do, and no amount of discussion

or thinking was going to change that. Even if she wasn't
permitted to momentarily die, she couldn't let Tyler's
sister suffer.

She might as well get this show on the road. Then, before she could chicken out, Anabel picked up the phone
and dialed the number Doug Polacek had given her.

He answered on the second ring. "Hello, Anabel Lee."
The evil reverberating in his flat voice sent a shudder
through her. After taking a deep breath, she didn't bother
wasting time on pleasantries. "I've made my decision. I
will agree to the trade. But I need proof of life."

"You already have that," he said. "Your ghostly friend
was in contact with his sister. I sensed his presence. Go
ahead. Ask him."

Stunned, she couldn't keep from glancing over her
shoulder, looking for Tyler. Of course, he wasn't there.
And she could no longer summon him by simply thinking
of him. "He's not around right now," she said—smoothly,
she hoped. "But I promise you I will ask him when he
gets back."

The silence on the other end of the line fairly crack-
led with impatience.

"Tell me about your boyfriend," he said, a thread of
ruthless anger in his voice.

She took another deep breath, grimly aware of the
way her skin crawled even talking to this horrible man
on the phone. She couldn't imagine letting him touch her.

"I don't have a boyfriend," she began.

"Don't lie to me." Snarling, he cut her off. "He called
me. We talked while you were in the shower. When I
asked him if the two of you had been intimate, he hung
up."

Stunned, she tried to gather her thoughts. "I had no

idea he called you. But that was Tyler, my ghostly friend, as you put it. How can one be intimate with a ghost?"

Polacek went silent while he considered her words. She waited with bated breath. After all, she hadn't lied. At least, not outright.

"So help me," he finally said, "if I find out you're not telling the truth…"

As threats went, it was an empty one. There couldn't be much worse than what he'd already proposed to do to her. She shuddered.

Forcing the thoughts away, she knew she had to focus on the task at hand. If she was going to succeed, she had to be extremely careful. "In the meantime," she said, "let's discuss specifics. I want Dena Rogers out of there so she can get immediate medical help. How do you want to do this?"

"You do understand that I can't personally be involved?" Was that amusement in his detestable voice?

"If I can, then you can," she countered.

"I'm a public figure in this town. An attorney with a successful practice, with hopes of being elected to the city council soon. While you are…" His voice trailed off.

Horrified, she stifled her instinctive reaction. "While I am what?" she asked, pleased her voice sounded level.

"Overwhelmingly despised and regarded with contempt."

Once, she might have felt his words like sharp knives. Even worse, she would have agreed with him. "You can say that after the show of support I received in the city-council meeting?" Her careless laugh came out perfectly timed, which did her heart good. "Anyway, we've already established that we don't like each other. I asked you how you plan to get Dena out. Are you going to answer?"

He went silent for so long she began to think he might have hung up.

When he finally spoke again, his flat, emotionless tone was back. "My assistant, Tammy, is going to help me. I believe you met her when you visited Dena's apartment."

Stunned, she couldn't speak. Although she'd feigned ignorance, Dena's roommate had already known Dena was being held prisoner when Anabel and Tyler had visited. That seriously pissed Anabel off. Still, since she could do nothing, she bit her tongue and stuck to the topic at hand. "How is she going to help?"

"Tammy, as Dena's roommate, is going to claim she found her lying in the field near the apartment parking lot. She will take Dena to the hospital and make sure she gets medical care."

This sounded too simple. "And what do you want me to do?"

Now the faint edge of malice tinged his tone. "You will enter the apartment and remain there while Tammy drives to the hospital."

Way too easy. Which meant it actually wasn't. "And you will be there waiting for me, I'm guessing?"

"Exactly. If you don't show up, Tammy will arrange a little accident for Dena."

A thousand possibilities opened up with his scenario.

"Oh, and don't even think about calling the police," he continued, as if he'd read her mind. "I've carefully set up everything to make it appear that you have been the one who's kept poor, little Dena Rogers prisoner and tortured her. Who do you think the Leaning Tree Police Department will believe?"

She couldn't resist. "Well, after your tirade about

witchcraft in town, I'm thinking more will actually lean toward believing me."

"Do I have your word or not?" he said snarkily, clearly not finding any humor or truth in her comment. This time, she didn't bother to hide her own amusement.

"You first. I want your word." Even though she privately considered it meaningless.

"I give you my word."

There. Now it was her turn. "Me too. You free Dena and get her to the hospital, and I'll wait for you in the apartment."

"Bound by oath," he intoned.

"Whatever," she muttered. "Now that we've settled that part of it, I need to know when."

"Tonight. And you'd better believe I will use a cloaking spell. So if you are foolish enough to call the police, Dena will die and Tammy will disappear."

Her move. She glanced at the clock. Short notice, but if Tyler would get back here, she thought, that might be doable. "Nine o'clock," she said. That would give her enough time to talk to both Juliet and Tyler.

"No." Crushing her hopes, Doug Polacek spoke firmly. "Now."

"No," she said back, using the exact same tone. "I need more time."

"For what?" Clearly, he had no intention of waiting for her to answer. "Either you be at the apartment in half an hour or Dena dies."

Even as she began protesting, he ended the call.

Crud. Half an hour. Thirty minutes. And with Tyler nowhere in sight.

Chapter 16

Heart pounding, Anabel scribbled a quick note to Tyler, snatched her purse and car keys and ran for the door. She'd call Juliet along the way. Without Tyler, she had no clue if her admittedly bizarre plan would even work.

Or if she even really wanted it to.

In the car, as soon as she started the engine, she scrolled through the contacts until she located Juliet. Punching Dial, she put the car in Reverse, after scanning one more time to see if she could catch sight of Tyler. Nothing, so she went ahead and backed out of her spot and pulled into the road.

Once Juliet answered, Anabel filled her in, leaving out the part about dying and then returning. What she had to tell her friend was already more than enough.

"No," Juliet immediately protested. "You can't go there alone. You must find Tyler. He has enough magic to help boost yours."

"I'm pretty strong," Anabel said grimly, surprised to realize she spoke the truth. "For whatever reason, I feel like a badass."

"Good for you. But you need to remember what Doug Polacek actually is. A Drakkor will kill a wolf anytime."

Stunned, Anabel considered her friend's words. "Are you saying you think I should change?"

Instead of answering, Juliet posed another question. "In what shape are you stronger? Human or wolf?"

Anabel didn't even have to think. "Physically, wolf. Magically and intellectually, human."

"What you need to figure out is what will best defeat him." Juliet's cryptic words were no help at all. "Tell me how to find this apartment and I'll come help you."

Horrified, Anabel thought fast. "There's not enough time. I've got to go." And she ended the call.

She made it to the apartment building in record time, parked and jumped out of the car. She sprinted up the steps, only stopping to take a breath when she stood outside the unit.

When she'd lifted her fist to knock, the door swung open before her knuckles even connected. She took a deep breath, collecting herself. One last time, she glanced over her shoulder, wishing for Tyler the ghost to appear, though she would have welcomed Tyler the man.

But it seemed for now, she was completely on her own.

Taking a deep breath, she lifted her chin and went inside.

The second she set foot in the apartment, Anabel felt the power coil around her like a hungry python. The stifling air lacked oxygen and light. She barely had time to gather her defenses before realizing she couldn't fight this. The Drakkor was too damn strong. She could only hope he'd kept his word and that Dena had been freed.

Though she knew he wouldn't kill her—at least not yet, not until he'd tried to use her as a breeding machine—evidently he meant to use his power to intimidate and hurt her.

Her last thought before she blacked out was of Tyler, of his chiseled, rugged face, fierce with love for his baby sister. And, if she dared to believe the impossible, also with love for her.

Though Tyler knew Anabel considered her plan a sound one, the powers that be did not agree. His request on her behalf had been denied, no matter how much he'd begged and pleaded. And all he was given by way of explanation was a few words of affirmation.

Trust in yourself.

Just that. *Trust in yourself.*

That was all well and good, but he would have appreciated a bit more assistance than that, maybe even including some detailed instructions on how to proceed.

Standing at the front of the motel, he ran through explanations a few times in his mind. He wasn't sure how she would take knowing her plan had been nixed. One thing for sure, they'd have to come up with something else. Meanwhile, the clock continued ticking. He could only hope and pray his sister continued to fight to live.

Knocking on the door to her room, he waited. After several seconds had passed, he knocked again. Then he tried the knob, which turned easily since it hadn't been locked.

"Anabel?" he called, not wanting to startle her. With the human body came new considerations. "Anabel?"

No answer. So he went ahead and entered, knowing she'd want him to.

The instant he stepped back into the room, he could tell something had happened. The entire atmosphere felt off—tainted, even. And when he saw Anabel's note propped up against the coffeemaker, he understood why.

She'd gone to meet Polacek. She'd even noted the time. Ten minutes ago. Thankful for small miracles, he bounded outside, eyeing the various cars parked in the motel lot and a few down the street.

There. The 1986 Camaro. Notoriously easy to break into and hot-wire. After he muttered a quick prayer of forgiveness for stealing, it took him thirty seconds to get the door open and another thirty before he had the car running.

And then he took off, heading for Dena's old apartment. Praying he wouldn't arrive too late.

He made it across town in seventeen minutes, glad the owner of the car had left the radar detector inside. Though Anabel had a decent head start on him, he hoped he could catch her before she did anything foolish.

On the way to the staircase, he looked around for Tammy's car, which Anabel had written would be carrying his sister to safety.

He saw nothing and no one.

Furious and frustrated, he took the stairs two at a time. He wasn't sure how late he was, but the churning in his gut made him wonder if Doug Polacek had lied yet again.

Worse, Anabel had to be already inside the apartment. Alone, with a monster.

At the door, he didn't bother knocking. Instead he tried to remember how he'd seen it done on television and attempted to kick it in. It barely budged. Now he definitely questioned the wisdom of him asking to be human. If he'd been his usual ghostly self, he'd already be inside.

He kicked again, cursing. Then he tried ramming it with his shoulder, which hurt like hell and accomplished absolutely nothing.

The door held solid.

Frustrated, he eyed the floor-to-ceiling window. Since he could see no other option, he ran downstairs, back to his stolen car and grabbed the metal toolbox from the backseat floorboard. As he'd suspected, it was heavy.

He lugged it all the way back upstairs, swinging it as he prepared to shatter the window.

Instead the apartment door swung open. Dropping the toolbox with a clatter, he rushed inside.

The apartment was empty. No Anabel, no Polacek, no Dena.

Empty. How in the hell was such a thing even possible?

After searching every single room twice, he stopped, his heart pounding. He'd lost her. The unbearable crushing pain inside him made him raise his face to the ceiling and howl. His body responded instantly, initiating the shift to wolf.

Clothes tearing, he hurriedly pulled them off so he'd have something to wear later. He'd barely shed them in time. The change took over, his bones lengthening so quickly he felt as if he were being pulled in several different directions all at once. At first he was too stunned to react. After an instant's consideration, he went with the flow, aware he could use his beast's heightened senses to try to track where Anabel and Doug might have gone.

As soon as the change was complete, he again made a search of the apartment, this time using his nose. Here.

And there. Anabel had recently been inside. Along with Doug Polacek and one more. Another person. Female. Another few seconds, and he realized who it was. Tammy, Dena's roommate.

Of course she'd been. She lived there, after all. But he had no way to answer the million-dollar question—had she been there at the same time as Polacek and Anabel? And what about Dena?

The Drakkor had promised to free his sister. If he'd lied... At the thought, anger filled him. With the fury came something else—power. As a ghost, he'd never felt its physical effects; nonetheless, he recognized them now. The tingling of his skin. The tightness gathering strength behind his eyes. And the roar of it through his blood.

As his lupine physical body vibrated, he wondered fleetingly if he'd turn back into a ghost, a wolf shade. Then he realized it didn't matter. He was here on borrowed time anyway. He needed to focus only on accomplishing what he'd come for. First he must make sure his sister was free and that she got medical attention.

And then he would locate Anabel. No matter what it took, he would find her. And Tyler vowed to make the Drakkor pay for daring to touch what should have belonged only to him.

A cell phone rang. As wolf, he located one lying on the carpet near the sofa. Anabel's.

Quickly he initiated the change back to human. Even though changing back and forth was exhausting, the chance that the call might be important was too great to risk letting it go unanswered.

"Hello?" he answered.

"I need to speak with Anabel Lee, please," a male voice said.

"She's not available," Tyler said cautiously. "May I take a message?"

"I guess so. This is pretty urgent. Please tell Anabel that a young woman matching Dena's description was just brought into the ER," the man replied. It took Tyler a moment to recognize who it was.

"Pastor Jones?" About to ask how the other man had gotten this number, he realized Anabel had exchanged information with him.

"Yes." The pastor's voice changed. "Have we met?"

"No, but Anabel has spoken of you. I'm a friend of hers. And I know Dena Rogers. She's been missing for a while."

"Yes. Yes, she has. And now someone has dumped her off at the hospital. She's very seriously ill."

"But alive, right?" After the other man answered in the affirmative, an awful thought occurred to Tyler. "Why did the hospital call you?"

"She asked them to. Apparently, she said my name and the name of the church before going unconscious."

Alive. Tyler said a prayer of thanks. "How is she?"

"They've moved her to ICU. It's going to be touch and go. Will you please let Anabel know?"

Tyler had to force the words past the lump in his throat. "I will," he promised.

"One more thing. You might head out to the hospital if you actually do know Dena. I imagine she could use as many friendly faces around her as she can get."

Tyler nodded, thanked the other man and ended the call. He wondered how Dena would deal with seeing her dead brother alive again, even though he knew such a thing would be forbidden. Regretfully, he had to stay away.

Plus, he still had to save Anabel. Figuring out where the Drakkor had taken her would be the first step.

Trust in yourself. The voice speaking inside his head was not his own. Yet the words made perfect sense.

He knew what he had to do. As wolf, all of his senses were amplified. He was in prime physical condition and could be a vicious fighting machine if necessary.

Taking a deep breath and praying for strength, he opened the front door and began to shape-shift back to his lupine form. Once again, he rushed the change, making it more painful.

But such pain was easily ignored. Wolf again, he lifted his head and scented the wind. He'd follow his nose and find Anabel.

When Anabel came to and opened her eyes, she was no longer in the apartment. Wherever she'd been taken, the complete and utter darkness felt suffocating. Pushing away the panic, she reached for consciousness, quickly, quietly, trying to regain her bearings without attracting the attention of the powerful Drakkor who'd brought her here.

She wondered about Tyler's sister. Had Doug Polacek kept his promise and set Dena free?

At the thought that he might not have, anger flared up in her, sharp and bright enough to vanquish a small corner of the all-encompassing darkness.

Interesting. Seeing this, she took hope. She'd never been completely powerless. The possibility that Polacek might have underestimated her buoyed her spirits. She was only as weak as she thought herself to be.

Good to know. Now she needed to set her mind to figuring out a way to extinguish pure evil.

"I'm not pure evil." A light clicked on. Apparently reading her mind or her expression, Doug Polacek stood in front of her, looking very ordinary and very human. "I honestly never intended to hurt Dena Rogers. I never intended to hurt any of them."

Of them. She should have been afraid, but instead she clung to her anger. "Yet you did. She's near death, and you still refused to let her go."

"I had no choice. She was my bargaining chip to get to you."

Queasy, she stared, wondering about Denise. Had he stashed her away somewhere too, as a backup plan? "I don't understand," she said, stalling for time.

He circled around her, like a hunter assessing his prey. "Of course you don't. How could you? You didn't even realize your own power until recently."

Though she wanted to lash out, she bit her tongue. Maybe if she learned the reasons for his actions, that knowledge might give her an edge in the battle to come.

"I still don't get it. Even if I am some powerful witch— which right now is highly debatable—what benefit is that to you?"

"Surely you've read up on your history," he chided her. "If so, you must know mine is a dying race. Our females are born sterile. The only way for the Drakkors to have any hope of continuing is to find females of another species who are strong enough to bear our young. A couple of us have been working to impregnate women of various shape-shifter races, in order to accomplish this very important task."

A couple of them? Horror flooded her as she realized what he meant. "You tried to do this to Dena?"

"Of course. Her and the others before her." He

shrugged, appearing completely unrepentant. "Both of my colleagues have had the same result. The females always perish, their bodies too weak to contain our seed."

Anabel actually caught herself looking for her cell phone. She needed to call Tyler, Juliet, anyone, and let them know what was wrong with Dena Rogers. That way, whatever hospital they rushed her to would better know how to treat her.

Seeing this, Polacek actually laughed. "I left your phone back in my apartment. You can't call anyone."

"Did you even release Dena?" Anabel demanded, tamping down the rising fury, aware she didn't need to reveal how anger fueled her power.

"Certainly, I did." He seemed affronted that she'd even asked. "Right about now, Tammy should be dropping her off in front of the Leaning Tree Hospital ER entrance. Of course, she won't be going in with her. She should be back here shortly."

The awful image made her wince. "Surely you don't mean to have Tammy roll her out of the car onto the ground or something, right?"

His answering shrug again filled her with impotent rage. Once more her power simmered, boiling under the surface. Taking note, she tamped it back down.

Clearly not noticing, he moved in closer. "You are very important to me, Anabel Lee," he said earnestly. "With your strength, you might very well turn out to be the savior of the Drakkor race."

"But what about the cost? You are destroying so many women's lives in search of something that might not even be possible."

He froze, rearing his head back as if she'd hauled off and slapped him. When he spoke again, his voice was so quiet she had to strain to hear him. "I do not have a choice."

"We always have a choice."

At her words, he turned away, holding himself so rigidly she figured the control he exerted over his emotions must be very fragile. If so, he could snap at any moment.

He let out a roar, the torment and pain in the guttural cry shaking her to her core. When he spun to face her, she saw his composed mask had slipped. The madness glittering in his eyes had her taking a step back. And then another.

She considered running, aware he wouldn't kill her but would use whatever means at his disposal to stop her, and judging from the condition of poor Dena Rogers, he wouldn't care if he hurt her. In fact, a wounded captive might even be preferable. Less resistance.

Trust in yourself. The voice came out of nowhere, speaking quietly inside her mind. Like balm on an open wound, the words soothed her indecision, enabling her to think clearly once again.

Trust in yourself. More than a mantra, but instruction. She could beat this man at his own game, and maybe if she succeeded, she could prevent other women from falling prey to his kind. Suddenly, she realized her temporary death wouldn't be enough. Even if he let her go, as long as this man—and his buddies—remained free, women would be captured and tortured, raped and killed.

Fighting and arguing wouldn't work. Nor would any sort of intellectual debate. Doug Polacek believed wholeheartedly in his cause and, like all fanatics who'd lived before him, wasn't capable of listening to reason.

He had to be captured, along with the other Drakkor he'd mentioned. As she puzzled out a method, she thought of another way. Convince him she was on his side. Or at least, on the fence, easily swayed in that direction.

"You know," she began, keeping her tone conversational. "I did read up on the Drakkors. I'd never even heard of them. From what I read, they sure were majestic."

"Are," he corrected her proudly. "We *are* majestic. Just because there aren't many of us left doesn't mean we're completely gone."

"How many of you remain?"

Narrowing his eyes suspiciously, he shrugged. "Not very many. Why?"

"Just curious. I mean, those of you that are still around must be very old. The way the books talked, your females went sterile a long time ago. How many years ago was that?"

"Long enough," he said shortly, sounding a bit more reasonable. "And yes, we that are left are aging."

Biting her lip, she decided to trust in her instincts and go for the gusto. "Look, I'm trying to decide if you're right or in the wrong. I still don't have enough information to make a choice whether what you're doing is justified or not."

"It is." He began pacing, muttering to himself. Anabel held very still, trying to remain as unobtrusive as possible, aware his instability continued to make him dangerous.

Finally, he came to a stop in front of her. "There are six of us left. Three males and three females. One female is paired to work with each of us males. Since she is sterile, my female helps procure the women we mate with and attempt to impregnate."

"Tammy?" Anabel guessed, wondering why he spoke of her as if she were chattel.

"Yes."

"She seems young."

He shook his head, his pride apparent in his stance. "Appearances can be deceptive. You of all people should know that. Tammy is over one hundred years old. I myself am approaching two hundred."

She didn't even have to fake her amazement. "All this time, you've been searching for a woman capable of continuing your species?"

His shrug was enough answer. She took that also to mean they'd never succeeded.

Still, there was one more question she had to ask. "How many women?" Voice raw with emotion, she forced herself to unclench her fists, hoping she managed to keep the anger from her voice. "Over the years, how many women have died at your hands?"

"I don't know."

His quiet, unconcerned-sounding answer infuriated her. Until she got a look at his agonized expression and realized despite his actions, some shreds of a conscience remained.

"Then why?" she whispered.

"Don't you see we have no choice? We are the last of our people. We wasted years while the doctors tried to find out what was wrong with our females. Now we do what we must, what we will continue to do until we can no longer function. We cannot let the Drakkor race die. No matter what the cost."

Heart pounding, she pretended to consider. Though his actions were awful, part of her could understand what motivated him. How terrible, to know that you and a couple of others were all that remained of an entire species.

Still, that didn't give him and his two other male Drakkor friends free rein to do whatever they wanted.

"You alone might have the power to change this," Polacek continued earnestly. "Never before have we tried to mate with a woman of magic. All of the others were either human or shape-shifter. None had your power. Our kind are beings of power. We draw strength for it. I believe joining our power with yours might be the key. You alone might have the strength to carry a Drakkor halfling to term."

"Halflings are numerous among shape-shifters," she mused, pretending to be considering the idea while inwardly she shuddered. "Though among all the various combinations of shifter and other, there has never been anything like this."

"Exactly." He couldn't contain his excitement. "Imagine the destiny of greatness a child of ours would be able to achieve. He might even rule the world one day."

He. She wondered what he'd do if they actually were successful and she birthed a girl child. Smother her at birth?

"True." Managing a smile, she looked down at her hands. "I'll need some time to think about it," she said, as if she truly believed she had options. "Plus, don't you need to wait until my next cycle so you can make sure I'm not already pregnant?"

He laughed, his eyes narrow slits. "I thought you said he was a ghost."

"He was."

"Then how can you possibly be pregnant? Quit stalling. What will happen will happen."

"My forty-eight hours are not yet up. I need at least that much time."

Crossing his arms, he regarded her. "Don't take too long. It's always easier if you participate willingly." The look he gave her made her skin crawl. "Though sometimes it's more fun for me if you don't."

Figures. That was when she knew she'd better start gearing up for a full-on battle. The more time she could postpone it, the stronger she'd be. Hopefully.

Sex. The ultimate sacrifice. Okay, maybe this was a bit melodramatic. Death would actually be the ultimate. But even the thought of letting Doug Polacek put his hands on her made her insides twist into a knot.

The only man she wanted touching her—other than David—would be Tyler. Forever and ever, amen.

As clear as a bell, she heard Tyler's voice, so close he might have been standing right beside her. *"Trust in yourself,"* he said. That same phrase. She tucked those words up, folding them deep inside her to use later, should the need arise. Which she had no doubt it would.

Polacek wouldn't kill her. At least not yet. He couldn't take the chance of ruining his potential baby-making machine. She wondered if he'd even considered what such a child might be. A wolf-dragon? Some sort of hideous combination of the worst of both beings? Or of the best?

No doubt his thoughts ran toward the positive. A child of his would embody all the powerful parts of the wolf and the dragon.

Since halflings—children who were half human, half shifter—were common among the Pack, and she'd even heard of children who were half shifter, half fae, plus a rumored vampire-shifter combination, she didn't really understand why the pairing apparently couldn't happen.

It had to mean the Drakkors were on an entirely different level.

Perhaps their line was meant to die out, for whatever reason. What other explanation could there be?

Though she couldn't understand why such a baby could not grow inside any of the poor women's bodies, she knew if they did somehow succeed, any child conceived this way would need both hope and prayers. And love, she thought. She couldn't help wondering if Polacek was even capable of the emotion.

Surely not all Drakkors were like him, were they?

Chapter 17

"What are the others like?" she asked. "The other Drakkors? And how long has it been since any of you have seen a child of your kind?"

One corner of his mouth twisted as his eyes narrowed. "Why do you want to know?"

"Just curious. I mean, if you intend for me to carry your child, I feel like I should know something about them. How will you even know if he or she is part Drakkor?" She held her breath while waiting for him to reply.

"You don't even need to worry about that." The confidence in his voice made her heart sink. "Once you are pregnant, it will be very easy to tell if you carry a Drakkor child or not."

"How so?"

"The same reason why most non-Drakkor cannot survive and carry our child," he continued, his smile full of malice. "Our young grow at a rate twice as fast as other species. And twice as large. Where humans or Pack might have a seven-or eight-pound baby, a Drakkor infant is fifteen pounds when carried to term."

The thought of that made her wince. "I see," she said weakly. "I have to say, that prospect doesn't sound appealing at all."

He shrugged in response. More than ever, she knew she had to figure out a way to beat him at his own game.

"By the way," Doug said, interrupting her thoughts, "I have your friend." He spoke as casually as if he were discussing the weather. "Denise what's-her-name."

Stunned, Anabel reared back. "Why?"

"To make sure I have your full cooperation."

She stared, feeling sick. "Denise is not part of this. Let her go."

"No."

"We had a deal," she began.

"And as you so generously pointed out, Denise had no part in that deal." His smug smile enraged her. "I kept my bargain. Dena is free. Now you keep yours. Or your luckless friend will die."

Hate filled her. "You're a monster," she cried. Under her skin, her wolf began to struggle, trying to break free.

"So I've been told."

"How do I know you don't plan to keep Denise in case I don't work out? How do I know you don't intend to hurt her the same way you hurt Dena?"

His smile spread across his face. "That's just it. You don't. Now take off your clothes."

She froze. Slowly shook her head. "No. I will not. I still haven't made up my mind."

Moving fast, he came at her, using the full weight of

his body to knock her onto his bed. He pinned her, with a savage grin on his face. "Time's up. But no worries on the clothes. I'll rip them off myself. Actually, I'll find that more enjoyable anyway."

His heavy body pinning her down made it difficult to breathe. Through a haze of pain and fear, Anabel registered the door opening.

"Stop." Tammy's voice. "Doug, stop. Don't do this."

Numb, Anabel wiped away the stray tears that kept sliding from her eyes. Swiveling her head, she saw the other woman silhouetted in the doorway.

"Not. Now," Polacek snarled, his jaw tight. "Get out."

"No." Tammy stood her ground. Tall and regal, she looked decades older and wiser than the young woman Anabel had met originally. "Get away from her."

"How dare you intrude?" he roared. "You know better. You know this is the only hope we have. Leave. Right now."

"There's no longer any need for you to do this. Our line will go on. I'm pregnant." Though Tammy spoke quietly, the words carried as much impact as if she'd blared them through a megaphone.

For the first time since pinning Anabel to the bed, Polacek faltered. "What?"

"I said, I'm pregnant." Though smiling, Tammy began to cry. "And I've already had this verified, not just through the at-home kit, but at a doctor. I've made it past the first trimester, so it's safe to say I will carry the child to term."

Slowly, Polacek pushed himself up, rolling away from Anabel to climb shakily to his feet. He dragged his hand through his already mussed hair, his expression telling them he still struggled to believe it. "How? When? Who?"

Still weeping as she tried to wipe her eyes with the backs of her hands, Tammy grinned. "The usual way, dummy."

"Is the father a...Drakkor?"

Now Tammy's grin wavered. "No, he's not. Of course not. You males aren't the only ones who've been working at keeping our species in existence. The other two females have been trying, as well."

Afraid to move, Anabel made a sound, low in her throat, enough to draw Tammy's attention.

The other woman moved closer, still wiping at her streaming eyes. "I'm sorry, Anabel. We were trying to save our species any way possible. It's generally been thought the women are sterile. For whatever reason, when we mate with our males, we can't conceive."

Anabel couldn't help wondering if it had ever been even considered that the men were at fault, rather than the women, though she kept this to herself.

When Anabel didn't respond, Tammy turned her attention back to Polacek. "We need to notify the others."

Though he nodded, he didn't appear entirely convinced. Anabel guessed the possibility that he was the one shooting blanks might be a hard pill for him to swallow.

"Who is the father?" he asked, his stony expression matching his flat tone. "You still haven't said."

Cocking her head, Tammy eyed him. "What's wrong with you? This is what we've all been hoping for. The Drakkor line will not die out."

"I want to know what species of being is the father of our next generation. Will the halfling dragon also be wolf or bear? Panther or cougar?"

Tammy laughed. "You'll just have to wait until I tell

the others. I can promise you one thing. My child will be very special indeed."

Some dark emotion flared in Polacek's gaze, but he only nodded. "All right," he finally said. "And congratulations. You have the honor of being mother to the savior of the Drakkors."

Dipping her chin, still smiling, Tammy turned to go.

"Wait," Anabel said, struggling to mask her desperation. "Don't leave me here with him."

Tammy's gaze flicked from one to the other. "He has no need for you now," she said.

"Maybe not," Polacek growled. "But I am still entitled to have a little recreation. Leave us."

For half a second, Anabel thought the other woman might refuse, might stand her ground and save her. But Tammy glanced at Polacek and sighed. "Have fun," she said, her voice full of disgust. Leaving the room, she closed the door behind her.

When Polacek turned back to face Anabel, she saw the rage in his expression and shivered. He might say he wanted the Drakkor to go on, might even mean it, but damned if he hadn't wanted it to be because of something he himself had done, not Tammy. Not a woman.

That instant she realized that if she wanted to survive this, she'd have to fight. She needed Tyler, she wanted Tyler, but if she had to, she'd manage to do this alone. She was strong, a powerful if yet untrained witch, and a shape-shifter to boot.

Holding her physical body perfectly still, she dug deep inside herself, reaching out for the spark of creation that resided in everything. This, the source of all, would fuel her magic and give her strength.

Briefly, she closed her eyes, aware he would take that as a sign of surrender.

After counting to five, she opened her eyes and fixed her gaze on him. "I'm ready," she said. "I would also like a chance to have a child who would be revered and considered a savior."

Surprise flashed across his face, making her see he'd been motivated by only his own lust, not of any other potential outcomes. "I like the way you think. Plus, we'll have a lot of fun." His leering smile disgusted her. "I knew you'd come around eventually. Most women can't resist a chance at enjoying my body."

Insane and vain. A dangerous combination. She kept a smile fixed on her face. At least she'd have the element of surprise on her side. Because if he thought she was going to let him lay one hand on her, he had another thought coming.

Since she hadn't been able to get up off the bed, she used her spot to its full advantage. Scooting over closer toward the edge, she pasted what she hoped was a welcoming smile on her face. "Kiss me," she ordered, trying not to gag on the words.

Eagerly, he rushed to comply.

Her fist met his stomach first.

"Oof." He doubled over, the desire in his eyes changing to shock and then rage.

She didn't hesitate, but came at him again, praying the element of surprise would compensate for her lack of strength. Pummeling him with everything she had, she kicked and clawed and punched. She went for his eyes, his man parts, anything she could think of to cause the maximum damage.

At first, he only defended himself, trying to fight her

off. When he finally went on the offensive, she knew she was in big trouble. One swipe of his arm as he back-handed her sent her flying into the wall.

Dazed, she didn't move. She tried to figure out an escape route, but first she needed to gather her strength.

Massive legs spread in a warrior stance, he appeared ready to come at her again if she so much as twitched a muscle.

Again her wolf tried to break free. Unsure, not trusting, Anabel barely managed to hold back the beast.

Eyeing the doorway, and noting that he stood between it and her, she wondered nevertheless if she could make a run for it. But even as she began to move to try exactly that, the air around Polacek began to shimmer.

Which meant the man was about to change into the dragon.

She'd had enough difficulty fighting him in his human form. She didn't stand a chance against a Drakkor.

In a few seconds, the flashing light show ended. The Drakkor, now solidified, appeared, his mouth blazing orange and yellow fire, his reptilian eyes glowing red. Despite herself, she noted and marveled at his beauty. He looked like a realistic stained-glass dragon with huge wings spread. Except he was real—and extremely pissed off.

If the intention was to frighten and impress, then he'd succeeded. At least with the *impressed* part. Despite his fury and his evil intent, the dragon was like nothing she'd ever seen. For whatever reason, she was not the least bit frightened. Instead she felt strong. Righteous, even.

Maybe because she'd finally had enough.

As the huge beast circled her, scales gleaming and glittering in an incandescent rainbow, she drew down deep, gathering strength, before beginning her own change into a she-wolf. She had no idea whether or not now was the right time, but since she needed to have faith in herself, she'd decided to trust her instincts. And her instincts told her she needed to let her wolf break free.

The change came too swiftly, just as it always did when she felt threatened. Her bones lengthened, her clothing shredded and she clenched her teeth against the sharp and sudden pain.

Momentarily, the sparkling lights that always accompanied shape-shifting blocked the circling dragon from her sight, a small blessing for which she felt grateful. She'd need every second she could gather to collect her strength and plan her course of attack.

Plan. She drew her lips back and sneered at the thought. As if she could even attempt to formulate a plan against a monster like Polacek. No, this bitch was acting on instinct. Nothing less.

She tipped her head back and howled. Her battle cry, if she ever had one. She was fighting not only for her honor, but for everything else. Everyone else. Especially for the ones the Drakkor had abused and tortured. She had to win to avenge all of the women who'd come before her and any Polacek might be thinking would come after.

He must be stopped. If the Drakkors wanted to try to keep their species from extinction, they'd need to find another way.

She'd fight for her life and her town, for Juliet and the coven, Denise and for Dena, and especially for Tyler. In a nutshell, she'd fight for everything that mattered.

A wolf, she told herself, could trump a reptile anytime. When her vision cleared, she saw the Drakkor had stopped circling and had reared back, eyeing her the way a hungry predator watched a fatted calf.

Except she wasn't. Nor would she ever be. She'd always been a hunter, never prey.

In her wolf shape, the magic residing inside her had become centralized and more accessible. Teeth bared at her enemy, she probed it carefully, understanding her magic had become a tight core of power, waiting for her to use as she saw fit.

She'd have to use magic if she wanted to stand a chance at winning with the fire-breathing monster.

To her right, something else moved. Registering the blur of motion, she noticed another wolf. Her heart leaped as she recognized Tyler. She didn't have any idea how he'd found her, but she was sure glad he had.

Tracking Anabel's scent, Tyler raced out of the apartment and down the steps to the parking lot. He stopped, sniffing the air, praying Polacek hadn't hustled her into a car.

To his shocked disbelief, the scent continued. Out past the edge of the pavement, through a narrow alleyway behind a convenience store and a fence, and to the open woods.

Something about this forest, this land tickled the edge of his memory. It didn't matter now. Polacek had taken Anabel here. He raced into the trees, following his nose.

A howl echoed in the forest. Not a mournful sound, but more like a battle cry.

He burst into the clearing, stopping short at the metal windmill. One of Anabel's landmarks.

Heart pounding, he spun a circle, scenting the air.

Anabel's scent was too faint, though still drifting in the slight breeze.

Trust in yourself.

As he remembered, he went absolutely still, listening. A faint sound came from the west, and he plunged into the undergrowth, heading toward it.

When he came upon the edge of the concrete structure, mostly submerged in the ground, he realized it was much larger than Anabel's drawing had shown. Then he spied the huge metal door, now open, and knew he'd found the Drakkor's lair. Rushing ahead, he ran down the steps into the massive underground room. Just in time to see wolf-Anabel confronted by a massive, fire-breathing dragon. A quick glance around showed neither Tammy nor Dena anywhere in sight.

Tyler didn't think, didn't hesitate. He just acted. Taking a running leap, he planted himself in between the Drakkor and Anabel.

Trust in yourself.

As he snarled a warning, Anabel moved up beside him, her shoulder bumping his. At the touch, energy flowed, as sharp as electricity, making his entire body tighten. Next to him, Anabel did the same.

They glanced at each other, and then Anabel's mouth curled in a wolfish grin. Just like that, he knew what they had to do.

Side by side, careful that they were still touching, they ran at the Drakkor. The beast only watched them come, a reptilian amusement glimmering in his exotic eyes. Apparently, he believed two wolves were insignificant against his monstrous might.

Normally, he'd be right. But he didn't know they'd

read up on him and his kind. They knew his weak spots, where he was most vulnerable.

Polacek sat upright, on his hind legs, leaving his unscaled belly unprotected. From what Anabel had told him, according to the books, the Drakkors could only be killed by being stabbed in the gut or in the eyes, or with poison. Since he and Anabel didn't have any poison, he figured their razor-sharp teeth and claws would have to be enough.

That and their magic.

One more quick glance at Anabel and he knew she understood what they needed to do. Moving as one, they leaped forward and up, avoiding the giant, three-clawed feet, clearly taking Polacek by surprise.

When Tyler connected with the Drakkor's soft underbelly, he slashed and ripped. Next to him, Anabel snarled and growled as she did the same.

Polacek let out a howl of pain, swiping at them with his front talons, knocking them away and sending them flying.

The instant Tyler hit the ground, he rolled and launched himself back up again. From the corner of his vision, he saw Anabel replicate his move.

Great rivers of blood streamed down the dragon's massive body. He shook his monstrous head, swaying as if dizzy. He roared fire at the two wolves, no doubt well aware that only fire or silver could kill them.

Though the flames singed the fur on his back, somehow Tyler miraculously escaped serious harm. Anabel yelped, and he spun to check on her.

Polacek's claw caught Tyler right in the stomach, knocking the breath from him. He felt his insides tear, aware the damage wouldn't kill him, as long as he avoided the dragon's fiery breath. He'd suffer, but he'd heal. What happened to him didn't matter anyway. No matter the cost, he had to protect Anabel and keep her safe.

He landed on top of her as Polacek fell. Pushing her, he rolled her aside just in time to avoid the dragon's last blast of flame.

Tyler tried to push himself off her, to nudge her with his nose and urge her to run, but he'd lost too much blood. As his vision grayed, he prayed the Drakkor would stay down until he healed, at least enough to run. Which, since Tyler was a full-blooded shape-shifter, wouldn't take too long.

That was his last thought before he blacked out.

When he came to, he wasn't sure how much time had passed. Anabel lay in the same spot, clearly still unconscious. The Drakkor also hadn't moved. But the air had filled with smoke, and as he turned his head to discover the source, he saw the forest was on fire.

If he didn't get Anabel out of here, that would mean certain death. He had to save her.

Dragging Anabel by the scruff of the neck, he pulled her as far into the underbrush as he could. Though he hated to leave her, he had no choice. He needed to summon help and he couldn't do that as wolf.

Anabel moaned, drawing his attention. He nudged her with his nose, willing her to wake. As he did, energy surged through him, like a sizzling in his veins, transferring to her. She whined and opened her eyes. The instant she did, she climbed to her feet.

He took a step away, indicating with his paw that she should follow. Once he was certain she could, he took off running with Anabel close behind.

Praying no one saw them, he raced toward the apartment building and up the stairs. He'd left the door open, and the instant they were both inside, he nudged it closed with his shoulder.

And then, side by side, they both began the change back to human.

As soon as he was man, and ignoring his own arousal, Tyler yanked on his clothes and went for the cell phone. He didn't have to look up the number; every shifter had committed the Society of Pack Protectors number to memory.

When the woman answered, he told her everything, including his location. No doubt used to receiving strange phone calls, she didn't even question him. She promised to send Protectors right away.

Relieved and spent, he turned to find Anabel watching him, wearing a too-large T-shirt she must have gotten from the closet, her copper-colored eyes shuttered, exhaustion carving out new hollows on her cheeks.

She looked so fragile he wondered if she'd break if he took her in his arms. Plus, there was his still-obvious arousal, and if there'd ever been a worse time for that, he couldn't think of it.

"Are you all right?" he asked softly.

After a moment's hesitation, she nodded. "I think so. Is that my cell phone?"

"Yep." Tossing it to her, he waited while she eyed the screen, where the last number called was still on display.

"You called *them*?" she asked, not needing to explain since they both knew whom she meant.

"I had to. They need to know about this. They can help us. We can't contact the human police."

Wandering over to the window, she peered out from

the dusty drapes as if she expected their enemies to make a sudden appearance. As the thought occurred to him, he went over and locked the front door. Just in case.

When he looked up again, Anabel once again watched him. "What about Polacek? How do you know he didn't escape?"

"I don't. But the Protectors know about him. And the Drakkors need to be held accountable for what they've done."

Wearily, she nodded. "Tammy's pregnant, you know. I'm thinking all along, the problem wasn't with the female Drakkors. I'm not sure what species the father is, but it doesn't matter. The Protectors need to know this so she isn't harmed."

Surprised, he nodded. "Even though their line is now secured, Polacek was still going to…?"

"Yes."

The one word made Tyler blanch. He nearly asked why and then decided he didn't need to. Doug Polacek had revealed his character in so many ways, it shouldn't have surprised Tyler that the man would continue to do such horrible things when the need no longer existed. "We have to make sure the Protectors know."

"I agree." She sighed heavily. "What do we do now?"

He looked around the small apartment, noting the framed photograph of bright flowers in a meadow. Dena had taken that. He noted several other small touches he knew she'd made—the bright yellow pillow on the couch, the book of photographs on the coffee table, the bright pink vase on the bar.

"I want to go see my sister."

She stared at him. "I know she contacted you and everything, but she probably thinks that was in her dreams, if she remembers it at all. Won't she find it weird to see a dead man standing at her bedside?"

Mentally cursing, he realized she was right. Which hurt like hell. But if he had to go back to being dead, he wanted at least a glimpse of his sister before he went.

"Not only that," Anabel continued. "Didn't you say it was some sort of rule that dead people couldn't materialize fully to the one they were closest to?"

He frowned. "I was only guessing." In fact, he'd actually really only said that to make her feel better about David not showing up. As far as he knew, ghosts could frequently visit their loved ones, though most times the person couldn't see or hear them. He wasn't sure why David hadn't bothered to try to visit his wife, especially since she was known in the spirit world as a person of power.

While his sister was captive, he'd made numerous visits to her to try to offer comfort. While she hadn't been able to see him, he'd tried his best.

And now no way would he let this golden opportunity slip by.

"I'd still like to see her," he said. "Even if it's only from a distance. Kind of like a parting present for myself before I have to give all this up."

She nodded, her expression going sad.

All this. Anabel. He got choked up just thinking about it. Which was probably pretty damn stupid. He wondered if Anabel would even miss him once he went back to being dead. Somehow he doubted it, especially if he managed to bring Dave to see her.

Unfortunately, Dave had never appreciated what he had. And now he most likely had only regrets. Maybe the meeting would bring them both closure. For Anabel's sake, Tyler hoped so.

As she watched him, Anabel's expression softened even more. "We can try. Polacek said he had Tammy drop her outside the ER. Let's check there and see if she's been admitted."

Using her phone, she searched for the hospital number and called. After a short conversation, she ended the call. "All the woman would tell me is that she's there. She said privacy laws prevented her from saying anything more."

Suddenly struck by the idea of actually seeing his sister, he took a deep breath. "Why don't you see if you can find something to wear and we'll head over there?"

Chapter 18

A few minutes later, with Anabel wearing an outfit Tyler recognized as one of his sister's flowery T-shirt dresses and strappy sandals, they headed down the steps and out to her car. As human, wedging himself in the front passenger seat felt downright painful.

Neither spoke much on the short drive to the hospital. Preoccupied with worry, Tyler hoped Dena had gotten help early enough to pull through.

Entering the hospital, which smelled, as all hospitals did, of that peculiar combination of antiseptic and sickness, they hurried over to the information desk. There they learned that Dena was in ICU. As for her condition, they'd have to speak to the nurse in that department.

"Are you family?" the head ICU nurse asked, eyeing them both sternly. Her sharp-eyed gaze looked friendly, if stern. "The police have been here and are trying to learn what happened to this young lady. She was left on the pavement outside of our ER, near death."

Tyler almost said he was her brother and caught himself at the last moment. "We're friends," he said instead. "Members of the same church."

The nurse nodded. "Usually, we only allow family in the ICU. But she hasn't had any visitors, so…" She tilted her head and gave a quick glance around the area. All the other nurses appeared to be busy. "I suppose you can take a peek in her room, one at a time. She's in Room 8."

"Is she…?" Tyler almost couldn't finish. His heart thumped so loudly in his chest he thought maybe she could see it. Clearing his throat, he tried again. "Is she conscious?"

"No, sadly, she is not."

"Is she going to be okay?" Anabel asked.

The nurse's face changed, becoming distantly professional once more. "I'm sorry. I can only discuss her condition with family members. Now if you want to have a quick visit, please do so. Otherwise, I'm going to have to ask you to leave."

"Sorry." Anabel gave a placating smile. "We'll just pop in for a quick visit and then we'll get out of your hair."

As they walked away, Anabel took his arm. "You go first," she said. "And be aware that we might be able to help her heal if we use our magic."

He nodded, unable to take his gaze away from Room 8, where the door sat partially open. "I'll do my best, but since I have no idea how to heal anything, I'm hoping you'll have more success than I."

"Just try," she said, propelling him toward the room and the sister he hadn't seen in person for so long.

Just inside the doorway he stopped. Dena looked so tiny in the white hospital bed, hooked up to various machines, every breath accompanied by impersonal beeps. He moved closer, holding his breath, but she didn't stir. Her eyes were closed and her gaunt face puffy from an array of bruises in varying shades of purple and red.

They'd cleaned her up, he supposed. Her long hair, her pride and joy, still looked lifeless, but at least he could tell it had been washed.

"Dena?" Speaking her name, he couldn't help wondering if she could hear him. He'd read somewhere that people in comas often did, and he took comfort in the idea that on some level, she'd know he'd come to see her.

Remembering what Anabel had said, he moved closer. After glancing around to make sure no disapproving nurse was about to bustle into the room, he touched his sister's arm.

Still soft, her skin felt cold. He wasn't sure exactly what he should do, so he focused on healing. Using the word *heal* as a mantra of sorts, he tried to send her some of the energy his magic provided. But he must have used up whatever supply he'd been given fighting the Drakkor. No sizzle, no spark, no blaze of power. Nothing but the aching worry of his love.

"I love you, sis," he said, over the incessant beeping and drone of the equipment. "You've got to pull through. I'm counting on that."

She didn't stir, but she was free now. She had a chance. He could only pray Anabel had better results, could help her heal fully after what she'd endured.

Turning to go, he took one last look at his sister, hoping he'd be able to visit her as a ghost once she was healthy and whole.

Out in the hall, Anabel took one look at his face. "Don't worry," she said, squeezing him in a quick hug. "She's going to pull through."

He nodded, heart in his throat. Unable to watch anymore, he moved away from the room to wait a short distance down the hall.

A few minutes later Anabel emerged. Her broad smile had his heart skipping a beat. "Come on," she said, taking his hand. His skin tingled at her touch. "I gave her some of my energy. She didn't wake up, but her vitals improved and she will soon."

He chose to believe her and they went to her car. Key in the ignition, she turned to look at him. "We should check and make sure the Protectors got Polacek."

"You mean call?"

Her shrug was artfully careless. "I was thinking more along the lines of we drive out there."

Instantly, he shook his head. "No. No way. If he's regained consciousness, doing that would be putting you right in the line of fire."

As she opened her mouth to argue, her phone rang. "Great timing," she said. "It's the Protectors."

From what he could tell of her side of the conversation, everything was under control. She let them know about Tammy's pregnancy and also about what Doug Polacek had tried to do even though he'd known.

Once she ended the call, Anabel confirmed what he'd guessed. "Polacek is in custody. The society is requesting a meeting of all the remaining Drakkors. From what I could get out of what she was saying, they are going to see if the other Drakkors are as crazy as Polacek. If they aren't, the society might release him to them for punishment."

He thought of Tammy and what Anabel had told him. "Now that one of their females was able to conceive, hopefully the other two will, as well. I do hope Polacek was an aberration rather than the norm."

"Me too. Their beast is beautiful."

"I agree." Oddly enough, he felt at loose ends. Though he didn't want to face up to the knowledge that it might be time for him to go, he knew he'd have to soon. "I think this is out of our hands now."

Anabel smiled sadly. "I guess it is. Now I just need to get my life back on track. I'll start with dealing with getting the insurance to pay so I can rebuild my house."

Without him. Because now that everything had been done, it would be time for him to go.

"I have one question," he said. "Earlier, you had your plan of trying to die and be brought back to life. I was told no, by the way, but I'm curious as to why such a thing would even occur to you."

She bit her lip, finding a sudden fascination with her fingernails. When she raised her head, the emotion blazing from her copper-colored eyes made him catch his breath. "Because I wanted to see if such a thing was possible. Ever. Being without you is unbearable to me."

Humbled, he forced words past the sudden aching in his throat. "You wanted to do this in case there might be a chance I could be brought back to life?"

"Yes."

That single word, so full of hope and yearning, nearly undid him. His heart sank. He knew what he had to do. The longer he stayed with her, the more Anabel would suffer when he left.

He'd been granted all this—from being allowed to contact Anabel as a ghost, to spending time with her as a real, live man. Much more than he'd ever deserved, a gift he appreciated from the bottom of his heart. He couldn't overstay his time and make the powers that be have to be the ones to call him home. He should initiate the process himself and go back where he belonged, leaving with dignity and grace.

Oh, but the thought hurt. Like a fire in his chest, cutting a jagged hole in his heart. The idea of leaving Anabel felt worse than his memories of the actual moment of his physical death. He could barely breathe. Even considering going away from her forever made him feel as if his entire being had been stabbed, shredded, spit out and stomped on.

At least as a ghost, he'd no longer feel physical pain. Though he should have taken comfort knowing that, he didn't care. He'd suffer this a thousand times if he could only stay with her.

No doubt his spirit guide, Elias, would inform him he had some fancy lesson to learn from all of this. Whatever it might be, he felt certain he didn't want to hear it.

He knew the truth. He knew how precious this love was, a love he'd found way too late.

During his time alive, he'd never been a saint, and after he'd died, he learned he'd passed roughly a third of the life lessons he'd needed to learn in this life.

Learning more he could deal with. He'd build on his strengths and overcome his weaknesses, and by the time he was ready to be born again for another try, he'd hopefully do better.

But the one regret he couldn't get past was that he'd never known true love while alive this time. He'd never even realized he wouldn't. Like most men, he'd just assumed that someday he'd meet the woman with whom he was destined to spend the rest of his life. Someday.

He hadn't even dreamed he'd meet her after he was dead. While she was still very much alive.

He'd found love with his eyes and his hands and his skin. With every fiber of his being, an emotion so strong that the sheer power of it had enabled him to briefly become human.

Worse, he'd gotten such a wondrous thing while his sister still suffered. He'd come back to this plane with one purpose—to save Dena. And while he hadn't failed at that, to finally experience the joy of meeting his mate and then being forced to relinquish her, leaving was a mighty bitter pill to swallow.

They pulled up to the motel and parked. As he got out and followed her to the room, he felt a tug inside his core, faint at first. A gentle reminder that he would need to go soon. If he planned to be the one to initiate things, he couldn't put it off. He knew better than to try to fight it.

Back ramrod straight, Anabel unlocked the door and turned on the lights. As she stepped aside to let him past, he took her into his arms. He needed to tell her the truth, say goodbye.

He tried twice to speak, failing each time. Her eyes wide, her mouth fell open. He thought she might have an idea, judging from the frightened expression on her beautiful face. Even her amazing copper eyes looked dull, all the shine gone from them.

"Don't," she pleaded, holding up her hand. "Please don't."

All the color had leached from her face. Worried she might faint, he supported her.

"It's all right," he said, helping her into the fake leather chair. "Take a breath. Let me get you a glass of ice water. You don't look good at all."

"No." As he went to move away, she grabbed his arm. "Come sit. Tell me what's wrong."

He took a deep breath. "We need to talk."

Her worried smile faltered. "Has any good conversation ever begun with those words?"

He only shook his head and went willingly when she pulled him down onto the chair with her. "Let me hold you," he said.

"For how long?" The sorrow in her voice made tears prick at the backs of his eyes, but he managed to contain them and keep his composure.

They sat that way, neither moving, for the space of several minutes. Breathing in her scent, that particular combination of cinnamon and flowers that would forever make him think of her, he tried to calm his racing mind.

"Whatever it is, we'll work it out together," she said, clearly trying to find a way to help.

The depth of the pain inside made him wonder how he'd bear this. Still… Taking a deep breath, he hoped they'd give him just a little more time. He'd take however long he could with Anabel. Maybe even long enough to give him a few memories to store inside him forever, memories to keep him company when he returned to the cosmos without her. Alone. Completely and utterly alone.

Devastation filled him at the thought. *Chin up,* he told himself. He'd been a soldier, a man's man. He needed to figure out a way to deal.

Except he couldn't. Truth be told, he didn't know how he would survive it. Loneliness wasn't as bad when you didn't know what you were missing. Now he did, which would make being alone unbearable.

* * *

Watching the emotions flicker across Tyler's handsome face, Anabel experienced them all at the same time. Soon, Tyler would leave her for good. Intellectually, she knew this. Emotionally, she could hardly face it. Even though they'd known each other only a short time, the deep connection she'd made with him felt like a marriage. Knowing he'd go soon wrenched her insides and made her feel as if she were being widowed a second time.

Since David's death, she'd gradually disengaged from thinking of herself as part of a couple. She'd come to understand there were only two camps—coupledom and singledom.

And when David got killed, she'd unwillingly switched sides. She was now alone—and would be the rest of her life. Now she realized she'd been living life as though she'd given up.

Until Tyler. Now this could end only one way. In pain and fire.

Ah, but the inevitability of it all meant she wanted to figure out a spectacular last day with Tyler. She'd been denied this with David. He'd died and she'd never be able to get back or repair their last conversation.

They'd been bickering. Nothing major. But in the middle of their argument, uncharacteristically, David had grabbed his gear and demanded she take him to the airport for his flight back to Afghanistan. Even though the plane wasn't leaving for another four hours.

Stunned and hurt, she'd snatched up her car keys and done exactly that. When she pulled up to the curb, at least David had leaned over and kissed her goodbye. Except it was more of a peck than a good, toe-tingling kiss between mates.

As she opened her mouth to protest, reaching for him to pull him close, he'd moved away and gotten out of the car. Grabbing his gear from the backseat, he'd dipped his chin in an impersonal nod and disappeared inside the terminal.

This was the last time she'd ever seen him. He hadn't called or anything for two weeks. The next thing she knew, two uniformed officers were at her door, telling her he'd been killed in an explosion. Worse, there hadn't even been enough of his body left to bury. They'd found his dog tags and his wallet and sent them home to her.

Pushing the memory away, she covered her eyes with her hands. She'd loved David, but he was her past, not her future. Still, that botched goodbye had to be rectified. She needed to see David one last time, even if only as a ghost. She wanted to tell him she was sorry, that she hadn't loved him the way he deserved to be loved.

The way she loved Tyler.

The realization crashed into her, though she'd known this all along. If only her magic, the wonderful gift she'd been given, was strong enough to enable her to keep him with her forever. But she knew it was not. There wasn't a single kind of magic that powerful, even the dark kind. Life was a precious gift from the Creator.

And she would do nothing to dishonor that gift.

Still, she selfishly hoped to keep Tyler with her as long as she could.

Though Anabel seemed lost in her own thoughts, the constant tugging that had begun inside told Tyler he needed to leave this earthly plane.

"Anabel." He touched her arm, unsurprised when she jumped. "It's over." Though he supposed they should have been celebrating his sister's freedom and Polacek's capture, he couldn't keep the sorrow from his voice. "I've got to go back where I belong."

She wouldn't meet his gaze. Upon a closer look, he saw tears streaming silver tracks down her alabaster cheeks.

Pain stabbed him. He refused to go with her like this.

Reaching for her, he pulled her close. Held her, breathed in her scent and smoothed her ebony hair away from her face. Though he ached to tell her how he felt, he knew a declaration of love would only make things worse for her.

So he kissed her instead. When his mouth covered hers, he tried to pour all of his longing and urgency and frustration into the kiss. She returned his kiss with fiery abandon. They both knew what neither dared say. But at least they'd have this, though a single kiss would never be enough.

The celestial tug came again, reminding him he needed to go. Rather than deepen the kiss, he pulled back, though it took every ounce of willpower he possessed.

"It's time," he told her softly, wiping her tears away with his fingers.

She nodded. "Remember your promise," she said, her tone as heavy as his. "No more ghosts."

"No more ghosts." And one other thing, though neither spoke it out loud. He'd promised to find her husband, David, and let her have one last conversation with him.

Though it ripped at his heart, he'd given his word. And since it was what she wanted, he'd move heaven and earth to give it to her.

"No more ghosts," he reminded her. "Except one. I promise I'll find the one you most want to see."

And with that, he stepped out of the motel room and headed toward the trees, wanting to spare her from seeing him leave this second, earthly body forever.

Once there, he breathed the damp, musty scent of forest and gave himself over to what must be.

This time, it didn't feel like dying. Instead, the simple action of stepping out of himself felt more like a caterpillar, shedding dull and tired skin, to finally emerge as another, much more beautiful creature. Being in the spirit contained an almost indescribable joy. Though this time, his transformation was tinged with sorrow.

Briefly, he looked back to see what had happened to his body, but he saw no sign of it. Taking a deep breath, he immediately went in search of his spirit guide, Elias.

When he found the other being, recognizable by his deep purple hue, Tyler bowed low. "I've completed my task," he said. "My sister is safe."

"And the Drakkors?"

"They have found a way to continue their species."

"Very good." Genuine pleasure rang in the other's melodic voice. "All beings are beloved by their Maker."

Tyler nodded, taking a deep breath. "As I'm sure you already know, I made certain promises to Anabel Lee in order to obtain her assistance."

Elias said nothing, merely continuing to glow his soothing and powerful deep violet hue.

"I've told her no more ghosts will bother her," Tyler began.

Elias laughed. "That is something she herself can take care of. All she has to do is close the door between realms. She herself opened it in her grief."

Though he shouldn't have been surprised, Tyler nodded. "I promised her I would do that for her."

Silence. Finally, Elias agreed.

Tyler wasn't entirely certain how his guide would take his next request, but he'd given his word and would do his best to ensure that he kept it.

"I also promised her she could see her husband's spirit one last time."

Now Elias radiated interest. "That will be easily accomplished," he said, clearly mulling over the right words. "Considering what is happening even as we speak."

Pleased, Tyler waited for instructions.

When Elias said nothing else, Tyler took a deep breath and asked, "Will you find his spirit and bid him to accompany me? I would like to bring him to Anabel Lee tonight, if possible."

At this, to Tyler's absolute astonishment, Elias laughed. "That would be difficult, if not impossible," he finally said. "Especially since David Lee is not here in the realm of spirit."

Tyler's heart sank. "Has he already reincarnated? It hasn't been very long since he died."

"That's the problem, actually. David Lee is not dead."

Stunned, Tyler didn't know how to react. "What exactly do you mean?" he asked cautiously. "Wasn't he killed in Afghanistan?"

"No. He merely made it appear that way. He escaped and is living in the Hindu Kush mountains with his true mate."

True mate? Tyler dragged his hand across his mouth, forgetting for a moment that he was not in his corporeal body. "But he's married to Anabel," he managed, well aware that such a thing clearly no longer mattered to David Lee.

"He is a deserter from his military post. AWOL. Plus, his actions when he set up the explosion to make everyone think he was killed resulted in another's serious injury. Until now, he stayed hiding as he couldn't let anyone know he's alive, or he would have to pay for his crimes. Not at all good for his soul."

Until now?

"I have to tell Anabel," Tyler said, feeling as if a knife had just stabbed him in the heart. "This is going to wound her. She holds her husband in high regard."

"And a traitor like him doesn't deserve that regard." Elias's tone sounded noncommittal, which didn't fool Tyler. He had become intimately familiar with the laws of karma. He knew whatever David had done in his single-minded pursuit of a new life would be something he'd have to face sooner or later. Every single casualty. Including his wife, who'd believed he loved her.

Somehow he had to protect her, if he could.

"I can't let what he's done hurt Anabel," Tyler said. "And yet I can't do her the disservice of giving her a lie."

Instead of reminding him about lessons and karma, Elias nodded. "Sounds like you have quite a dilemma," he mused. "Unfortunately, you will not be allowed to deal with it. This is Anabel's lesson to learn."

Again Tyler felt that tug, even stronger this time. Which made no sense, as he had already left the physical realm for that of the spirit. But it came again, making him stagger. He tried to reach out for Elias, but his guide only smiled benevolently at him from out of reach.

And then blackness.

When Tyler vanished right in front of her eyes, Anabel told herself she wouldn't keep crying. After all, they still had unfinished business. Tyler couldn't go on to his heavenly reward until he kept the promises he'd made to her. She'd see him again, at least once more. She had to.

A few minutes after Tyler left, the phone rang. Not her cell phone, but the hotel landline.

If not for that, she probably wouldn't even have bothered to answer. Knowing what would soon come to pass had made her numb, and Tyler disappearing the way he did made her want to weep.

No one had this number. No one.

The absurd thought crossed her mind that somehow it might be David, calling from heaven. And so she crossed the room to the countertop and picked up the handset.

"Hello?"

The first few words didn't register. She'd been so certain the call would be something from the realm beyond that she had trouble taking in that it wasn't.

Snippets of the conversation finally reached her, spoken in that all-too-familiar, überformal tone used by the military.

The voice spoke a name. David Lee. Her husband. But the rest of what the stranger said seemed incomprehensible.

When the caller asked her if she'd understood, she didn't at first respond. How could she, when she wasn't even entirely sure she wasn't dreaming this entire conversation?

After all, the phone that had rung was a motel phone, not her personal cell. Most likely it was someone making a very bad joke or one of the still-absent remaining Drakkors, trying to extract some sort of bitter revenge at her expense.

Because what the caller said simply could not be true.

David wasn't dead after all. David was alive, a deserter, and living in the mountains of Afghanistan with another woman and a child.

When pressed, she finally murmured something in assent. She thought. Yet there wasn't one bit of this making the slightest sense.

She was told David would be court-martialed and tried, most likely there in Afghanistan. She would not be permitted, at least for the time being, to see him.

See him? The only reason Anabel would want to do that would be to ask him for a divorce.

After assuring the caller she'd contact him if she had any questions, she gently replaced the receiver in the cradle and swayed.

Chapter 19

When she turned to make her way back to the living room, she nearly fell. But somehow she reached the couch and allowed herself to drop onto the overstuffed cushions.

Then she tried to think about what she'd just been told.

Allegedly—and as of right now she still couldn't bring herself to believe it was true—her beloved husband, the man she'd considered her soul mate, the soldier she'd held in such high regard, had not only deserted his post, but staged his own death. His doing so had caused others to be seriously hurt. His fellow soldiers, men he'd worked with, men who'd trusted him.

Worse—was there actually anything nearly as bad?— the military had caught up with him. He'd been found living in some remote mountainous village, along with a native girl and their child. Which meant that he'd staged his death knowing he'd gotten the woman pregnant.

The thought that he could do such a thing—not only to her, but to the men in his unit, men who'd relied upon him to have their back as surely as they had his—didn't match up with the man she thought she knew.

Painfully stunned, she wasn't sure how to react. Eighteen months ago, she'd grieved for David. She'd fallen down a well of sorrow so dark that she hadn't known if she'd ever be able to climb back out.

To learn that all that time, while she'd been weeping and trying to figure out how to manage to live without him, he'd been making a new life with some other woman and their child felt like the worst kind of betrayal.

Especially since David hadn't wanted kids. When she brought the subject up not long after they were married, he'd told Anabel he never wanted children. Apparently, he just hadn't wanted them with her.

If the call had even been real. If it hadn't, then the remaining Drakkors really knew how to mess with her head.

Unfortunately, it didn't take long for Anabel to verify that the phone call had indeed been true. Her first hint came from the incessant ringing of the hotel room phone. The second time she answered, it was a reporter from one of the national television shows, wanting to interview her about David.

She didn't know how they'd gotten the number, and after five minutes of nonstop ringing, she no longer cared. Unplugging the phone, she sat down on the edge of the bed and tried to figure out what to do.

Had Tyler known? When he'd promised her that she could speak to her husband again, had he known all along David wasn't dead? She found it hard to believe he would have lied to her, but she also would never in a million years have suspected David of doing what he'd done.

Finally, she began to make a list. Number one on the list was file for divorce. Number two was to find the man her husband had caused to be injured and learn if there was any way she could help. It seemed like the least she could do.

Plus, action might help take her mind off missing Tyler.

A commotion outside the motel had her peeking out from behind the curtains. The parking lot had filled, not only with vehicles bearing the insignia of most of the large news networks, but with people. Reporters carrying cameras and microphones. All camped right outside her room.

She made a quick phone call to the Leaning Tree Police Department, asking Captain Harper for help.

"Unfortunately, you're in a public place," he drawled, sounding not the slightest bit sorry. "If you still had your home, they couldn't come on your property without your permission. But since you're at the Value Five, as long as they don't try to come inside your room, the media are well within their rights."

After vowing not to speak with anyone until she sorted things out, she decided she needed to purchase a laptop computer, even if doing so would tap her already low funds. She put on dark sunglasses and a scarf to cover her head. Then she hurried from her room to her car and did her best to ignore the camera flashes and shouted questions. The way they surrounded her Fiat as she tried to pull away reminded her of what she'd seen on TV with the paparazzi and various movie stars.

Careful not to run over anyone, she finally broke free

of the throng of reporters. A few of them tried to follow her, but she knew this town like the back of her hand, and she managed to elude them.

As soon as she'd purchased her laptop and a few other supplies like bottled water and snacks, she headed back. Again her Fiat was instantly surrounded, and she had to battle her way to her room.

Once inside, she locked the door with a sigh of relief and got set up. Since the Value Five had free Wi-Fi, she got on the internet and read everything she could find about David.

Some sources were reporting that his actions had killed a fellow soldier, while others claimed several other men had been wounded, one of them grievously. The seriously wounded soldier had gone from Kandahar in Afghanistan to the Landstuhl Regional Medical Center at Ramstein Air Base in Germany. Since he'd been badly burned, once stabilized, he'd then been flown to Brooke Army Medical Center at Fort Sam Houston near San Antonio, Texas. As far as Anabel could tell from what she could glean on the internet, he was still alive.

She refused to cry, at least not for David. She'd done all her weeping over him eighteen months ago. But for this man her husband had hurt, she allowed herself to shed a tear or two.

Next, she researched divorce attorneys. As soon as the media storm died down, she planned on filing. Until then, she thought a trip to Texas might be in order. She owed David's victim an apology for what her husband had done and her support and prayers for his continued healing.

The last straw to a very long day was a phone call from a man who identified himself as David's attorney. "I'll be representing him in the court-martial," he said. "Though he has serious criminal violations in the UCMJ—that's the Uniform Code of Military Justice—at least he's not a murderer."

"Yet," she muttered. "I'd like to see the man David caused to get hurt," she said. "The least I can do is apologize for my husband's actions."

"There's no need. Like I said, he's in a coma. He won't even know you're there."

Every instinct, every bit of magic she possessed, urged her on. "I don't care. I need to see him. Can you arrange this or do I need to start making some phone calls?"

"Doing so might look bad, as if you believe David is guilty."

"Don't you?" she asked, incredulous. "I assume you've talked to him. What does he have to say for himself?"

The silence on the other end of the line told Anabel the attorney clearly just now realized David's wife might not feel too charitable toward his client right now.

Clearing his throat, the lawyer asked if she planned to travel to Texas.

"Yes. I'm driving to the city and to the airport this afternoon." Before she left, she delivered Leroy to Juliet, who'd agreed to watch him.

The uneventful flight, with a layover in Atlanta, gave her time to think. Though she kept her book open in front of her and pretended to read, she couldn't help rehearsing what exactly she'd say. Even though the soldier might be in a coma, she had faith that the magic inside her could help him to heal. After all, she'd been able to assist Dena Rogers.

At the thought of Tyler, her firm, steely grip on her composure slipped. She missed him, more than she would ever have believed possible. She'd have given much to be able to fill him in on this latest development. Assuming he hadn't already known.

Once she arrived in San Antonio, she took a cab to the hospital. Apparently, someone had alerted the media about her arrival. The instant she pulled up to the hospital entrance, she saw they'd assembled in wait for her.

Though the reporters took pictures and shouted questions, she kept her expression remote and stared straight ahead, putting one foot in front of the other and plowing forward. The multiple camera flashes disoriented and disturbed her, but the knowledge that the press—at her request and backed up by the US military—would be denied entrance to the hospital itself gave her a bit of relief.

Once she was inside, the instant the automatic doors closed behind her, the roar of the crowd cut off. That scent particular to hospitals—a combination of cleaning agents and sickness—assaulted her nose.

No matter. She was going to visit the man whom her husband had hurt. Hopefully, the magic inside her would be enough to help him heal.

Somehow she had to make amends. Her magic was all she had.

The two military policemen at her side stopped at a closed door. "He's in there, ma'am," one of them said, inclining his head.

"Please wait outside," she said, keeping her voice gentle yet knowing if they balked, she'd do whatever she had to in order to make sure she entered the room alone.

"Of course," the man replied.

Relieved, she took a deep breath and placed her hand on the knob and turned it.

Entering the room, which was silent except for the thrum and low-level beeping of the machines, she approached the bed. And stared. Hand to her heart, which now had begun beating madly, she looked skyward and muttered a quick prayer of thanks before turning her gaze back to the rugged features of the man lying there.

How could this be? Yet before her eyes, indisputable proof.

Her legs quivered and threatened to give out on her. She sank into the chair next to the bed. Tyler, alive. Not dead after all, even though he'd appeared to her first as a spirit, a shade.

Fleetingly, she wondered how he'd been made human and then realized maybe with magic and love, anything was possible. In the end, she decided none of that mattered.

He was here, alive, and she might be the only one able to bring him back from his coma with her magic.

Or with her love. Maybe the two were interchangeable.

Trust in yourself. Again the voice in her head, the same one from when she'd had to fight the Drakkor.

So she would, she decided. She'd trust in herself and more. She'd trust in what she and Tyler had made together. She'd trust in them.

Approaching the bed, she took in the various machines keeping him alive. At least he breathed on his own, one blessing. Machines regulated and monitored everything—there were so many she didn't know what each was for.

He didn't move. His wonderful, beloved features looked the same. Puzzled, she eyed the rest of him, swathed in bandages. She'd read that he'd been badly burned in the explosion and she realized the bandages covered his burned skin. Both hands and arms, chest, stomach and legs. Most of his body, as far as she could tell. She wasn't sure how his face had escaped serious injury.

And then she knew. David. David had done this to Tyler. The man from her past and the man she believed with all her heart would be her future, interwoven together like strands of an intricate web. And neither was dead.

Tyler. Her heart sang. The magic racing like a dizzying current inside her veins would help him, save him, bring him back to her, where he belonged.

So she leaned close, inhaling his wonderful scent, fainter now, but somehow still redolent of mint and trees. And then she touched her lips to his and kissed him.

Softly at first, the barest whisper of her mouth. He didn't respond, of course. Not yet. But she hadn't unleashed her magic.

Not wanting to overwhelm him at first, she kept the kiss gentle. Slow, and warm and sweet, using her lips to try to coax a response. Still, he didn't stir. The machine continued beeping with his heartbeat, slow and steady. Unmoved.

She broke away, studying his rugged features, so full of love for him her chest hurt, and knew she couldn't fail.

This time when she placed her mouth on his, her kiss became a command. *Come back to me. Come back to me.*

Slanting her mouth over his, she poured everything she had into this kiss, parting his lips and trying to reach his soul. Deliberately drawing his face to hers in another embrace, she stroked a gently growing fire, and when she felt the first answering spark from deep inside him, her pulse fluttered with joy.

Spirit soaring, she continued, stroking his hair, the side of his face, willing him to return. The dreamy intimacy building between them filled her tired soul, and when he finally moved his mouth under hers, tears filled her eyes.

"Tyler." She pulled back, holding his hand as his eyelids fluttered open. She willed him to feel the almost tangible bond between them. "Tyler, it's me."

Finally, he looked at her, his beautiful hazel eyes at first disoriented, gradually becoming sharper when it dawned on him that she was there.

His gaze locked on hers, and a warm glow ran through her. Though she locked her jaw and tried to be strong, she couldn't stop the tears from spilling down her cheeks.

"Anabel?" His voice a rough rasp, nonetheless it was his, sounding the same as he spoke her name. "Is that really you?"

Wiping at her eyes, she nodded, temporarily unable to speak. He pulled her to him and kissed her again, as if he needed the touch of her lips to convince him she was real.

The machines began wailing, a claxon sound that brought a nurse running. She spoke into a small phone clipped on her belt, and the room filled with people.

"I'm sorry, ma'am," she said to Anabel. "But I'm going to have to ask you to wait outside the room."

Anabel didn't move. How could she leave when they'd just found each other again? Instead she backed up in one corner, making herself as unobtrusive as possible, while a team of people worked on Tyler.

What did this mean? His eyes remained open, and a flicker of annoyance crossed his face as they all poked and prodded at him.

"Stop," he finally ordered. "I just woke up from a coma. I'm starving and I'd really appreciate you getting me something to eat."

Startled, the assembled medical team momentarily fell silent. And then one of the nurses chuckled, shaking her head. "Damned if you don't sound healthy."

"I am healthy," Tyler shot back. "At least as healthy as a man can be who was caught in an explosion and has had numerous skin grafts."

"You remember that?" This time the white-coated man, clearly the doctor, sounded shocked.

"I do. Now if you'll leave me alone with my Anabel—" Tyler cast his gaze toward her, making her smile "—I'd really appreciate it. It's been way too long since we've been together."

The doctor nodded and began inspecting the machines. "Pulse and blood pressure are fine. Oxygen saturation is great. I'd say he's well enough to have something light to eat. And visit with his lady friend."

"Light?" Tyler protested. "I need a steak and baked potato."

The doctor laughed. "All in good time, but not just yet. You've got to give your body time to adjust to regular food." Then, scrawling notes on a clipboard, he motioned to his team and they all left the room.

"Anabel." Tyler beckoned her close. "What the heck is going on? I think I remember, but I can't be sure. I was dead..."

Her heart turned over. When she could find her voice again, it trembled, but she didn't care. "You were never dead. Even when you were a ghost and visited with me to save your sister. Apparently, you've been in a coma all along."

He grimaced. "I wasn't dead," he repeated, confirming her statement. "Does Dena know?"

"I'm sure they must have told her, before all this happened. As soon as either of you is well enough to travel, I'm sure you two can talk about it."

Worry clouding his eyes, he nodded. "How is she doing?"

"Last time I checked, she was being moved out of ICU. Beyond that, I'm not sure."

"And David?"

She tried to speak, failing miserably. But as she gazed at him, she realized she didn't have to. One look at his shuttered expression told her everything. "Did you know all along?" she asked, holding her breath for his answer.

"No. I didn't find out until I left you that last time and asked to bring Dave's spirit to meet with you," Tyler said, his voice gentle. "And that's when I learned that Dave wasn't actually dead."

She nodded. "And his actions nearly caused you to be killed."

Astonishment widened his eyes. "Dave did this?"

Keeping her words as terse and factual as she could, the same way she'd been informed, she told him what she knew. "I mourned a man I didn't truly know. He lied and cheated and almost caused someone else—you—to die."

She took a deep breath. He started to speak, but she waved him away. She hadn't finished yet. "David is not who I thought he was. Everything he did, in the end, was for himself and his Afghan family. He didn't care who else got hurt when he faked his own death. And clearly, he didn't give a second thought to me, the woman he'd left behind, the woman he'd married, who once actually believed him to be her mate."

"Are you all right?" he asked, his voice soft.

"I think I am. I will be." Lifting her chin, she met his gaze. "Even though I realize clearly now that David was never my mate, still I did nothing to deserve to be treated as if I didn't matter. Instead of sadness, all I feel is anger."

"What will happen to him now?" she asked. "Once he's court-martialed? They've assigned him an attorney."

"It will be just like any other trial, only military. If he's found guilty, he'll go to prison."

She nodded. "What of his…girlfriend and their child?"

"They'll remain in Afghanistan." His familiar hazel gaze searched her face.

"I didn't even hear whether it's a boy or a girl."

Watching her carefully, he nodded. "I guess you could ask his attorney."

"Maybe I will." Heart heavy at all the hurt her husband's selfish actions had caused, she walked to the hotel window. Pulling aside a sliver of curtain, she stared out at the parking lot.

"Will I be able to see him again?" she asked, turning just in time to see a naked look of pain cross Tyler's face before he rearranged his features.

"I'm sure his attorney could arrange that." Tyler shrugged. Then, speaking carefully, he asked, "You still want to see him?"

"Yes, I think I would." Anger still fueled her. "I'd like to demand an explanation. Plus, he'll need to sign the divorce papers once I have them drawn up."

He froze. "You're going to divorce him?"

"Of course I am. Wouldn't you?"

One corner of his mouth lifted. Not quite a smile, so she wasn't sure if he found her question amusing or not.

"You should probably think about this," he said carefully. "Consider whether or not you want to give him a second chance."

"A second chance?" She could hardly believe what

she was hearing. "After what he's done? Not only dishonorable, but—"

"You made mistakes too. And I think you've been relieved when people finally forgave you."

What the heck was Tyler doing? Playing devil's advocate? Yet, to her teeth-gritting irritation, he was right. At least about the part where she'd made mistakes. Still, that didn't change how she felt about either man.

She took several deep breaths, trying to see past the righteous and wounded anger. "Forgiveness is one thing," she allowed. "And if I have enough time, I might be able to give him that. But a second chance? I don't think so."

The tense lines on his face relaxed. "As long as you're sure."

"I am." Crossing to him, she gently lowered herself next to him on the edge of the bed, taking his hand. "You're not getting rid of me that easily, my love."

Satisfaction and love blazed from his gaze. "I think that's my line. I love you, Anabel Lee. Surely you've already realized that."

She couldn't tear her eyes from him. "I love you too. How foolish I was, believing I knew love before you. You're my mate. We were…"

"Meant to be together," he finished for her. "And as soon as you're free, I'd like you to be my wife."

Happiness filled her, wrapping around her like a warm blanket. "As soon as you're well enough too," she teased.

"My strength is returning rapidly," he warned, pulling her down for another kiss. As she opened her mouth for him, thrilling to the familiar shiver of awareness, she dimly registered the sound of someone clearing her throat.

"Excuse me." The first nurse had returned, carrying

a tray. "When you said you were hungry, I thought you meant food."

Feeling her face color, Anable scooted back, unable to hide her smile.

Tyler's annoyance vanished, replaced by anticipation. "Great," he said. "We were just talking about me needing to regain my strength."

The nurse placed the tray on his bed table. "Enjoy." Her shoes silent on the floor, she turned and left the room.

Grinning like a kid at Christmas, Tyler lifted the silver cover from his plate. His expression fell as he saw what he'd been given. "Soup?" He sounded incredulous. "And crackers? Oh, look, they gave me lime gelatin for dessert."

Anabel couldn't help it; she laughed. "I'm going to go check into my hotel and give you some time to rest. I'll be back this evening."

He grabbed her hand. "Don't be gone too long," he said. "We've been separated for longer than I ever want to be again."

Heart full, she promised.

In the days that followed, Tyler made a rapid recovery. A miracle, his medical team called it. The skin grafts healed far quicker than they had before Tyler awakened. The hospital physical therapist marveled at his progress—soon he could walk laps around the hospital.

Anabel spent all her time with him, even sleeping in the chair beside his bed most nights. She refused to grant any interviews, giving her standard "No comment" to the reporters when they confronted her.

Finally, Tyler was deemed well enough to leave the hospital. Since the insurance company still had not settled on her house, despite the arson investigator's report that he didn't believe she'd set it, they'd have to return to the Value Five Motel.

"Or—" Tyler's eyes crinkled at the corners as he smiled "—we can see if the McGraws will let us rent one of their cabins at Wolf Hollow. They're so much nicer—and more private—than that motel room."

This time she was willing to consider the idea. To her surprise, the McGraws agreed, stating they had no problem with her staying there. For this, as so many things lately, gratitude overwhelmed attitude. She felt truly blessed.

Tyler purchased a car in San Antonio, using some of the pay that had accumulated during his eighteen-month coma. They drove back to New York together, both still full of wonder at the love they'd found.

David made no attempt to contest the divorce. He signed the papers immediately after receiving them, giving her everything. Which, at the moment, was a whole lot of nothing since she still owed money on the house that was nothing but ashes.

They moved into a lovely and secluded cabin at Wolf Hollow, and the McGraw family made both Anabel and Tyler feel completely welcome.

Once the uncontested divorce became final—rushed through the court system in a miraculous six weeks—Tyler took her shopping for a ring. Despite her protests that she didn't want anything fancy, he purchased her a gorgeous diamond. He said he wanted to find a ring as spectacular as her.

They were married on a brisk fall evening, in a clearing in the woods near their cabin. Though originally Anabel had planned a small wedding, half the town apparently wanted to come, so they made it like a party, with a potluck dinner. A local band provided music. There was dancing, and for the first time in years Anabel felt like part of the town, of the local family.

But the best moment of all was hearing the vows Tyler spoke. They'd each written their own, and she'd told him how he completed her and of her great and everlasting love for him. She could have sworn he wiped a tear from his eye when she finished.

"Now my turn," Tyler said, his voice loud and strong and sure. "I love you, Anabel. I vow to protect you and cherish you, for all of our lives until beyond. Because what we have is so amazing and so strong, not even death can tear us apart."

Anabel was sure none of those assembled understood why she laughed. "Not even death," she repeated.

And they sealed their vows with rings and a kiss.

* * * * *

Linda Thomas-Sundstrom writes contemporary and paranormal romance novels for Harlequin Nocturne and Harlequin Desire. A teacher by day and a writer by night, Linda lives in the West, juggling teaching, writing, family and caring for a big stretch of land. She swears she has a resident Muse who sings so loudly, Linda often wears earplugs in order to get anything else done. But she has big plans to eventually get to all those ideas. Visit Linda at lindathomas-sundstrom.com or on Facebook.

WOLF BORN

Linda Thomas-Sundstrom

To my family, those here and those gone,
who always believed I had a story to tell.

Chapter 1

Everyone had demons.

"Some species are just closer to them than others," Colton Killion muttered as he ran beneath the light of a huge Miami moon. For a werewolf like himself, the desire for what the moon offered fit into another category altogether. But now wasn't the time for beastly antics. He'd had an emergency call.

Drenched in moonlight, and in human form, he sprinted over a wide stretch of dirt and grass. The night air, filled with the scent of the ocean and a dozen kinds of Cuban food, burned his throat as he sucked in it, and left a warm sensation in his groin.

Running appealed to his animal nature.

At the moment, though, he couldn't afford to blow his cover. Two other cops were on his heels, running as fast as their human legs would take them. The radio on his shoulder kept repeating directions interspersed with static.

"Officer down. All units on the south side respond to the following address. 521 Baker."

The harsh words wouldn't have been half as bad without the address the dispatcher had given out. Damn if his family didn't live on the same street.

Colton lengthened his stride to reach an area of what in Miami passed for a forest of trees. Liquid moonlight had already begun to move through his veins as if he had injected it into an artery. The phantom sensation of an elongated muzzle made him reach up to check that it hadn't materialized yet.

Those cops behind him couldn't see that. There was no way they would understand having a Lycan in their midst, and that a searing, breath-robbing heat was spreading outward from deep inside his chest where a sleeping beast lay curled, craving the night, awaiting its freedom.

"Killion! Wait up!" Julias Davidson, the officer responsible for this beat yelled, the strain in the man's voice due to him being shamefully out of shape and having to run to the cruiser parked on the street.

Colton didn't care about the identity of the officer loping along in Davidson's wake. He was more concerned that Davidson, usually nosy as hell, hadn't asked why Colton had been passing through this way in the first place when he was officially off duty.

Good thing he hadn't been asked that question, since Colton didn't know the answer. He'd just acted on a feeling that something was up with this park and had dropped by for a look. Most of the time, he paid attention to those little sparks of intuition.

"Hell." In deference to the unanswerable *why* he was

here, Colton found himself in a precarious state. With the muscles of his neck throbbing and the skin on his bare arms undulating like disturbed water in a pond, restraining his lupine abilities took every ounce of willpower he possessed.

The moon called to him, but there was also an officer down just two doors shy of his parents' house. And the sudden notoriety of an injured or, God forbid, dead police officer would be unwanted attention for a family like his that had a lot to hide—and even more to lose, if they were identified as Lycan.

"Hellfire!"

The whitewashed oath didn't satisfy him, or take the edge off his anxiety. "I've got a bad premonition about this dispatch to Baker Street," he whispered hoarsely. In fact, his gut told him he shouldn't wait for the others, and that he would get to the crime scene faster if he ditched the limiting human persona.

Too late now. He had company. Turning, he said to a breathless Davidson in a steady voice, "I'll go ahead," as Davidson hit the edge of the trees.

"On foot?" Davidson tossed back.

"I know a shortcut through the park."

"This park's dangerous enough with three of us out here."

"There hasn't been much real trouble since Scott, Wilson and the other boys cleaned it up last year," Colton said.

Key word there: *Other* boys. Capital *O*. There weren't many completely human bones left in the bodies of detectives Adam Scott and Matt Wilson, whose lives had radically changed after receiving rogue werewolf bites less than a year ago, and who now had their own secrets to keep.

"Yeah? Well, suit yourself, Killion," Davidson said. "Some bastard shot a cop, and we need to be there."

Without stopping for anything longer than two quick breaths, Davidson and his partner took off again. Colton watched them go, his own breath regulating now that he was about to be alone.

Or almost alone. That initial spark of intuition nagged at him again. The night had a strange feel to it that was thicker, denser than a normal night. It felt to him like too many unseen things moved through the dark, taking up space and crowding the atmosphere. Notable oddities like these seemed to hint at an unusual kind of energy massing on the park's periphery.

He could taste that wayward energy. The word to describe it was *wild*.

Raising his face to the moon, he absorbed the tingle of light on his skin, and sniffed the air. Most of the scents under the trees were familiar to him. He often worked this part of Miami.

He sniffed again and waited to make sure no intruders appeared, knowing that he had to let the moon have her way this time. He had to let the beast out because of his need to get somewhere fast. Werewolf speed was legendary and what he needed right now was to beat the other officers to the crime scene.

In order to beat Davidson and the others to the crime scene on Baker, Colton Killion, officer of the law, but also much more than his seemingly human appearance or profession, needed to morph into a creature that really wasn't an entity other than himself, but an integral part of him.

Not a metaphorical twin or the symptom of a split personality with an evil side, his beast was something he birthed by merely turning himself inside out to expose what lay beneath the surface of his skin.

All true Lycans, with pure, undiluted Lycan blood in them, were born to this. Lycanthropy, the oldest form of werewolfism, meant housing a rare blood disorder that predated history, escaped explanation and encompassed the strongest, fiercest of the beings falling under the heading of *wulf.*

Man-wolf hybrids. Not wolf, but *wulf.* Royal-blooded werewolves, able most of the time to blend in with human society in a world that had unknowingly absorbed them.

"Okay," he said with calm finality. "Bring it on."

Lupine euphoria hit before he finished the invitation. His body quivered with excitement. His core temperature rose in a lightning-fast ascent, reaching the level of "sizzling" before his next intake of air.

Claws popped from the ends of all ten of his fingertips like spring-loaded blades. Brief, swollen seconds of what felt like dark-dipped madness came and went, a throwback to a state people once called Lunacy. And then the process of a man becoming a werewolf took over.

Bones snapped. Ligaments stretched. The sound of hot, wet flesh tearing echoed in the night as his muscles redefined themselves. Colton's stomach knotted and clenched, doubling him over at the waist for a few more tense seconds as rich brown fur sprouted from his pores.

When he again stood upright, feeling inches taller than his usual six-two, and confined and claustrophobic in his clothes, he opened a mouth full of razor-sharp teeth and issued a low guttural growl that mimicked the sound of distant thunder, a sound that was both a response to the

temporary pain of this shape-shift and a keen acknowledgment of being something other than one hundred percent human.

Following that, he belted out a harrowing, piercing
howl that rolled through the park's vast emptiness with
a feral quality that would have sufficed to make any animal's skin crawl, and was meant to do just that.

But as he gathered himself, ready to utilize the animal's agility and superior speed, Colton's senses suddenly
jerked again to a state of full alertness. The feeling of not
being alone made a comeback.

And then, out of the silver-coated darkness, came the
surprise of an answering howl.

What the hell?

Had he missed something out there?

Colton's fur stood on end. He backed up a step,
stunned as another howl followed the first. This one
was higher in pitch than his own vocalization and no
less menacing. But it was also tantalizing and seductive.

Colton glanced up, thinking that the moon must have
been playing a trick. But a third sound came soon after
the second, closer this time, and from ground level.

Haunting, preternatural, seductive in nature, this howl
originated from the part of the park where he'd sensed
strangeness but had seen no one. No human, anyway.

The wulf's immediate natural instinct was to find
what had made that sound and mount it, instead of dashing off in the direction he needed to go. The animal's
need to chase down whatever had made those wolfish
sounds was so strong and insistent that Colton tightened
his mental leash on the beast.

Despite the check of restraint that had him frozen to
stillness, Colton's insides writhed with the new dilemma

he faced due to hearing that answering howl. Should he hurry to Baker Street and see what had happened there, or take the time to find out who or what else roamed this park?

He and his beast weren't completely at odds over voting for the last one. It was, however, an unexpected trip in the agenda when timing might be critical.

Waiting out several more thunderous heartbeats, the blood inside his distended arteries began to burn. Judging by his arousal, he knew that the unexpected visitor was female.

Not just any female, either. Not with a voice like that. This was a she-wulf—powerful, practiced and pure Lycan, or he was a sorry son of a bitch who didn't know a Lycan from a hole in the ground.

Who are you?

Where did you come from?

He hadn't met many purebred female Lycanthropes.

The rarity of full-blooded she-wulfs was the reason true Lycans as a breed were slowly dying out. Females often weren't wired correctly for the transition from human to werewolf, and many of them didn't make it past the Blackout phase of their coming-of-age party for reasons no one actually knew. Special Lycan matchmakers traveled the world to find females to bring home to a qualified clan. He, himself, had been waiting ten years.

And what? One of those rarest of creatures has just announced her presence here in Miami, on the edge of this park? To me?

The acknowledgment of this possibility hit Colton with the force of an oncoming train. His wulf-heavy limbs shuddered. His teeth snapped together, filling his mouth with the acrid taste of his own blood. He grew hotter, and a little confused.

Hell, his human side wanted to chase after whatever had made those sounds as much as the beast did. Finding a *She* fulfilled a powerful need and provided a possible solution to a lot of problems of sheer physical necessity for a male. *Keep the line going. Keep it strong. Choose a mate.*

But damn the timing of finding this female. Not only did duty call, it also called with an overriding personal necessity that meant the possible welfare of his family. He had taken an oath to protect and serve not only the population of Miami but the few Lycans left in his scattered clan. Oaths were binding for werewolves, and lifelong.

In addition to that, he might know the cop who had been shot.

Shit. He visualized the scene. There would be officers, CSI techs and television crews all over the place, knocking on doors.

And a she-wulf appeared now?

Really bad timing. Effing bad.

Worse yet, his beast had already driven him to take a step toward the female's invitation, stretching at its leash.

Colton hauled himself back with difficulty and a barked chastisement. *Can't have this. Get a freaking grip. There's too much at stake.*

Good advice in the best of times, but the beast's needs were elemental and approaching the point of no return. It was hungry to bury its cock in that female's damp, furry, feminine folds, and angered by the restraint.

He had to get away, though leaving this spot would be one of the hardest things he had ever done. He had to ignore this she-wulf, knowing the odds of ever finding another one.

Resolutely, regretfully, he echoed the she-wulf's call with a low-pitched howl that could have been translated as: *You have no idea how sorry I am for having to go.* Though it actually meant so very much more than that, and perhaps even the extinction of his family's line.

Stepping out from under the trees, and filled with regret, Colton took off. Alone. Into the night. Toward the scent of a downed cop's blood in the distance.

Chapter 2

Rosalind Kirk dropped to her haunches and slammed a furred-up fist into the ground to keep herself from following the Were in the park, whose scent was new, feral and overtly masculine.

Her hackles rose with a mixture of curiosity and anger.

That wulf had ignored her invitation.

She stared at the way he cut a smooth swath through the trees, running faster than anything she had ever seen. He was a big werewolf, tall and powerfully built. His brown pelt blended with the shadows. Highlighted by moonlight, it appeared that he wore clothes.

Strange.

Although anger flared over his rude rejection of her call, Rosalind's heart raced as she watched him run. She felt the rhythm of the movement of the brown Were's legs in her muscles, and heard the harshness of his breathing echo inside her chest. All this made her feel disturbed in a way she'd never experienced before.

Her fur ruffled.

Her chin lifted.

Finding a male of her species hadn't been the reason she had slipped her father's net when he wasn't looking, but suddenly seemed like a bonus.

She'd been homesick for her bayou property, where she could run unhindered. Here in Miami, where her father had accepted an invitation to visit the Landaus—an ancient Lycan line as old as her own—she had been quarantined on the estate's grounds. Her father had forbidden her to go past the expansive property's stone walls.

Right. Like she'd listen to that, or be chained to a ridiculous confinement, however lovingly the directive had been issued by a father who said he had her best interests in mind.

Like she had ever met his expectations.

I'm a woman now.

Even her father, an elegant, intelligent Lycan, had no idea how elevated her metabolism became on a night like this one.

Sure, it was dangerous being out here in wulf form. There were plenty of risks in ignoring the rules and restrictions. It was equally dangerous to expose herself to a member of another pack without being properly introduced. Yet her boundless need for freedom resonated in every bone and cell in her body. The moon's influence blasted through her like some kind of invisible ray, dispersing her humanness almost completely.

She had too much pent-up energy, and her search for freedom had been interrupted before she'd used it up. Her focus had been riveted to a big brown werewolf sprinting in the opposite direction who hadn't paid any attention to her at all.

Didn't you hear me, Were?

Shaking her head without taking her eyes off him, she leaned forward, into his scent. A series of disgruntled growls rumbled in her chest, registering her displeasure. Maybe Miami Weres held contempt for those outside of their packs, and that's why he had turned from her.

His loss. She was lithe, smart, fast and strong—a worthy mate for a purebred male. In spite of that, she had been shielded from all eligible partners and kept from pursuing any outside company at all, leaving her to wonder what everyone had been waiting for.

She was sick of the tight ring of supervision surrounding her, and ready for her first close-up with a prime example of her species.

Like you, pretty, brown-pelted wulf.

Wasn't finding a mate what she was eventually supposed to do?

Had the brown Were considered her unworthy, when the whispers behind her back at the Landaus' place had described her as special?

Special...

The dreaded Blackout phase wired into her family's line had come upon her at thirteen, instead of the usual age of twenty-one. Surviving her body's internal rewiring at so young an age had caused her to acquire a stellar repertoire of abilities.

Special...

At fifteen, she outdistanced her father in races. By sixteen, she could painlessly shape-shift in seconds whenever she chose to, with or without the moon. Even her father couldn't do that.

Tonight, at the matronly age of twenty, eight-foot-tall stone walls hadn't stood a chance of containing her. One agile leap was all it took to escape the Landaus' boundaries.

Piece of cake.

In her defense, she hadn't planned on being outside those walls for very long. Merely one good sprint to calm her had been the justification…

Until she felt the ongoing song of this male's Lycan blood as if that song had been written for her. Until she had sensed him in the shadows as clearly as if he'd stood five feet away.

Even now, his earthy, alluring scent pulled her like some sort of unavoidable undertow.

Unsure of what to do next, because she actually was socially inept, and had been more or less a prisoner in her own home all of her life, Rosalind didn't completely understand the feelings of wanting to catch up with the brown wulf in spite of his rebuff.

Seconds ticked past as she stood there, longing to give chase. Her legs trembled with the desire to move. Her dark muzzle quirked at the thought of werewolves having one-night stands in public spaces, and how that would go down.

So, which way to go? Back to her father, or after the rude brown Were?

With a glance over her shoulder toward the Landaus' walled border in the distance, Rosalind straightened to her full five-foot-five-inch height. Her black pelt—thick, rich, shining like polished obsidian in the moonlight—reflected the bright look of rebelliousness in her amber-green eyes as she made her decision.

* * *

As Colton had feared, the five-hundred block of Baker Street crawled with people. Too many people gumming up a crime scene always made a bad situation worse.

He hit the side of a building hard with his left shoulder to shock his wulf side back to reality. Closing his eyes, blowing out a breath, he willed his beast into the background and corralled it with a word of promise. *Later.*

The reversal of his shift was equally as hard on his body, but one hell of a lot quicker. Everything rearranged with a soft snapping of ligament and bone. On human legs, Colton cut a path through the hordes of neighbors out in full force behind fluttering expanses of yellow crime tape. But after those few moments of letting the beast out, the sensory bombardment of being near to all these human bodies weighed him down. Fresh from his run, his thermostat had yet to settle. He was damp with perspiration and needed about ten more deep breaths in a quiet place where he could fully recover before showing himself—a luxury he didn't have.

In spite of the distraction in the park, he had beat Davidson to the scene. Six other cruisers were parked along the street. Two emergency vehicles were in attendance with their back doors wide-open. Uniforms moved like an army of ants up and down sidewalks in the dark.

Colton grabbed hold of a blue uniform whose name tag said EMT Smith. "What happened here?"

"Homicide," Smith said after checking out Colton's badge.

"Where? Who?" Colton's voice cracked with emotion.

"Name's Connelly. And one officer was shot after arriving at the scene."

"Connelly." Colton processed the news. "Which Connelly?"

"All of them."

"What?"

"The whole family was killed. Two adults and two kids. It's one of the worst scenes I've been to. Blood and body parts are spewed all over the place. The house looks like a freaking horror movie set. No offense or disrespect, Officer, but I need some air. I've only been on this job for three weeks."

Colton felt a rush of adrenaline returning in a bad way. He knew the Connellys. His parents had socialized with that family on occasion. A year ago he had helped to build their kids' swing set.

But the arctic adrenaline dump jarring him was also an indication that he needed to chill out in public. EMT Smith was still looking at him as if the guy awaited permission to be dismissed, so that he could slink away and hurl his dinner.

"Thanks," Colton said. Staring at what Smith had called a house of horror, he added, "The injured officer? How is he?"

"He's been taken to Miami General. Took a bullet in the upper abdomen, but it looks like the gun might have belonged to one of the other victims, perhaps shooting at whatever moved. I heard another EMT say that if he's in good shape physically, he'll probably make it."

"His name?"

"Don't know. Sorry. Got to go." Smith hurried back to his truck.

Colton looked down the block to where a city streetlight should have been glowing and wasn't. The bad feeling in his gut quadrupled in intensity. His parents' house sat beneath that blown-out bulb. The front windows were dark.

He ran. Ducking under the yellow tape with his eyes locked on his parents' house, he rushed across the lawn and up the front steps. Forgetting himself and his innate strength, he tore the screen door off its hinges and reached for the knob.

He stepped across the threshold, where the brutal odor of blood and exposed Lycan secrets hit him in a moment of monumental frenzy, and the severed head of his proud Lycan father lay on the carpet at Colton's feet.

Stunned by the sight, Colton let out a wail of anguish that nearly buckled him at the knees.

Chapter 3

Rosalind heard the sound of a Lycan's roar and froze midstep. Registering the sounds as pain and loss, the intensity of the emotion in the roar rocked her. Hearing something so personal made her want to run away. Stubbornly, she stayed.

Drifts of a dreadful odor hit her, tearing her from the shadows. *Enemy stink. But what kind?*

After the darkness of the park, the revolving lights on the police cars hurt her light-sensitive eyes. She was in werewolf form and in danger because of it. She couldn't be found like this. She didn't dare follow the big male's muffled howl of pain. She wasn't used to crowds. With so many people around, changing back to her human semblance wasn't an option, since she'd be naked if she did.

Nevertheless, she was drawn to the sound of the brown Were's pain, and moved through the dark spaces between houses on the opposite side of the street, her black pelt acting as camouflage in the night.

She was stopped by the sight of three human police officers heading toward where she hid.

Time to get away.

She had to leave the wulf and what had happened here, and didn't want to. That sound. The pain in it. *Where are you?*

She had been gone for a long time now. Her father would be frantic. Still, she couldn't dismiss her feelings of connection to this male, or what might have happened here. His pain had become her pain. She hurt, and shared his sorrow.

Hugging the building, she watched the scene with her heart in her throat. *Go, or stay?* For the second time in so very few minutes, the decision of what to do was a heavy weight on her shoulders.

Colton's world began to spin. Walls closed in.

He made himself stand still and forced down another scream, too shocked to regulate his breathing. If this was what was left of his father, he definitely didn't want to stumble upon what might be left of his mother. He couldn't pinpoint her life force amid the carnage when he should have been able to. Her amiable presence didn't call out to him like it always had.

His body wasn't so frozen by shock that he didn't feel his heart break. His insides roiled. His mouth was dry. At the same time, a nagging insistence warned that he had to move, had to take care of this. Officers might knock on the door any minute now. Beyond family, there was a secret to protect.

The cop side of his training began to seep through the

sickening whirl, perhaps as a defense mechanism for coping with a loss this great. With that training, one thing became perfectly clear: whoever had enacted this rampage of evil deeds not only knew who the werewolves in this neighborhood were, but how to kill them.

Silver bullets in the chest or a full beheading were the only ways to truly rid the world of a strain of very powerful Lycans. The Killions had been around for more years than a human could count. They knew how to defend themselves and should have scented trouble before it arrived.

Why then, how then, had his parents been taken down in their own home? The answer came to him in the form of a jolt that further messed with his head and equilibrium.

No human did this.

What about the Connellys then who, according to the young EMT, had been slaughtered? Not beheaded, but "slaughtered." Could those poor people have been decoy killings to cover up the murder of his family?

His parents had been down-to-earth in their day-to-day living. His father had been a college professor. His mother had worked in a dress store. They hadn't concerned themselves with their royal genes or the special Lycan blood in their veins that made them honored within their species. They had raised him in the same down-home way, and instilled in him their values.

The Killions were protectors. Had always been protectors…of Lycan secrets, of their Lycan blood, in their low-key relationships with the humans they lived among.

"Not just paranoia," Colton snapped. "There's more here to discover."

He smelled something beyond the cloying odor of Lycan blood. In order to identify this, Colton made himself breathe. Through the forced intake of air he began to soak up anomalies in the environment, realizing that every minute he stood there in a state of silent agony was a minute wasted in going after the monsters responsible for this heinous crime.

"Who were you?" he demanded angrily of the invisible, murderous fiends, tuning in to clues by opening up his senses up full throttle.

"Help me, wulf."

The arrival of his beast's keen awareness came to him like a swift kick in the solar plexus as it melded with his own intuition. Colton glanced up. Hovering near the ceiling lay a subtle scent, hardly there at all, that made him sway on his feet.

"Can't be," he objected. "Look again."

The wulf growled adamantly.

"Christ! Vampires?"

Colton took the sudden weight of his beast pressing against him as confirmation of the deduction being correct. Could it honestly be true, though? "Yes. Hell." Only the dead would stink like old soil and sour, aged, rotting wood. Nothing else could possibly smell like that.

There were vampires loose in Miami, and this was very bad news. The worst kind of news. And a Lycan's age-old enemies had found his family.

Not many humans knew about the presence of werewolves in their communities. If the world wasn't ready for werewolves, how would people feel about a new breed of enemy that amounted to a plague of murderous bloodsuckers in their neighborhoods?

"Shackled." Colton's voice broke. The awful truth was that he couldn't warn the world to be on guard. He couldn't tell anyone what had happened here, or allow this scene to come under public scrutiny. He was therefore virtually shackled to silence.

"Besides, who would believe it?"

If this had been a vampire kill, no evidence would have been left for CSI teams to catch. There'd be no fingerprints or footprints or detectable stray hairs for any system to analyze. For all the advances in human technological wizardry, as far as that technology went, the dead were dead.

Still, other than trained werewolf hunters, only vampires would know exactly how to take a werewolf down. Unlike with human criminals confronting a powerful Were family able to hold their own, vampires couldn't easily die trying to tackle a wolf-human hybrid, since vampires had the advantage of being dead already.

And damn it, if the rumors were true, those fanged children of the night were the fastest creatures on the planet. One blink, and they could be on you, then gone before your last breath rattled.

Reason this out. Why did they strike at us here?

Reasoning was another important part of the cop game, as was following suppositions with hopes of getting somewhere.

It was possible that his parents, with the addition of the Connellys as a distraction for the law enforcement system, had died because of a centuries-old vendetta between species. Vampires and Weres hated each other.

Then again, maybe a vamp had merely stumbled upon his parents somehow and had been hungry.

"No. That's not it," he shouted, because vampires hadn't been here for a drink. Bloodsuckers couldn't ingest werewolf blood of any kind. Lycans were poisonous to them.

"Premeditated strike, then."

If his family had been outside tonight, conversing with the full moon, they would have been ten times stronger and able to withstand an attack. But for some reason, they hadn't made it to the door.

"Hate crime."

The mortal world was filled with such things in this day and age. So was the supernatural one.

The more Colton thought about it, the more likely it seemed that the Connellys had merely been in the wrong place at the wrong time. After the carnage here, it was possible the pale, dead, fanged bastards had worked up an appetite.

Besides all the usual gangsters and gangbangers around, vampires were a horrific addition to Miami's rising crime wave, and what had happened on this block might be an indication of things to come.

As Colton stared down at his father's silver-haired head, he felt the rise of a blazing anger at the atrocity committed to a man he dearly loved. He couldn't stay here to grieve, though.

"They're all gone." He whispered this with a grim finality that made the beast inside him spasm with anger and disgust. He and his wulf shared the agony because they were one, one and the same with the same memories.

With a brief glance to the door, he remembered that there was a young EMT named Smith outside who had run from a gruesome sight a few houses away. He wondered what the poor guy would think of this.

"No one will know that two sets of murders have been committed tonight," he said. For now, he had to manage his pain so that he could find his mother.

Stepping over the body of his father, he searched the room, then the house. His hopes rose, as hopes always did, despite his inner premonition. Maybe she had been spared. Possibly his mother hadn't been here, which would have been a rare occasion, since imprinted pairs wouldn't tolerate separation.

Colton searched all over again, feeling each agonizing second that hurtled by.

Then he found his mother on the back porch step, half in the house, half out, as if she'd been reaching for the moon. The brutality that had been dealt to her washed over him like an icy wave. Nausea threatened. She also had been beheaded.

"Damn those filthy bloodsuckers!" he cried.

Two members of one of the oldest Lycan families in existence had been taken out. And the stench of the undead hung over the tidy backyard like an insidious vapor.

Despite the gnawing ache growing by bounds in Colton's chest, he'd have to invent a way to cover this up. His pain, great enough to be nearly intolerable, had to be internalized. In order to go on, he'd have to focus elsewhere.

"Vengeance." His whisper fell flat. Vengeance was an emotional state Lycans had tried to outdistance as human populations began to rise and the sheer number of humans forced Weres into hiding. Revenge was a reaction Weres had learned to tamp down in favor of more peaceful aspirations and acceptable coexistence.

Contrary to all that, rage was overtaking him. He felt sick, shaky, pissed off and ready to do something about it.

As Colton lifted his mother's limp, desecrated body in his arms, his beast, tucked inside him, trembled with rage.

* * *

Aware of the disturbed emotions surfing the air, Rosalind had to move. She ran past the hordes of cops and stopped when she spotted a house that radiated the familiar scent of Were. Silently, she crept up the steps and through the open doorway.

The front room was dark and empty, but it reeked of both sadness and Lycan damage.

Not just Were. Lycan.

The reality of that turned her stomach. Chills covered every inch of her body. Did the brown Were live here? What had happened in this place?

She rolled a series of throaty growls meant as a warning that if someone was in this house, they now had company.

No reply came.

Exploring on bare, padding feet, she found two bodies on a bed in a small room, and choked back a cry. These were dead Lycans. Someone had placed them there.

The scene seemed insanely surreal, but the room also gave off the scent of the male she had followed. He had been here mere seconds before she arrived. She hadn't missed him by much.

Leaping over the furniture, feeling her anger sift to the surface of her skin, Rosalind raced for the back door. Then she was out again, in the moonlight, back in the relative comfort of the cover of darkness.

Chapter 4

Vampire tracks weren't easy to follow. Nevertheless, Colton knew a trail of rot when he smelled one.

The alley behind the houses snaked through the neighborhood, eventually leading back to the park. Colton started that way without getting far. An icy prickle at the base of his neck made him spin around. He scanned the dark. This section of the alley seemed too quiet. No one was out. Not one dog barked.

Standing in the open, he allowed moonlight to caress his human hands and forearms as he waited for his senses to skip past the tragedy and delve into the arena of hunter and prey. Red flags waving in his mind told him the vampires had been this way not long before. More than one of them, by the intensity of the odor.

It was no wonder that the neighborhood dogs had run. Rolling his shoulders helped him to gain control of his tension, but his nerves felt like long threads of fire. Inching sideways, closer to a fence, he cocked his head to listen for clues. All the while, his beast pummeled at him, wanting to be free, its desire to take over the hunt stirred by a cop's ingrained need to catch some killers.

But freeing his animal side was not doable at the moment with uniforms swarming around a short distance behind. He had to fight the moon and the wulf for the time being and hope he'd win.

"No movement. No sound."

Gazing through the shadows of the alley, Colton felt his knuckles ache from holding back his claws. The sinister stink of these particular blood-drinking intruders was especially bothersome to his beast.

Colton had never seen a vampire up close, yet his soul seemed to recognize them. The wolf particles embedded in his long-term memory knew the smell and taste and feel of an ancient enemy.

"Burned toast," he said, picking a valid description of the sum of all those parts. "Disgusting."

The beast gave a rattle that shook Colton to his boots. The closeness of monsters was luring his animal instincts to a riotous state that messed with his hard-won self-control.

He flinched as the ligaments in his shoulders and knees began to stretch, and exhaled some air as the skin covering his biceps began to bubble. The whooshing sound he heard was a claw bursting through his skin. Another claw appeared. Then more, until all ten fingers were lethal.

Did this minimorph mean that the wulf knew something he didn't? He was willing to bet that it did.

A shout came from behind, untimely as hell because

it came from a cop who had no doubt seen something in the alley. Colton was in uniform, but his body was half in transition and burning badly with the need to chuck the binding accoutrements tying him to a human's sense of justice.

"Hey! You!" the uniform said from the other end of the alley; a cop who couldn't help here or offer moral support. A human, either in or out of uniform, would in fact be easy pickings for any walking undead hanging around.

He had to remove the cop from this equation.

"Killion," he shouted back to the officer, his voice gruff. He coughed, unlocked his throat and added, "Metro PD. I'm on it. All is clear. No sign of anything back here."

"Okay," the cop shouted back.

"Killion?" Davidson's familiar shout followed the other one.

"Yeah. It's me," he said.

"You're one fast son of a bitch. You actually beat me here?"

"Pays to be in shape."

"Not if that doesn't include pizza."

More footfalls, then Davidson's final remark. "We'll go around the other way. The bastards had to come and go from somewhere."

After agonizing seconds spent waiting for the men to disappear, Colton's internal heat finally overwhelmed him, and his clothes ripped apart at the seams.

Rosalind watched the brown-furred werewolf hurdle the wooden fence as if it were nothing as soon as the humans at the head of the alley had gone. She covered the length of that alley in twelve huge strides. One good leap after that, and she, too, was over the fence.

She had seen the beautiful Lycan before and after his shift, but this time she had been close enough to take stock—a second rare occurrence in the highly personal world of werewolves and only, she supposed, because he had been distracted to the point of not recognizing the presence of another wulf in the area.

Her brown wulf had been incredibly handsome as a man. His face was angular. Tanned skin stretched over high cheekbones. His mouth was wide, his eyes deep-set. Dark, slightly wavy hair framed those features, long enough to cover the tops of his ears. Each strand glinted like gold in the moonlight.

The man side of the Were was tall, his physique leanly muscular, with broad shoulders and a narrow waist. He had spectacularly molded thighs that hinted at a Were's hidden strengths. Rosalind guessed him to be in his late twenties, though it was hard to gauge werewolves, especially since she had met so few of them.

This one had been not only beautiful, but naked. Her first naked male of any kind. And he was definitely a perfect specimen that she imagined most women would call mouthwatering.

The skin of his bare back and buttocks had shined with a tanned tautness that suggested he saw a lot of sun without wearing clothes. No white lines traversed the flowing, golden flesh. Nor did he bear tattoos, other than the ring of scar tissue on one upper arm in the shape of a wolf's bite that all true Lycans possessed.

Rosalind passed a clawed hand over her own similar mark, taking this as a further sign of an unmistakable bond with whoever he was.

She had held herself back so he couldn't see her when he'd turned. She had observed how a light drift of masculine hair ran the length of his powerful chest and over his sculpted abs to become even darker as it nestled between his legs. The feature that had been momentarily displayed between those thighs made Rosalind flush.

And then there was the werewolf.

The beast that unfolded from all that glorious humanness had brown-auburn fur the same color as the man's hair. Denser than his human form, and heavier with tension-loaded muscle, this werewolf was also damn near perfect, and too magnificent to be real.

Rosalind fielded the arrival of a full-fledged hunger for him. Battling sensations that were new, instinctual, primal, she wanted to wrap her arms around him and lick his golden-brown neck.

Her sexual appetite intensified with each ripple of his incredible Lycan muscle. But Rosalind also sensed a pain-filled anger that would prohibit him from shifting in such close proximity to others. His body visibly shook with that anger.

In spite of all the possible repercussions of empathy with a stranger, as well as a fair amount of misplaced erotic hallucinations, Rosalind followed him when he moved, as if she were his shadow.

He had ignored her in the park, not because she was a stranger, she now knew, but because he had been needed elsewhere. He hadn't rejected her out of choice.

Picking up her speed when he started to run, she raced in his wake, keeping back apace, watchful, careful, realizing that she was going to pay for this in one way or another when she got back to Judge Landau's place.

Then again, surely her father would understand the situation once he heard about the Lycan killings, and comprehend her need to help this wronged Were. Maybe she could lead this male to the Landau retreat, where he'd be safe and among friends, even if Were packs were private and didn't usually mingle.

At that moment, she was willing to place her own life and secrets in jeopardy for the chance to offer comfort and support to the first young Lycan she had ever come across, one who made her feel viciously alive.

Silent words tumbled in her throat.

You are not alone.

My strength will come in handy. I give my strength to you.

As Rosalind sprinted after him, she felt the chill of a terrible premonition about what awaited them both in the cover of darkness. The night rippled around them as though tugged by an unseen force.

If werewolves had pockets for cell phones, she'd have sent an SOS to her father. Still, in whatever faced them out there, two Lycans were always better than one.

Pity the poor soul, she growled, *who finds this out firsthand.*

Colton ran like a fiend, working with each stride to maintain enough humanity to keep his reasoning powers functioning. He couldn't afford for Otherness to overtake him completely—or for his pain to overwhelm him.

Once he was through the last of the suburban homes, his vision sharpened. He sped across open ground on the west side of the park, heading for the trees, calculating how many buildings rose in the distance on the eastern and southern sides.

He knew the night creatures hadn't headed toward

those buildings, toward civilization. Rationalization told him that perhaps they hadn't been randomly hungry, but on a mission. There had been plenty of opportunities in the surrounding neighborhoods between here and his house for a freak's blood buffet, and yet they had picked his street.

So, where are the murderous vipers headed?

North of the park lay the posh estates of prominent Miami citizens wealthy enough to enjoy the luxury of space and privacy. Big houses protected by security gates. Lycan presence lay in at least one of them. The famous Landaus, head of their own pack. Surely no fanged monsters existed near there.

His knowledge of the habits of vampires was insufficient, and that was a snag. Did they have clans, packs, dens? Did the presence of these few mean, like cockroaches, there were others in the area?

What sort of weapon would de-animate a creature already dead? The mythology listed wooden stakes, exposure to sunlight and beheading. Thinking that holy water could do the trick had, so rumor said, always been a mistake. Garlic as a deterrent was laughable.

The only question remaining was about how many vampires a werewolf could handle at once with his bare hands.

No matter. Have to try.

Finding his rhythm in much the same way that real wolves chased down prey, Colton took in great gulps of night air that were like candy to a beast so hot inside and out. Apprehension was in itself a kind of narcotic.

He ran, driven by what may have been his own kind of bloodlust, able to tell he was getting closer to the vampires. The mood in the park changed, darkened, intensified, along the park's edge.

Movement.

Rustling in the shadows.

Don't vampires know that Lycans can hear?

Colton veered to his right with his nerve endings blazing in time to see an outline of whatever was out there coming on exceptionally fast. A fuzzy blur.

His senses all but exploded. He had time for just one more breath and to bare his teeth. Then they were on him.

Too many of them, maybe, Colton acknowledged as his claws began to swing.

Stunned for a moment by the sight ahead of her, Rosalind slammed to a halt some distance away from the disturbance to get her bearings.

These weren't humans the Were had gone after. She didn't immediately recognize the scent, but the odor of maliciousness these creatures gave off saturated the otherwise spring-flavored night with something similar to the iron-like taint of blood.

They were a kind of creature new to her, and they moved too fast to see details, or get a head count. Ten of them, maybe twelve, she figured. Fifteen?

Dropping from the trees like winged bats falling on an insect, they had either been waiting for some other poor, unsuspecting soul to trespass here, or else they had laid a well-planned ambush for the brown Were, having expected him to pursue.

She gave a soft roar of sympathy as she carefully studied the scene.

The big Were rushed through the blur of monsters. The beautiful werewolf who had been a golden-skinned man not long before this tore into the attackers with aggressive, fluid skills and a look of pure madness on his face.

She caught a word from the brown Were's mind without knowing how she could do that. *Vampire.* That's what this werewolf faced.

Her blood began to pound in her veins. Some distant part of her recognized the concept of bloodsucker even if she didn't fully understand it. What she did realize was that a masterful, powered-up Were didn't stand much of a chance here without the aid of several more like him. There were just too many monsters in this fight.

Also clear was the realization that she truly couldn't leave him to fight alone.

I'm here.

Moving in from the werewolf's left side with the fury of a black tornado, Rosalind plowed through the haze of bodies, wielding her claws like the weapons they were originally intended to be, slashing at everything in her way.

The shockingly gaunt, fleshless creatures targeting the brown Were shrieked when hit, and came back at her baring long yellow fangs. Up close, their faces were spectral and expressionless. Dull red eyes sank deeply into bottomless sockets. They had Lycan blood on their breath.

The brown Were, too busy to acknowledge her help or toss her a look, had felled two monsters by landing well-placed swipes to their necks that cut cleanly through to the bone. When those monsters sagged, their bodies exploded into a rainfall of foul-scented gray ash that drove the remaining creatures into a frenzy.

Only two down—out of too many.

Using the Were's technique as an example, Rosalind

aimed for their necks and exploded one bony mass of her own.

Her first kill.

An odd sensation flowed through her, as though she had swallowed the wind and it continued to churn her insides. As gray ash clouded the area, her beast's energy began to blaze. Surging ahead like a caged animal that had finally been freed, she felt a new and terrible energy take her over; it flowed through her muscle like a river of fire, and left an icy residue.

She doubled her efforts.

More vampires came on, each of them fighting with ungodly speed and an unearthly agility of jaws that housed far too many gnashing, needle-sharp teeth.

The new, crazed kind of energy fueled Rosalind's fury. An unrecognizable thrill for battle made her fight on without thinking of the consequences. She was fast, strong and good at fighting. She felt as if she were made for this.

She wanted to kill them all.

Driven by that objective, she whirled, bit and clawed at the corpselike flesh around her. As she took another vampire down, Rosalind howled.

The air trembled with her silent battle cry.

Death comes to all who oppose me!

Colton fought with all his might. To the right. To the left. Coming from behind. Dropping down from above his head.

He barely heard the sounds over his own rattled breathing. He was moving so fast, he'd lost some control over his actions. His arms were tiring. He'd lost count of how many vampires he'd taken down, but had taken several vicious blows himself.

He smelled blood, and knew it was his. His face was damp, and it wasn't sweat. In five years on the police force, he had garnered a reputation for fearlessness, driven by a werewolf's need to protect innocent citizens and the knowledge of how fast he would heal if he were ever to be injured on the job. But this was no street gang or worrisome mob. This was a nest of particularly blood-thirsty monsters, attacking with intent.

More of them arrived. Each kill was replaced by another set of snapping teeth. Another Were had arrived from who knew where, but he had no idea what was happening to that beast, and had no opportunity to look. He thought he could hear that other Were close by, making growling sounds that mirrored his own. But the fight had gone on for so long, with no end in sight, that Colton wondered if they'd make it out of this one.

He fought with a renewed vigor, bolstered by the thought that someone had come to his aid. He swung his arms, swiped through fetid vampire flesh with his claws, and bit through the bones of several hands and many thin necks. And still the monsters came on; an unending supply of mindless foes animated by something purely evil in design.

God, where did these monsters come from?

I'm sorry, he wanted to say to the Were that was someplace beside him because, too late, he had realized that this may have been a trap.

Rosalind slashed her way through the flood of fanged monsters, determined to beat her way to the brown Were's side. But as she finally reached him and saw the wounds he had already taken, she opened her throat again and let out a howl that rose from the depths of her soul.

Her beautiful Were's face and shoulders had been slashed nearly to pieces. He was covered in blood that seemed to drive the monsters mad. And still, as his limbs moved, weaker now but with whatever determination he had left, the brown Were was a magnificent beast.

Her howl echoed in the park with the effect of a sonic boom, a throwback to ancient times when like called like, and species survival was paramount. The call was answered.

Sounds rose above the fighting, rolling like thunder over the bloodstained grass. She recognized her father's voice, alongside the furious vocalization of another wulf. A third howl arrived, and a fourth. From just past the trees, harrowing werewolf voices lifted in an eerily beautiful Lycan symphony, crowding out the grunts of the remaining bloodsuckers. These were low, aged voices—terrible, experienced and deadly to all that would stand against their song.

Rosalind's big mistake was stopping to listen.

She heard the terrible growling breath that escaped from the brown Were's throat, knowing with a sudden and overwhelming feeling of horror that she had hesitated a mere minute too long.

Chapter 5

Rosalind couldn't stop pacing. Her heart continued to race as she moved back and forth in the hallway leading to Judge Landau's living room. She felt caged, and anxious. The walls were closing in. She needed to be out in the dark, under the moon, where she could breathe…but she couldn't go anywhere.

Her father faced her, sitting on a step, observing her motions in a quiet manner.

"He will heal?" she asked him.

"Not completely, I'm afraid," he replied.

"We always heal, miraculously," she pointed out.

"This is different, Rosalind. He has been torn to pieces by vampires. It's a miracle that he survived at all."

Rosalind shook her head, and continued to pace. Her heart was racing. She hadn't been able to ease the edge of her anxiety since her father and his friends had turned the tide of the fight, and then brought the severely injured brown Were here.

Her brown Were.

"The wounds have ravaged his immune system. If he comes out of this, he will be changed," her father said.

Rosalind paused, every muscle feeling strained. "How, exactly, will he change?"

"We don't yet know the full extent."

"Then how can you predict that he won't completely recover?"

"You saw him not minutes ago, Rosalind. What did you see?"

"He is alive, and breathing much easier than he did two days ago."

"What else?"

"His wounds are already better. Less vivid. Closed over."

"Please state the obvious, Rosalind."

Her father expected a reply. She didn't offer him one.

"His color has changed," her father said. "You saw that. What was he before this happened?"

Her father was in the way. She could have leaped over him, but knew that he was keeping her from going upstairs, to the wounded Were's side.

"Brown and beautiful," she said. "He was brown-pelted, and beautiful."

"And now?" her father pressed.

"His hair is white. His skin is pale. But maybe that will change again."

Jared Kirk shook his head. "White Weres exist only in legend, or so we thought. No one here has ever seen one, and the minds of the Weres visiting the Landaus go back quite a distance."

Rosalind noted how her father paused to allow her time to soak that information in.

"He won't be what he was before this if he heals enough to open his eyes," he continued. "He's a ghost, Rosalind. That's what legend calls a wulf who shouldn't have survived such horrific trauma, yet somehow did."

Trauma. Was that the right word for near total destruction? Rosalind didn't like the description. It left a bitter taste in her mouth.

"If he were to continue to get better," her father went on, "he will likely choose to walk his own path, because he will have one foot in this world and one in the next. He has straddled the fine line at the end of his own existence."

Rosalind ignored the fact that her father was eyeing her closely. She held her breath until he spoke again.

"Ghosts see out of the eyes of both worlds. This wulf was strong, and of royal lineage, but who could be the same after what has happened?"

"He is a wulf, and a cop. He will know what to do," she protested.

"Rosalind. Listen to what I'm telling you. No soul can survive the cost of those kinds of internal damages intact. He wasn't just wounded, he was mauled by vampires. Their blood has mingled with his. This fight didn't kill him, but it has changed him. He has been altered. The white hair proves that. The best healers can't change or reverse the process."

No, Rosalind silently protested. She had just found her brave, lovely Were, and wasn't ready to let him go. She was eager to find out why she felt connected to him, and why she wished so fervently for him to heal.

She desperately wanted to be near to this wulf—ghost

or otherwise. She could feel him upstairs. She wanted to go to him.

"Maybe those are just stories, about the ghost wulf," she suggested.

This strapping Were could not have been broken by vampires. Fate couldn't be so cruel.

"Truth often fans the flames of myth and rumor, as you well know," her father counseled.

"And some rumors are just rumors."

"Werewolves, to the human population, are a myth. But we exist. We blend with humans because we choose to. We keep our secrets because it's better for everyone that we do. A ghost wulf who has had a life here won't be able to blend so easily. What will his friends think when they see him? How could he go back to work, or explain?"

Rosalind stopped pacing and looked at her father.

"He will leave them behind," he father said. "He might choose to live in the shadows, on the fringes, not because he will be forced to, but because he will have to make peace with what he has become."

"Which is?"

"An old legend, made new. A ghost wulf. Part man, part wulf, and for all we know, part vampire."

Her father sighed, as if these explanations were a chore, and painful for him.

"You don't know that. You're not sure of anything," Rosalind said.

"You're right. Time will tell. But the elders who have tended to him have noted that something new has entered his bloodstream, and that out of necessity, this new thing will likely change his soul."

This information didn't sit well with Rosalind. In spite

of everything being told to her, she still felt connected to the Were, oddly enough, now more than ever.

She had rushed to his side when the other Weres had arrived. She had seen him close his eyes, and fall to his knees.

She had pressed her mouth to his while the others finished off the vampires, and breathed into him some of her own chaotic energy.

If he was changed, as her father was saying, theirs would be a sympathetic bond. She had been forced to be a loner, almost held captive by her father for most of her life. She could relate to being apart from others, and living on the fringes. She had been called special. Which also translated to mean different.

They were both different.

A ghost and a loner. She and this injured Lycan were perfect for each other.

Her father's voice dropped in tone. "You can't wish him back to normal, Rosalind. You must accept this as fact, just as the Were upstairs will have to accept his fate."

Rosalind squeezed her eyes shut to avoid her father's wary expression. But the thought persisted that he had kept her from all Weres in the past, and that maybe this warning was just another example of her father's overbearing overprotection.

Well, she wanted to say to him, *I can't be kept from this one. I won't be kept from him. Not this one.*

"He's a ghost because of me," she said. "The responsibility is mine."

"Not so," her father countered vehemently. "A vampire attack caused this. You were brave, but also foolish to have joined in such a fight. It's a miracle you weren't hurt equally as badly, and that Landau and the elders were with me, searching for you. You could be lying in a bed upstairs. What would I have done then?"

"Those monsters killed his family. He went after them, just as you or I or Judge Landau would have. He did this alone."

A long pause preceded her father's next remarks.

"Rosalind. It's important that you hear what I'm going to say to you now. You and I will go home tomorrow. You have to let this wulf go. We will leave him in the Landaus' care."

"No."

"I'm not blind or insensitive to your feelings, but this male is not for you. He wouldn't have been compatible before this event, and certainly isn't now. You have no idea what would happen if..." Her father's voice trailed off, then returned. "You have no inkling of what his life might be like if he heals well enough to keep it."

You have no idea what would happen if...

If what? Rosalind wanted to know, picking up on the unsaid portion of an argument and tasting the tang of withheld secrets.

Rosalind chilled up as she stared at her father with a new thought. *Has he been keeping secrets from me all this time?*

"I want to stay with him," she said.

"That's impossible." Her father shook his head.

"Judge Landau will let me stay, if I ask."

"You won't ask. I forbid it."

"Then the wounded Were can come with us."

"You cannot have your way in this, Rosalind. My decision is final. You might be in real danger here, now that vampires have your scent in their filthy noses."

"The bloodsuckers were killed."

"They can transmit signals we have no notion of."

Rosalind stubbornly stood her ground, legs splayed, hands on her hips. "It was my fault he was hurt so badly. My inattention did this. I owe him. Don't you get that?"

"The Landaus are a powerful clan with powerful friends, and are experienced healers. He needs time, and couldn't be in better hands."

"He could be in mine."

Her father got to his feet. "You can't help him. This is a fact. Moreover, you cannot remain near to him. It's imperative that you two are separated, the sooner the better."

The authority in her father's tone had hardened his formidable features. In the firm set of his mouth, Rosalind sensed the gap in his explanations. Her father's secrets were heavy enough to be like the aura of another person in the room.

"Are you going to tell me the real reason he can't come with us, without going around in circles?" she asked.

"It isn't time for that, or necessary."

"I'm not a child."

"I know that. But two such extremes are destined never to meet, if in fact they could exist at all," her father said.

His reply came with a sting. An unspoken message resided in what her father had said a message so terrible it couldn't be spoken. A dark secret?

Extremes, he said.

Two such extremes are never destined to meet. If they could exist at all.

Her father had just called her a freak, without coming right out with the word.

He had uttered this remark as if he'd been near wit's end and it had merely slipped out. Whatever he held inside didn't want to see the light of day; a secret that if spoken, might come to pass all the quicker.

But she couldn't accept that, and needed to have things in the open. Her father was keeping something important from her. And even though knowing he thought his daughter a freak hurt like a knife to the chest, she had to stand her ground. What other option was there?

"Not good enough," she said. "Nothing you've said is good enough to change my mind about this Were."

You aren't the only one with secrets, she wanted to shout.

Separating me from the wulf upstairs will do no good, because against all odds, he and I have already bonded. And bonds between Lycans are unbreakable, except by death.

She had another secret. Her insides ached with longing for the Were upstairs. Her womb thrummed for the golden-fleshed man who had shed his clothes in the moonlight. She hungered for his gaze, and for what hung, hard and swollen, between his powerful thighs.

Instincts trumped innocence here, and she wasn't to have that? Wasn't to see him again?

"I know better than to argue with you," she said.

Indeed, nothing would influence her father once his mind had been made up. Still, she was responsible for the Were's injuries, at least in part. If she had gotten to him sooner, fought harder, not stopped to listen to the calls in the night, he might have been spared some of his wounds.

She looked past her father. The Were upstairs was stirring. She felt this, and her fingers twitched in reaction. Her inner defiance against her father's restraints rose again.

There was more truth she had to hide from her father.

Another secret pain that she didn't understand. When she had issued the howl in the park that had brought help, something had happened to her. It was as if restraining straps had been unbuckled, setting part of her free that she'd had no idea existed. Wild. Complicated. New.

God, there was more, yet. *The worst part.*

In hearing her cry, the fanged monsters attacking her had stopped their attack. After that cry, they had transferred all their attention to the brown Were, leaving her alone, leaving her standing there, unheeded, untouched, while her golden-skinned, brown-furred male, heavily outnumbered, was ripped to shreds.

After her call, the fanged creatures had bypassed her as if she no longer existed; as if she had suddenly become invisible to them, and no longer mattered.

I'm not quite right inside. But how do I tell you the extent of this, Father? Your wizened eyes, gazing at me, suggest that you might know the reason for this, and possibly even why those bloodsuckers had left me alone. Freak, is what you were thinking. Not the time for reasons, you said.

Everyone, it suddenly seemed to Rosalind, had secrets. But so many secrets made the world a much darker, more unbearable place. She was going to get some answers. Now.

Colton wasn't sure if he had died. His first thought was that he must have.

The last thing he remembered was that his heartbeat had slowed to near nothing when the last wave of fangs hit him. He recalled shutting his eyes when the pain had become too great and his limbs had stopped working.

Soon after that, he had fallen into a dark tunnel, listening to the sounds of a continued battle all around him without being able to participate.

As he lay where he was now, wherever that might be—heaven or hell, maybe—his thoughts kept returning to that brave Were who had come to his aid, and was little more than another smudge of darkness in his mind. He had, for the briefest seconds of time before his fall, imagined that other Were to be female. Maybe her lips had touched his, he thought, or else he had been dreaming.

Female werewolves were nearly as able as males, and he had sensed one in that park, earlier. But the werewolf fighting beside him had torn through the vampires like a creature hell-bent on utter destruction. That dark-coated werewolf, merely a blur in the night, had been nothing less than a total fighting machine.

Had he died out there? Was he in shock? There seemed to be a disconnect between his mind and his limbs. It didn't hurt him to think, and his thoughts kept returning to the same questions. If he had died, had the other Were who'd helped him died, as well? Had she whispered something to him out there as his eyes had closed? More important, had those fanged vipers who had stolen the life from his family been defeated?

Colton's pulse gave a sudden kick. He groped for the reason for this sudden alertness.

There was no sense of anything waiting to take him over. No overriding awareness of angels or demons surrounded him. The blanks in his mind were holes occupied by swirling drifts of a silver-gray mist. In that mist, he thought he saw Death's outline hovering. He was almost sure he heard Death's call.

The cop side of him wanted to fill the holes in his reasoning so he could understand his current state. Cops were trained to fill in gaps and connect the dots. But he just didn't seem able to do that.

Pertinent lapses in memory could be his mind's way of reaching for a temporary peace after encountering the rabid side of chaos, he reasoned. Those lapses could just as easily mean that consciousness continued for a time after the body formerly housing it had succumbed to its final loss of breath.

But he hadn't lost his breath.

He was breathing now.

Colton suddenly sensed something else. He reached out to this new presence with his senses.

"Hey."

The voice cut through the swirl of gray. He classified the sound as a word. Beyond it lay a familiar fragrance that was nothing at all like the stench of vampires.

Flowers. Musk and flowers.

Not hell, then.

"Can you open your eyes?" the soft voice asked.

It was an odd request, he thought, since he'd been sure his eyes were already open.

"Can you see me?"

This was said in the slightly husky tone of a female's whisper.

Turning his head took effort.

"I'm not supposed to be here, but I had to see you," she said. "My father will take me away tomorrow."

Father? Some feeling came, centered in Colton's chest. He knew that particular word because he had a father.

Sharp pain struck without warning, as though an arrow had pierced him. It was the arrow of past tense. He'd *had* a father. But not anymore.

"Can you talk? Will you make the effort to speak to

me?" the female asked, her breathy voice bringing with it another hint of the taste of a floral bouquet. Roses. Bloodred roses, rich in color and sprinkled with dew.

No. Not dew. These roses were covered in fur.

Black fur.

Memory zigzagged. Colton wanted to slap his head to make things work more smoothly, but couldn't move his arm.

A Were with a black pelt? Had he seen that out there? *Absurd.*

Why should he remember that, when there were no true black-pelted Weres? Dark brown, yes, but not black. The color itself denoted unfathomable darkness. Even black-haired Weres in human form shifted to a different color.

"Yes," she, whoever she was, coaxed. "I'm here. If you open your eyes, you'll see me."

The voice struck a distant chord. It was filled with submerged emotion and as demanding as it was inviting. This voice was the human equivalent of the howl of invitation a she-wulf had issued to him in that blasted park.

It's her.

You.

Wanting nothing more than to see who was near, Colton struggled to do as she asked. His eyes hadn't been open, after all. He opened them, sorry that he had when a glare of hurtful light hit him.

"Wait. I'll dim the lamp," she said. "It's just one lamp, by your bed."

Absorbing the ache that followed so much time spent in darkness, Colton forced himself to focus. His vision took a while to get into working order, and then he found himself gazing into a pair of large green eyes, very near to his.

His insides stirred restlessly.

There was something about those eyes. Not exactly familiar, but...

A surge of heat broke through his numbness. Again, he heard a howl, far away now, but there, all the same. He saw a dark-pelted wulf charge in to help him, and join in the fight.

His nerves began to simmer, then fry, which in turn caused feeling where there had been nothing but a wasteland.

The fire spread.

Hunger came upon him, heated, and with a ravenous need for the *She* with that mesmerizing voice.

His biceps tensed. His toes curled. He heard the crack of his spine straightening as whatever power those green eyes held hurled him toward full consciousness.

The flames tearing through him called up his beast. His wulf unfurled as fluidly and easily as if he'd merely spread his arms, the shift silent and uncommonly fast. It came on in a wave, similar to a smooth ruffle of air between two breaths. No extra pain. No forethought. No moon necessary.

Left panting from a transition that had no right to have happened in the first place, Colton, in werewolf form, squatted on a soft blue cloudlike surface, trembling and in shock. All he saw was the brilliance of the green eyes across from his that had not wavered in intensity or retreated by so much as an inch.

This female wasn't afraid of him.

I know you, he thought again.

His growl was the sum total of his strange new feelings of hunger and longing, and lingered in the space around him.

"I knew it," the green-eyed woman beside him said. "You're still in there."

Rosalind felt the throb of this werewolf's blood in her veins. The erratic rhythm of his heart spoke of the depth of his inexplicable need for her.

There was no second-guessing what this need was. It came across as primitive, hotly sexual, and was, Rosalind would have known without the rapid acceleration of her own pulse, very much reciprocated.

She wanted to be with him. Be like him. She wanted to meet him wulf to wulf. Wanted everything this male had to offer.

Exerting pressure to control herself, Rosalind knew that she had been right. They had imprinted not long ago, without their eyes meeting, a fact as unusual as this wulf's snowy-white pelt. Their hunger was mutual, no matter what shape he was in.

Rosalind was glad she had locked the door. As she stared into his eyes, she could barely keep her hands off the wulf on the bed. Her beast was starved for his beast. She craved his touch, and was left trembling.

"Yes," she whispered. "We have bonded."

Tremors rocked her. Similar tremors moved through the white wulf beside her. He was sharing the effects of their bond. He felt what she felt.

"I don't understand why they would separate us," she said, tilting her head, trying to speak slowly. "You'll need details of what happened, some of which you probably already know."

Rosalind swallowed her beast's needs down and lowered her voice. "You've been badly hurt, attacked by bloodsuckers in the park. The same suckers that killed your family, I suppose. We've taken care of those fiends, got rid of them. My father and the judge brought you to Landau's house. Judge Landau's wife has been treating you."

Placing a hand on her chest, as if that would slow her racing heartbeat, she continued. "These vampires were savages. The Landaus say you've knocked on Death's door and stepped across the threshold, only to be pulled back by the strength of your will."

It was impossible for her to slow down. A deep breath didn't help.

"You're alive, but changed. I don't know how, exactly. I'm not sure what your white pelt means. They won't tell me everything. They never have."

The creature her father had called a ghost remained almost motionless, though his white fur rippled with the force of his pulse.

"I'm Rosalind Kirk," she said. "My father is Jared Kirk. You'll need to know those things in order to find me."

The white wulf stared at her soundlessly.

She fell silent for a minute, maybe two, noting how the room at the top of the Landaus' house that posed as a one-bed makeshift hospital ward smelled of clean laundry and antiseptic. It was sparsely furnished, with a large bed, one soft chair and two bedside tables. The window in the wall opposite the bed was open. The curtains moved in a faint breeze.

Rosalind had no idea what kind of care they had given this Were, or what those treatments entailed, but he had pulled through. Her actions in the park hadn't killed him.

She blinked slowly to take that in.

On the surface, most of the stink of the vampires had been wiped clean from this wulf, and from the room housing him. Underscoring the room's aura of calm, however, Rosalind still perceived hints of vampire. Black glittering molecules, as shiny and sharp as polished shards of glass, seemed a part of every breath she took.

Wary of this, and mindful of the fact that she had sneaked upstairs when the judge's wife had gone for food, Rosalind went on.

"You're at the Landau estate at the edge of the park. Since you're a cop and a Were, I'm guessing you know Judge Landau and about some of the secrets kept in this place."

The white wulf growled softly, as if trying out his voice through a throat the bloodsuckers had ripped open several times over. It seemed to Rosalind that she might have made a similar sound without realizing it, because her own throat felt raw.

The eyes looking at her were intent, piercing and the palest green. They were ringed by deep purple circles, leftovers indicative of how badly his face and body had been injured.

She didn't want to think of how he had looked when her father and the others had come to the rescue. All that blood. And she had seen glimpses of bone beneath his torn and mangled flesh.

At the time, it seemed that a true miracle would be necessary in order for him to survive. "You look better," she said, hoping this might calm him.

And that was true. He did look better. Already, after just two days, new skin covered bone and sinew, though several patches of fur and flesh were missing from his neck and shoulders, leaving lines of raw, reddened flesh. Red welts lined his face like the stripes of a tiger, but they were no longer oozing blood.

His moon mark, an indication of his superior place within their species, showed through the colorless fur of his left upper arm. It was riddled with tiny puncture holes, as though the vampires had purposefully gone for it with gusto, hoping to tear the mark clean off.

For a Were, removal of a moon mark was a blasphemy. For this big male, it would have been a forced emasculation. But the filthy blood drinkers hadn't tackled this Lycan easily. He'd fought hard before succumbing to the sheer number of attackers. Burned into her mind was the image of the brown Were feverishly taking on the monsters.

"Brown or white, Were or ghost, you are the most beautiful, the most courageous being I have ever encountered," she said.

And I have nearly caused your death.

"I'm to be taken away," she repeated. "They will separate us, and it will hurt, when you've already been hurt so badly."

Another growl came from him, noticeably stronger, and meaning for her to go on. Coming from this formidable creature who had looked Death in the eye, the sound seemed strangely exotic, and took her breath away.

"I come from the bayou country. I'm seldom allowed out from under my father's strict supervision and rules. We have no modern forms of communication there. No computer, no television, no phones. Only a radio," she said, pausing as the absurdity of these facts registered. "I learn about the world through that radio."

They had, in fact, been living like they were deprived

backwoods folk. Compared to the Landaus, they were decades behind the times. Backwoods cousins.

"This is the first occasion the Landaus have hosted us as guests, and I think this was due to an important meeting between Lycan elders. For me, it's a quick visit here, and then back."

They had so little time. She could hear it ticking away.

"Landau's son and some of his pack aren't here, though I've heard them talked about. I've seen no one my age, and only briefly have met Landau and his wife. I don't think I'll be allowed here again after this."

She waited out a span of several shallow, rapid breaths before continuing, needing to get all this out in the open.

"There are other secrets hidden here. I don't pretend to understand what's really going on, only that some of those secrets pertain to me. I can sense being the focus of this meeting, and believe those secrets are why I've been kept away from other Weres, and ultimately why I'll be kept from you. There is, I think, something wrong with me."

Do you want me to go on?

The wulf continued to study her intently. He hadn't moved.

"I understand the pain of loss." Her voice was beseeching. "My mother was killed by hunters. Not vampires, but monsters in their own right."

The white wulf blinked slowly, as if he was riding out a wave of pain.

"My father says that your fur has turned white due to the intensity of the injuries you have sustained. It might also be a physical manifestation of devastation and loss."

She cleared her throat. "I wish I could take away the anguish of that."

It had taken more than a dozen vampires to gain hold of him. This Were had fought like he was the right hand of Death, when even death, as vampires proved, didn't have to be the end.

"I feel your pain. And I am so very sorry."

She was hurting for herself, and for him. In sharing his heartache, she had to let him know how sorry she was that he'd been injured so badly. As much as she could bring herself to confess. When their imprinting was complete, he'd find out her secrets by easily reading her. They would eventually share thoughts.

"I didn't help you enough out there," she said, noting the alertness in this ghost's eyes.

She couldn't go on, was unable to utter the words that might have freed her from the terrible, plaguing guilt. If she spoke the truth in its entirety, if she confessed what she had or hadn't done now, her white wulf wouldn't want her. There was no way he'd come after her, find her, mate with her, when she wanted those things so desperately.

"I—" She paused when the green eyes across from her began to recede, and the white wulf shape-shifted in a slick, soundless, reversal.

"I couldn't leave you to face them alone," Rosalind whispered as the man from the park, who was now just as captivating with his white hair framing his wounded, angular face, reached for her.

Colton jumped to his feet. With both of his hands on Rosalind Kirk's shoulders, he backed her into a corner so quickly that her breath escaped in a startled hiss of surprise.

He gave her no opportunity for further sound or protest. His mouth covered hers as if her breath alone could make him whole again. As if the beating of her heart against his bare chest could jump-start his, and prove finally, absolutely, that he was alive.

His need was all-consuming. His body was on fire.

He drank her in as if his survival counted on those things.

The fragrance of her breath seemed familiar.

Rosalind Kirk was a young, black-haired, oval-faced vision, and slight to the point of an ethereal thinness. Although her mouth was momentarily motionless beneath his, Colton sensed with every instinct he possessed how much she wanted to respond.

There was a possibility, he realized, that she didn't know how.

Her lips were warm, supple, tender, sweet and not in the least bit rigid. In her stillness came a reminder of what she had told him. She had been kept from others. She'd been sheltered from actions like this by an overprotective Lycan father. She had no family or friends. This might, in fact, have been her first real kiss.

He wanted her in that moment as much as his beast had desired her in the park. Every inch of him yearned for her, now that he'd been awakened, and had captured her in his arms.

Had this slight, ebony-haired creature truly fought beside him, placing herself in jeopardy in order to help? Was she the one who had come to aid him in a time of trouble?

"You," he whispered with his mouth on hers. "It really was you."

Ignoring shaky limbs that refused to behave properly, and his heart's offbeat rhythm, Colton leaned into her. Licking gingerly at her lips, nipping lightly at the corners of her mouth before again sealing his lips to hers, he took her breath into his lungs, and felt that breath warm him. One word resonated in his mind, on its own loop, playing over and over.

Mine.

He wasn't dead. This moment was real. Where there was feeling, there was hope, and he desperately needed some.

He kissed her, and the kiss drew a gasp. The raspy sound of Rosalind's breathlessness shuddered through him as the pleasure of being close to her far outweighed the nagging internal pain he harbored.

His captive wore a black shirt he hardly noticed, except that it felt cool and silky against his bare chest. His current impulse was to tear the shirt from her and get down to it, chest to chest, groin to groin. This was his animal side taking over. His beast voted for that.

Injuries be damned! This Were female had a name that rolled easily on his tongue. *Rosalind.* A name as creamy as the sexual act itself.

Her black hair, worn long and straight, spilled over her shoulders in a gleaming cascade. Her face, with its prominent, sharp-edged bones, would suit few people, but somehow suited him. She had a small, tapered nose. Perfectly arched eyebrows looked like dark smudges of paint on ivory skin decorated by huge, penetrating green eyes.

Her shoulders were narrow, her hip bones like blades. Lycan females never had overindulgent curves or ponderous shapes due to their super-revved metabolisms and the frequent nighttime sprints, and Rosalind didn't break that mold.

Small, firm breasts, perfectly proportioned to the trimness of her body, pressed against him through her shirt, begging to be touched, licked, suckled, by someone who would understand what she needed in a mate.

She was no mere pretty young thing. This was a category of female he had never expected: unique, sensual, animal and almost supernaturally beautiful.

Mine.

Colton's wulf roared, possessive and protective of Rosalind Kirk in spite of the fact that she had been a freaking lightning-quick fighting machine in that park.

Couldn't have been her, his mind still argued. The female in his arms had a trembling, succulent mouth. The Were in the park had been lethal, black-pelted and incredibly fast.

Thoughts fled as her lips parted and her tongue, extremely hot and seductively moist, tentatively met his. The action cued something in Colton's body that had long lain dormant. It was a real need for her, having nothing whatsoever to do with the concept of superficial. He longed for closeness and connection. He wanted to hold in his hands something fine and special and long-term. In the face of those needs, self-control was not an option.

The heat of her presence pushed his pain aside. Colton had a sensation of his strength returning by bounds, as if she were the one pulling it back, inch by agonizing inch, and as if the kiss connecting them was drawing his better parts out.

Her arms encircled his neck. Their hips ground lusciously together. Through the silky cloth of her shirt Rosalind continued to radiate the kind of enticement that he imagined would be similar to getting too close to the sun. *Pure, radiant fire.*

He groaned when her hands touched the nape of his neck, and he repeated the sound when her fingers moved upward into his hair. She grabbed hold of a handful of strands and tugged, trying to pull him closer. But the only way they could have been closer was for him to be inside her. And there was no way to describe how much he wanted that.

His body responded to hers as if he hadn't been hurt. His erection was proof that a Were's ability to heal was indeed nothing short of magical.

Rosalind's touch made illness seem distant and irrelevant. The swift return of his libido told him that if his body wasn't fully recovered, he was well enough to oblige the desire to claim her, and to enter the blistering heat he knew would be waiting for him if he did.

"Ties that bind. You and I, Rosalind," he whispered to her, allowing her only a very small breath.

It seemed to him that the female whose tongue now swept boldly across his had somehow created an energy flux that encompassed them both. Maybe it was only a male-female attraction that had made him get up from that bed, because hell, he didn't know how he could be standing up when he had only opened his eyes a short time ago. He wasn't entirely sure what had happened to him out there in the dark.

Nevertheless, there was healing in her fingertips. Her breath rammed a steady stream of energy into him as she willed him to take her, and urged him to hurry.

She was a fast learner, an apt pupil. Already she kissed him back with enough fervor to melt away the doubts.

Oh, yes. One of his dreams lay within his grasp. All he had to do was what came naturally to them both.

But, his mind nagged, *they are going to take her away.* Away from him. This seemed a ridiculous impossibility, now that he had found her.

Dampness broke out on his forehead. Rationality warned that they were guests in someone else's house, and that the door might open any minute. Rosalind had mentioned the name Landau.

Still, Rosalind's fingers moved like little bolts of lightning across his upper back, scorching his tender skin, making him wince from the sheer intensity of the pleasure. She was exploring him, as well as the other way around, and she liked what she found.

He seemed to hear her whispering to him, though his mouth on hers left her no ability to do so. "Now," she was thinking. "Seal our fate."

Chapter 6

Reluctantly, Colton pulled his lips from hers to gaze at her flushed face. How far would she go? How far would she let him go? The she-wulf was looking back at him. Their gazes met, held.

He had a sensation of falling, though he was on his feet. His body imploded with the desire to have all of her; every last bit. Wrapped in her heat, he could almost forget the vampires and what they had done. He stood a chance of sidelining his need for vengeance.

When he tore at her jeans, neither of them spoke or moved apart to make access easier. Rosalind's palms were like burning coals when she placed them on his chest.

With ease, he lifted her from the ground, turned and threw her on the bed where he'd been tended. Rosalind was, he noticed, barefoot, her feet delicate, her toenails unpainted.

Her jeans were discarded in seconds. The blue underwear beneath them was destroyed in less time than that. She lay half-naked on the bed, her hair and her silk shirt glistening in the light from the bedside lamp. Her eyes told him that she anticipated what might come next.

Colton crawled up to arch over her on his hands and knees, so that the only thing between them, below the hem of her shirt, was his thrumming cock—the dusty, unused body part of a werewolf who had been too long without.

"Mate," she said huskily through pink, swollen lips, her eyes wide and as brilliant as emeralds.

"Yes," he growled.

Her hips rose to meet him when he slid both hands beneath her slick, bare buttocks, buttocks that were as sleek as her shirt. Her legs were endlessly long, and stretched out beneath him. Her thighs were shaped with lengths of strong, lean muscle.

"Some other time and place," he told her, "this would take much longer and move much slower. Hours. Days. Weeks."

"Find me. Promise," was all she said in return.

Somehow, Colton knew there was no time for foreplay and that the needs driving them ruled out any effort at further restraint. With trembling fingers, he explored the spot he needed for entering her body. Although she might have been kept from this in the past, Rosalind was more than willing. Between her thighs, behind a wedge of dark fur, she had dampened. With his fingers pressed against her, she growled low in her throat.

When her legs opened for him, he forgot everything else. Time, and all that had gone on before, seemed to slip away.

Easing the tip of his cock inside her, Colton closed his eyes. He didn't want to move, wanted to linger and soak up this wicked heat, but he had to continue. His body demanded satisfaction.

With an agonizing slowness, he began to make tender stroking motions, moving his hips, dipping in and out of her meagerly at first, amazed that he could exert this much will over himself when what he longed for was a singular thrust hard enough to fill her completely.

He shook with the intensity of that desire.

He and this stranger had imprinted. And this sealed the deal. That's the way this went: eyes, thoughts, body, then soul. They had bonded, and all he knew about her was her name, and that she had pulled him up from unconsciousness, and how extremely hot she was.

Inside, she was tight and beautifully lush. He stroked her gently until that tightness began to relax and a rush of cream surrounded his erection. Even in man form, he nearly howled.

As he pressed himself farther inside her, Rosalind made more encouraging noises in her throat. When he stopped moving, she seemed to stop breathing altogether.

"I will find you," he said with a pledge that seemed to have been dragged from his heart.

Though she gasped, Rosalind didn't open her eyes.

"You understand what this means?" he asked gruffly, because her body, and what she was allowing him to do with it, had stolen his own breath away.

Her eyelids fluttered, the long, midnight-hued lashes dark against her flawless ivory skin. As he studied her face, her chin moved up and down once. She understood perfectly.

"All right," he whispered to her. "God. Okay."

His plunge into her rich depths brought another, louder, sound from her throat. It was a purr of encouragement. A nod to pleasure.

Colton withdrew, then sank his length into her again and again, building a rhythm that took him deeper and deeper, trying not to burst with the pleasure this gave him. He hung on to his sanity by a thread.

When waiting was no longer an option, he lowered himself to her body and drove himself into her with a force that rocked his body and hers.

Unparalleled gratification careened through him that was as violent as live wires crossing. And when Rosalind bent her knees, grabbed his buttocks with her hands and invited him to partake of the last remaining barrier, he felt the rise of an oncoming orgasm that would truly weld them together for life.

With his scent on her, and imbedded in her, no other Were could hope to gain her interest. That's also the way this worked. She would be his. *Forever. Until death do us part.*

And when she drove her hips against his, he tumbled over the rim of an abyss. One more move of his own hips, and he executed just one more powerful thrust; the exact one he had longed to make.

He reached the molten center of the female beneath him, not thinking of taking or claiming her now, but offering himself to her in a union that was tantamount to the binding of their souls.

"Rosalind."

The rumble started in his back, spread to his torso and careened between his legs. A similar rumble, like an approaching earthquake, tore through Rosalind, hitting and then overtaking them at the same time.

The room exploded with a light that seemed to carry in it all the emotion of the life Colton had lived so far. With their moist bodies pressed together in a rigid few seconds of suspended stillness, and their mouths locked together so that no sensation could go unresolved, the suddenness of the intensity of their mingled ecstasy ripped through them.

But so did something else.

One last peripheral sensation slid through Colton unexpectedly as he reached his peak.

In that moment of heightened awareness, as his body convulsed with pleasure, he was sure that Rosalind tasted not only like wulf, but of metal.

In her feverish mouth, and at her heated core, lay a hint of what he imagined silver to taste like. Silver, a concoction that was the bane of all Weres, purebred or otherwise.

Absurd.

He let the notion go as he rode the crest of a wave of ecstasy prolonged by each tremor that shook her.

And when the storm finally subsided and some time had passed without sound or motion, Colton was afraid to move. Afraid to believe. Opening his eyes, he again found Rosalind's eyes waiting.

Problem was those eyes were no longer green.

Liquid darkness swam in Rosalind's irises, drowning the color, turning them black. It was like watching a curtain drop over a verdant landscape. Like a dark veil descending suddenly to cloak something fine.

The sudden strangeness made Colton draw back. The skin on his neck prickled. His jaw tensed.

"What the—"

What had happened to Rosalind? Hell, had he just

linked himself to a Were who might be something more than wulf?

He heard the word *special* in his mind, and knew it came from her thoughts. He didn't like the questions turning up.

Was the key to Rosalind's well-guarded seclusion the fact that she might not be just any *She* after all, but something else? Something far more dangerous?

Was that why she wasn't allowed out, when Lycan females were so scarce, and why she felt she was different?

Perhaps also sensing this, or seeing the concern in his expression, Rosalind opened her mouth to protest the look on his face. After a brief hesitation, she uttered a strangled cry.

Between her beautiful lips, so swollen and lush and pink, lay a pair of tiny needle-sharp incisors reminiscent of no wulf canines that Colton had ever seen. On her lower lip lay a fine sheen of pooled red droplets where she had bitten herself during their moments of shared passion.

Blood. On her mouth.

Dark blood, red as roses.

Before Colton caught a startled breath, his lover, his she-wulf, the female he had sealed himself to forever, moved from under him with an astonishing speed that was little more than a time-slip of barely disturbed air.

She leaped gracefully onto the sill of the tall, open window, where she paused in a crouch to draw her fingers across her mouth. Glancing at the smear of blood on them, her body visibly shook.

For a moment more she remained there, outlined by the night beyond, her silk shirt shining, her long, loose hair billowing in the breeze.

She looked at Colton with a shocked, pleading glint in her wild black gaze as she held up her hand to show him the red stain on her fingers. Then, uttering one more sound, a sob, Rosalind turned from him and jumped out.

Chapter 7

"**W**hat the hell are you?"

Colton swore to himself, shocked as he sat back on the bed where he had just made love to a...what? Certainly not the she-wulf he'd assumed her to be.

His heart was thundering. She'd looked like a vampire. Like one of the creatures that had killed his parents.

He felt weak, shaky, and not all from the surprise of having his new mate turn into a vampire-like creature before jumping from his window. Sex had taken effort he'd barely been able to muster before she had arrived. With Rosalind gone, and twisted by shock, he felt completely drained.

"Have to get up. Must find out what's going on."

Where was he? What was he to do now? Rosalind, God, whatever she turned out to be, had brought up the Landaus. Everyone in Miami would recognize that name.

Prominent Judge Landau and his socially adept wife were Lycans from way back who obviously knew how to fit in with humans and had created a compound for their pack members.

He was in their house. Landau's house.

Colton got to his feet. Chills covered his body as he stumbled to the window. Rosalind had left a spot of blood on the sill. Seeing it, his stomach seized.

He looked out, seeing nothing below but the glow from windows that were lower to the ground than his. Backing toward what he assumed was a closet, he braced himself against the doorjamb as he opened it. After pulling on someone else's jeans that he'd discovered on a shelf inside, Colton limped out the hallway door and down a wide wooden staircase, the drag of one foot awkward beneath a numb left leg.

"If I have to crawl, I will find out what that was, and where she has gone."

This wasn't a choice. He had promised, if not verbally, then with his actions. He had fully imprinted with what he'd believed to be an eligible female Were; one who had the courage to follow him into a vampire ambush. Now, hell, she looked a bit like one of those same monsters. How was that possible?

He remembered the black pelt, and shuddered.

"She could have been injured in the bloodsuckers' attack, as I was," he said, needing to hear his thoughts. "If that were to be the case, and her fangs were the result, I am ultimately to blame."

She had seemed as shocked as he had been when she stared at the blood on her hand. He'd never forget the flatness of fear in those big eyes. He had hurt her with the shocked expression in his.

She hadn't known what would happen to her.

"Bloody frigging damn!" He staggered to a stop, catching sight of himself in a long mirror in the hallway. His legs threatened to give way as he stared at his image. It had to be someone else. Couldn't be him. A ghostly form looked back at him from that mirror, its colorless skin marred by red slashes, its long hair freakishly white.

"Christ, what happened to me out there!"

Rigid with the horror of that, Colton limped on, putting distance between himself and that image. He had to get outside, get air, find her. There was no time to ponder what he might have become. If he had hurt Rosalind, he had to put things right.

The Landaus had tended to him on the top floor of a three-story house. As he neared the bottom of the stairs, Colton pictured Rosalind jumping from such a great height. Did this mean she'd be dead, sprawled on the lawn? Weres were notoriously strong, and possessed the agility of big cats, but what would a dose of vampire do to that scenario?

His heart sputtered as if unable to rev properly. He wasn't sure he'd have the energy to make it to the front door, but he did. No one appeared to stop him from pushing through that door when he reached it.

The suddenness of leaving a closed space and stepping off the boards of a large covered veranda, into the night, offered up yet another surprise that stopped Colton in his tracks.

The night was composed of fragments of pure sensory bombardment that rushed at him from all directions at once—a barrage of sight, sound, scent, taste, arriving to flood and overwhelm his overworked, not yet up-to-par system.

This bombardment was like being caught in a whirlwind and felt like sharp knives were being worked into his eye sockets. It felt as though the mother of all migraines had rained down to provide a wallop, when the night and the moon riding high in it shouldn't have been anything other than normal fare for him.

Then again, he was no longer normal. He'd seen himself in the mirror and was pretty sure the world had made one too many wrong turns while he'd been asleep.

Sucking in a breath of sensory-filled air forced him down to one knee. What energy he had left seemed to have deserted him in a time of need, but he lifted his chin in stubborn defiance, determined to face this. He took in another breath that tasted strongly of wulf, and then he saw why.

Weres were waiting for him out here, as motionless and silent as a line of marble statues, on Judge Landau's front lawn.

Rosalind sped through the night, chased by fear, driven forward by a newly discovered, terrible speed that felt like flying.

She had landed on the grass outside of the house without injury. Springing to her feet, she had sailed over the wall before even making up her mind to do so, and was running to escape from herself. From what she had become.

It had to be part of that same thing her father had neglected to tell her about.

She'd had her first kiss, as well as so much more. And the experience had been beyond imagining. The sensations of their lovemaking remained. The spark her ghost wulf had ignited still flickered deep within her.

Though she kicked up her speed, there was no outrunning the fact that something had happened to both her and the brown Were in the park that had made their needs a priority. She didn't fully understand what that might be.

If she went back there, to the same spot under the trees where she had first laid eyes on the Were, maybe she'd find out what the key to their connection was. If she found more vampires, she'd wring the truth out of them. She had to try. Emotions were rife, and cresting.

The sickest question of all, one that followed her like a shadow, was about how many freaks the Were community might sustain in their midst.

Second in order of horrific fears was her new paranoia about being sealed off for good on her father's estate for having the wrong kind of fangs, never to set foot beyond its boundaries again.

The shocked look in the ghost wulf's eyes dogged her. That look had warned her about her changes. The blood on her fingers had confirmed it.

But she and the ghost wulf had fully mated. Their connection had been consummated. Two entities in transition, and who hadn't a clue as to what they were becoming, had kissed and then bedded. And despite the push to run away, Rosalind desperately wanted a rematch with him. Her body ached for another bed, or a stretch of green lawn…anywhere private enough to have the ghost wulf inside her.

"I have fangs. What does that make me?" she shouted into the quiet night.

Half-naked, she moved between the trees as if she'd become a part of the breeze blowing through them. After her shout, she clamped her jaws and tried not to swallow the sickeningly sweet thickness of the blood filling her mouth.

Out here, unprotected by fathers and fences and a hundred acres of bayou swampland, she had to find answers or die trying. She was both herself, and not. A glob of darkness had partially taken her over, and if that darkness continued to spread in so swift a manner, there would be no gauging how long she had before being completely overcome by some new entity.

What would such a thing do to her mate? To their connection?

If she were no longer Lycan, would their imprinting fade?

If she were to become a vampire, they would be enemies.

The outline of the first large tree lay ahead, an old tree with scarred bark. Glancing up at it, Rosalind bent her knees and jumped, landing on the lowest branch perched on both feet, and with perfect balance.

She uttered a hoarse, muffled cry of terror at what she had just done. Kneeling now, she compressed herself into as small a mass as possible, with her arms wrapped around her knees. The vampires they had fought here had been hanging in these trees like bats, and she seemed precariously close to doing the same thing.

That seemed unthinkable, unreasonable. To the best of her knowledge, she hadn't been bitten or scratched when she'd joined the fight. Vampire blood and venom couldn't have reached her bloodstream, so there was no reason for vamp fangs to have appeared inside her mouth, and no explanation at all for being in a tree when werewolves were earthbound creatures.

She looked at the ground, thinking about how the

bloodsuckers had stopped attacking her after she issued the howl that had summoned the other Weres. She was unable to see anything in it that would have caused the startling changes taking place.

So, why had the vampires backed off her before that fight had ended?

Why had she always been kept away from other Weres?

Did the answers to those questions go hand in hand?

Damn it, didn't her father understand that she, of all Weres, needed to know these things, and that it would be impossible to go on without knowing? Look what was happening to her now!

Blinking back tears of frustration served to clear her vision. Inhaling the night opened her senses enough to recognize the strong scent of humans strolling through the corners of the park, probably lacking the courage to trespass deeper into it.

She smelled their clothes, all the way down to the fabric and dye. She smelled their musky perfume.

"Nothing extraordinary," she whispered with relief. "Just more wulf senses."

Beneath her, the odor of vamp ash had gone. In the distance, behind Landau's protective walls, she sensed the ghost wulf moving.

"We're mated, and I don't really know you."

Rosalind hated the tears that ran down her cheeks.

Chapter 8

It took a full minute for Colton's eyes to adjust enough to pick the Weres out of the dark landscape, then he counted six large bodies in man-form before getting to his feet.

He glanced up at the sky to gauge the position of the moon, then focused on the Weres who weren't furred-up because the moon had passed her full phase.

"Landau's pack, I presume?" he said, feeling unnaturally winded and as if he might be sleepwalking. How long had he been here? he wondered.

"Did you see her?" he asked.

"Who?" one of them replied.

"Rosalind."

"Rosalind Kirk?" another Were queried.

This speaker was a big man. Tall, well built, fairhaired and recognizable as Miami's Deputy District Attorney, Dylan Landau was Judge Landau's only son and

pure Lycan through and through. Dressed casually in
tan slacks and a soft blue shirt that spoke of wealth and
privilege, and without one hint of the stink of the pre-
vious night's vampire attack on him, Dylan was a key
figure in the fight against crime in this city, and lethal
in his own right.

Beside Judge Landau's son stood another outstand-
ing specimen of Werehood, slightly on the rougher side.
Brown-haired, hard-featured, this guy's strong shoulders
were shown off by a tight black T-shirt. His faded jeans
were threaded with a belt that had a badge pinned to it.
The golden shield of a detective.

This guy with the badge was Were, but not purebred
Lycan. And since he was here with the Landaus, it had
to either be Adam Scott or Matt Wilson that faced him,
both of whom had been inducted into the Were clan after
they'd been bitten while on the job. Both had helped to
clean up a werewolf fighting ring last year run by a creep
named Chavez. That feat alone could have earned either
Scott or Wilson access to Landau's full-blooded pack.
Among Weres, the Red Wolf and Wolf Trap cases were
hailed as notorious.

He guessed the Were in the T-shirt was Wilson, without knowing why. Any other time, he would have been
honored to meet the guy in person.

"Then you haven't see her," Colton said, straining to
see beyond the line of formidable muscle barring his exit.

"No one has seen her," Dylan Landau said.

"She exited from that window." Colton pointed up at
the house. Talking took a monumental effort. "I need to
find her. You can help by pointing me in the right direction if your senses are working better than mine at the
moment. I seem to be stuck in healing overload."

When Dylan Landau shook his head, the shoulder-length blond hair he was famous for spilled over his shoulders. "We're not supposed to follow her."

"Rosalind," Colton said. "Her name is Rosalind."

"Yes, I know," Dylan said.

"Then you do know about her."

"I know *of* her."

"What does that mean?"

"As I said, no one here has seen Rosalind. We've only heard rumors about her, and we've just returned to the compound several minutes ago."

"I'll be on my way, then," Colton said.

Landau and Wilson stepped forward at the same time to stop him. Colton nodded in understanding. "You're here to keep me from leaving?"

"Are you ready to leave?" Wilson asked.

"Don't I look like it?" Colton replied cynically.

He had avoided Miami's underworld of werewolves in order to better keep his own family's secrets, and regretted that decision now. Like him, these Weres used their special abilities to fight the bad guys, and wore their secrets well. They were distant cousins, of a sort. Comrades, if their packs were ever to socialize.

Yet he still felt coated in something heavy that dragged at the edges of his awareness. And the female he had bedded had sprouted fangs, jumped from a three-story window, and had gotten away with it.

"Actually, no," Wilson said. "You don't look like you're ready to go anywhere, especially if that means seeing people you know, or encountering the sort of creatures that seem to be making their home in the park."

Yes. The albino hair would be hard to explain, Colton admitted to himself. He'd have to shave it off before he

showed up at his apartment. As for seeing others, these
Weres were right, of course. He wasn't ready to go anywhere. He could barely handle being around those of his
own kind. His senses were firing on too many cylinders.
The night was filled with external chatter and the mingled smells of way too many things.

He felt sick. He felt different. And his face looked like
a Frankenstein creation.

Worse than that, strange impulses flowed through him
that he didn't dare to address, shouting at him with all
the hype of his brain being hit repeatedly with a Taser.
These Weres were kin, if not by line or by blood, then
by species, and yet he wanted to kill them all for getting
in his way. For stopping him from going after Rosalind.

But then Weres didn't kill other Weres, except out of
dire necessity, when no other course of action was fea-
sible and trouble rained down.

Colton had to pry his mouth open to speak, and fisted
his hands to keep them still. "The question remaining on
the table is whether you're the welcoming committee,
or actually here to keep me from following Rosalind."

Dylan Landau spoke again, probably afforded that
leeway because this was his family's house. "This isn't
a prison, Colton. It's a place of healing. A safe haven.
We know what those suckers did to your family. You are
welcome here."

It had been a long time since anyone had called him by
his first name, and Colton took another hit of regret. He
had to close his eyes briefly to sidestep a rise of emotion
that caused a tug-of-war with his darker side.

Closing his eyes turned out to be a terrible idea,
though. The night crowded in, clamoring with noise not
unlike the static from his police radio, turned up to max.

His ears rang. His head began to pound. He had no idea what frequency he was tuning in to, or what could be happening to him.

As his legs faltered, Colton caught himself before going down.

Landau had taken another step in his direction. As he did, Colton began to hear and comprehend that Were's thoughts, as well as the thoughts of the others. Those thoughts rushed in, overlapping, getting louder.

"What's going on?" he muttered, keeping his hands at his sides with a concerted effort.

The voices of the Weres across from him were like raised shouts.

Can we help him, after what's happened and what he has become? he heard one voice ask.

Ghost wulfs are creatures of legend. How can this be possible? said another.

He feels different, smells different.

Vampire scum did this. What can we do to help? There must be a way. He's one of us.

How could he have seen her, when no one else has?

Why is he asking for the freak?

Colton spoke to stop the deluge of what had to be a sudden arrival of a telepathic link to all of them. The chatter was driving him mad. He didn't like the word *freak*.

"I don't know what I am. I believe I might no longer be like you," he said, hanging on to his anger by the thinnest thread of self-control. "Something happened to me. I don't belong here."

"Let us help." That was Dylan.

"I need time to heal."

"You can do that here."

"I have to find Rosalind. If I'm like this, I have to know what has happened to her."

Dylan spoke again in a quieter tone. "I'll just ask you to think twice about disrespecting a father's wishes for his daughter's safety and well-being, whoever she is. We were warned against trying to see her."

"I have no intention of harming her." Colton cleared his throat, feeling as though something had gotten stuck in it.

"Then why the claws?" Wilson asked.

Colton looked down in surprised confusion. His claws had sprung, and were on full display. These Weres would be wondering how he managed that without a full moon.

He was equally as curious.

In the presence of a full moon, the others present would have to assume he was angry. Emotion tended to let transformations slip now and then. But here, now, their faces were dark with worry. None of them knew how adept he was at changing any time the mood struck him, rather than having to wait for the moon's permission. Only his family's line could do that, another reason for the Killion's remaining apart from the others. Nevertheless, the claws were a problem. He hadn't invited them into being, or even felt his hands change. One moment the claws weren't there, and the next moment they were, which meant that another potentially harmful secret had just escaped its net.

"I've been ill," he said, growing more and more anxious about the expressions on the faces in front of him. Inside him, his wulf gave a perfunctory whine.

"My beast takes advantage of the opportunity," he said, with no idea how or if these Weres would accept such an explanation. He'd never messed up like this before. It was as if his will were sliding back and forth between forms and he could no longer be entirely certain which shape was which, or who was in charge. It was as if the beast no longer lay curled up inside, awaiting its turn, but actually coated the surface of his skin.

He felt as though he had one foot trapped inside the tunnel of night that had swallowed him out there in the park, and like he had stumbled into a pit of quicksand.

Through it all, because of all that, a need unlike any he had ever experienced drove him, compelled him, toward what light he imagined remained open to him. He had to reach that light, find the one voice he craved above all others. He had to find Rosalind. Only then could he find himself.

Rosalind didn't care about the white hair. She'd seen the ghost, seen him. She had encouraged him to open his eyes, and then had opened her legs. And she had been right to warn him that being separated from her would hurt.

The desire for Rosalind was bigger than that, larger than the universe, and in this kind of need had to rest the answer to the riddle that had struck him in darkness.

Why had the vampires arrived here, now?

"Colton?"

Adam Wilson called him back to a reality that had him facing a wall of wary, sympathetic faces.

"I know a place where you can take all the time you need to get better if you're worried about staying here," Wilson said.

"Speaking as a friend or the shrink you once were?" Colton asked.

Wilson smiled. "I wasn't aware that anyone knew of my former profession."

"Everyone at Metro knows. You're a hero there for what you did to help take the Chavez gang down."

"Okay. Then I suppose the next question is what you'll do when you find Rosalind?" Wilson said.

"You mean while I'm like this?" Colton ran a claw through his white hair.

"Yes," Wilson replied frankly. "If you don't know what's happening to you, how can you be sure Rosalind will be safe?"

"I gave her my promise not to worry about that."

Wilson nodded. "Then you have seen her, spoken to her."

"Were you thinking that I might have made her up?"

"Of course not. But other than a handful of elders, we just learned that no one here has known for sure of her existence before tonight. We only found out that she'd been here when we returned to find her scent in the air. Female Were, but nothing usual. Maybe you can tell us why the secrecy surrounding her is so great, and what the hell happened here while we were gone."

Again, Colton felt his human physical form begin to waver. His hands and face pulsed as if a full shift were imminent. He actually began to fear what that shape might be, since he felt so strange.

"Colton," Wilson said.

"Yes, I've seen her," Colton muttered. "She's beautiful."

When he looked at the faces staring back, it was to find that the Weres had stepped back and drawn together in an automatic pack response to sniffing out trouble.

Colton glanced down at himself to see patches of white

fur covering his bare arms. He felt his body starting to strain against the tightness of the borrowed jeans.

"Well, well," Matt Wilson muttered with a sharp intake of breath. "What have we here?"

Chapter 9

Rosalind swiped at her tears.

Glancing down at herself, she saw that black fur covered her bare legs. Though the transition to wulf appeared to have stopped halfway up her shivering body, she sighed with relief, taking the fur as a good sign.

Her apprehension returned when she noticed that the overall scent of the park had changed. Its feel had changed.

She glanced toward the Landau compound with the certainty that her ghost wulf would soon come after her, and that she had no way to prevent it. She didn't want him to see her like this.

Another smell came to her unexpectedly, delaying her departure. People. Two of them. Male humans in pressed pants, wearing shoes with rubberized soles. She caught a whiff of leather, mixed with bits of metal and the dampness of perspiration.

Reflexively, she backed up on the branch, and pressed herself to the tree's resinous bark.

"No one has seen the bastard since the Tuesday night," a gritty voice remarked.

Rosalind recognized something familiar in the slightly nasal tone.

"He didn't show up for work. We learned that his family lives on the block where the other family was murdered. No one has heard from Killion's people, either. Neighbors say they're reclusive, travel often, and therefore might have been out of town when those killings went down."

"Lucky for them," the second voice chimed in.

"Yeah, so where is Killion? I saw him in the alley behind his family's house, then he disappeared."

"Maybe he knew those people and he needs time to mourn."

"He's a cop, Jack. We mourn with expressionless cop faces and then come back for more. You know that. He didn't call in, just up and disappeared. It's strange."

Rosalind placed the middle-aged voice and where she had heard it before. It was in the alley behind her brown Were's family's house. The brown wulf had talked to this man before hell had risen in the park.

Their scent filed into a reasonable order that began to make sense. These were cops. They were looking for the big Were, who'd gone MIA. She couldn't help with that unless he came now, hunting for her. If he did come, white and faded and ghostly, there would be trouble with these cops who were looking for him.

The strange thing was that trouble might have arrived already. Her jaws ached from the sound of these voices. Her body pulsed with the scent of blood. One of the men had cut himself, and the odor of crushed aluminum ema-nating from that tiny wound had the same effect on her as inhaling an oncoming storm system.

Her teeth began to chatter. Rosalind felt her lips curl away from her fangs, leaving them wickedly exposed. In horror, she realized that she had stood up, driven to her feet by a faint inner warning suggesting that she could easily hurt these men if she wanted to, and that if she did, no one else would find her mate.

The thrill of fighting the vampires returned to course through her. The fury of battle, the sound of slashing claws and gnashing fangs came back like distant echoes. So did an imagined sensation of biting into solid flesh, of sinking her teeth into a soft neck. Decent werewolves didn't bite innocent people. They weren't supposed to bite anything at all.

Her teeth were snapping. Her jaws were straining.

"No. Please, no," she whispered. "I'm not a monster."

In order to escape, she'd have to wait until the men moved off. She couldn't afford to let them see her. They were good guys, but they carried guns. Although she had been taught that a bullet, unless it was silver, wouldn't kill her, she'd also been taught that a bullet would hurt like hell and sorely slow her down.

Dizziness hit her, nearly knocking her sideways. The fur that had stopped halfway into its transition wavered as if a hand had run through it.

One of the men on the ground beneath her slapped a hand to his ear, glanced at his fingertips and looked up. There was a drop of blood on his hand.

God, had she shed some of the blood in her mouth without meaning to? Worse, had she bitten a cop without even realizing she had moved, her sinister action hidden in those seconds of brief dizziness?

"No!"

She had to take a chance and get away before anything else happened, and before these men found her. She had to get away before she hurt them, or herself, for real.

With a fluid leap that she hoped would be too fast for human eyes to capture, Rosalind landed soundlessly on the ground in the shadows. Whirling on her bare feet, she called up her wulf, hoping more than anything that the wulf would still listen.

"I think you should go back inside," Dylan Landau suggested with earnest concern. "It would help if we all knew what's going on."

Colton shook his head. "I told you I'm ill, and that this is the result. There's no time now for the explanations I need as much or more than you do. Rosalind is out there, alone."

"How do you know she's out there?" Wilson asked.

Colton patted his chest with a fist, an action reminding him of Tarzan. The pain she was experiencing centered in his chest as if it were his own. He shared that, as well as her anguish.

"It doesn't matter what we say?" Dylan queried.

"It can't matter. She's hurting. And I'm…this."

There wasn't going to be much more communication. Colton's face burned like a son of a gun, unlike the smoother morphing of his clawed hands and furry arms.

"What about you?" Wilson said. "Maybe there's a way to—"

"Reverse the damage?"

"Heal the worst parts of it," Wilson finished.

Colton stared down at himself. White fur now covered his chest, a discovery not all that comforting.

"You need to get out of my way," he warned in a deep, guttural tone.

"And you need to remember where you are, and who you are," a tense, authoritative voice said from behind Colton.

Colton spun with his claws raised. That fast, he had shifted and dropped to his haunches in a position of fighting readiness.

"We are not the enemy, my friend," a tall, thin man said from the porch steps. "Quite the contrary in fact, if you'll recall."

"Jared. Stay back," Dylan Landau cautioned.

Colton cocked his head at the sound of the newcomer's name. Jared. Jared Kirk. This was Rosalind's father. Rosalind had told him he'd need to know this name.

Ignoring Dylan's warning, the elder Were, dark-haired and dark-eyed, moved closer and spoke again to Colton. "Do you know where Rosalind has gone?"

Colton rose slowly, hearing the question echo hollowly inside his head.

"Can you lead me to her?" Jared Kirk asked. "She can't be loose in the city. It's imperative that we get her back, then return to our home. It's crucial. You must trust me on this."

By the time Colton stood, he was in man form and as close to being Colton Killion again as he was probably going to get.

"The questions can wait," he said gruffly, his vocal cords lagging behind in the latest shift.

"Yes," Jared Kirk said with a grateful nod of his head. "They can wait. Finding my daughter can't."

"We'll go," Dylan Landau said. "We'll search for her."

Ready to quelch that suggestion, Colton spun around. But Rosalind's father replied first to the crowd.

"I'm sorry I don't have the time to name you all, but please trust me when I say that I appreciate all of your offers of assistance. However, you're not fully equipped to take on my daughter at the moment. Only this Were can, I believe, if indeed it can be done at all."

Jared Kirk had alluded to Colton with a wave of his hand. Dylan fell silent, possibly due to the rebuff that Kirk hadn't in any way meant as a slight, and only a statement of fact, one that Colton had already started to realize.

Only this Were could find her, Rosalind's father had said. Meaning him. Another freak. A ghost. Rosalind's mate. He and Rosalind were different from the other Weres present and connected by an unbreakable link.

He scented Rosalind out there, not too far away. He knew she was thinking about him, and that she was scared. Inhaling her lingering fragrance amounted to a directional beacon guiding him to his unusual lover.

Colton turned his head. Dylan, Wilson and the other boys were staring at him, perhaps hoping to see what tricks he'd perform next. He tuned them out.

What is she? he wanted desperately to ask Rosalind's father, when he had just agreed to forgo the questions in lieu of finding the girl.

He nodded to Jared Kirk. Turning toward the eight-foot wall edging the lawn near the end of the driveway, and bypassing the astonished members of the Landaus' pack at a lope, Colton parlayed his limping pace into a run.

Chapter 10

Colton raced through the park with his hackles raised. Rosalind's scent had changed again, going from familiar to foreign and then back. She was melting back and forth between forms, just as he was.

He howled his displeasure over the situation, and the roar carried. No howl answered his.

Come back to me, my lover.

His head hurt. Sharp pains pierced his limbs as his injured body adapted to what he was putting it through. He hadn't healed completely, and the wulf internalized that pain.

Pure need drove him on.

Sensations of his own oddness tingled through him, but the act of running calmed his lust for the familiar. Most of the smells in the park were ones he recognized.

He had to keep focused. The sound of voices, some of

them in the distance and some inside his head, refused to allow him the moments of quiet he needed in order to get his thoughts together.

He let a second howl rip, and caught a whiff of flowers nearby.

She's here.

Colton slowed when he heard voices.

"Jesus! What the hell was that?" a man said with fearful agitation.

"I don't know. Probably a bird."

"Pterodactyls are extinct!"

"A neighboring dog, then, would be my second guess. What are you doing with your hand? Is that blood?"

"It isn't food coloring. Something bit me. And that sound was like no dog I've ever heard."

"Could have been a big bug that bit you. Who knows what's in these damn trees? But no dog I know of can fly high enough to nip at your ear, so chalk it up to really hungry mosquitoes. Man, though, this place is creepy. I'll give you that."

"We've probably seen enough of this cursed park to know there's no trace of Killion here. I'm heading back to the boulevard."

"You're not interested in finding out what made that growling noise?"

"Are you kidding?"

"Yeah, I guess so."

"You don't sound convincing."

"I like the guy, okay? Killion is one of us. I'd like to find him."

"He's not here, Davidson, so we can look someplace else."

"All right. Let's head back."

"Wait. What's that? Hell, I think that big dog is loose!"

"I'd hate to hurt a dog of any size, them being man's best friend and all."

"Even if it comes after you out here, like a four-legged maniac?"

"Is that it over there? Come on, I swear I just saw it."

"Hell with you, Davidson. I'm not going after that thing. I'm out of here."

Colton growled again as he crept toward the spot where his fellow cops had been standing, hearing them kick up dirt and grass as they trotted toward the street. There was no way he could call out to them. Though he wanted to do just that, and his heart hurt, he had to let them go.

Beneath the tree, he dropped to the ground, able to smell the blood crushed by the officers' boots.

Rosalind's blood. Fresh.

She had to have heard his call. To call again with the officers so close would be species suicide.

Colton raised his head, sniffed the air, then took off.

I might be hurting, he thought, *but my wulf knows what has to be done.*

Hearing the ghost wulf's roar, and feeling it rip through her, Rosalind's steps faltered on a cracked section of a concrete sidewalk. She had reached the street.

Moving cautiously, Rosalind noted the scent of a particular newcomer too late. Before she had made it to the nearby covered structure, a hand reached out to stop her.

"Do you really think that's a good idea?" a female asked, with a grip like a steel trap on Rosalind's right arm.

Rosalind turned. The newcomer's scent was Were, but not Lycan. Not from an ancient bloodline.

She withheld the desire to knock this wolf to the ground and be on her way. She had to be civil, and keep her damn fangs to herself.

"Where did you come from?" the woman asked. "Where are the rest of your clothes?"

Rosalind shivered. When had she again changed form? The full shift to her human shape must have been swift and automatic. It had to have occurred as she'd left the fringes of the park. Without fur-covered legs, she was half-naked, with only the hem of her shirt covering the tops of her thighs.

This had to be an odd sight. What should she do now?

The woman beside her was a dark-haired Were of about the same height as Rosalind, and young. She wore a uniform like the one the brown Were had worn until he'd been catapulted onto a divergent path. The name on her chest pocket said *Delmonico.*

Another cop.

Before Rosalind could summon the wits to reply to this female officer's question, another voice rang out from behind them.

"It's okay, Officer," said her lover, her mate, in a tone that set Rosalind's teeth on edge. "This is my problem, so I'll take it from here."

Rosalind and the woman holding on to her turned toward the speaker in unison. A ghostly figure stood beneath the branches of the last line of trees. His pale skin was shocking. Long strands of pure white hair fell across a portion of his handsome, hardened face.

He seemed twice as formidable as he had been before the vampire attack. The red welts crisscrossing his forehead and cheeks, when added to the light skin and dark-ringed eyes, would make him scary to onlookers of any species. The sight of him took Rosalind's breath away.

But whatever it was that she had become, the effects of their mating ritual hadn't been lost, or forgotten. Her cravings for this wulf hadn't diminished; had in fact grown stronger in her brief absence from him. Even the dark thing taking root inside her wanted to rut with him here, now, without a care for who might be looking.

She recognized the same cravings in him, and she stole a glance at the Were female cop whose grip hadn't lessened.

The cop blinked slowly and sniffed the air. "Don't know you," she said to the wulf in the distance.

"Came from the Landaus' place a few minutes ago," he said. "Chasing after an escapee."

"You know him?" the cop asked Rosalind.

"No," she said, struggling against the idea of shifting into the dark thing with needlelike fangs so that she would scare the hell out of this officer and be able to get away as planned. The emotions inside her were becoming oppressive. Every thought, action, desire, seemed larger than life and potentially overwhelming.

The Were cop sniffed at the air. "I can smell him on you," she said. "I also smell something else."

Facing the ghost, the officer named Delmonico added, "Different. Wounded. Lycan. Are you Killion, by any chance?"

Killion. The name brought on another flutter. Rosalind wrapped her tongue around the sound. It was his name. Had to be.

"I was the man you're asking about," her lover replied.

"Something happened to you after the deaths on Baker," Delmonico said. "This is the result?"

"Yes, but I can't speak of it."

"Everyone is looking for you. The force is exploring all avenues. Will you be coming back?"

"I don't think so. At least not for a while. Did they find…?"

"No. Not many know about your parents. We handled it. They've been taken away."

"We?"

"Adam Scott and myself."

"Thank you," he said sadly, soberly and with obvious relief.

The cop named Delmonico nodded and addressed them both. "It's safe to turn her over to you? You are all right, at least in part? Enough of a part?"

"No," Rosalind replied. "Not safe."

The emotional turmoil inside her was staging a comeback. She could hardly speak, was afraid to open her mouth and expose what lay inside.

"It's the only option," her ghostly mate named Killion said. "Her father is waiting. So is the Judge."

Delmonico nodded again. "Do you know who I am, Killion?"

"I do," he said.

"And why I'm concerned about wolves in this park, and about what I feared might have happened to you?"

"I know the details of what secret circles call the Red Wolf case, and about the rogue named Chavez. Adam Scott was your partner, and he was hurt. But this—" he alluded to the wounds on his face with a wave of his hand "—wasn't due to those things."

The cop let go of Rosalind's arm as if the white-haired

Were had uttered a magical sequence of words that rendered him worthy of her trust. She spoke directly to Rosalind. "Best not to have anyone else see you like this. People here wear clothes. Will you go with Killion, or should I accompany you?"

"Can't." *Don't you see why? Can't you sense the changes?*

Before Rosalind had time to register the expression of surprise on Officer Delmonico's pert face, her ghost wulf had closed the distance and had swept Rosalind into his arms. With a respectful incline of his head to Officer Delmonico, he left the street behind, carrying Rosalind toward the shadowy spaces where the concept of normal in no way applied.

"You don't mean that, about not wanting to come with me," the ghost said. "I can read you like a book."

Carting her as if she weighed little, he ran like the wind in human form toward the Landaus' walls...where instead of returning her to her father, as promised, he shoved her up against a patched section of the stone barrier, lifted her legs and wrapped them around his waist.

He pinned her hands above her head with his large, shaky palms, and leaned in. The stone scraped at her flimsy silk shirt and dug grooves into her bare lower back and hips, but that was nothing. The eyes boring into hers weren't questioning or accusatory. They didn't seek the truth behind the fangs, or why she had left him so abruptly.

Killion's eyes, though pale, were bright with uncontrollable desire. He shook with the attempt to restrain that desire, just as she shook to restrain hers.

"You bite me," he whispered in warning with his face an inch from hers, "and I'll bite you back."

"Promise?"

With an exhaled breath and palpable anxiousness, he said, "Let me in, Rosalind. Now. Here. Take me in before I tear you apart."

Rosalind shut her eyes to manage the frightening, rising dark. With a rush of desire, she felt this ghost wulf's glorious cock sink into her womb possessively, aggressively, in response to the soft sigh of her breath in his mouth.

Chapter 11

The ecstasy of being inside Rosalind again was similar to the pain of being torn apart by enemies and then waking up alive, Colton thought.

Each thrust seemed an earth-shattering event. Every soft, very real sound of encouragement she made hurled him toward hot, sweet, ecstasy.

She was so very...fine.

This couldn't go on, of course, his mind warned. They couldn't continue like this because they wouldn't be allowed to. Rosalind's father waited on the other side of this same wall, and he was going to take her away.

Colton realized that the roughness he used to get at her was tearing Rosalind apart, and he couldn't help it. His mind was set on having her in every possible way, carnal and emotional. If she was to be taken away from him for any amount of time, he needed sustenance.

Rosalind accepted the roughness of this act as if she had been born to it. As if she had to have this as badly as he did, if only to put off and outrun her own demons.

She writhed against him, opened herself, rose to meet him. Her body took him in, massaging his hardness, accepting him with a passion that was ferocious and feral.

This wasn't merely good, it bordered on insane. And not once did she ask him to stop.

He had bites all over his mouth and cheek and neck from Rosalind losing herself in this mating. Colton smelled the blood that seemed to drive her further into a state of euphoria, and let that pass. He would confront that issue another time.

Touch, feel, taste and the sleek, silken sensation of being inside her rendered him worthless in curbing his need to possess her. Being embedded in her blistering heat was everything.

It was life itself.

It was as if he somehow temporarily shared hers.

When the crescendo inside him had built to an impossible level and screamed for release, he penetrated her just one more time with a deep, forceful thrust.

Rosalind moaned, then cried out again, vocalizing her gratification, forgetting where they were.

He came. With her. Simultaneously. The flood gates opened, and his soul's liquid ecstasy mingled with hers. Theirs was a unanimous gasp, a last reach for something beyond themselves that crowded out all other thought... for a while.

And though he wanted to stay buried inside Rosalind, their shouts had an unanticipated domino effect.

An instantaneous response came from beside them;

a gruff, angry stringing together of senseless words intended as a warning, and quite possibly as a threat.

In the time it took for Colton to zip up his jeans and turn Rosalind to face him, he found himself surrounded by Weres that had appeared from nowhere. All of them were elders, all of them were in human form, their auras saturated with hefty, polarized power.

With terrible timing, Jared Kirk had arrived with the big boys in tow.

But before any of them could offer up a protest or more harsh words on Kirk's behalf for Colton taking such liberties with the Were's daughter, a terrible new odor flooded the area on the south side of Landau's wall.

Everyone turned to face this new wave, including Colton.

"They have arrived," Rosalind's father grimly announced.

Vampires.

Above the loaded silence that followed Jared Kirk's remark, Colton heard Rosalind's soft growl of fear. His own fear took shape. He had faced these creatures before. He glanced nervously to each elder Were. As far as he knew, none of these Lycans could shift shape without a full moon. As men they were exceptionally strong, but against the supernatural flood of danger rushing in, they were much more vulnerable.

Taking a step back, Colton pressed Rosalind to the wall, placing himself protectively between her and whatever approached. His hunger for her was barely appeased, but Rosalind's father stood beside him, too close for comfort and reeking of anger. A tall, broad man with silver hair and a long face crowded him on his other side.

"Surely that's impossible," Colton said, his anxiousness escalating as the foul odor of sour earth wafted in. "Bloodsuckers don't dare to trespass here, so close to Were boundaries."

"Nothing about this is usual," Jared Kirk snapped, scanning the park where the trees were the densest.

"Luckily we're prepared," the silver-haired Were remarked in a voice backed by the steel of a practiced authority that made Colton sure this was the infamous Judge Landau himself.

"There may be no moon," said another of Landau's friends, as if he had read Colton's mind, "but since we have fingers and pockets, we have the next best thing."

The familiar smell of metal wafted to Colton, a smell he had lived with nearly every day on the job with the Miami PD. These Weres had weapons. They had guns.

"You don't imagine that will do the trick?" he protested impatiently.

"Special guns," one Were said. "Wooden bullets should do the trick."

Rosalind squirmed behind him, registering her tension with a sound that made the hair at the nape of Colton's neck stand up. She knew a fight was coming. Maybe out of all of them, and with her new fangs, she had the most to fear.

Her father stepped closer to her wearing an expression of wary concern. "We'll go now," he told her. "If it's not too late."

"We can hold them off," Judge Landau promised. "As soon as you go, I'll call the boys."

Kirk took his daughter by the hand. It could be that Rosalind's father realized what had happened to her the night Colton had become a ghost, after all. But maybe not. What was fair to assume, however, was that Kirk and the other elders had been expecting something like this and were ready to take on an influx of fanged parasites.

God help us all if there are hundreds.

"I'll help," Colton volunteered, looking around, sensing the vampires' closeness.

Turning to look at Rosalind, he saw that her eyes were downcast and cloaked by fluttering ebony lashes. She was fighting feelings that none of them really saw or recognized. He also noted that a single streak of white hair, two or three inches wide, ran from her forehead to the tips of her waist-long tresses. He had no idea what had caused this, or if he could simply have missed the discoloration before.

Now wasn't the time or place to address it.

"Rosalind," he whispered to her. "Tell me what this is. What comes here?"

"No," Kirk protested. "It's too late now. You've helped to cause this, and must help get my daughter to safety. Get her away from them. You must guard my daughter with your life."

All eyes turned to Colton, except for Rosalind's. She seemed to have retreated into herself. But her heartbeat had become his heartbeat, pounding, thundering in their arteries.

He wanted her all over again, here, now. He had to be inside her. Nothing else would do. No one else would do. Below his waist, he was still hard, still aching for Rosalind's molten sweet spot.

Yet the way the elders were staring at him put a quick end to his lust. Lycan anxiety filled the area with a palpable heaviness.

Colton didn't like how cold the night had grown in direct correlation with his thoughts about what hid in the park's shadows. And though he wasn't sure what the next vampire onslaught would entail, he sensed that Rosalind knew they were near, and that her current quiet exterior was misleading.

Jared Kirk seemed privy to this, as well. Rosalind's father knew the real answer as to why they all believed these vampires were coming for his daughter. Rosalind had confided to Colton that this council of elders kept secrets, and that she feared they had met to discuss her.

Without waiting to see what Landau and the others had in mind—besides wooden bullets—Colton, for the third time since he had met Rosalind, gathered her in his arms. Not because she was weak or helpless, but because of his intrinsic need to keep her close. Though her dark eyes glowed with rebellion, and her breath hissed out, she allowed his closeness, and seemed to understand how necessary it was.

Ignoring her father's expression of worried anger, Colton said, "Guard her with my life? Gladly. I probably owe her my life, or what's left of it. So, what are you waiting for? Lead the damn way."

He tossed Rosalind atop Landau's eight-foot stone wall with a seemingly effortless grace that left his weakened arms shaking, and left the others murmuring incomprehensible phrases behind him.

Chapter 12

Rosalind couldn't speak. But she did know that with one concerted physical protest, she could get away from all of them, and that if she did, the others here would be safe, at least for a while. Her white wulf, Killion, would be safe, too, except perhaps from his own demons.

Yet swell after swell of longing for him washed over her, as did the fear that if she left him now, he might never find her again. She might be alone forever after knowing the pleasures of bonding with this magnificent male.

Terror over that was like an added layer of pain.

If her father knew what they had done, and what their sex had accomplished, he made no mention of it. Things had too gone far. All was chaos, her father was thinking, and he was right. After planning to separate her from her white wulf, he had asked that same wulf to protect her.

On Landau's side of the wall, she allowed herself to be

led away as if she were a senseless child. Her father's grip on her arm pulled her forward. His anger pushed her on.

She felt every step her ghost mate took. Each labored breath he took moved through her lungs as if it were her own. His pain was becoming her pain, as if such things were contagious. She still felt him between her legs…a ghostly leftover sensation of their lovemaking. She felt him sliding in and out of her, hard and dangerous and filling, with each pulse that struck her throat. Yet her father would see that it didn't happen again.

As they moved away from the park, Rosalind also knew that the effort to escape another vampire attack would be in vain. The Weres here would face them any minute now, and she would be gone.

Deep in her gut, she sensed that the fanged monsters would find her eventually, wherever she was, because of something she had done while in their presence that had exempted her from the fury of their fangs.

The call…

It had been that soulful howl she'd made out there that had slid her closer to the unforeseen abyss where vampires lived.

Making their way past the Landau house, where outside lights now blazed with the wattage of full daylight, Rosalind saw more Weres running for the wall. Young males turned to look at her only once before obeying the call to arms.

Landau's pack. They were all preternaturally beautiful, and terrible in their own right.

I have done this. Brought anger to them all.

One lapse in the rules, and the world had gone mad, taking her with it. No matter how much she wanted or wished, it was too late to change anything.

Hunger. Hunt. Kill. Rosalind flinched as the remembrance of vampire hatred invaded her mind. The rancid emotion behind those words caused her to stumble, catching her father off guard. He dropped his hold on her wrist, and glanced behind them.

Rosalind spun toward the wall in the distance with a shriek of despair on her lips. She felt heavy, awkward now, as if the enemy's existence, so close, was causing her to drown. Unfamiliar fangs were extending, slicing through her gums, bringing hot jabs of discomfort. She could barely move her legs.

Her lover's arms encircled her waist. Killion. Cop. Were. Lycan. Ghost. "No, Rosalind," he said in her ear. "Whatever is happening, you can rise above. Bring up your wulf. Use your strength."

To her father, he said, "They're here now. We only have minutes."

"How do you know?" Jared Kirk demanded.

"Look at your daughter."

Her father, to his credit, showed no sign of panic as Rosalind's body transformed in her lover's arms, surrendering to the cult of the moon, and to his closeness. Only her white wulf's humanlike grunt of approval filled the silence for several seconds as his arms tightened around her.

For the briefest of moments, her eyes met with his. She saw herself in the brilliance of his gaze. Black wulf. Small, sleek, but with one noticeable difference: a vampire's fangs.

The white wulf wanted her desperately. She read that in him. He wanted to take her right there. Throw her down and impale her with the evidence of his glorious sexual vigor. A growl had stuck in his throat. Yet he was also afraid.

"The car is by the garage," her father barked.

There was a sudden rumble of a well-oiled machine. Someone had started the car's engine in anticipation of their departure. As they approached the vehicle, a dark-haired young woman stepped out of the SUV. Rosalind recognized the she-wolf. This close to Killion, she heard his thoughts.

Good cop, he thought. *Bless her, Delmonico is on our side.*

Though Rosalind growled, Officer Dana Delmonico, whom they'd met on the street, faced them as if they were old friends. And the white wulf's thoughts told her that Delmonico was soon going to be Dylan Landau's wife.

"Small world, after all," she heard Colton say as he opened the back door of the black SUV and waved Rosalind inside.

Her father nodded to Delmonico and jumped into the front, behind the wheel. He stomped on the gas pedal with a heavy foot. As the car screeched out onto the asphalt driveway, her mate's thoughts transmitted one more thing before the world went dark with images of bloodsuckers cutting through a line of Weres:

Delmonico and Landau. A pure Lycan and newly inducted Were have bonded together. Further proof that rules can be stretched or broken by a concept as simple as love.

They drove a long time, heading west from Miami and then south toward Florida's gulf.

Colton kept his eyes on Rosalind. One of the first things she had told him was that she came from the bayou

country. This could have meant anywhere in several
Southern states, but in Florida meant the Everglades. The
last road sign Colton noted was of a place called Cape
Sable before he finally succumbed to sleep without meaning to beside Rosalind, who had faded back into human
shape once they'd left the Landau compound behind.

She hadn't said a word. Neither had her father.

When he woke, dazed, startled, the sun had risen, and
he was alone in the car.

He sat up straighter, experiencing a rush of disorien-
tation. His muscles were painfully bunched and aching.

How long have I been asleep?

Where the hell am I?

He felt sick, tired and apprehensive. The sunlight hurt
his eyes. His joints were rigid.

"Rosalind?" he whispered, reaching for the door handle.

The clunk of the SUV's metal was the only sound in
an otherwise silent clearing when he stepped out. Panic
kicked at his stomach.

Colton waited, straining to hear any sound at all, and
finally heard birds and the oddly foreign croak of frogs,
signifying how close they were to water. There were no
traffic noises. No planes passed overhead. There wasn't
one sign of the everyday cacophony of people rushing
around.

"Everglades," he muttered with distaste. "Jesus."

As a city boy, he felt adrift in unknown territory. He'd
never even visited here. This was a foreign landscape, as
different from his world as being dropped onto another
planet. There wasn't even a sidewalk, or a streetlight.
There was no movement at all, save for the quick rise
and fall of his chest.

Colton glanced down, half expecting to find an alligator at his feet, and stubbed at the dirt with his foot. He expected to see something else in the lush jungle greenery surrounding him: vampires, hanging upside down from branches. But that was an impossibility, he realized with relief. Bloodsuckers were creatures of the night, and had to hide from the sun.

With a sweep of his gaze, he saw the house, or what posed as a house. He hadn't considered the sort of residence Rosalind and an elder Lycan like her father would call home, but this was a surprise.

The small, squat building was really a cabin built of rough-hewn timber log walls, with some sort of gray-green mortar packed in the cracks. It couldn't have contained more than a few rooms, beneath a green-hued pitched roof and a couple of chimneys made of river rock. A wide covered porch wrapped around the front and sides. The windows next to the front door had glass in them and the shades drawn, giving the place an abandoned look.

His cop background made him take a further survey of the site. Foliage, thick and riotous near the small garage, had been cleared fifty feet away from the cabin's foundations. The SUV was parked on a dirt road that wound in a curvy manner through the center of a particularly dense grove of unrecognizable trees.

Cop or not, Colton felt utterly alone as he stood there trying to get his bearings. Rustling sounds roused him. He braced himself, called out "Rosalind?"

The cabin's front door opened, but it wasn't Rosalind who stepped out.

"My daughter is resting," Jared Kirk said from the top of the steps.

Colton nodded without moving to meet him. He remained wary, and on guard. "Is she okay?"

"That's a matter of one's point of view, I suppose," Kirk replied frankly. "Sedation will become Rosalind's best friend in the days to come."

"Why? We're far from the vampires, aren't we?" Colton pressed.

"You don't understand what it is that you've vowed to protect, do you? What you've dared to love and befriend?"

Colton said, "A very hyped-up she-wulf, hyped because of reasons I can't yet fathom."

"Ah, then you have your eyes closed to the possibilities, my friend," Jared Kirk remarked.

The elder Were was being purposefully cryptic, and that was flat-out unacceptable after everything Colton had been through. Still, his training mandated that he remain calm and start the necessary interrogation.

"I've been hurt," Colton said. "My world is changing, as, it seems, are my alliances. I've just left everything I have always known and loved behind, most of it lost to me, so why don't you fill me in on a few things that might make this trip to the middle of nowhere make sense."

"Will details affect your willingness to protect my daughter?"

"Do you really expect me to answer that ridiculous question?"

Jared Kirk descended one step slowly, in the manner of a man who had been pushed to his limits. "You made a vow to guard Rosalind, and I will hold you to that vow."

"I've never broken a vow."

The elder Were's voice remained steady, in spite of

how tired he looked. But Colton needed to know what was going on.

"Do you believe I'm responsible for what has happened to her?" he asked. "What *is* happening to her?"

"No. I'm not stupid or unreasonable. My daughter would have had problems with or without meeting you. Her acquaintance with you merely brought her to that end result quicker."

"You'd better explain that," Colton said.

"I'm not sure it's my place to try to dissect what no one truly understands."

"Try." Colton was adamant, his voice firm. Cop voice. Cop demand.

"Very well. I suppose you'll have to know some things if you're to comprehend what guarding her entails."

Kirk took another step with his hand on the carved porch railing before going on. "Rosalind is not like you."

"And?"

"She comes from Lycans, and our blood is in her veins. But she is also something else whose shape has been handed down from a distant side of her mother's family."

The rare black fur. Yes. She was different.

In the silence following Kirk's announcement, Colton got a question in. "How can Rosalind carry the scent of a full-blooded *She*, as well as the mark of the moon, if she is something else, as well?"

Jared Kirk managed to descend the last two steps. Facing Colton, he raised his hands and let them fall back to his sides in a gesture that suggested the futility of attempting to answer Colton's question correctly.

"Issues of the blood are tricky," he finally replied. "With those distant genes remaining dormant, my daughter had the potential to become so many things. We hoped she would be fully Lycan, and only that. Only time would tell us this."

Colton fisted his hands in frustration. The conversation wasn't moving fast enough. Nor were they getting to the heart of the matter in a clear enough fashion to satisfy the needs welling up inside him.

"I'm afraid I don't understand," he said. "You're either Lycan, or you're not. Half-breeds are another thing altogether. Bitees are still more distant."

"Are you prejudiced against diluted blood, Colton?"

"Certainly not."

"What if that diluted blood came from a vampire?"

"Can't happen. Our blood doesn't mix."

"Can't it? You were injured by vampires. The brutality of their attack and the venom in their fangs has changed you into what you are now. You're Lycan, but fully? Do you know that for sure?"

The allusion to his current condition was for Colton like a sudden slap in the face. He waited, speechless, for the elder to continue, considering the possible ramifications of what Kirk had said and feeling unsteady in his open-legged stance.

Kirk's hand again moved, reaching for the railing as if groping for support. He spoke in a lowered tone. "The medication the Landaus gave you will slowly leave your system. It has temporarily given you access to some of your former strength, but what is left after that's gone is anyone's guess."

Hell, this was ominous news that Colton didn't need or care to dwell upon at the moment, though he probably should have cared. He was tired, sure. Bone-weary. But his wulf was still there, coating his insides, waiting for a chance to be freed.

If they thought he might become something other than wulf without special medication, as Kirk had just suggested, then why would the Were entrust him with his daughter's welfare?

The last thought was accompanied by a tingling sensation that rivaled the moon's influence on his bones. Seconds of light-headedness came and passed that could have been an omen of the nebulous future Kirk had hinted at, if Colton believed in omens. As it was, he just took it for another symptom of fatigue.

Nevertheless, the situation here remained unclear. Shoving the hair back from his face and looking directly at the Were in front of him, Colton asked with trepidation, "Did the vampires bite her? Is that what you're alluding to?"

Kirk eyed him wearily before speaking in a voice hushed by sorrow. "They didn't need to bite her. In order to change my daughter, those creatures only had to get close to her. They only had to touch her, brush up against her, exhale their foul breath on her."

Colton observed Kirk closely, thinking his response ridiculous.

"This is why I've kept her from the world," Kirk explained, without having actually explained much at all. "I have sequestered her here for the same reason I would have kept her away from you and any other potential suitor. I had to explain to Landau and the other elders why Rosalind can't be in their gene pool. It's not your fault this has happened. It's mine, for taking the risk of having her with me at the Landaus'. I couldn't allow them to come here when this place has to remain secret, and I couldn't leave Rosalind here alone."

Colton's unease had grown by bounds. He felt extremely uncomfortable now. The tingling sensations on his face and hands had gotten strong enough to resemble a swarm of insects walking around. The muscles of his upper back twitched with the intensity of a recurring spasm.

He was shirtless, and shivered in spite of the muggy heat of the place. In his peripheral vision he watched strands of white hair blow in an unusual breeze that smelled sultry but brought on a chill. Those colorless strands in his face were locks of his own hair, longer than he remembered, thicker than before and peppered with Rosalind's floral scent.

With that scent, memories flashed.

A call in the park from a she-wulf.

A black whirlwind tearing into the vampires, fighting savagely by his side.

Rosalind in his arms, leaving bites on his mouth, face and neck.

Rosalind on the windowsill, holding up her shaky, blood-tinted hand.

The heat of Rosalind's insides as he thrust into her.

Her groans of pleasure. Her blackened eyes.

Her shock over discovering that her mouth was filled with something no other wulf had. Needle-sharp fangs.

Those fangs dragging across his skin when he had...

"It would seem," Jared Kirk said, "that Rosalind's genes didn't remain dormant, and that they are showing up in full force. If she had been near to you first, Colton, she'd have been like you. Lycan, for all intents and purposes. But instead vampires overpowered her senses with their insatiable thirst and their craving for blood, and my daughter has taken on some of their characteristics."

Kirk's voice cracked with submerged emotion. After a long, deep breath, he went on. "If we hadn't gotten her away from them quickly, her adaptation likely would have been more complete than it is. From what I've seen, Rosalind is stuck midway through a transition between wulf and vampire that none of us recognizes. Maybe it's not too late for her to change back. Perhaps there's hope. I pray for that."

Colton stood there, feeling completely useless and only partly appeased. He supposed there was light at the end of this explanation, but he wasn't able to reach it. Though he opened his mouth to speak, no words came out for some time.

"That's why you have allowed me to come here with her, and to hold her," he finally managed to say. "You're hoping that between the two of us, between you and I, she will revert back to normal? To wulf?"

Jared Kirk shook his head and pointed at Colton. "Normal? You think you're normal? Look at you. No, my current fear is that if you get near her again, she may take on more of your ghostly attributes. That has already started. You've seen the white in her hair. But you were the second thing to change her, not the first. The result of being with you is more subtle. The vampire traits remain, though yours seem to have influenced Rosalind, as well."

Colton stared at Kirk.

"Hell," Kirk said. "My daughter is now part wulf, part vampire, and part whatever else that you are going to turn out to be, with the multitude of bites you received in that park."

"Yet I remain wulf," Colton said, "in spite of my injuries. Other than the color of my hair, I feel Lycan. A ghost of a wulf is better than a creature of the night."

"True," Jared Kirk agreed. His expression didn't soften. He didn't seem to realize what effect on Colton his words had; the suggestion that Colton might lose the wulf, and himself, in the end.

"So here we are," Kirk said. "You and me and whatever now swims in Rosalind's veins."

The sickness in Colton's stomach worsened, threatening to bring up bile. His legs had grown more and more restless. His mind warned that he should run now, get away from this crazy interlude...but he was still in the dark in more ways than one, and the Were across from him seemed to hold a handful of clues as to what that iffy, nebulous future hanging over him might bring.

What I might become if I don't fight for myself. And for her.

"I won't change," he said to Jared Kirk.

"Who can be sure?" Kirk tossed back.

"Yet you asked me to protect Rosalind."

Kirk nodded. "I don't know what else to do. You've bonded with her. Maybe you can influence Rosalind in ways no one else can. I will hold you to that promise, as I will hold you to a promise not to touch her again until we see what your changes might bring."

Colton shook his head. "How can I protect her if can't be near to her?"

"You must promise me, Colton, not to touch her."

"You know that we have imprinted."

"Yes. But I repeat that if you have a care for my daughter's safety and her future, you must comply. You must honor my request not to touch her again."

This was an utterly useless warning, Colton wanted

to shout, and quite impossible. Even sick and shaky, he wanted Rosalind so badly, he had begun to taste her presence in that house. In his mind, he saw her outline. She was lying on a bed, with her long hair fanning over the edges of a pale pillow.

So very lovely, and so very silky, her midnight-black hair had spilled like that across his skin when he had taken her. When they had joined their bodies and their souls. He could taste her, feel the exquisite texture of her body, still.

He rolled his shoulders to stop the insanity.

"I'm not sure I can stay away," he earnestly confessed. "Not now. You don't understand."

Kirk held up a hand to stop Colton's protest. Colton ignored the Were's warning.

"I'm to stay here, be her guard dog, without getting close? How close is too close? How is that kind of relationship supposed to work? You have to see how absurd your requirement is. What about her? What she wants?"

"Her needs don't count. Cannot count."

"It's to be one freak protecting another, then?" Colton was angered into taking a step. "Is that it?"

"No. It's a male who has accepted a female, taking care of that female. Your police training will come in handy here," Kirk said. "I can't be sure they won't find her here. I can't be sure they won't try. If they don't, others will, now that she has come of age. Now that you've opened the door to her womanhood and dispersed the scent of her uniqueness into the world."

What Colton wanted to say in response to this absurd diatribe was *You are a crazy bastard*. The words he managed to get out were "What do you mean by *Others*? Others trying to get at her?"

He had heard and internalized the meaning of that special emphasis, the capital *O*. But it soon became clear that Jared Kirk had said all he was going to say.

Looking bone-tired and far older than his years, the Were's broad shoulders drooped. His face had taken on a gaunt, sunken appearance. Rosalind's father was worried. There was no doubt about that. Jared Kirk honestly feared for his daughter, and who might come after her.

Turning from Colton, Kirk said in a wavering rasp, "There's a place for you in the shed, and clothes and boots in the wardrobe. You must be hungry. I'll bring some food."

Then Rosalind's father was gone, closing the door on what Colton supposed had to be only the beginning of a brand-new nightmare.

Chapter 13

Rosalind stirred. Feeling a sensation of coolness on her cheek and a burning sensation below her right knee, she awakened fully, overcome with a sense of impending doom.

She wasn't drowning, running, howling, or pressed up against a stone wall by her lover. She was in her room, on her bed. Familiar scents were everywhere. Waning daylight seeped through the curtained window, casting long shadows along one wall.

Covering her eyes to close out the suddenness of the light, she waited for whatever would come next.

The room was quiet, undisturbed, but her heart drummed, its rhythm chaotically rising and falling without perceivable instigation or trigger. The nag of an awful pain below one knee demanded her immediate attention. Between her thighs, a flickering spark informed her that her lover was near.

She sat up and looked to the door expectantly.

"I'm here," her father said, dashing her hopes for the big ghost wulf as he appeared in the doorway too quickly to have been anywhere else. "You're safe."

The throb in her private places didn't lessen. Her wulf was near. It hadn't been a dream. None of this was her imagination. She could almost smell the magnificent Killion. Her body was telling her that she couldn't bear to be long without him in spite of recent events.

"Where is he?" she asked her father.

"Who?" he replied. But Rosalind read him easily enough, and in her new, even more impatient incarnation, despised the old games they played. She was no longer a child, nor childlike. In the past few days she had become someone else. *Something* else.

"I know he's here. I can sense him," she said.

"Colton is outside."

Colton. Hearing his full name brought her pleasure. Her lips parted as she sucked that pleasure in.

"Your protector is standing guard," her father explained, his voice backed by the strain of this announcement. He wasn't happy about having the ghost here.

Rosalind swung herself to the side of the bed in an attempt to get to her feet, and was yanked back before getting far. Tossing the blanket aside, she found the reason she couldn't budge, and the source of her leg's burn. She looked at her father questioningly.

"It's for your own good," he said, sadly.

"It's a chain."

"Yes. You might have chewed through a rope."

Automatically, Rosalind put a hand to her mouth.

"The fangs will probably appear as soon as the sun goes down," her father said. "Yet I'm hoping for progress since you're awake in the daylight and adjusting to the silver chain, when those things should have been problematic."

Waves of fear hit her and retreated, carrying flashes of memory and feelings of dread.

"What am I?" Rosalind demanded, tugging against the restraint, wanting to tear it off.

Her father crossed to the bed and sat down beside her. As his weight hit the mattress, Rosalind suddenly understood about the necessity of restraint. If she'd had fangs, she might have used them. The urge to do so, and to be free of the damn chain, was there, lurking in the darkness of her soul.

"I believe you're a mixture of vampire and Were at the moment, with the latter maintaining some hold," her father said.

"Secrets," Rosalind muttered, pointing to the chain. "Is this the result of withholding things from me?"

"I doubt that any explanation would have curbed your enthusiasm for ignoring rules, Rosalind. As parents, we can only do so much."

"Then the fangs are penance, payback, for desiring freedom? Could you possibly think that? How did this happen? I'm owed an explanation."

Her father patted her hand, allowing his fingers to rest on hers as he leaned in to place a kiss on her forehead. "I'm sorry," he said. "I prayed this wouldn't happen to the extent it has, but saw it coming long ago. I tried to keep you from it, and assumed that if you didn't know what resided within you, that thing would stand no chance of showing itself."

Another wave of darkness hit Rosalind. The shadows

from the window had moved to the bed. The closer those shadows got, the more restless she became.

"How can I be part vampire?" Her tone was insistent. "And how could you have watched for it? That's insane."

"The Blackout," he whispered.

The sheer weight of her father's closeness and the kiss he'd placed on her forehead temporarily robbed her of the terrible, irrational urges to tug on the chain. His scent was familiar. His face was very dear to her. He was worried, and not bothering to hide it.

"It was different for you," he went on. "The Blackout phase came on earlier, and so very intense. As your body rewired to allow your wulf in, there were signs of other changes, as well. In your fever, your body mimicked other things, the likes of which I had never seen, as if those things had somehow gotten in through an open door."

Her father winced, remembering. "You shifted in and out of form relentlessly, fighting to be what you needed to be. You pulled through. Your abilities and powers grew, almost as if there weren't enough abilities to master, and then you furred-up into a rare, very beautiful, black-pelted wulf."

"Go on." She had to stop for a breath before finishing what she wanted to say. "Tell me more. Tell me everything."

Her father waited an unconscionably long time before obliging. Rosalind forcibly withheld her claws from springing. Already there were gouges on the walls of her room from the misplaced anger of her youth. Had this been part of the anomaly her father had seen in her early on?

"Your mother told me stories about an ancestor who possessed abilities like yours. She told these stories to me so that I would watch for signs. Watch *you* for them, just as her mother had watched her," her father said. "I conferred with the elders at Landau's compound, fearing what your future might hold. They had to know about you, and why I hadn't presented you to one of their sons."

"So, what am I?" she demanded, dreading the answer to the question, and knowing she had to have it.

"Werewolf," he said. "But with something else at your core. Not just a she-wulf, Rosalind. Nor just showing vampire traits. I believe you are part something else, as well."

His expression had grown dull with sadness and regret. He spoke again before she could protest or argue.

"You have in you the traits of another supernatural creature, one that is noted for announcing oncoming death. Legends abound of this creature in other countries, but not so much here."

"What are you saying? What creature?"

"I fear that you are, deep inside, a hybrid. As far as I know, there has only been one such mixture, and that was your great-great-grandmother. The tale says she was a Lycan who was saved by the very Death-caller slated to announce her death. She lived, and went on to mate with another full-blooded Were. But there was a consequence for cheating Death. In being saved by a creature that was destined to cry of death, some of that spirit's traits passed into your relative. The offspring of her and her Lycan mate was unique. Special, with special skills like yours. She was called Night Wulf."

Rosalind scooted backward on the bed until she felt the hard support of the wall against her back. It seemed that her father would allow her no room for avoiding the secrets she had been asking for, but each one seemed like a blow.

"I guess," he said, "that those stories were true."

Rosalind wanted to shout for him to stop, and tell him she'd had enough. But she was riveted. She was starved for explanations for the turmoil that had always roiled inside her.

"Go on," she said.

Her father nodded. "From this incident, we must assume that your form can vary according to the species you focus on. You fought vampires, and so you became somewhat like them. You got their fangs."

He took a breath. "We must see if you'll change back to Lycan after leaving the bloodsuckers. I have no idea what to do if you don't. I doubt if anyone would know. The elders of the Landau pack saw you. They saw the fangs. I've promised to keep you away from the world until we do know what's to happen, for your protection and theirs."

Rosalind felt a howl rising that was frighteningly similar to the one she had issued in the park. She didn't dare allow it to escape. Her father's explanations had alleged that the other call had risen from unknown depths because she possessed depths she wasn't aware of. What was a Death-caller? What did that even mean?

He was also telling her that she had become stuck physically between Were and the vampires she been attempting to kill while aiding her big brown werewolf. And that her body also hid something else that labeled her a Night Wulf.

The title itself was ominous, and produced a shiver.

If that wasn't bad enough, her father truly believed that she had become infused with the particles of a fanged, blood-drinking species that was her enemy. And it was true. Her Lycan teeth had molded to resemble those of another species.

"What's wrong with my pelt?" she managed to ask. "You say black as if that has meaning."

Her father got to his feet. He looked down at her with the same expression of frustration that he'd worn whenever she had ignored his counsel in the past. "There are no black-pelted werewolves, Rosalind. It was the first sign of something being amiss. An early warning."

Too stunned to speak, Rosalind watched her father head for the door. She felt sick. Her father hadn't wanted her to know any of this, but how could he have kept something so important from her? What had he been thinking?

She supposed he hadn't wanted her to feel different. Then again, maybe, just maybe, he'd had the protection of others foremost in his mind as he had harbored and basically held her captive all her life.

Black pelt, black heart?

Freak.

"I've protected you. I warned you about that excess energy," he said as the door began to close behind him. Before the metallic click of the lock, his voice took on a hint of her own level of despair. "God knows I tried."

Rosalind stared after him, hearing his words repeat over and over in her head. Inside her, alongside her wulf, lived some kind of Otherworldly chameleon that had to be chained now that it had shown up.

Could she be, in part, a creature that was a harbinger of doom, whose purpose was to announce the death of others, without knowing about it all this time? A creature able to absorb the traits of Others, and make them her own?

God…

Was that what a *Death-caller* was? Another word for Banshee?

Hadn't she heard in that disturbing howl in the park the unspoken message "Death comes"?

"Heaven help me."

All those secrets she had so desperately wanted to know about, all those whispers about being special, had turned out to be really bad news.

Chapter 14

Colton sat with his head in his hands on a cot in a room no bigger than eight square feet. The quarters were too small for pacing and too big for hiding from the current level of his pain, half of which he attributed to the surprise of so many recent discoveries.

Jared Kirk had told him that his pain might return, and the elder had no idea what that diagnosis meant. If the pain got any worse, he might lose his mind.

Nevertheless, he'd had to take the time to settle down and focus on the fact that rationalizations were the bane of his new existence.

He was becoming an entity that had no name other than ghost, and it was possible that term was indicative of the hazy area between being Lycan and some other nameless surprise.

There was also a fair chance that being a ghost meant

inhabiting the colorless, amorphous space between life and death in such a way that he might never get over it, or back to normal.

He had looked Death in the eye, he'd been told, but he didn't remember Death looking back. All that he knew for certain was that he had dreamed of a female's soft lips on his, of a hissed breath into his lungs, of consciousness slipping away...and that when he had awakened from the void, following his fight in the park, he had sealed himself to a female also in transition. His lover, in truth, had taken on aspects of the same monsters that had murdered his family.

"Vampire," he said with distaste.

In strange surroundings the word sounded even worse than usual.

If Rosalind evolved into being more like a vampire than she already was, what came next for her? A desire for blood?

Would their bond be broken by the same unseen force that had put them together, if that were the case? What if it wasn't? Would he eventually want to harm her for those new fangs or, God forbid, would she want to hurt him?

"Fine mess."

He wondered if vows had a pecking order that required the first one to take precedence. His allegiance to his family came first. It's what he had meant to take care of in that park.

Now, he had promised to watch over a female he was supposed to stay away from; one her father had insinuated might very well turn out to be a danger to others. This all seemed too much of a fantasy to be real...until he looked at his hands, which were ribbed with the evi-

dence of wounds that a Lycan would be able to heal, if a
Lycan were pure Lycan.

"Has all this come out of my wish for vengeance? In
following my anger, have I somehow accidentally unleashed dark forces that are beyond my comprehension?"

His question fell flat in the wood-paneled room.
Colton glanced to the window, high above the cot, for
enlightenment, needing to feel the sun on his face, wanting a reminder of the touch of Rosalind's healing heat.
Wanting her lips, her eyes and her luscious body.

Was Rosalind's current transition his fault, since she
had been helping him when it occurred?

Each pulse that thrummed against his neck brought
with it a ribbon of pain, and at the same time, an un-
quenchable carnal craving for Rosalind. The image of
the savagery of his parents' deaths had dimmed for the
moment, overtaken by a new threshold of lust for Rosalind, whatever the hell she was to become.

And whatever the hell was to become of him.

What if he proved to be the last of his clan, and this
imprinting had gone astray?

Conversely, even if he had let his parents down by not
being able to protect them from all existing evils, couldn't
he make amends by saving Rosalind from a similar fate?

Jared Kirk had said that vampires might come after
her here. Not only vampires, but other things, as well.
Colton had no idea what that meant. Police training was
so far from the parameters of this world, it did him no
good at all. Otherwise, he might question why the Landaus, who had brought him back from the brink of death,
couldn't have helped Rosalind in some way.

"Well," he whispered, watching dust motes dance as

his palm hit the surface of the cot, "I suppose we didn't give them the chance."

It was a moot point now. They were tucked away in the Everglades. He truly was out of his element in this balmy jungle. What help he could offer here might turn out to be minuscule at best.

Another ribbon of pain struck somewhere behind his rib cage. He wondered if it might just be his heart, aching.

"Rosalind," he whispered, needing to say her name. Needing to see his body's reaction to the thought of her, and if that reaction had dimmed with the meager attempt at reasoning.

Nope. He wanted to see her right now. He was tired of waiting this out.

"Rosalind," he repeated, louder.

The effect she had on him hadn't been lessened by the shed's thick wooden walls. If he turned his head, he knew he would see her. If he stopped the tumultuous thoughts from whirling, he'd hear her calls.

Thinking that, Colton's heart gave one hardy kick, as if starting back up after a stall. That kick was for Rosalind, the woman he wanted so completely. Her heat beat at him in waves, and as though she was there, by his side. Her voice was in his ears, her own need reflected in the eyes he couldn't actually see.

"Sweet wulf."

My lover. For better or worse, my mate.

Frustration ripped through him as Colton got to his feet.

"Who else will come for you?" he remarked as the idea of Others arriving weighed heavily in his mind. Jared Kirk obviously feared who and what those Others might be. The elder Were did have his daughter's safety at heart, and that was why he seemed like her jailer.

"A freak to protect a freak," Colton whispered.

Kirk knew how hard his request would be, to protect Rosalind without touching her. Colton wasn't sure he could honor that request, despite its significance. Rosalind was like catnip to his wulf, and she called out to him now, in his mind, in a voice like fire.

Or was that fire merely another stab of pain related to his injuries?

No matter which thing it turned out to be, and hoping to keep his sanity intact for a while longer, Colton covered his ears.

Evening arrived. Before checking the clock on the table, Rosalind knew when she woke up that the sun sat lower in the sky. She'd grown colder and more restless. She hadn't meant to sleep, dreading the coming of night, but had been so tired.

The ache of the chain around her ankle had doubled. As if the links had been dipped in flames, they now robbed her of breath each time she moved. But her jaws were taut in a way that wasn't normal, and had to be indicative of the awful changes in her mouth that her father had been waiting for.

Hell, she really was a mixture of Lycan and monster. More than just a freak, she was an abomination. And yet it was curious how much she felt like herself, in spite of all that.

Tugging again at the chain, Rosalind glanced to the locked door, then to the window. She had always been strong, and felt a surge of strength now. She had never craved freedom more than she did at that moment. Freedom, and a big brown werewolf's overheated loins.

Bracing herself on the edge of the mattress with both hands on the chain, she yanked as hard as she could. The chain stretched by inches. The wall behind the bed groaned. Crawling on hands and knees, Rosalind found an iron ring embedded into the wall's support beam. That beam had cracked slightly.

Riding out a wave of dizziness, she stared at the heavy metal piece that had to have always been there, hidden, for such a time as this. For a time when her father's long-anticipated fears might come true, and an abomination would need restraint.

Her father had planned for this. He had been prepared.

"Damn him. Damn everything."

Her body tightened by anger, Rosalind tugged again at the chain, utilizing the power of her bunched muscles. She heard a crack, and fell back as the ring came free.

Quickly, she got to her feet.

Dragging the short length of metal links, Rosalind crossed the room. The chain clanked on the floorboards as she opened the window, and again when she climbed onto the sill and was met by a dark, damp, slightly sinister Everglades breeze.

"Haven't you heard of doors?" someone asked as her two bare feet hit the ground outside.

Rosalind stayed in a crouched position, ready to spring away.

"It's not safe for you to be out here," Colton Killion said. "Not tonight, or any night in the near future, I imagine."

Rosalind straightened slowly and narrowed her gaze

on the space beneath the grove of trees bordering the driveway. A lightness shone there that wasn't affiliated with the moon. It was her ghost wulf's paleness.

Her heart dialed into the rapid rhythm of his, finding it familiar, liking the sensation of two hearts beating as one. She easily scented the passion he withheld, and headed toward him, drawn by the pheromones in the air.

"Wait," he cautioned in a tone tinged with uncertainty. "Don't come closer. You can't get closer."

She paused to absorb what he had said. The warning hurt more than the fangs stretching her mouth out of shape.

"So," she said, searching for control that was already slipping. "You believe my father."

"Don't you?"

"I have fangs, so what's not to believe?"

"Do you have them now?" he asked tentatively.

"Yes."

To his credit, Colton didn't wince or drop his gaze to her mouth.

"Your father says that touching you will make things worse," he said.

"I wonder if anything could be worse."

"It's torture," he confessed in a voice hushed by strain. "You warned that it would hurt if we were separated. Being here and unable to touch you trumps that."

Rosalind was afraid to shut her eyes or ignore his warning. What if the things they had been told were true, and instead of him changing her, she'd hurt him instead? His musky, masculine presence hadn't been dulled by his circumstances. He seemed to fill her vision, larger than life, every bit as sexy as he had been. Her longing for him threatened to outweigh any scrap of common sense she tried to drum up, when she had never been particularly good at common sense in the first place.

"My father didn't tell me enough. I don't think he knows what to do," she said, lowering her gaze.

"Neither do I," he confessed.

"Did he tell you what to expect? Why I'm chained?"

"Chained?" her ghostly lover repeated, as though his throat had gone dry.

She moved her foot. The chain made a dull thudding sound in the dirt.

"Hell. I had no idea," he said.

"Now that you do?"

"I'm staying. I'll try my best to keep them from you if your father is telling the truth. But who, I wonder, will be able to keep me from you?"

Rosalind hated common sense almost more than anything, but couldn't give in this time. Not yet. The male across from her had been hurt enough already, some of it at her expense.

"Who does he believe will be coming?" she asked. "He failed to mention that to me."

"He's guessing that vampires may have your scent, and now that you're more like them it will be easier for the vipers to find you."

"Why would they want to find me?"

Hearing his short bark of frustrated laughter, Rosalind looked up.

"I suppose," he suggested, "that they might want what I want, if they had any normal body parts left."

The laughter hadn't reached his eyes.

"But the thought of anyone else getting near you for any reason whatsoever is not only unacceptable, it's outright disgusting."

He paused to draw in a breath. Rosalind did the same, as if their lungs were united in the search for air.

"If they arrive, I'll fight them. This I swear," her ghostly protector said.

"And if they don't come? If no one arrives and this is nothing more than supposition and my father's personal fear?"

He touched his mouth, his gesture alluding to her fangs. "Don't those make your father's fear reasonable?"

"Yes." Her voice was faint.

"Vampires are the children of the night, Rosalind. Perhaps we only need to worry about that."

"Night has always been our time, too. Wolf time. Are we to ignore what we are?"

"For a while, we'll have to fight our nature. In the meantime, it isn't a good idea for you to be out here after sundown."

"But I have only just found you," she said, taking one more step toward him and changing the subject completely. Or maybe just bringing their attention back to it. "And you're to stay away from me."

"I'm here," he reiterated, his expression highlighting the dark circles under his eyes. "I'm here for you. Trust me on this."

"Maybe never to touch me again?"

When he didn't reply to that terrible question, Rosalind shook her head. "Guarding me won't be an easy job. I'd rather face what's coming now than let this draw out."

"Please, Rosalind. Listen to reason." His hands were raised, as though he had already forgotten that he wasn't to touch her.

She held up a hand. "Your wulf calls to me, and I have to refuse that call. The night also calls to me. If I can't have one of those two things, I'll take the other, or go mad."

Her anger faded when sadness replaced all other emotion on her ghostly lover's face. That sadness overwhelmed her, though there was nothing she could do to stop it.

"You are Lycan," he said. "As am I. We can withstand this. We face what life brings, and land on our feet."

Rosalind looked at him with pangs of regret so deepseated, it felt to her that her soul was aching. This brave Were had been wounded while trying to avenge his family, and might never be the same. There was no greater show of respect for his family than that kind of sacrifice. And he'd do it again, for her.

She had tried to help him, and honor his fight. The result had joined them together, and at the same time brought them more pain.

She could not remain apart from him, and feared to try. Colton was the epitome of what every Were should be. Still, she so very badly wanted him to forget about honor and promises, and pretend they were back at the Landau's wall, in each other's passionate embrace.

The remembered heat of that meeting made her thighs quiver. The ridiculous idea that vampires could possibly experience emotions like regret and sorrow made her feel slightly less frightened as she stared at Colton. And because she felt those emotions, and so much more, she supposed that she couldn't really be like the creatures her father feared would find her. Her mind was her own. Her lust for Colton was the desire for mating with a Were, wulf to wulf, not for biting him with another species' teeth.

Her body thrummed and twitched for the kind of mating that had sealed them together in the first place. She wanted him, now; everything he had to offer. She wanted to kiss him, straddle him, take him into her body and make him howl with delight. She wanted to tell him this.

If he'd believe in her, she could confess such a thing. If he would meet her halfway, anything was possible.

Please take that step, she sent silently to him.

I need you. Can't you see?

"Rosalind," he whispered, as if her name were some kind of magical talisman for retaining his wits. In his voice lay traces of the dilemma he faced with her father's mandate. This magnificent male was choosing to do the right thing.

Rosalind backed up, fighting a lump in her throat, sure she'd choke if she spoke again.

"What is it?" he asked, concerned, striding forward to stand in all his white glory near the base of the steps. Tall, proud, Were, in spite of the visible remnants of his injuries and the draining away of a golden future, the sight of Colton Killion hurt her. They both wanted the same thing. Yet he was unable to throw her to the ground and do to her what they both craved because...

"You made a promise to the wrong Kirk," she said to him.

His interrupted breath moved her lungs. Her pulse matched his, beat for beat. And she couldn't have him because they were both something other than what they were supposed to be.

"It's too much," she added.

Cursing the initial rise of rebellion that had gotten her to this point in time, she whispered, "If you can't touch me, then you can't stop me."

Spinning as if the links attached to her ankle were no

more than a nuisance, Rosalind took off at a dead run in the opposite direction, refusing to allow her tears to fall.

"Shit!" Colton shouted. "Are you insane?"

His words hung in the air, useless. The fanged, feisty Rosalind had already disappeared into the tangle of trees.

He took off after her. What he would do when he caught up with her was anyone's guess. If he didn't touch her, he'd have no way to bring her back. Reasoning hadn't done the trick.

Where the hell was her father, anyway?

The house was dark. No lights lit the porch or yard; just the faint glow of a partial moon behind the trees. Didn't Kirk believe in electricity? Without lights, anything could hide in the dark.

His heart rate peaked as he stretched his stride. Rosalind's special scent saturated the air, and in that scent, he could perceive the state of her emotions. She was angry, nervous and sad. A terrible mix for running through a night that might be populated with monsters.

He glanced at the trees as he raced by, thinking how bloodless Rosalind's beautiful face had been, and of the wildness in her eyes.

"Rosalind! Stop!"

He was feeling at odds with the world around him.

Dismissing the pain shooting through his torso, and on legs as heavy as lead, Colton ran. He hoped Rosalind wasn't actually as nuts as this action made her seem, and prayed that the bloodsuckers actually had no way of tracking what their now doubly dead pals had witnessed in that park.

It took exactly twenty more big strides for him to find out that his wishes weren't worth much.

Chapter 15

What lay hidden in the dark made the rest of the already strange night seem tame by comparison.

Colton stumbled to a sudden halt. Hate twisted his gut. The vampires had arrived like a plague of bloodthirsty locusts. A series of eerie, high-pitched signals arising from corpse-like throats rent the croaking, frog-infested night. And then the frog sounds ceased.

There was no more pain in him, only cold. It felt to Colton as though his life was slipping away from him one chilled inch at a time as he waited for whatever would happen next.

"You can't have her. I'll die first," he shouted as the weight of the vampires' presence added to the thickness of the dark's unsettled atmosphere.

He cast glances in all directions, whipping his head from side to side, seeing nothing, but sensing the dead gathering someplace not too far away from where he stood.

Without stopping to wonder why he sensed this connection to them, Colton strode forward, heading for the trees. He knew better than to shout for Rosalind because if she answered and the vamps hadn't already found her, they certainly would after that.

Heaven and hell were here, on both sides of him. A succulent lover vied for his attention, as did the plague of blood-drinking creeps.

"I suppose I've already cheated Death once," he muttered. "Maybe I owe him one."

Rolling his shoulders, he moved on, determined to see this through. Damn if he didn't hear Rosalind's voice before the protective thoughts had dissipated, though.

Her voice was raised. She was egging the bloodsuckers on, taunting the monsters, inviting them to find her.

A horrible thought entered his head that caused him to stagger. What if Rosalind was hoping to die, and in that way set both herself and him free from this ongoing nightmare?

The thought was so dreadful that Colton shook off his hesitation and sprinted toward the echo of her voice.

The brush he fought his way through was thick, damp and clingy. His borrowed boots sank into a half inch of mud that slowed him down by tugging at his steps like quicksand would have in some other godforsaken place.

Pushing through the foliage fiercely, he managed to find a path fragrant with Rosalind's scent. Out of necessity, he ventured a whisper.

A reply came in the form of a startled roar of protest. *Not Rosalind. Someone else. Not vampire, but Were.* Colton spun in place, sniffing the air. Detecting a

Lycan presence behind him, he leaped to one side of the path and vaulted over a fallen tree as the newcomer's presence grew stronger. No full moon rode the sky tonight, which meant that this Lycan walked in man form. Since this place was so remote, there was only one Were this could be.

Jared Kirk appeared on the path, wearing dark clothes that blended with the surroundings. A dangerous expression hung on his features. Grasped in his hands was a strange instrument Colton had seen in history books that had been modified with a futuristic flare into a lethal-looking crossbow.

"I asked you not to touch her," Kirk said as he approached. "In light of that, I figured you can't fight this one alone."

Colton nodded, relieved.

"How many monsters are there?" Kirk asked.

"More than one. Do you have any idea where Rosalind would have gone?"

"I think I do. How close are they?"

"Their foul stink is all around us, but they must have gone ahead, after her, alerted by her voice."

Kirk nodded. "She wasn't always so foolish. Not until this."

"She's leading them away from the house," Colton said, only then realizing that this was true, and that something in her scent had communicated her intentions to him. "Leading them away from you, is my guess, and away from me."

Kirk seemed to momentarily slump before regaining height aided by a rigid spine. "All this sacrifice nonsense is for the birds. I don't want to lose her."

"Neither do I," Colton confessed.

Their gazes met.

"So be it," Kirk concluded with a wave of his hand. "Do you have any more secrets that might help, other than having already survived a vampire attack, and having some inner connection to my daughter?"

"As a matter of fact, I do," Colton said. "Small help as it may prove."

Calling up his anger, letting the night breeze waft over his tingling skin, Colton tore off his shirt, unbuttoned his pants and kicked off the cumbersome borrowed boots. With a glance to a sky mostly hidden by the tall trees, he envisioned the moon shining there, and opened his eyes wide to let that light in.

An incendiary heat began to churn in his muscles as he began his transformation. In the blink of an eye, he was a werewolf...big, strapping, white-furred, with an insatiable appetite for kicking vampires back to the hell they had arisen from.

Facing Jared Kirk with trepidation over what this new kind of confession might bring, and with his razor claws raised, Colton let out an ear-piercing howl.

"Dear God," Kirk whispered, letting the oath fade as Colton turned toward the rose scent that he knew would lead him to Rosalind.

The monsters had heard her call, Rosalind thought.

She should have been scared out of her wits. Instead, her rage for all the changes these creatures had brought to her life gave her the fuel she needed to fight them now.

The first gaunt, white-skinned spirit appeared as if it had risen from a bog. The second one dropped from a tree in the same way its malevolent brothers had fallen on Colton that other night.

They didn't immediately attack; just stood there looking at her as if they were waiting for something or someone else. Rosalind gritted her pointed teeth.

"I'd rather be truly and completely dead than be like you," she said when neither of the monsters moved.

The creatures didn't respond. When one of them cocked its bony head with a stiff movement more reminiscent of a robot than anything that had once been human, Rosalind remembered how she'd used her claws to tear through the necks of their brothers, and how simple that had seemed at the time.

"You're not welcome here," she said.

The cold brush of a third vampire came in from her right side. Rosalind ventured a glance. This one was by itself, and had stopped several feet away from where she stood.

It resembled the other two. Nothing she noticed made this sucker seem different. Yet the way the two vampires on her opposite side focused intently on the newcomer suggested some sort of vampire pecking order.

"Go away." She directed this warning to the tall, sinewy creature with frozen, emotionless features. "This is wolf ground and you are trespassing."

"Wolf?" the vampire repeated in a dry, mocking voice.

"I'm still one of them in spite of some recent additions," Rosalind warned. "Don't be fooled. I'm more wulf than not."

The other two vampires made stunted, grating sounds as if tendons had to move in order for them to use their voice boxes. The ugly noises matched their grim exteriors.

Rosalind's claws burst through her fingertips. She hid her hands behind her back. Simultaneously, or at least in rapid succession, her incisors began to lengthen. She didn't dare cry out against this, sensing that any move, even the slightest visible flutter, would set these creatures off. She had to stand her ground, hide her fear and catch them off guard, if that was at all possible.

One of the monsters inched forward.

Rosalind screamed inside at the intrusion. The back of her neck chilled up.

As if it had heard her feral protest, the vampire who had spoken to her grinned. There was no mistaking this show of exaggerated fangs for anything other than scare factor. Between pasty lips were two sharp, yellow teeth that were much longer than her own.

"We came for you," the vampire announced, the weakness of its voice yet another example of deception, and of an untapped hidden agenda.

"Go back to wherever you came from while you're still able to," she shouted.

"We came for you," one of the others echoed, confirming for Rosalind that vampire thoughts ran along one thread.

"Tough luck," she snapped. "I'm happy where I am. If you get any closer, I'll show you just how happy being a werewolf makes me, and how good at it I am."

A silent alarm went off inside Rosalind seconds before two of the monsters lunged. Chattering fangs came at her as she ducked sideways and raised her claws.

The first swift strike hit one vampire in the chest and sent it staggering backward with its sorry excuse for flesh torn down to its ribs. Thin blood, black in color with a putrid odor, gushed from the wound.

Rosalind didn't have time to see if that freak was out of commission. Another vampire was at her throat, tearing at her shirt as the third bloodsucker looked on. She fought the attack off with a grunt of disgust and a rising rage, moving fast, striking hard.

The ferocity of her hatred for these creatures caused a dramatic internal burn. Her throat heated up. That heat quickly spread to her shoulders, arms and finally to her chest, where it called up a glimpse of unfamiliar power, a power out of focus and comprised of sizzling crimson sparks.

When she shoved the monster off her, it flew through the air. Unfazed, it leaped back to its feet and came at her again. Before it reached her, though, the toothy vampire she thought of as the leader of this group had her by the throat in a tight grip. So fast, she hadn't seen this coming.

Its bleached, awful, angular face came close. "Not wolf," it said with a jaw-shattering snap of fangs. "Not anymore."

Vampires flowed through the trees as though the night itself had become liquid. Shades of dark on dark. Stealthily creeping shadows.

Colton jerked to a stop with Kirk at his back. His lure had worked, at least in part. The howl had brought some of the monsters to him, and every one of them attending this little hunting party would be one less to reach Rosalind, wherever she was.

He sensed five bloodsuckers and smelled another three in the distance. The odor of those distant three had mingled with Rosalind's scent, which meant that if they hadn't yet found her, they were close.

He roared with fury.

Kirk had the crossbow in position, sited on the path. The elder Were gave an angry grunt as the vampires came on, temporarily setting aside his innate fear about what Colton had turned out to be. Colton matched that grunt with a growl that rolled threateningly through the tangle of trees.

A pair of vampires materialized together. Eyeing him with red-rimmed eyes as if unsure of how to proceed against some new thing that reeked of power and death, their uneasiness rumbled through them in discordant hisses and squeaks.

Perhaps they recognized the results of their damage to his face. Maybe they smelled the strangeness in his blood, there because he had survived an attack from their own kind.

Their hesitation worked to Colton's advantage. Kirk's bow sang with a high note, striking one monster in the chest and passing all the way through. The silver-tipped wooden arrow had staked the creature's withered heart, and shattered the viper into a shower of dust. But such a weapon also had in its makeup the promise of a dual purpose. Its silver tip could just as easily bring down a werewolf, or the ghost of one.

Had Kirk been late to this gathering because he was adding the silver coating to the arrows, thus hedging his bets?

There was no time to consider that. More vampires dropped in, their ranks totaling four. This might not have been a problem, once upon a time, but with one Were in man form, and one still wobbly on his legs, it posed a threat.

The four vamps charged as a team. Colton's claws, like moving gears of revolving steel, cut cleanly through the first. A second arrow from the crossbow took down another. As Kirk reloaded, Colton felt the Were hesitate for a moment before shooting wild, missing an oncoming bloodsucker by a hair.

"On your right!" he shouted to Colton, and Colton whirled in time to fell a vampire with a staggering blow of one swinging arm. Seconds later, he was on the creature, straddling the downed freak so that he could get a better look at it.

Black eyes, intently focused and devoid of emotion, stared back as the creature writhed on the ground. It moved like a rabid dog, its fangs snapping in an attempt to get at Colton.

Colton's growl, as he tore the creature's head off with both of his hands, avowed: *She is not like you, and never will be*.

Bouncing back to his feet to grab hold of the bloodsucker that had leaped onto Kirk's back, he added: *Neither am I*.

Kirk wheeled and ducked, dislodging the attacker. With surprising dexterity, the Were was up again. His next arrow slashed through the bloodsucker at close range, and the fanged viper exploded in Colton's face.

Where is she? Colton silently demanded as the ashes rained down. Brushing the gray dust from his face, he turned toward the scent in the distance. Kirk followed his gaze.

"Go," Kirk said. "Save her."

Needing no such permission, Colton took off, utilizing every bit of speed he possessed even as he started to feel his energy drain away. It was too soon for a battle like this. He'd faced Death not that many days before, and hadn't finished healing. Although rage drove what strength he did possess, he wasn't right inside. He knew this. So did Rosalind's father.

The situation was extremely precarious, and the silver tips on Kirk's arrows were meaningful. Maybe Kirk knew something Colton didn't about what being a ghost meant, and that bit of unshared knowledge was what hung like a barrier between them.

Rosalind.

Chanting her name made Colton feel closer to her as he chased after the fragrance of roses, sensing that trouble wasn't far ahead.

Chapter 16

Rosalind stared into the eyes of pure evil, meeting the gaze of the monster holding her with a black gaze of her own.

Likely she didn't fear this as much as she should have because her wulf waited, held back for now, but clawing at her insides, ready for action. It was possible these monsters didn't know about her ability to shift with or without the moon's permission. It was also possible that the vamps wouldn't know what to do with a Night Wulf, if the darkness she had hidden inside her were to suddenly unfurl.

"What do you want?" she demanded, her breath nearly completely cut off by the vampire's grip on her throat.

Her demand was met by silence. She considered whether these monsters had limited resources for speech, and if this one had used up all of his. Its eyes glowed like polished stone.

She sensed something else. There was mist on her skin, and then a sudden temperature drop in the small clearing where she and two of the attackers stood.

The vampire holding her lifted its head. Its comrade uttered a whine. And before Rosalind could allow her senses to form an image of what was about to happen, a white beast, huge, muscled and angry, shot forward with the speed of a bullet, and she was knocked to the ground.

The werewolf was lethal in the cold swiftness of his strike. It was also a sight she would never forget. This wulf was much fiercer, much more dangerous than she remembered. Dark stains ringed his muzzle, matching the circles beneath his eyes. His chest was as broad as a lion's. His teeth were bared.

It was her lover.

The sudden silence in the clearing was alarming. As one vampire went down beneath the ghost wulf's hurtling bulk, the remaining vampire with a hold on Rosalind began to drag her toward the trees. But its grip on her neck had slackened when she fell.

Wresting herself free, Rosalind jumped to her feet. Lunging at the creature, she shifted shape. With the power of her wulf flowing through her, she drove the monster back with black-as-midnight furred arms and a vampire's lethal incisors.

She pinned the monster to a tree before it had time to register what had gone wrong. And as she stared at what she held, her vision went red, as though the night itself had changed in color and texture.

Rosalind blinked, listened. There was silence in the empty chest of the monster. There was no breath.

Not like you.

Her head bent forward. Her fangs grazed the monster's neck as she sniffed out the perfect place for a final kill. But she was torn from her attacker by the muscular power of a larger beast, and flung to the side. Leaping back, Rosalind fixed her gaze on the frozen face of the surprised vampire who dared to trespass on private property this night, as the white ghost of a once golden-brown Lycanthrope dealt that monster its fatal blow in her place.

Ashes swirled in the energy-enhanced space with the fervor of a small tornado. The night turned from red to gray. And then her white wulf turned to her, covered in ash.

He reached out to her with his arms open, wulf calling to wulf, and it seemed to Rosalind that those arms were all that mattered in the world.

She went to him, and felt his arms close around her. Enfolded inside his revved-up heat, she experienced a moment of pure bliss, and a sensation of security that she'd never felt before. That moment, however, was followed by a jolt of unexpected pain that shook her head to foot.

Alerted by the sound she made, the white wulf let her go.

Not me, she sent to him.

She wasn't hurting. It was his pain she was feeling; pain that continued to rip through her even though they no longer touched. Jolt after jolt of physical agony blasted her. Swaying, she closed her eyes.

A growl brought her back. Colton's growl.

She could hardly tune in with her attention. He was trying to tell her something. Confused, racked with the knowledge of how Colton was really feeling, though he managed to appear in control of his injuries for the most part, Rosalind glanced down.

She was still furred-up. Her muscles were tense and corded with strain. But her pelt was no longer a pure, midnight black. Fine streaks of white, like a manifestation of the streaks of Colton's pain, ran through her fur, a matrix of ghostly lacings that altered her appearance completely.

Dazed, Rosalind looked to the ghost wulf that now stood a few feet away. He met her gaze knowingly, his wolfish face registering an emotion much deeper than either surprise or fear.

Her father might have had been right, and Colton had finally realized this. By falling into his arms, she had taken on some of the outward aspects of yet another entity. A ghost wulf's characteristics. If she had stayed there, in his embrace, what would have happened? Did any of them know?

She ran her tongue over her fangs. Still there.

Looking up at the sky, Rosalind opened her mouth. Her howl, which seemed to go on endlessly, rang out with a disturbing blend of anger, frustration and utter despair.

Colton melted back into human form. Somehow, he had to reassure Rosalind, comfort her when neither of them knew what was going to happen next.

"It's all right," he said. "It has to be all right."

She had again closed the eyes he desperately wanted to see return to their former emerald green.

"Change back," he said. "Change now."

Rosalind did as he asked. In a swift download of human traits, she lost the wulf parts and stood there facing him, the defiance in her expression gone, her hair tousled and half in her face.

Her sleek, bare skin glowed with a faint sheen of moisture. Her long hair covered her breasts. Her legs were unsteady.

Attached to her slim ankle was the short length of chain that her father had tried to bind her with. Its cuff had branded her flesh with a reddish ring that resembled a burn.

Colton studied her naked loveliness. In human form, the only sign of her body having adapted to anything ghostlike were the number of white streaks riddling her hair, and the fact that she had gone pale, to the point of being as white as a sheet.

He exhaled, restraining himself from grabbing her. Maybe the white hair and paler skin wasn't too significant, but what the hell did he know? Each time he touched her, would she change more? Because of her nature, and what lay in her bloodstream, would she beat him to what he was going to become?

The effort of restraint cost him. His energy had diminished. He had so little of it left.

"Don't presume to know what's best for me," he gently chastised, with his theory on her having run away to save him from vampires in mind. "Because anything having to do with you getting hurt would be the end of me."

She remained motionless. Not even a hand moved.

"What's to become of me, Colton?" she asked. "If I'm not to be Lycan, then what I am is anyone's guess. I swear I didn't know this when I came to you. When we…"

"Bonded."

"Yes," she whispered.

"It doesn't matter," he said. "I was attracted to the Lycan in you, and I see it in you still. You're beautiful, Rosalind. You're my wulf, and it's too late to take back anything we've done. Nor would I want to."

After a beat of silence had passed, she said, "He will keep me here forever. You know that."

"Surely that's important, at least for the time being. You do see this?"

Her gaze slid past him. "How many more of them will come?" She then repeated a question from their earlier conversation, as if it had more meaning for her now. "Why do they want me?"

"We'll have to find out. It will be our goal."

"I want to touch you."

"I'd like nothing more."

"I want more than that."

"So do I."

"How can anyone like us be isolated without going mad?" she asked.

"You're not alone. I'm here."

Rosalind raised her chin, and turned her head. "I won't be chained," she said to her father as he approached. "I may be an abomination, but I still have my mind."

Kirk set down his crossbow, and removed his shirt. Careful not to move too quickly, he draped the shirt around Rosalind's thin, shaking shoulders.

"All right," Kirk said, his voice low, almost ragged. "No restraints."

And then, unexpectedly, Rosalind's father slid soundlessly to the ground.

Colton could now see that the shirt covering Rosalind was stained with blood. He smelled the iron in the air.

The vamp that had jumped on the elder Lycan's back had to have dealt Kirk a blow that Colton had missed at the time. Blood ran from the wound and dripped down his left arm, but Kirk's neck was clean. The blood drinker hadn't taken a bite out of the elder, and for that, Rosalind's father was extremely lucky.

Rosalind fell to her knees beside her father before Colton had drawn a full breath. She didn't need to address the blood pooling on the ground beside him. Demonstrating the truth in her statement about retaining her wits, she said, "The wound is deep, but not from teeth."

Colton nodded. "If there are more bloodsuckers around, they'll be on us like flies."

Gesturing for Rosalind to step aside, he picked up her father and slung the big man over his shoulder. He wasn't going to mention how much this hurt, or how very weary he was.

"Do you know where we are now, and how to get back?" he asked Rosalind.

"I know exactly where we are," Rosalind said with a sweeping glance that covered the area. "This place is sacred. It's where my mother was killed."

Colton took seconds to confront that news and the pain Rosalind had to be feeling on top of all the other things going on. But there was no time to spare for condolences, and no time to think about his parents.

"Let's get your father home," he said through gritted teeth, fearing that calling up his wulf again so soon after losing his strength wasn't in the cards. He'd have to carry Rosalind's father the old-fashioned way and hope the cabin wasn't far. He had to make sure nothing further happened to Rosalind on the way.

Cop and Were, he thought. He'd never needed the strength of being either of those things as much as he did right that minute.

"Lead the way," he said to Rosalind. "Be on guard."

"I swear to you that they will never sneak up on me again," she promised.

And he believed her.

Chapter 17

No vampires appeared or attacked on the way back to the cabin. Nor did Colton smell their nasty presence.

Rosalind had adopted a pace that was sensitive to his burden. Jared Kirk was a large man and a wulf. The combined weight of both proved formidable for the ghost of Colton's former self.

However, having Kirk injured meant the Were couldn't take care of his daughter for a while. In his favor, as an elder, Kirk would be able to heal quickly enough and be back on his feet soon. In the meantime, without Kirk acting as guardian, would their deal of keeping his hands off of Rosalind be honored, or broken?

Colton's sable-haired lover seemed to walk a fine line between fragility and a noticeable toughness of spirit. It had to feel to her like she had a split personality; a tug-of-war between the wulf and the darker forces trying to get at her.

Seen from behind, in human form, partially naked, and moving gracefully through the brush, Rosalind looked much the same as she had before this latest fight. She smelled the same, and that fragrance continued to affect him in ways too personal to acknowledge.

Still, he'd seen something in her eyes, and had heard a chilling note in her voice when she had promised him that vampires wouldn't be able to sneak up on her again. Because of what swam in her blood besides wulf, she had the ability to hide things from him that otherwise would have been in the open between an imprinted pair.

Rosalind seemed to glow in the night, her skin lit from within. Every move of her shoulders, legs, head, brought home the fact that he had only held her for seconds, and she was already showing changes. She moved like an animal.

He now understood the danger of Rosalind being close to others, but had yet to notice how the vampire attack tonight might have altered her further. He hated himself for watching her so closely, searching for a glimpse of evidence that she had slipped a notch further away from wulf.

The path widened at last. They had reached the clearing and the cabin. Rosalind spoke over her shoulder as if reading his mind. "I can do this."

"I know you can," he agreed.

"But you're worried."

"I've been worried since I woke up in a Landau bedroom."

"About me?"

"And about me."

"Well, at least you're honest." She waved a hand at the house. "Can you bring him inside?"

"Yes." He had just about enough strength left to get up the stairs. After that…

"It's probably best if you stay here until I get him there," he suggested.

Rosalind's slender fingers raked through her streaked hair. She stared at the tangle of black strands laced with white and said as he moved up the steps, "Why were you a cop?"

"To take care of people, and out of an earnest desire to see the little guy kept safe from the big bad predators of the world."

"You didn't have to put yourself out there for anyone," she said.

"Didn't I?"

"So now you'll take care of me."

He nodded, and shifted Kirk's weight. "Maybe I can redeem myself in some way."

"For what?"

"Not protecting my family when it was needed most."

Rosalind fell silent, probably hearing his unspoken amendment. He would have added, if he had both time and more breath, that if he couldn't do this one task, he wasn't worth the space he took up on the planet's surface. And that the goal of protecting her might in fact be the only thing keeping him on his feet at the moment, as well as keeping him from going stark raving mad over the injustices in the world.

"Meet me here after I put him down," he said. "We should talk about what to do. Together, we can reason things out."

Rosalind's eyes were hooded by rich, lush lashes that Colton wanted to feel feather over his skin. No matter how tired he felt, his feelings for her remained savage in intensity.

He swallowed back the urge to take her now, here, and shout to hell with all the rest.

Damn that vow. Damn your father for making me agree to such a promise.

Rosalind, in all her Lycan glory, with no hint of vampire fangs showing at the moment and the percentage of white in her hair gaining on the black, said, "The first room on the left is my father's."

Colton trudged slowly up the steps. He needed rest, sleep and the food Kirk had neglected to bring. More than any of those things, though, he needed to stay awake and keep Rosalind in sight. For now, anyway, and until he was relatively sure she was okay, he had to remain vigilant.

He also had to make sure that holding her for a few precious seconds hadn't done more damage to her continually rearranging system than what immediately met the eye.

As for himself, he was going to be cursed if he did or didn't do what he wanted to do...*Throw you on these steps and take all the pleasure from this union that we can get. Forget the consequences. Give in to our spirits.*

The thought had merit. Fighting it took all of his willpower. The idea of never being able to touch her or get close to Rosalind made the world and his place in it unthinkable. But the ridiculous idea that they would be compatible if she were to also become a so-called ghost was nothing more than a nagging suggestion.

Colton kept walking.

The house lay cloaked in a darkness he'd grown sick of. He crossed the floorboards to a back room, and laid

Kirk on a quilt-covered bed. He then headed outside where the breeze, though humid and filled with strange swampy odors, made him breathe easier.

Rosalind was waiting for him, and so damn beautiful he fielded a spasm of pain separate from what he had so far been tolerating.

His arms were covered in her father's blood. He looked from her to those slashes of red. "What about the..."

"Blood?" Rosalind finished for him.

She was gazing into the distance, possibly gathering information he couldn't process.

"There's hardly a moment that doesn't include thirst," she confessed. "I'm not sure if it's theirs or mine. It comes and goes, but I don't think the thirst is for blood. Not for me, anyway. It's more like an urge for something I haven't yet figured out."

"What could that be?"

She cocked her head in thought. "This feels a little like lust. And like hate. The feeling contains all of the characteristics of a rising addiction that can't be escaped no matter how hard I might wish to be free of it."

She left him with that, floating up the steps effortlessly with her long hair flowing behind her.

He almost caught her hair in his hands to tug her back to him. Watching her go, though it was only into the house, was torture.

Not knowing what else to do, Colton sat on the steps with his head in his hands. He felt ill; worse now that he'd heard Rosalind's confession. He was confused, but it was imperative that he go over the options for guarding the area, as if he actually had some. This wasn't Miami. Every direction looked alike. The isolation of the Kirks' property could either be a boon or one hell of a continuous problem.

He had no inkling of how much time passed, other than noticing how the moon's path across the sky had progressed. When the smell of food reached him, his stomach roared to life. He got up on shaky legs as the door behind him opened.

"I heard your stomach growling from in there," Rosalind said, holding a plate in one hand and a glass in the other.

"What?" she added. "Preparing food isn't a talent you'd expect from a black-pelted vampire-wulf hybrid?"

Colton eyed her curiously in the faint light from the lantern she had looped over one elbow. In spite of the situation, he smiled at her remark. Funny, he thought, how normal some moments could be in the midst of chaos.

In the flickering light, he searched Rosalind's face for evidence of the black tornado he had once seen. The fighter. The empathizer. The hybrid. All he found were those large eyes looking back at him. Eyes that made his wulf stir restlessly.

"I'll be back after I finish bandaging my father," she said.

"Will he be okay?"

The conversation was stilted. Their mouths wanted to be used in other ways that involved a meeting of their lips, hot, moist tongues dancing in tandem, and drowning deep kisses.

"He'll live, just like we all seem to," Rosalind said.

Colton stared at her, not with the gaze of a protector, but with the focus of a predator. Although he had Rosalind's father's blood on his arms, her addictive scent masked it; that dark floral mixture that was almost fe-line, highly sexual and impossible to resist.

He finally looked down at the plate in his hand. Temp-tation, he'd learned the hard way, was one hell of a beast.

Chapter 18

The chain attached to her ankle had become a pain in the ass, but Rosalind no longer felt the burn of the metal. She moved her foot impatiently, and strained to hear the night sounds. All she came up with was Colton's quiet breathing, coming from outside, and the slow thump of his heart. He hadn't moved. He was waiting for her.

Her desire to go to him burned in her like a wind-whipped fire, but she was scared, and didn't dare act on her urges. She sensed that something darker than her fears was approaching, out there beyond Colton's heady presence. The oily feel of this encroachment slithered across her skin, dirty, evil, foreign.

The monsters had found her again, and she was on her own. Colton could barely move. Her father was flat on his back. It wasn't right to involve them, see them hurt again, when this was her fight and her strange destiny.

She'd have to face this alone.

She bit her lip hard, tasting blood, regretting the secrets she hadn't shared with her lover, and wondering if omissions counted as lies.

She'd told Colton that the sight and scent of her father's blood didn't affect her, when it did. She had wanted to rub her face in the bloody rags at first. In the swamp, she'd fought the impulse to suck her father dry for keeping important information from her.

"What if you knew that, my lovely ghost?" she whispered. "And that the growing darkness inside me is like the creep of filthy fingertips up my spine. Insane, and quite inhumane."

She blinked slowly against the intensity of her regrets.

"When you opened your arms to me, I began to slip away, as if slowly losing my grip on reality."

She had assumed for a brief time that she might become one of the same shadows she had always despised. Worse yet, something her father feared.

"What would be left of me if I were to give in to that darkness? If I were to fade away, allowing others to dictate my future and how my life would or wouldn't go after this?"

Blinded by the terror of those thoughts, Rosalind looked to the window. She could use it to sidestep Colton's watchful gaze. She could go out there and meet her future face-to-face.

Get it over with.

Which choice would hurt her lover the least?

"I wish you could help me," she whispered to him.

And as fast as that, Colton was in the doorway. She wasn't really surprised. She should have realized he could hear her whispers, and possibly some of her thoughts.

His troubled eyes met hers. His heart was racing. But he would not touch her again, she heard him thinking, hating that reminder. He didn't dare hold her, because if he did, some new hell might carry her away.

Always, his thoughts were to protect her.

"I feel the same," she said, and felt her face drain of all remaining color. Though Colton's closeness brought a much-needed heat, the disturbance in the distance had grown icy.

"You're not alone in this," Colton said.

"Are you afraid of me?" she countered, searching his face.

"No. Other things, but not you."

"What other things?"

"The silly ones you're about to embrace."

Rosalind's hands fluttered by her sides. The pull in the distance dragged at her soul.

"Tell me what's out there," he said.

"Monsters."

He nodded.

"You're in pain," she said.

"Aren't you?"

"This close to you, I share yours."

"Then it seems true that your changes might have to do with emotion and feeling. A saturation of empathy."

"And the vampires? Did I empathize with them?" she said.

"What did you feel out there, the night you followed me and helped me in the park?"

"Hatred."

"Why hatred?" he asked.

"For what the blood drinkers did to your family. For what they had done to you."

"You didn't know me."

"I wanted to."

He took a moment to think about that, then said, "What did you feel, Rosalind? Exactly. Can you describe it?"

"I was angry. You had spurned me. That's why I followed you."

"When did that change?"

"After going inside your house. Hearing your howl of grief."

Colton nodded again, as if this had started to make sense to him. Excitement pitched his voice. "You helped me fight them. You sympathized with what had happened, and fought the bloodsuckers, by my side. You transferred your anger to them."

"You think that's why I became like them? Anger did this?"

"Emotion could have done it," he said. "Maybe hatred was necessary for you to access the strength to fight, but it also allowed whatever is in your blood to manifest against the creatures you fought."

Rosalind saw how serious he was. "Are you suggesting that I might take on the aspects of the creature producing in me the strongest emotion at any given time?"

"It's an idea worth considering, isn't it? Better than nothing? A starting point?"

Rosalind touched her hair. Several streaked strands slid through her fingers. "My feelings for you make me more like you? I transferred my emotion back to you after the attack tonight, and that could have saved me from adopting further vampire traits?"

"And caused the white in your hair," Colton said. "But I'm still wulf. I truly believe that. I will heal completely.

And if I'm right, this could be the reason you remain wulf after we touch."

Rosalind tuned in to his excitement in the same way she adapted to the way his heart was beating.

"Come here," he said. "Closer."

She balked at his invitation. Both of her hands clutched tightly to the windowsill beside her.

"What if," he began, "you only have so much space in you for changes? What if most of that space is filled with something other than vampire?"

She read his thoughts. He couldn't remember much about the laws of physics or mathematical averages, but the suggestion about space had a certain rightness to it that spurred him on.

"Who's to say that if you felt strongly about something other than vampires, you couldn't lose the fangs and replace them with something else? Something better?"

Rosalind turned. "My father must know about this." She thought of the metal ring in the wall that had awaited the possibility of a chain attached to her ankle, and the reasons for remaining secluded from other Weres. "He's the only one who might."

"Then he will have to enlighten us. In the meantime, we can hope I'm right, can't we?" Colton said.

She took a second wary step toward him, hungry for his enthusiasm, compelled by their imprinting to further the bond.

"You want to test this theory out on our own?" she asked.

"Don't you?"

"No."

"Why?"

"Because if I become more like you, and we're not

sure about what that is, what could be waiting for me, for us, might not be the better thing. If you're wrong about this theory, and even about feeling like a wulf, it could turn out bad." She took a breath and added, "I could turn out bad."

She watched Colton raise his hands as if he couldn't stop himself from comforting her. Although Rosalind wished he would actually cross that line, she couldn't let him know that. Her bed was in the corner, just four feet away. Her thighs were quaking for a stroke of his bare hands on her naked flesh. She desired real closeness and a respite from thought. She wanted him inside her, filling her, his actions erasing all the doubts.

But her assessment about his condition had been correct. He was in pain and barely managing to control it. Instead of healing completely right away, as he should have been able to do after his injuries, the visible evidence of how close he had come to death had stayed with him, lingering like a layer of fog.

How much of that pain was due to the injuries he had sustained? Did his theory about Others cover him and his condition, as well? Was he becoming something other than Lycan, with ongoing pain as the symptom of that eventual change? Part of that change? The catalyst for it? What was a ghost, if not merely an awkward color discrepancy?

She was visibly trembling now, and desperate for comfort. Yet she had every right to be afraid. They could not connect without the possibility of further consequences.

Although her lover was hurting, he was hard, swollen with the anticipation of sharing her breath. Again he was reading her thoughts. *Just a hand on hers. His mouth on her mouth.*

It was at that moment Rosalind felt herself again start to fade. Her spirit flickered in and out of the present as if losing its form.

She dropped to the floor, sat down hard and lifted her face to her lover. Her lips parted. "More of them are on their way."

He turned to look behind him, then crossed to the window. When he pivoted back, she found herself standing by his side without knowing how she had gotten there.

They were inches apart. The souls of their wulfs were mingling.

"How do you know?" Colton asked, his face tense, his shoulder muscles bunched. "I can't smell them."

When she offered him a sad, mirthless smile, he said nothing about the evidence of the sudden enlightenment that protruded from between what she knew were two bloodless lips: fangs. Longer than before. Sharper than ever. A telling sign about exactly who was coming for a rematch.

She watched a thought about the kind of shape he was in at the moment flit across Colton's features. She felt his heart sink into an uneven rhythm.

"Where are they?" he asked. "How far away?"

She gazed beyond him. "Not far."

Her white wulf swore under his breath. She thought his face shifted slightly to the vague outline of his wulf. "How many are there? Can you tell?"

"Let me go to them," she said.

When her eyes met his, her stomach clenched. Colton's wulf was burning hotter than ever, and a kind of sweet oblivion rested in the acknowledgment.

"And do what?" he demanded, his eyes not leaving hers. "Surrender? Give in to them? We don't know what they want with you, or what might happen. We can't know that without some guidance."

The spike in his pulse spiked hers. He'd wanted to bed her, protect her, be her mate, and all those needs were becoming tangled, mired in mystery.

"I can find out what they want," she said. Her voice quavered.

"At the risk of placing your life in peril? Forget it, Rosalind. Whatever they want, they want badly enough to come here in waves. I don't like the notion of that, and what it might mean. Master plans, as part of a vampire's vocabulary? Strategy? It's unheard-of."

Rosalind made herself turn to the window. If she maintained eye contact, her heart would break. No matter how determined Colton was, if she closed the distance, he would cave to his beast's superior urges.

"I don't see that we have another choice," she objected. "I started this. Me. I won't see you or my father harmed any more than you've been harmed already."

"Then it's a good thing you have no say in the matter."

Though they had bonded, he wasn't her captor or keeper. He was older, and maybe wiser in the ways the world worked, but she also was fluent in wulf. She knew these woods. This was her playground. And out there, tonight, she hadn't even begun to fight.

"We have to bring your father back to consciousness," he said. "He'll have to provide some answers, quickly. Can we wake him up? Do we have time?"

"Not much time."

Again, she watched Colton search the night beyond the glass. Though his skin was feverish, he was riddled with chills. Still, at that moment, when confronted with an immediate problem, Colton Killion looked every bit of the strong, virile Were she had first seen.

His head was lifted. His eyes were wide. She took a step that brought her closer to him, fighting the instinct to rest a hand on his rigid back.

"Do it," he said with the gravel of pain in his voice. "Wake your father now. Wait this out. Give me more time."

It took a gigantic effort to back away from him and turn for the door. Only then, when an unuttered sob of distress closed her throat, did Rosalind realize how long she had been holding her breath, and that the monsters in the trees had stolen it.

Chapter 19

"**K**irk," Colton said to the Were on the bed in a tiny room no larger than Colton's room in the shed.

Green eyes met his.

"The vampires are staging a comeback."

Kirk's eyes closed.

Colton spoke again. "You told me Rosalind will attract others now that she's reached a certain age. Why vampires? What others, and why? How would anyone know about her, so far out here?"

"She's more than Lycan," Kirk said softly. Speaking was obviously difficult for him.

"Yes, you mentioned that. I've seen her change, and I think those changes might be due to a state of heightened emotion. Am I right?"

Jared Kirk turned his head and opened his eyes. "What did you say?"

"Emotion. Rosalind may be reacting to emotion, to strong feelings in others and in herself."

"That isn't what a Banshee does," Kirk said.

Banshee? Colton was blown backward by the term. He found himself on his feet, with his jaw tight, sure he'd heard that term somewhere.

"Explain," he said, not sure Kirk would be able to utter ten more words in his present state. "Quickly."

"A Banshee is a feminine spirit." Kirk's voice was faint, but accommodating.

Colton leaned closer to the bed. "And?"

"Said to be an omen of impending death, or doom."

"What?"

"They are spirits often associated with families and bloodlines. Rosalind's mother's family had one, though that kind of spirit had never come to rest in the blood of the family it had attached itself to until..."

"Until what?" Colton asked impatiently.

"Until one did."

Colton felt like a Were with a one-word vocabulary. Harsher this time, he said, "Explain."

Kirk gasped to draw in more air. "The MacAirlie clan's Banshee, what they called a Death-caller, was to warn of the death of one of them, but had grown too close to the woman she was to have given over to Death. Maybe that Death-caller craved the kind of life others around her had. No one knows for sure. That Lycan female lived to mate with the Were who found her alive at Death's door."

"Yes." Colton's skin had grown colder. "Go on."

"The result of this Lycan union was a Night Wulf. A black Were that carried the moon mark on her arm, but had other abilities, as well."

Night Wulf. This was the source of Rosalind's unique

black fur. She carried something else in her blood that came from long ago. Could this be true?

"Who was that child the Banshee saved?" he asked.

"Rosalind's great-great-grandmother."

Colton had to take a minute to process that information. He wished he could calm down. "Does this explanation imply that a Banshee's spirit might have become housed in the Lycan she saved? That's how the unusual characteristics and black pelt come in? It reflects the Death-caller's presence? Jesus. How does something that happened so long ago affect Rosalind now?"

"I don't know. Maybe part of that Banshee's spirit has been handed down to Rosalind, and she's showing herself. Maybe, as you say, emotion calls that spirit closer to the surface. Possibly, a threat of imminent death is what a Death-caller would recognize. God knows what resides inside Rosalind. I prayed that nothing would show up at all."

The expression on Kirk's face made Colton's throat seize. He barely got the next question out. "But you know about it. About that spirit. How do you know? Has it shown up before this?"

Kirk turned his head on the pillow and said with a reluctant sincerity, "I'm afraid I've seen it before."

"When?" Colton's cop voice had taken over. He was the interrogator who demanded answers.

Kirk's voice sputtered, as if the words were painful. "In Rosalind's mother."

Colton didn't remember getting to his feet or placing his hands on the mattress. His face was close to the elder Were's when he spoke again. "Her mother was a Night Wulf?"

Kirk tried to nod his head. "Rosalind doesn't know.

I didn't tell her. I was sure it couldn't happen again, so close in time. After her Blackout phase had passed, I saw that it could."

Colton pushed off to pace the room, again thinking about Rosalind's shiny black pelt, and recalling Lycan legend about how impossible a pure black pelt was supposed to be.

"Bullshit," he said, glancing at Kirk. "Right? Are you putting me on, hoping to chase me away?"

He'd mated with a creature that also had the ability to herald death? Could that be true?

Another memory returned, throwing him back in time to the night in the park when he'd heard Rosalind's howl—the sound that had started all of this by alerting him to the presence of a she-wulf.

"Hell," he whispered. "Had she been calling me or keening for the death of other Lycans?" Which turned out to be the slaughter of his family.

Had the events that transpired that night been enough to have kicked a latent spirit into action?

Or…God, had a wulf with a Banshee inside her been howling for *his* death?

Impossible.

This wasn't Ireland or Scotland, for Christ's sake. It was Florida. He was alive. Changed, but breathing. So, what did any of it mean?

Unless…some of her spirit had been passed to him that night, so that he would survive.

Colton considered that possibility now. Had Rosalind saved him in order to become his mate, just as the other spirit had done one hell of a long time ago? Could a dormant spirit in her blood have manifested that night in the park?

It was crazy. Far-fetched.

"Okay," he said, out of shocked frustration. "Tell me how we help her."

"Keep her safe."

"Surely," Colton said, "you knew better than to think she would remain here forever, or even be willing to?"

"Here, she was Lycan, like me."

"It was an artificial life, Kirk. A kind of forced stasis. She wasn't who she was destined to be. If what you say is true, part of her soul was sleeping."

"Yet she remained Lycan. The longer she did, the better."

"Yes, and look at her now." Colton leaned down again. "You do know how to help her in some way, if you were with her mother?"

"It was her mother's wish to live here and to segregate ourselves from the others. My mate never set foot outside of these grounds. She never went through this. I came here by invitation from my wife's father, and I stayed."

"Knowing what she was, you stayed?"

"Yes." Sadness lowered Kirk's voice. "And I never regretted it. Not for one single second."

"Yet you would scorn me for wanting the same thing?"

"I would have saved you, or any other suitor, from the isolation that both I and my daughter have endured."

Colton put a hand to his forehead, then ran his fingers through his hair. "Well, it's too late to worry about that. I'm bound to Rosalind, as she is to me. I want to help her, now more than ever, and I'd like you to tell me how to do that." He faced the closed window. "Emotion has to be the key to her unwilling transformations. She loved you and was therefore like you all this time. She wanted me, and…" The white in her hair. The lightened skin.

He returned to Kirk's bed. "None of that explains why vampires might want her. Why would they come here? Bloodsuckers are already dead. How could a Death-caller be of use to them?"

"I don't know." Kirk cleared his throat, and grimaced at the effort it took. "Vampires could be attracted to the dark spirit in her. They might sense the likeness of a Death-caller. On the one hand, she would know how to find death because she feels it approach. With that ability, she could easily alert them to the location of their next meal."

"And on the other hand?" Colton pressed.

"She can alert mortals, or any other species, to the approach of monsters."

Kirk tried to sit up, and made it to his elbows. It sounded to Colton as if the Were said, "There's more." But when he looked, Kirk had fallen back, his energy spent.

"One thing is for certain. It's no longer safe for her here," Colton mused. "Vampires know where she is, and want something. The bastards have arrived."

"Then we must take her away," Kirk said.

"Where? To a more populated place where there are far more emotions running rampant than in these woods?"

The question hung in the air as another sound reached Colton, drifting in through the windowpanes. Rather, the lack of sound is what caught his attention. Outside, at that moment, there was no noise at all.

"As I said, it's too damn late now," he said regretfully, heading for the door.

Rosalind dropped to a crouch on the porch. She snapped her head from side to side, searching the night.

A wave of palpable tension ran through the trees, leaves shuddering in its wake. The air felt dense. In the distance, she perceived the stench of death and destruction.

Without turning to look, she was aware of Colton's approach. She didn't acknowledge him, unable to speak and afraid to try.

He came close, but she was beyond fear and running on instinct. Straightening, she backed up and away. "Can't touch," she said. "Not now. Not yet."

She tried to make some sense out of it for him, perceiving his distress. "If I'm like them, I can feel them. It's best that I do feel them because I'll know where they are."

"Do you know a way around this next confrontation?" he asked.

"There's no way around it."

"What are you feeling when you say you can sense them?"

"A rising blackness, bleak and dreadful, unfurls inside me, almost as if they're pulling that darkness to the surface."

"God, Rosalind, I —"

By the time Colton had stopped whatever he had been about to say, she was already at the bottom of the steps, facing the trees on the south side of the house and the path leading to the swamp.

"There are five." She glanced at Colton over her shoulder.

"Is that all?" he said drily, following her gaze.

Her big Were didn't look frightened, though Rosalind observed how his body had stiffened with this news. His anxiety had mostly manifested in his rigid arms and back. He rolled his shoulders and clenched his hands.

"Please don't imagine that I'll allow you to run off by yourself in order to meet them face-to-face, because that's not happening," he said. "There's a chance you can control what happens to you."

She swayed slightly. "How?"

"I have no idea, really, but what if it's like controlling your wulf? You learn to stifle the urges and tuck them inside. You start to appreciate the changes and what they mean."

Rosalind studied him, reading the truth of this statement in his face, and sensing that he believed it.

When she turned her head, he jumped down to meet her.

"What? What is it?"

"They're moving," she said. "Heading toward the place where my mother was killed."

"Tell me how you know this."

"The ripples in the night are the wake of their movement. See it in the trees? Vampires run like a dark wind, like nothing else on earth that I've seen. It's as if they don't possess bodies at all, and are some kind of misty substance that can defy the laws of nature."

She added, "Scratch that last part. We already have seen evidence of lapsed laws of nature, haven't we?"

Colton said nothing. She heard his heart thundering.

"Also, it's like I have a homing beacon inside me," she went on. "My inner darkness is attracted to their darkness, like mercury coagulating or drops of liquid merging with a larger pool. I see them clearly in my mind. I can nearly make out every detail."

This statement was met by more silence. She guessed he didn't even know where to start in tackling that.

"I have to go there, Colton. They're defiling my

mother's memory. They won't stop harassing me unless I do something to make them stop."

"Maybe that's their point," he said. "They zero in on that particular spot because it has the most emotional ties for you, hoping to lure you to them. Otherwise, why wouldn't they just come here?"

She met Colton's gaze and could tell he was assessing the situation, determining what to do. In a gleam of moonlight, she saw his claws spring forth.

"It's me they want," she said.

"Over my dead body."

Oh, yes. God, how she loved him, right then, right there. She loved this ghost with all of her tormented, black-tainted heart. Colton Killion was willing to lay down his life for her. She had observed the signs of this kind of selflessness in him before.

Were. Cop. Gentleman. Lover. Fighter. Protector. He was all of those things, rolled into one...

And that was the reason she couldn't allow him to fight her battle. The world couldn't afford to lose him. Lovers didn't lead their soul mates to their deaths.

That thought brought her out of a trancelike state. Excitement began to simmer in her nerves. She looked at Colton and almost smiled because she didn't see his death here. She didn't sense it. Didn't feel it. If she housed a creature that announced death, as her father had inadvertently told her, through Colton, then surely Colton was not going to die tonight. She was closer to him than to anyone. She would know this.

In a flash, she was off and running. For the first time in a while she felt ready for whatever these monsters were going to dish out. If instinct was all she had, it was conceivable that she and Colton would come out of this alive.

Black fur, soft and familiar, sprang from her pores to cover her legs. Her arms looked thin, pale and human before they began to shift shape. She ran her tongue over her slowly descending fangs and howled passionately with a Lycan call that sounded like the cry of an exotic bird.

Death to them all. Save my own.

There was a scrambling noise behind her, and nothing she could do about it. "If you're determined to follow," she shouted to Colton before her wulf completed the takeover, "you'll have to keep up."

Chapter 20

Rosalind's life passed before her eyes as she ran. The stink of vampires wound itself around those memories, becoming more intense with every stride.

Not long now, and I will find you.

Back again into the past she went, sliding down memory's tunnel with the hope of discovery.

Her Blackout phase, her father had told her tonight, had been the start of his recognition that she was different. But she didn't remember much about it. She'd heard that few females survived the process of the human body rewiring itself to become Were. Yet she had embraced that new life with her arms open, relishing her wulf's powers and constantly gaining more.

Her early rebelliousness now seemed to have been a selfish, frivolous trait, and highly dangerous. Then again, what was the point of lingering on that time when she'd moved so far past it?

Besides, that same stubborn streak is what had brought her to Colton. In no way could she ever regret that. The ghost behind her understood that she was different, and still wanted in.

She wished she had known her mother. There had been no women or she-wulfs in her life. She had always felt empty, despite her raw strength. And all that time, the empty space inside her had been nothing more than a sleeping Death-caller waiting for a chance to awaken and declare itself.

Yes, she wanted to shout back to Colton, she had heard every word her father had told him.

A branch hit her in the face. Rosalind growled, and heard that same branch hit Colton. Her lover was here. He was close.

It took real effort not to turn around and jump into his arms. She knew that once she was in his embrace she would feel only Colton's love, both physical and spiritual, pouring in.

Her mother had had her father to care for her, until Analise MacAirlie Kirk had been cut down by hunters who had either been after the pelts of mammals or out to bag a gator.

Had her father tried hard to protect his wife? She had no doubt about that. The question was how a bunch of bloodsucking fiends from hell knew about the sacred location of her mother's grave.

Along the lines of Colton's theory, could vampires also read and crave the highs of emotion?

Another growl bubbled up from her throat.

"Rosalind." Colton's voice was gruff, but he hadn't shifted.

Of course he read her. Their souls were entwined.

I have done this to you, she longed to say to him,
knowing he wouldn't turn back no matter what excuses
she flung his way.

I'm not worthy of your love.

She dared a glance behind her.

Colton's chiseled angles produced their own shadows.
He wore her father's blood on his left shoulder, and on
both arms. The welts of his wounds were now a pinkish-
white, crossing his cheeks in raised parallel lines of scar
tissue. More lines encircled his neck, at the base of his
throat, looking like a necklace of lace.

He had meant to say something else. Speak meaningful words that would equal a different kind of sentence,
trapping her in a world that wouldn't allow for the small-
est, slightest touch between lovers.

How much more distance could she stand? A lifetime's
worth? Sixty seconds?

She wished for just one more kiss.

Yet if his lips were to feather over hers, it wouldn't
be enough. There would be no holding back the advanc-
ing degree of her needs. Even in her wulf's shape, her
arms tingled and twitched. Her breasts strained with the
memory of his hands on her. Phantom fingers seemed to
cup the private place between her churning thighs, calling up the fires she had to tamp down.

Her fur was mottled now. Black and white. The ghost's
spirit was spreading through her as she moved on, ignoring the impulse to turn back and face Colton instead
of the vampires.

*Please. Save yourself from what hides in the night,
my love.*

Wishful thinking was bad, and a distraction. The place

was crawling with vampires, and all she wanted was to end this and have Colton for herself.

She was brought to a staggering halt by his hand on her arm. Guilt flowed through her. Had she driven him mad by telegraphing her own desires?

A snap of his arm turned her around. "Shift," he said in a voice as ragged as she felt.

She looked into his eyes.

"Shift back," he repeated. "Please, Rosalind."

It took her seconds to comply, despite the danger around them.

"This is what we have to look forward to," he said. "This is what's in store for us. Danger and mystery and monsters. But let's not lose sight of the end result, whatever turns up between now and then."

"Promise," she said. "Promise me that will be true."

The lips she had stared at, wishing they would meet hers, did just that. Colton's mouth closed over hers savagely, as if he needed to prove something to her. As if he would be the only one to devour her.

He didn't touch her in any other way. His body remained apart from hers. Just lips on lips. His mouth on hers. And the fire that raged in that kiss seared the air between them, turning the chill of a monstrous night to a molten red-hot.

Colton's mouth was reaffirming his promise as the ground rippled beneath their feet. The earth seemed to be warning them of supernatural trespassers getting closer and closer, of other beasts in the landscape rushing in.

For a few seconds, though, stolen from time and backed by the exquisite seduction of her lover's mouth, Rosalind began to believe they could do this, that somehow, it would work out.

In Colton, there was hope.

The second his mouth left hers, blackness descended.

Blinded by the shock of losing what she held so dear, Rosalind tore herself from her lover and spun around to confront whatever was out there preventing this future.

To confront the advance of five fanged blood seekers that would mess with her for reasons of their own.

Vampire stink flashed like a yellow beacon in the dark.

Colton watched Rosalind twist away from him, her body already half covered in fur and strung tight with tension. She tore through the brush, toward the awful odor, leaving him standing there, staring. Then, as though he'd been infused with a shot of liquid adrenaline, he called up his wulf.

His beast came on like thunder rolling down a runway, hard and fast, in a transformation that left him panting. Sinew snapped. Tiny bones broke and realigned as his flesh expanded. His blood began to boil, as if he had swallowed a furnace.

The whole wulf universe rushed forward to banish what was left of the human. For an indeterminate amount of time, there was nothing but the sound of his pulse accelerating, and then something inside him screamed for him to take a breath.

An awareness of the position of the moon came to him, as did the direction of the wind that ruffled his white fur. Animal smells crashed in, and the foul odor of evil at its basest.

The beast's heat took the edge off his pain. Power replaced it. On legs like steel, he took off after his mate, angry, hungry, with the beast's undivided attention locked on the path the she-wulf had taken.

He was fast and incredibly fleet, and caught sight of Rosalind before a full minute had passed. She made audible sounds that reached him like tortured syllables, but if Rosalind was speaking, he didn't understand the language. The possibility of this being some sort of vamp communication made him angrier.

There came an answering cry to her jabber. More of a shriek, really. Rosalind had lunged upward on her Night Wulf's powerful hind legs to dislodge a vampire from a stunted tree, and had the pathetic bag of bones on the ground before he reached her.

Clawlike hands tore at her. Bottomless black eyes refused to close as she straddled the creature, roaring her displeasure.

And then another vampire hit the dirt on Colton's right, followed by a third.

They were lightning fast. Like wind, Rosalind had told him, but they were more like a blur of dark on dark than a streak of displaced air. The blurs danced and swirled, taunting him, never in one place long enough for him to land a swing. The monsters seemed to suck all the air out of the area, though vampires didn't breathe.

He caught one by spinning on one heel, and with a well-placed canine of his own, tore through the skinless flesh. Black blood dribbled down his chin to dampen and discolor his snowy-white fur. A little jolt went through him, as if he had bitten through an electrical cord.

The wulf knew what to do, and the man inside it went along for the ride with his human thoughts intact. *Help Rosalind. Keep my promise.*

Given that, and the powers he and the Night Wulf beside him were seemingly able to access once their bodies were in sync, this attack should have been laughable. Only five vampires, total, against two furred-up creatures that only existed in legends?

Yet Colton's attention was divided by the demand to see to Rosalind and the need to watch her back. So when the vamp in his hands exploded into a storm of putrid gray ash, he jumped onto the chest of the freak she had on the ground, tore at the branch above his head and, with the jagged edge of his makeshift stake, went for the spot that would effectively terminate that monster's useless, lifeless life.

Rosalind was already on the third. Colton grabbed the fourth, wondering briefly about the location of the other remaining bloodsucker.

But there was no stopping these wulfs.

With uncanny speed and a raw, unleashed fury, Rosalind exploded the flailing vampire in her grip. Colton took care of his. When the dust had settled, they stood with their backs pressed together in the small, muddy clearing.

A slight smoky smell reached them. Colton glanced around, preparing for the next onslaught. But no other vampire arrived to try its hand at boxing with a ghost and a wulf-Banshee-vampire hybrid. In fact, no further sound reached them at all.

Colton looked to Rosalind.

Her dark eyes looked back.

In the distance, a low rumble started up. Quickly, the noise got closer, louder, becoming mixed with the silky sound of brush being trampled.

Rosalind bolted—not away from the oncoming rumble, but toward it.

Here we go again, Colton thought, tearing through every curse his Miami PD partners had taught him.

When he rounded a grove of trees, he saw a dark SUV skidding to a stop. At the same moment Rosalind landed on its roof with a metal-denting clank of her ankle chain.

"Get in," Jared Kirk shouted from the driver's seat. "It's not what you think. The vampires weren't alone. There are others here."

Colton knocked Rosalind off the roof with a swipe of his left arm. As she dropped to the ground, they both shifted shape. He wrenched the door open. In a chilling replay of their escape from the Landau compound, Rosalind preceded him into the backseat, and then her father, grimacing with pain as his hands yanked at the steering wheel, stepped on the gas.

Chapter 21

The SUV swerved on a soggy section of the path, then righted its direction, heading, Colton guessed, back toward the house. Kirk was hunched over the steering wheel. His back was heavily bandaged. His knuckles were white.

"Others?" Colton demanded. "What the hell do you mean?"

Before Kirk could answer, Rosalind made a soft sound beneath her breath, as though she had an idea about what her father had meant.

Her face, colorless before, had gone translucent. Her skin seemed thinner in the light of the dashboard, showing every one of her fine lavender veins. Eyes, dark just moments before, flashed with a hint of their former emerald green.

"Others?" Colton repeated more forcefully without

taking his eyes from her. "Rosalind said there were five vampires. We're missing one of them. Is that what you mean?"

"Not vampires," was Kirk's slurred reply.

"Not werewolves, either," Colton snarled in frustration. "There's no moon. So what does that leave?"

"Demons," Kirk answered in a whisper that no one other than a Were could have heard.

Colton's insides churned as if his beast had grabbed hold of him. His claws, an automatic result of that strain, punctured the leather seat.

"You're kidding," he managed to say.

"You'll just have to take my word, wulf."

Rosalind's avoided his eyes. Her features were benign, showing no emotion at all. They could have been taking a ride for the enjoyment of taking a ride, for all that look told him.

"What does everyone bloody-well know that I don't?" he shouted, so very tired of being the last one to the party. "Demons? What makes you believe that?"

Kirk didn't have time to answer. As they spun wheels past the garage, the acrid smell of smoke grew stronger. Something was on fire. It was the house. The roof was blazing with flames, and had partially caved in. The porch was an inferno.

Beside him, Rosalind made a small sound of regret deep in her chest. Both that sound and her skin's translucency made her seem terribly vulnerable, young and small.

He wanted to hold her, now more than ever. For all her former fierceness, his lover's sudden sadness was like a strike to his own heart.

"To hell with this," he said.

"Don't," her father warned. "Colton, listen to me. Do not touch her. Please. For her sake. For yours."

The idea that he should listen to her father and go against everything he felt at the moment made him take another swipe at the seat. As the leather tore, Rosalind's eyes met his.

She was trembling, and chilled to the bone without her fur. Her slender hands covered part of her face.

He just could not take much more of this, because he knew that she couldn't take much more. He didn't see how things could possibly get worse.

"Demons did that? Started the fire?" He felt uncommonly winded with the return of the pain that had been pardoned by his wulf.

Jared Kirk had gone silent, the last of his energy all used up. Nevertheless, the Were had found enough energy to try to remove Rosalind from this new mess.

Kirk had loved Rosalind's mother and had guarded her from this sort of thing for years. No doubt he saw reflections of Rosalind's mother in Rosalind; maybe even in this current replay of events. Hunters after pelts and gators, Rosalind had told him in regard to her mother's death. But odds were that wasn't true.

The stiffness of Kirk's neck told Colton that the elder Were had been through all of this before.

Colton faced Rosalind helplessly, hurting for her, for himself and for her father. He pondered where they might go if hell's doors had been opened for some reason, and why vampires and demons were prolonging this mess.

His heart shattered into pieces too fine to easily reunite when Rosalind's hands fell from her face and he saw a tear slide down her frozen, expressionless cheek.

"I'm sorry. You'll have to drive," Kirk suddenly

announced. Pulling the car to the side of the road, he slumped forward. "I'm not quite myself."

Colton was beside him in a flash. Warning Rosalind to stay back with a guarded glance, he felt for the Were's pulse. "Weak, but there."

After lifting the big Were and placing him in the back of the SUV, Colton got behind the wheel. He allowed himself one comment on the issue facing them all.

"Damn it to hell and back, where was he taking us?"

"Back to the Landaus'," Rosalind replied, keeping vigil over her father. "Who else might know what to do with creatures like us?"

There was, Colton thought, just no arguing with that.

The lack of scraping sounds meant that Colton was keeping his claws to himself. Rosalind sensed his anger and his frustration.

Her suggestion to go Judge Landau's had been met with a grunt of disapproval, though Colton was already driving at breakneck speed in that direction.

They had gone a good distance before he spoke again. "Why demons, Rosalind? Do you know anything about this?"

"Sorry," she said.

Another span of silence followed that she was afraid to break.

"I'm not sure Landau will want us," Colton finally said. "Let alone know what to do about recent circumstances. We will have to tell him everything. You know that."

His eyes were bright in the rearview mirror.

"The judge can call the elders back if they've gone," she said. "One of them has to know what this means."

"Demons, Rosalind?"

"It isn't your fault. None of it is. If I had an entity inside me all along, it would have eventually come out anyway, in one circumstance or another."

"But it was me you followed that night."

"Yes. So what if I was supposed to follow you, and there is something at work here other than chance?"

She could see him thinking about that.

"I'm changing," he said. "Without the wulf's power, I'm barely hanging on. It's as though I'm growing thinner, losing substance. Strange, isn't it, when you're gaining substance? I'd almost tend to think you were finding mine."

"I'd release you if I knew how," she told him, her stomach in knots at the thought of that. "I'd break the bond. You don't deserve this."

"Your father didn't ask to be released," he said. "Do you imagine I would want to?"

"Fathers have to love their daughters, even if they're different."

"He must have loved your mother tremendously."

Rosalind considered his remark.

"Like me," she said. "My mother was like me. That's what he told you."

The tension in Colton's tone had been negligible, and meant that he was withholding something. A thought, or another theory?

"I'm sorry," Colton repeated.

She climbed to the seat beside him. The leather felt cold on her bare legs. "What are you thinking?"

He gave her a sideways glance. "You're not the only one."

She let that settle. "Night Wulf," she said. "My mother was one."

"You did hear what your father told me?"

She nodded.

"Then you know there was no way you could have avoided what's inside you," he said. "Yet you are blaming yourself."

Each time Colton pointed the car in a new direction, Rosalind groped for new meaning. Her mother had been a Death-caller. She was like her mother. In a strange, roundabout way, this brought some comfort. A little, anyway.

She moved her foot. The chain attached to it jangled against the floorboards. "Just in case, my father said. I suppose he meant to keep me from going after the vampires like the rebellious idiot I have always been, but I took this chain to mean that he thought I was the monster who needed to be shackled."

"God, Rosalind…" her white wulf said, without being able to finish the sentiment.

"Here's what else he said, at the Landaus'. 'I conferred with the elders, fearing what your future might hold. They had to know about you, and why I hadn't presented you to one of their sons.'"

Banshee. Death-caller. Night Wulf. Shape-shifter. She was all of those things, and had to be watched for the signs of something odd making an unscheduled appearance, in the way her mother probably had to be watched.

"I am like my mother," she said, solemnly, swiveling on the seat to get a better view of Colton's silhouette. "Maybe my mother wasn't killed by random hunters or by accident."

With utter and complete sadness, her lover, her protector, her mate, said, "Maybe not."

"Not that it makes me feel a whole lot better," she remarked, waiting anxiously to see the lights of Miami that would eventually appear in the distance, and hoping demons were really a myth.

Chapter 22

By the time they reached Miami, silence had fallen between them. Colton headed for the Landau estate less eagerly than he would have imagined under the circumstances. He had no idea how this freakish little party of tired, filthy, undressed beings would be received by another wulf's pack. For the Landau family and their elegant associates, the hasty return of a ghost and a Night Wulf might come as a shock.

Hell, he already owed them more than he could ever pay back.

When Rosalind finally spoke from the rear of the car, where she again sat with her prone father, he guessed it was because she had seen and recognized the pillars of stone marking the Landau gates.

"Will you stay near me?" she asked.

"I won't let you out of my sight," he replied. "For any reason short of…"

"Death?"

"Yes."

The tall iron gates were closed to intruders. As the SUV pulled up to them a siren went off in a single burst of sound, and more lights came on. Immediately, two men flanked the vehicle, appearing from nowhere and looking as dangerous as the rest of Landau's Weres had been when in man form.

Colton wasn't sure what he'd say or how he would explain his presence here. However, instead of engaging Colton in conversation or asking for identification of any kind—which would have been impossible for Colton to produce anyway—the Were nearest the driver's-side window nodded his head, said, "Killion, right?" and stepped aside.

As the massive gates swung open, the overhead lights dimmed back to a wattage more reminiscent of starlight than a prison yard. Reluctantly, Colton pressed on at the slowest pace possible, in the SUV's lowest gear. With that kind of introduction—the siren and the lights—Judge Landau and everyone else here were sure to know they were coming. It was also obvious that Landau felt he needed this kind of beefed-up protection.

Colton dreaded this visit. Yet Rosalind's safety, as well as her father's, had to outweigh his own discomfort.

Tonight, after hand-to-hand combat with vampires, finding out that the she-wulf he'd mated with was actually some sort of throwback to a Celtic death spirit, and that a bunch of demons, unseen but felt, had burned Rosalind's house down…facing the Landau pack in a prettily decorated living room with explanations about their arrival had to circle the bottom of his all-time worst wish list.

Landau had been left with rabid vampires on the rampage the last time they had met. The guards and the lights were a symptom of Landau's estimation of more trouble brewing. *Smart man, Judge Landau.*

"We're back," Colton announced.

Two more Weres awaited them halfway up the mile-long driveway, wearing dark clothes and carrying weapons. Colton was surprised to see that those weapons were crossbows similar in design to the one Rosalind's father had carried.

Vampire trouble, then.

The Weres didn't stop him, nodding as he passed them by, but Colton wanted to speak to these guys. Landau's personal guard force, members of the Landau werewolf pack who were more like himself in his Miami PD gig, were doing their bit to keep the peace in a city that had no idea there were werewolves in their midst. Or vampires.

For the first time, Colton wasn't sure how well the simple rules for being a protector that he had lived by would apply in the future. He'd be facing other Lycans of equal status who would expect him to come clean about everything. To top it off, he looked like an albino. Would anyone here take him seriously?

Colton blinked slowly as the house came into view. It was a formidable place modeled after a plantation mansion. Three stories tall, with a facade of brick, its main feature was wraparound porch. Tall pillars supported the roof of the wide veranda. It seemed that all sorts of things with calm, genteel exteriors could be deceiving.

As Colton braked by the front steps, he counted three more Weres waiting for him. Two men, and a woman. It wasn't difficult to recognize Judge Landau, with his silver-gray hair. Beside him was Landau's son, Dylan. He guessed the third had to be the Judge's wife, the healer who had tended to him during his first visit. If it had been any other time or circumstance, he would have brought her flowers. Maybe even kissed her cheek.

He cut the engine and got out of the car as quickly as he was able to, given his disintegrated levels of strength. He was hanging on by a thread, but he had to see this through.

"Killion," Judge Landau said in greeting.

Colton heard no irony or sarcasm or hidden meaning in the welcome, and experienced the first bump in his resolve to remain as distant as possible. In that greeting lay no hint of an acknowledgment of Colton's white hair and skin being anything other than normal. He found no inkling whatsoever of the dislike of having to face a freak.

"Hello," he returned. "Sorry to trespass on your hospitality again so soon. Jared Kirk has been hurt and his daughter is in the car with him."

Landau passed his son a look, and Dylan turned to go into the house. Rosalind was likely the cause of Dylan's hasty retreat. The judge was taking no chances with a strange, death-related entity, even after more or less accepting the presence of a ghost among his brood.

"We'll see to Jared at once," Mrs. Landau said, moving toward the car. Speaking directly to Colton, she added, "Perhaps we can see to Rosalind's comfort before we do that?"

Landau joined his wife. To Colton he said, "Rosalind can have the same room she had when last here. She might feel better in familiar surroundings."

"Would that room include a bolted door and bars on the windows?" Colton asked before thinking about how rude that might sound. "She already has a chain on her ankle. A gift from her father before he was hurt."

Mrs. Landau looked earnestly stricken.

"Actually," Landau said, nudging his wife toward the SUV's rear door, "the room has a pretty view of the backyard, as well as new curtains made by my wife."

Colton wanted to hide from Mrs. Landau's lingering gaze, but the stronger motivation was to protect Rosalind, and in doing so, honor the promises he had made.

"She'll probably like that," he said. "And maybe we can think of a way to remove the chain before too long? It's done real damage to her ankles and shins."

Colton was close enough to the elder Were to see Landau's eyes shut briefly, as if word of that chain had somehow tortured him. "I'll get the tools," he said, "and come right up."

Colton's tension eased a bit more at the sight of the Landaus' concern for Rosalind. He inclined his head to them. He had to trust these Weres because no other option remained.

"Rosalind," he said gently as the rear door opened. "It's safe to come out."

Jared Kirk moaned as the car's interior light hit him, and tried unsuccessfully to open his eyes.

Rosalind, on the other hand, was nowhere to be seen.

"Need I ask if this isn't a good development?" Judge Landau observed, taking in Colton's surprise.

Colton didn't answer. The way his stomach had begun to knot seemed answer enough.

Landau gestured with a hand, and out of the dark two Weres responded. The big Weres with arms like professional wrestlers. Carefully, they lifted Kirk up and carted him away, under the judge's wife's supervision.

"You look beat," Landau said to Colton.

"Beat doesn't even begin to cover it. But I'll find Rosalind. She can't have gotten far."

Landau came closer. "I don't usually man the place like this. It's highly unusual. That last vampire sighting, when you were here, led us to believe that the imbeciles have become more aggressive. And now, for a while at least, we have to be overcautious about safeguarding our own."

"They didn't actually come here?" Colton asked.

"We didn't let them get this far."

"How did that turn out?"

"It was nothing we couldn't handle. Nevertheless, that made two attacks on Weres in a few days, and they were too damn close to these walls. I'm sorry about your parents, Colton. I didn't have the chance to tell you so before all of this. It couldn't have been a random targeting. I fear that kind of horror might be the start of a vengeful retaliation against those of us keeping watch over our more vulnerable human neighbors."

Colton nodded. "Has there been anything with the vampires since then?"

"Not even a fang," Landau said.

"I'd stay prepared, then. According to her father, they're likely to know Rosalind has returned."

"Then it isn't safe to go out there alone," Landau advised.

"Thanks, but I'll manage."

Colton hoped to God he'd be able to find the strength to go after her, and prayed that no one else, fanged or otherwise, would find her first.

"Wait," Landau called after him. "I can't let you go alone. You'll need help. Give me a minute."

"Who would you send to accompany me when I'm hunting for a Night Wulf, Judge? You've kept Dylan and the others from knowing about her for quite a while."

Landau's jaw tightened, probably due to the name Colton had given Rosalind. Yet Landau had been in on some part of this revelation for a few days now, and couldn't pretend otherwise.

"I was volunteering myself," Landau said. "A minute more, while I pick up a weapon or two, won't get her into more trouble."

"So you might think," Colton whispered as Landau sprinted up the front steps. "If you didn't know her as well as I do."

Since the Landau estate was now overrun with Weres, Rosalind could only ponder the chances that the folks inside those gates didn't know what she was by now. What were the odds they'd allow her any freedom or shelter when she was a monster magnet, and there might be demons on the loose?

Her legs weakened at the thought of what a creature with that kind of moniker might be like, but she kept walking, directionless.

She didn't know anything about Miami or cities; hadn't a clue where to go now that she had run away from Colton. Her father would be in good hands, though. She'd seen what the judge's wife had done for Colton, and the care they had taken to be kind to another Lycan line.

Colton had told her he felt like he was growing misty inside and less like his old self. Though he wasn't sure what that meant, Rosalind wondered if that felt anything like her new sensations. Her heart went out to him. Her body wanted to go back to him.

She felt him thinking about her. He was worried, and struggling to come to terms with her vanishing act. Her pulse erupted to match his, so far from his. His lure remained strong and nearly all-consuming.

She felt sick.

Glancing over her shoulder at the Landaus' walls, she fielded a tinge of regret that came with a renewed swell of fear. Going back would place all those Weres in danger. She had caused enough trouble already, had brought enough pain to her father and the others. No way could she hit them with the possibility of yet another breed of monster.

"Going back is an impossibility," she said aloud. "What do I do next?" Would demons come this far to find her, and skip the compound if she distanced herself from it?

She had no money and no clothes. Without a doubt, she looked like the monster she was, and was still dragging the damn chain around.

She didn't get far before her legs finally gave out. She sat on the grass, surrounded by the foreign smells of a foreign city.

If she was so special, then she had to dig into that specialness and come up with a way to combat what was happening to her while keeping everyone else safe. She had to at least try.

Determined, and with the help of a tree, she got to her feet. With her hands hanging limply at her sides, she struggled to formulate a plan that didn't involve being scared out of her wits.

First, she had to find clothes. Then she had to find a way to remove the chain.

"How do I accomplish that?"

Frantically, she tuned into her surroundings, scenting humans in the distance and also…someone walking atop Landau's stone wall.

Not Colton. Female. Recognizing this particular smell, Rosalind stood tall, with the hair at the nape of her neck bristling.

The female walking along the top of the wall had the grace and flexibility of a cat. Slim, and not too tall, she wore her dark brown hair at shoulder length, and out of her uniform, in jeans and a sweatshirt, looked just as formidable as she had the last time Rosalind had seen her.

"Delmonico," Rosalind muttered, recalling the name that had been engraved on the officer's name tag.

It didn't take Delmonico long to sense Rosalind watching her. "Who's there?" she called out softly. "Show yourself."

Rosalind nervously stepped out of the shadows.

"You again," Delmonico said, widening her dark eyes.

"Naked this time," Rosalind returned.

"Why is that, exactly?"

"I'm on the run, and didn't have time to address wardrobe malfunctions. Plus, my house was burned down tonight."

"There's blood on your legs."

"Some of it is my father's blood. He's inside your walls now."

"Jared Kirk."

"Yes."

"You haven't run very far, then. He has been taken inside. Why are you out here?"

"No one would or should willingly accept an abomination into their homes. That warning should be cross-stitched, framed and hung above every front door."

Delmonico blew out a breath. "I see."

"I'm pretty sure you don't."

"Then why don't you enlighten me?"

"I'm afraid of people running away if I do."

"Has anyone run away from you?"

"Very few know about me, to date. That doesn't mean they have to accept what baggage I bring with me when they do know."

"Is that why we weren't asked to go after you?" Delmonico asked.

"Neither Colton nor Judge Landau would allow contact, I'm sure."

"Then you must be pretty lonely."

For the second time that night, tears gathered in Rosalind's eyes. She tried desperately not to let them fall. All she had to do was jump over the wall Delmonico crouched upon, and her mate would be there. She wasn't sure how she could want him so much, and miss him so ferociously. Every cell in her body called out to him.

"Heck, I don't see anything wrong with you, except for the lack of clothes," Delmonico observed. "And the blood. Come with me and I'll outfit you."

"No. But thanks."

Delmonico looked into the distance. "They're coming after you now."

"I know."

"Can't I help?"

"Would you help, against their wishes?"

"They are my pack, and my family. They'll be yours if you'll give them a chance."

"I'm a different kind of wulf. Beyond that, I harbor a darkness that draws darkness to me. My father called me a Death-caller. I'm probably not safe to be around, and won't see anyone else harmed."

She had no idea why she was telling this to a stranger, and a member of Landau's pack. Maybe it was because she'd never been around another female.

Delmonico had a pretty, wise, intelligent face, and wore a calm expression. As a police officer, she'd be used to freaks...that's what Colton had thought when the three of them had last met on the city street.

"That's an altruistic plan," Delmonico said. "And complete hogwash, just so you know. More than a few of us also possess an intrinsic need to help, and to protect. If we tempered that need to only include the morally pure or the physically weak, what kind of world would this be?"

"Mine," Rosalind replied.

"I think you'll find that isn't true. I'm willing to help you." Delmonico pulled her sweatshirt over her head. Shaking her hair free of the collar, she tossed the shirt to Rosalind, then straightened up and reached for her zipper. "I don't keep many clothes here. I'm a guest, but Dylan can spare me something."

Climbing out of the jeans, and dropping them to the ground, she added, "I'll come with you, wherever it is you're going, if you'd like me to. However, I strongly recommend that you either let the white wulf catch up with you, or that you get behind these walls. The night has a strange thickness to it that I don't like."

"Colton, the cop you knew of, the white wulf, is what he is because of a vampire attack. He went after the bloodsuckers that killed his parents, and was hurt."

"I know about his family. I also know that there's nothing wrong with being different," Delmonico said, standing on the wall half-naked in some sort of flimsy undershirt and a pair of black lace underwear. "Wouldn't most people be surprised to find out what we are?"

Rosalind stared at the jeans before picking them up. They smelled like worn denim and the perfume Delmonico probably wore when around humans for any length of time.

"Your mate is lucky," Rosalind said to the off-duty cop, meaning it. She liked Delmonico. "And I appreciate the offer."

"But no thanks?"

"I'm poison. I have to go before that poison chokes you."

"Suit yourself," Delmonico said. "You know where to find me."

Rosalind nodded, and with Delmonico's gracious gift of a sweatshirt and jeans in her hands, and Colton's scent and mystical allure getting stronger by the second, she turned back to the park to find a hiding place.

Chapter 23

"It's odd," Judge Landau said as they scrambled over the wall, "how I can't find her scent."

Colton scented Rosalind easily, and could also make out her aloneness and her fear. "She smells like night, and like wind in the leaves."

"You have her scent in you, Colton?"

"It has become a part of me."

"Then you actually have—"

"Yes. We have mated."

They leaped to the ground on the far side of the wall and stopped short. Landau turned his head. "Dana?"

"I'm here," a soft voice returned, after which Officer Delmonico, minus her clothes, landed soundlessly beside them on bare feet.

Colton sucked in a breath. The last time they'd spoken, Delmonico had been in uniform, with a grip on

Rosalind's shoulder. Up close, and out of those unisex clothes, Dylan Landau's she-wolf looked beautiful. Her fighting-fit body showed sculpted, long, lean muscle. She had long brown slightly curly hair, an oval face and large eyes, dark in color, that were fixed on him.

"Sorry if this embarrasses you, Killion," she said. "As it happens, I gave my clothes away not more than five minutes ago to someone who needed them more than I did."

"Rosalind." He reacted with the familiar nerve burn when he said her name.

"Actually, the name she gave herself was Night Wulf," Delmonico said.

Landau interrupted. "Did you see where she went?"

"Yep," Delmonico said. "She headed west. I've never come across anyone like her. Her shape seemed to fuzz at the edges when she spoke to me, as if she wasn't quite solid. I thought to myself that she may be tough, but she's also scared. She wouldn't come with me when I asked her to, which doesn't say much for my powers of persuasion. Sorry." She patted her bare thighs. "I didn't have my cuffs with me."

"She's hurting," Colton said, gazing at the park, thinking he could almost see Rosalind there, and that her presence was, for him, like a strong radio signal.

"She had a chain wrapped around her ankle," Delmonico said. "That has to hurt."

Colton hadn't forgotten about the chain. Thinking he could hear its echo rattling as Rosalind ran, he set off after her, rudely leaving Landau and Delmonico behind.

Rosalind, he silently called. *It's all right. I'm here.*

Her fear breezed over his skin like a layer of ice over heat. The taste in his mouth as he took in air was again like crushed aluminum. Rosalind would be in human shape and wary of another change. Yet outside Landau's compound lay a strange human world unfamiliar to her.

Landau caught up, forcing Colton's attention to split. "She's not the only one out here," Landau said. "This time, it's humans, up ahead."

Colton smelled those humans who had a preference for artificial fragrances like aftershave, scented soaps and shampoos—things most Weres shunned in light of their heightened sense of smell. Another odor emanated from the park, as well. Metal. This new flavor of a scent kindled a memory he didn't have time to explore.

He and Landau jogged toward the center of the park, where Rosalind's trail guided him. Having Landau beside him felt curiously similar to running with his father. Some of his sense of loneliness faded to a dim, dull throb as he locked the memory of his father away with others that were too painful to confront.

"She's weaving through them," he explained. "No trouble this time. Nothing she isn't capable of handling, I hope."

Landau grunted in reply, perhaps not wanting to waste his breath as they picked up their pace.

It wasn't long before they saw the men they had scented. Aware of Landau's hesitation, Colton slowed. As soon as he saw who strolled in this park, he slipped behind a tree, leaving Landau to face them. For their sake, not his.

"Judge Landau?" Officer Julius Davidson, of all the rotten luck, said in a surprised tone. "What are you doing out here at this time of night? You do realize how dangerous this place is?"

"Out for a run," Landau replied, faking a shortness of

breath. "My son is out here somewhere, so much faster than his old man that he'll beat me to the street."

"Mind if we accompany you to that street?" Davidson asked in that way cops had of giving people the feeling they were going to do what they wanted, no matter the response.

"Not necessary," Landau protested.

"I'd feel better about it," Davidson said stubbornly, and also a bit reverently…perhaps out of respect for the elder man, Colton guessed, and possibly also to score some future points in court.

Landau had the sensitivity not to look where Colton had hidden himself. "Well," he said to Davidson, "I've probably lost the bet already, anyway. I'm not as young as I used to be, you know. Dylan will win this race, hands down."

"How about if we pretend I didn't hear anything about a federal judge's personal gambling habits," Davidson joked. "If you want to jog ahead, we'll follow. Doesn't running without shoes hurt your feet, though?"

It's useless, Colton sent silently to the Were. Davidson, attitude aside, also wore the badge of a protector, and most of the time he took that job seriously. *Change of plans.* Landau had to lead the cops to the street. The judge, for all his Lycan power and strengths, had an image to maintain. That image, and the shape that went with it, were human.

His own forced companionship with Landau had been terminated. Colton felt sorry about that.

Raising his chin, he sniffed the air. The really disturbing thing about this encounter was that the officers' weapons hadn't been what saturated the area with the odor of metal. Nor had anything the judge might have been carrying in his waistband and pockets triggered the smell. Something else was causing it. Colton glanced across the grass in time to see a flash of what looked to him like the backside of a man's naked body, streaking through the trees.

His heart gave a thump of disapproval.

His beast growled a warning.

The bad wolf criminal element had been wiped from this park a while ago, and cops had been on patrol tonight. So whatever was here had eluded the park's human guardians.

His claws sprang through his skin in reaction to whatever his beast had sensed, and the familiar undulations began in his shoulders as his ligaments began to stretch.

This naked streaker had been no vampire, so what did that leave?

Colton's chest heaved. His ribs cracked, with his spine following suit. He tore his borrowed shirt open and unbuttoned his pants without too much thought about how many times he had stripped lately, and how outrageous the events of the past forty-eight hours had been.

"There is no earthly way a demon could have found us so quickly," he protested as his wulf unfurled. But then demons, by their very definition, weren't earthly.

Once his shift was complete, Colton ran so fast that he virtually skimmed the ground. If it had been a demon he'd seen, and if it had been hunting for Rosalind, he had to be there when the cursed thing found her. He had to hope to God that a demon wouldn't touch her.

As if Rosalind had left a trail of breadcrumbs, her lightly floral scent beckoned to him. She hadn't lost that fragrance or left it behind in favor of others crowding her system. That one thing alone gave him hope. Amid all the changes, Rosalind's she-wulf maintained a firm enough hold on her to overpower the rest.

That she-wulf was what he wanted to find, coax forth, capture, bed and love. They'd had sex in human form, and it had been good. Many more experiences like that, and their wulf sides would want in on the deal. He couldn't imagine how that would go down. Wulf to wulf...

Another flash of white downgraded his speed to a lope. Keyed up, his fur rippled with tension. This wasn't a damn demon though. The bright spot of light turned out to be a lamp post marking a driveway, the first of many driveways bordering the neighborhoods surrounding the park.

Rosalind had gone into public territory, for who knew what reason, with what might or might not have been a demon trailing behind. Being anywhere near to a human neighborhood like this one amounted to a dangerous setback.

Growls rattled in his throat.

He bared his teeth.

Damn it, he had to lose the fur. Things were bad enough without giving the people here a reason to call the cops.

How strong were demons? How crafty, fast?

This didn't have to be a demon.

Jogging, naked, Colton veered off the sidewalk, aiming for an alley behind the closest row of homes and praying that in one of those backyards he'd find some clothes to borrow, hanging on an old-fashioned line. And that the presence of a Night Wulf would scare barking dogs indoors.

Chapter 24

Rosalind had known the exact moment something new began following her, and tried to process the symptoms of this acknowledgment.

Whatever the creature was, its presence made her head hurt. The vicious pounding behind her eyes caused the landscape to swim by in a blur of movement. The lights she passed beneath were like streaks of pain. Her mouth hurt from clenching her teeth hard enough and long enough to fracture a jaw bone. Her wulf exhibited signs of a rare distress that had made her muscled hindquarters quiver.

Her heightened senses didn't like this new thing shadowing her.

Outlines of fences, formerly solid, melted into wavering liquid forms. Buildings became fluid, their edges filmy and undefined. The pavement she raced across buckled in her peripheral vision, though it seemed okay when she glanced at her feet. Either the world was actually losing its shape, or she was losing her mind.

The only thing completely in focus now was the feel of the entity behind her. Awareness of it had become a distress.

Not human, not vampire, not Were. *Demon? Really?*

Afraid to face such an entity in the open, in the darkness from which both it and she had been born, she had instead brought it to civilization. Still, the artificial lights people needed to make them feel safe did nothing to lessen her fear, and streets of houses filled with sleeping humans seemed utterly alien.

Why had she come this way?

Realization struck when she found herself in a corner yard. Familiar smells stopped her cold. This was where she had heard her lover's wail of grief, and where she had viewed the cause of his despair. On this street sat the house where Colton's parents had lived and died; now a place where no one would want to willingly return to.

Over the fence in a bound, Rosalind fled to the alley where she had once watched Colton shift shape. In her mind's eye she saw him there, golden, angry and hurt. That image bolstered her courage somewhat. They had both been Lycans then, at least on the surface, and ignorant of what lay ahead. She had been young in spirit and very naive.

She found the house that still reeked of Lycan death. In the yard behind it, she pulled up to make her stand.

"Come and get it, you bastards," she said.

Dread set in the minute Colton's feet hit the pavement. Rosalind had made a beeline for his parents' house, forcing him to confront his compartmentalized feelings about the terrible events that had taken place there.

He hadn't lived on this street with his parents for years, but had spent a lot of time with them. For that time, he'd forever be thankful. Again, though, why would Rosalind come here?

Vaulting over the fence and landing in the alley, Colton paused to listen for whatever a demon might sound like, not expecting crackling hellfire and devilish laughter. An atmospheric heaviness covered the entire area, as if something not of this world had punched its way through.

He heard nothing at all for the span of several shallow breaths, and then perked up. A growl.

His body lurched into action. Hopping one more fence, he sighted Rosalind crouched on his parents' back step.

Glorious, rare black fur covered her legs and arms, and her claws were raised and gleaming. At her feet lay a pile of clothes that didn't smell anything like her, and probably would have confused any creatures coming her way.

Although she might have been scared, Rosalind was magnificent in the fierceness of her pose. Her she-wulf had taken over, leaving no room for debate about the mastery of her Lycan bloodlines. Even in the face of danger, she radiated with the scent and strength of a pure, dangerous wulf.

She made no gesture of acknowledgment. Her eyes were trained on a darker area near the garage. When she growled again, he turned in what felt like slow motion.

He didn't see a damn thing, though the mere thought of a demon in this yard was viscerally disturbing. Adding a menacing growl to the echo of Rosalind's, Colton stayed frozen in place in case the thing by the garage advanced, feeling sick over the fact that the yard still smelled like blood.

Rosalind balanced on her haunches over the exact spot where his mother's headless body had lain.

Narrowing his concentration, Colton awaited what would come next, afraid that if he moved he would spark an unconscionable reaction in one of hell's denizens.

He felt Rosalind shift position and reluctantly looked to her. When her dark eyes darted to meet his, his heart began to hammer. She was gearing up for a strike, no longer content to play the waiting game.

The air tensed around him. An ungodly, otherworldly shriek that completely stole his breath tore through the quiet. High-pitched and ear-piercing, it shattered the windows beside where Rosalind crouched. A rain of broken glass showered everything, looking like a typhoon of confetti.

In motion, Colton's first thought was for Rosalind's safety, and to hell with the demon. But she jumped to her feet and met him on the walkway before he had registered her astonishing move.

Something else met them in the center of the yard: a glistening, hard-bodied entity with a humanlike shape and no eyes in its twisted face. This thing rammed into Colton so hard, he stumbled sideways. After quickly regaining his balance, and with the sound of his own blood rushing in his ears, Colton stopped, stunned.

In the seconds he had taken to right himself, Rosalind had fallen to the ground, and the demon was leaning over her.

Raging, Colton lunged and knocked the demon away. Whirling, he showed his teeth, ready to take on this thing.

But the demon seemed to have vanished, taking its filthy intentions with it.

Colton fell to his knees bedside his mate, who had shifted back to human form. Without giving a damn about what damage further closeness to her might do, he gathered her to him, cradling her body, rocking her gently and growling her name.

At first glance, he saw no evidence of serious injury. Her fur had protected her from most of the glass. Splinters of it sparkled in her hair like pieces of fallen stars. Only one jagged shard angled through the smooth, flushed skin of her right cheek.

Instincts screamed for him to go after the demon that had hurt her and tear out its throat with his bare hands. A wildness flowed through him that he had only experienced once before, on the night his parents had died.

Sanity seemed to be slipping away from him by degrees.

When Rosalind's eyes opened, she gazed up at him calmly. Raising a hand to touch his white muzzle, she said, "Stay with me, wulf. No one dies tonight."

He had to honor her request. He had to let the demon go. She needed him.

He saw no sign of demon in Rosalind. This monster hadn't touched her. But he had.

With a swift reverse shift in shape, Colton watched the last of the white fur disappear from his arms. He waited for whatever Rosalind's reaction would be. The answer came as he looked into her eyes, which were not black or green, but gray, and continuing to fade.

"Are you all right?" he demanded, wary of that change being related to him, and unable to do anything about it. Unable to let her go.

"Hold still," he crooned, fingering the piece of glass imbedded in her cheek. With a gentle tug, and not so much as a grimace from Rosalind, the glass came free. Colton tossed it away and pressed a finger to the wound to stop the trickle of blood seeping from the cut. Then he bent down to kiss the spot, startling them both.

The moment stretched in complete silence, broken only when he asked, "Has it gone?"

"Yes."

"It didn't reach you."

"You didn't give it time."

"I'd have killed it if it had."

"I could feel it," she said. "I could feel the soulless be-ing's spirit trying to get inside me."

"Did you tell it there's no more room?"

When she shook her head, glass scattered, making tiny tinkling noises as the pieces hit the concrete.

"I want so badly to go on holding you," he confessed.

"I want that, too. I feel your pain, way down deep, Colton. How can you stand it? How can you stand up and face that kind of pain?"

"Job to do," he said tenderly. "Though you're making that as difficult as possible."

She smiled, and the wound on her cheek oozed more blood. But that smile was worth everything to him. It was the first one he had seen in a while, and was as daz-zling as it was brief.

"I tried to get away from you and the others," she ex-plained.

"Yes, and how well did that work?"

When she smiled again, dusted with glass and as white as a sheet, Colton was sure his heart would break.

He uttered his vow...to her. To the night. To the moon,

and whoever else might be listening. "I will do anything and everything in my power, forever, to protect you, and keep you selfishly for myself."

Her hair, as white as it was black, her gray eyes, her light skin... Was a ghost so bad? Two ghosts?

He lightly kissed the lips that had temporarily up-turned. He kissed her forehead, her injured cheek, her hair, her long, graceful neck. His free hand moved over her, exploring, seeking anything unfamiliar that he'd have to deal with. That *they* would have to deal with.

If Rosalind could become what others around her were, she would remain Lycan. *I'll see to it.*

His mouth came back to hers. He deepened the kiss, separating her lips with his, daring her tongue to dance with his. Her breath was shallow, though her heart raced. Though he felt her energy charging upward to engulf him, she didn't wrap her arms around him, afraid of what else she might do.

He was nearly blinded by his desire for her—for possessing her in every possible way. He had never been so hungry, so demented by the emotions flooding his body and his mind.

Reason, like a blinking light way off in the distance, warned that he couldn't devour her now, here, in this place. It wasn't right. There wasn't time. And yet with one more stroke of his lips across hers, and upon hearing her gasp of reciprocated longing, some of the horror of what had taken place in his parents' house began to fade.

He wasn't alone. He and Rosalind, whatever incarnations they ended up in, would be a family.

As if his life's blood had begun to return, one precious drop at a time, Colton's pulse steadied. Utilizing what was left of his willpower, he drew back just far enough to speak.

"Rosalind, what did the demon want?"

"It wanted you," she replied.

Chapter 25

The meaning of those words eluded Colton at first. Maybe, he thought, he hadn't heard her correctly.

"Me?" he said, his mouth still hovering over hers.

She couldn't have meant that the demon had been waiting for him, as in him personally? Nevertheless, the remark had a haunting vibration that sped through his mind like the tail of a comet.

"Is somebody in there?"

An unfamiliar voice broke through Colton's mental jumble with the force of an unexpected electrical discharge.

"Who's there?" a second voice demanded with stern authority. "We heard noises. Stay where you are. We're coming into the yard."

It was the police. Colton smelled them.

Obeying that command, of course, was utterly impossible. Colton shot to his feet. The uniforms couldn't find him like this, and see what had become of him. Not only did he have no badge or ID, both he and Rosalind were stark naked, breathless, rather scary-looking and sprinkled with broken window glass. To an observer it might look as though they'd tried to break into the house.

He turned his head. Dana Delmonico had told him that the terrible event on this premises had been taken care of, no doubt by Weres on the force who found it in their best interest to help cover this particular murder up. If that cover-up hadn't been accomplished correctly or had been done too hastily, the current window breakage would result in further investigation.

These cops weren't Were.

"We've got to get away," he said, tugging Rosalind to her feet.

She was light. Her thinness had been further accentuated since he'd first seen her. Her ribs were countable. Her arms seemed frail.

She stood proudly before his scrutiny, comfortable with her nakedness, as all Weres were, but trembling from the circumstances they found themselves in. Rosalind didn't fear vampires, and maybe not even demons, but she wanted nothing to do with the Miami PD.

Colton wanted to feed her, fatten her up, pacify her fears. He wanted to keep her within the circle of his arms and assure her that nothing outside their relationship mattered. But he saw, as she moved with the grace of a panther beside him, that her waist-length hair, salt-and-pepper-colored moments before, was now completely white. No black remained, and therefore no evidence of the Night Wulf.

This was the result of a kiss, and of holding her in his arms so briefly.

"Ghost," he said softly, tenderly, as the uniforms on the other side of the fence fumbled with the lock in the gate.

"Landau's is the safest place now. Are you good with that? Will you trust me?" he said to Rosalind. "They will help. I'll be there with you, and it will be all right."

She nodded.

"Promise you'll follow me there," Colton said. "Promise now."

"I promise," Rosalind said, reaching for the pile of clothes on the steps.

Having gained that assurance, Colton leaped through the open window of his parents' house with Rosalind in his wake just as the backyard gate finally swung open behind them.

"Wait. Stop!" both officers directed.

"Sorry, boys," Colton tossed back.

Seconds later he and Rosalind were out the front door and sprinting with a speed that matched the sound of the wind in Colton's ears.

They moved in tandem, side by side, in a rhythm that made Rosalind's heart pound. They were leaving the human neighborhood behind, but the imprint of the demon's silent message stayed with her.

It hadn't wanted her.

It wanted Colton.

She was afraid to slow down, afraid the demon's evil intentions would make her turn around and hunt for it, so that she could wring answers from its scrawny neck.

The hellish monster hadn't had a mouth, or eyes. It was composed of mounds of tight skin stretched over an otherwise humanlike form, with exceptionally long arms. It had communicated through vibrations in its body, by rubbing bone against bone.

It had followed her, but didn't intend to harm her.

It had wanted Colton, but hadn't stuck around.

The thought made her ill and threatened to topple every theory they had pieced together so far. Things were quite the opposite, in fact. For whatever reason, that demon had used her to get to her mate. She had led it to him.

Her thoughts reformed as she ran beside Colton, with terrible results.

If that monster hadn't wanted her, was there a chance the vampires hadn't wanted her, either? Could they also have been after her lover? But...why?

There had to be more to this story than met the eye. The pairing between Colton, specifically, and herself was what her father had actually been afraid to let happen.

She and Colton. Two entities able to shift shape at will, unlike other Weres. Special beings. Wulf. Now, one of them was a night creature and the other an entity out of Were legend.

She didn't like this terrible line of thought. Now that the floodgates of thought had opened, though, her ideas took on a life of their own. What-ifs became directions.

If a demon wanted to find Colton, and that applied also to the vampires, there might be a possibility that the bloodsuckers that had murdered Colton's family had done so in order to call *him* out, knowing he would follow them with a Were's need for vengeance. They hadn't gone away, but had been waiting in the park.

"Colton!" she exclaimed between breaths, her body again filled with dread. "Colton. No!"

If any of those thoughts proved true, Colton was in the dark about what was happening, and was in real danger. He was the one who had to be careful. She had a Death-caller inside her, and yet her lover might be the entity in trouble.

"Colton," she said again, softer this time, almost pleading.

How had all this started, she wanted to ask him, if not by her coming to his aid in the park? If not imprinting with him immediately, with the first glance in his direction, before fighting off the vampires?

What had made her want to belong to him, and him to her, in a relationship with a supersonic ascent?

His wail of agony.

Not hers.

Rosalind focused on that memory and dug in with her razor-sharp claws.

The sound Colton had made, exemplifying his grief, and in this very neighborhood, is what had chased away her anger over his early rejection. His wail of unimaginable pain had to have been what succeeded in sealing her soul to his.

His wail. *His* call. The pain and death in that heart-rending sound he had made after finding the remains of his loved ones was the language that a Banshee, whose deal was to announce those same things, would recognize and identify with.

She had been drawn to his pain. It had been love at first sight. Like calling to like. She had accepted this, confronted it, reveled in it. Did that make her a cohort of the monsters in the area? Had her need kept Colton from seeing the possibility of his own peril?

She, usually so fleet on her feet, stumbled.

The data seemed flawed, the gaps insurmountable. Colton had been right. Judge Landau and the elders were their only option for finding the truth.

Perhaps sensing her distress, Colton slowed. In the heat of the balmy night, chills covered his naked body, mimicking hers. Having told him something of the demon's desire, his mind would be as active as hers in attempting to process that information. There was so much going on in her mind, she couldn't enter his.

Rosalind shook her head hard to clear it.

There was someone up ahead.

A silver-haired man was headed their way beneath the lights of the tall Landau gates. Backed by the two big Weres that had stood guard at the gate, the silver-haired Lycan tossed some clothes to Colton and gestured for the gates to be closed after them.

Colton's sigh of relief when the sound of iron hitting iron resonated in the night moved through Rosalind as if she'd made it.

Chapter 26

There were more Weres on the front lawn than Colton had ever seen. Young Weres and old. Landau, his wife, his son Dylan and Dana Delmonico were the recognizable few. Beyond their somber presence stood the rest of the Weres Colton had met in this same area the last time he'd faced a welcoming party.

Had that only been two nights ago?

The difference was that he felt almost glad to see them this time.

"I'm truly sorry about that," the judge said as the gates closed. "I couldn't get rid of those officers in the park. They wanted to drive me home. Then they waited here for a while. Is everything all right?"

"Not unless you can discount the presence of a demon in Miami," Colton replied.

"A—"

"Demon," Colton repeated. "An eyeless, mouthless bastard that Rosalind says was looking for me."

He turned to Rosalind, who was inches from him and staring nervously at the reception line. "Do you want to go inside? Your father is probably waiting to see you."

When she shook her white-haired head, a rustle of murmurs went through the gathered crowd. Colton had forgotten how her appearance had to have surprised them. The younger Weres, Dylan and his pack, had never seen Rosalind. They hadn't been allowed to see her.

Here she stood. A creature possessed by a spirit that none of them understood, although it would have been easy for them, as Weres, to pick up on the subtle Otherworldly aspect of her aura. It was all there in her scent, along with that seductive fragrance of flowers.

Rosalind, just inside the walls, had donned a blue longsleeved sweatshirt and a pair of jeans. Her feet were bare. Her hair was tangled and she was covered in blood. Looking battle-scarred, she faced them all defiantly. Truly special. One of a kind.

He knew she was shaking inside.

Colton stepped in front of her possessively to ward off the stares. To the judge, he said, "Do you have any idea why a demon might want to find a wulf?"

Landau frowned. "I've never heard of a demon actually existing, not to mention showing itself in public."

"I have," a woman said, stepping forward and into the light of the porch.

All eyes turned to the auburn-haired beauty who was flanked by Matt Wilson, the Were detective Colton had met the other night.

"I run a facility not far out of the city center," she said. "A psychiatric hospital. A few days ago I felt a presence hanging around outside and went out for a look. I saw what I now presume might have been your demon skirting the perimeter of the fence. When I turned on the lights, it slunk away."

"Then there's a chance it wasn't after me," Colton said, turning to Rosalind. "I've never seen that place."

"It was looking for you," Rosalind confirmed.

"Why?"

"Black heart," a deep voice said from behind them, and everyone in that yard spun to find Jared Kirk, standing in the house's open doorway.

"What's that?" Judge Landau barked.

To the judge Rosalind's father asked, "Do we want to talk about this here or in private?"

"I think it's gone too far to be considered private," Colton replied in Landau's place.

Judge Landau glanced to his son, and to his pack of gathered Weres. Dylan spoke up. "I think we need to know what's going on. We're the peacekeepers here. How can we do our jobs if there are secrets we aren't privy to, or if some of this missing information can put not only innocent bystanders, but those we love in jeopardy?"

Kirk stiffly took a seat on a bench. He gathered his thoughts before speaking again.

"My daughter," he said, "is not just Lycan. She is part Death-caller, a Celtic spirit who deals with death. Not handing it out, not walking hand in hand with Death. A Banshee, as some call them, merely acknowledges the coming of Death, and warns humans of its approach."

His voice had dulled, but he continued. "The spirit in Rosalind is a messenger from the Otherworld, and something we know little about. Hence the need for protection and seclusion."

"That doesn't mean she's a danger to others," Colton said, realizing how rude it was for them to be speaking of Rosalind's secrets, and about her, as if she wasn't there.

"I believe that she's no danger if the spirit is contained," Kirk said.

Colton was of a mind to pick Rosalind up and take her away from this. But she needed these explanations as much as any of them did. Probably so much more.

"I didn't guard her for other people's safety, really. I guarded her for her own welfare," Kirk said. "Telling myself otherwise, and allowing myself to believe it was for the sake of others that she had to be hidden away, was perhaps my best way, my only way, of finding justice in keeping her apart from all of you."

Dylan Landau spoke up. "You said black heart as if that's something significant. What does it mean?"

More murmurings went through the crowd.

"Rosalind will become something else if she…"

"What will she become?" the judge asked when Kirk let the explanation die.

"Night Wulf."

Colton heard Rosalind's soft, lamenting whine before her father's explanation had concluded. It drove him forward so fast, he shocked Jared Kirk into silence when he faced the elder Were from a closeness of less than three feet.

"Maybe I spoke too soon and she has heard enough for now," he said.

"Yes." Kirk nodded sympathetically. "But this affects you, Colton, if you're the demon's target."

Colton nodded for him to go on.

"I had to accept that you had mated, and along with that the possibility, the hope that you would adhere to my request never to touch her again until we knew what the situation was. In ignoring my request, you've placed her and yourself in danger. The others who come after her will want to be rid of you. You now stand in their way. As her mate, they need your removal in order to make Rosalind realize her full potential."

Light-headed from the strain of standing up to this after all that had gone on before, Colton raised a hand to stop the Were. Rosalind had other ideas. She appeared beside him to stare at her father.

"Black heart," she said. "What is that?"

Kirk looked pained by the smooth deception of his daughter's calm expression. Though his reluctance showed, he met her gaze.

"A Night Wulf is created if you, Rosalind, were to mate with a species in whose chest rests a black heart. An evil heart. Rogue vampires, demons and fallen angels will all fight for the right to turn you, to possess you, in order to bring this thing into being."

"I thought that's what I am already," Rosalind said weakly.

"No. Not yet. Not ever, hopefully. Because that creature would, I believe, have the potential to rule any species she chose."

Colton put his arm around Rosalind's waist, able to feel her tremors roll through him.

Her father spoke again. "Keeping you from actualizing such an inheritance has always been my goal. Keeping you hidden from those kinds of beasts was all I ever wanted."

Colton staggered forward. "You thought I'd have such a heart? Because I'm what you've called a ghost?"

Kirk's patience was worn, his face haggard. "I didn't

know what the vampires had done to you. I thought you might be the key to a Night Wulf's conception. I was wrong."

"Who killed my mother?" Rosalind asked. Colton thought her voice sounded sad.

"Something other than demon. Something worse." Kirk's wide shoulders sagged. "They all came eventually, after so much time without a sighting or hint of their presence. And they came at once. I didn't know until it was too late. Your mother slipped out to meet them without my knowledge, and while you and I slept. She sacrificed herself for you and for me, knowing we would go through it all again when you were old enough, but wanting to give us some time."

There were tears on Rosalind's face when Colton pulled her closer. The tears streamed down. With gentle fingers he stroked her face, wiping away the dampness. "You are blameless, innocent and vulnerable," he said to her. "I don't care who is after you or me. We can beat this and find the truth."

She looked up at him with pale gray eyes. "They nearly killed you the first time I followed you. Your parents dying was bad enough, but that didn't have to be connected to me, to what I am."

Then she stiffened and looked to her father. "I didn't know Colton until the night the vampires attacked his family. Those monsters couldn't have been trying to take him from me."

Leaning over, she spoke to her father clearly. "Secrets. There are more. I can taste them."

Kirk shook his head as if some parts of this mystery were too hard to comprehend.

"The ridiculous part of all this," Judge Landau chimed

in, "is how they can think they can tackle a werewolf pack to get what they want, when what they want is for the most part Lycan."

The judge approached Rosalind cautiously, not afraid, Colton sensed, but taking care not to alarm her. "What else can you tell us about this, Rosalind? You must know something."

"Colton and I were meant to be mated," she replied without hesitation. "I don't see how vampires could have predicted that ahead of time and gone after his family."

Landau appeared to consider her statement. His gaze fixed thoughtfully on Jared Kirk.

"Do you understand that, and what might cause her to believe she's right?" he asked.

In the lull of silence following Landau's inquiry, Rosalind repeated her tiny sound of distress. Whether or not her father fully comprehended what was going on, Rosalind had forged some sort of link to the truth, and knew it.

"What is it?" Colton asked her.

She turned her luminous eyes to him. "Memories."

"Tell me about them."

"I have to speak with my father alone first."

"Use the house," Landau said.

Reluctantly, Colton stood aside so that Rosalind could see the doorway. "I'll hate every minute you're in there, and out of my sight," he confessed. "I won't leave the porch until you come out, or call."

Kirk looked pretty much like a doomed man, Colton thought, as the elder Were, with hunched shoulders and a solemn expression, followed his daughter inside.

Colton placed his back to the doorjamb and stared out at the gathering of Weres. "Any problems with this?" he asked them. "Or with hosting us here until we figure out what to do next? Because if there are, we'll honor that, and go."

"No problems," Judge Landau replied, as spokesman and Alpha of his pack. "None whatsoever."

The rest of Landau's pack hadn't moved a muscle.

Chapter 27

Rosalind preceded her father into the Landaus' living room, feeling trapped there. Feeling wild, and way too feral to make use of a chair.

She began to pace.

"The last time I was here," she said, "I eagerly waited for Colton to heal, naively believing that everything might be okay once he did. It was you who frightened me with hints of the secrets you were keeping. Maybe things would have been easier if you had shared those secrets with me."

"You have matured," her father said in response. "Quickly. I'm not sure you would have listened or understood just days ago."

She retraced her steps. "'This male is not for you' is what you told me. And that Colton wouldn't have been compatible before the fight, and certainly not after it.

Also, you said that I'd have no idea what would happen if..." She let that empty sentence linger a while. Her father didn't break the silence.

"You said that I couldn't help him, that I couldn't remain near him. It was imperative, you told me, that Colton and I were separated, the sooner the better."

She hesitated, and looked her father in the face. "But the thing I remember best of all was that you said two extremes were never destined to meet."

Rosalind walked toward the window, able to feel Colton out there. Allowing his presence to calm her, warm her.

"Two such extremes, Father. A Lycan with an unusual spirit inside her, and a Lycan warrior who had nearly lost his life and retained it as a ghost of his former self."

She was again standing above him. "How did you know what to expect? Because it's quite obvious to me now that you did."

Her father's Lycan-green eyes were bright in the indoor light. "I didn't know anything for sure," he finally said. "Until I heard this ghost's name."

"Killion."

"Yes. Once I'd been made aware of that, I realized that it was probably already too late for the both of you."

Rosalind put her hands on the arm of his chair. "Too late for what?"

"To reverse or withhold your bond. It was, you see, more than a case of like meeting like, and after all this time..."

Circles. They were going in circles, when all her father had to do was tell her the truth.

"I don't think anyone comprehends what this bond

means," her father continued. "How could they? I'm not sure I believe it."

"They? Who do you mean? What do you mean?" Rosalind demanded.

"The monsters."

"What wouldn't they believe?"

He looked directly into her waiting eyes at last, and she saw the resolution on his face. "That you, of all Weres, could have met up with the heritage of that damned Banshee who started all this," he said.

She waited for that to make sense, but it was gibberish he'd fed her. Not the truth at all.

"Heritage?" she echoed.

Her father waved a hand at the door. "Colton Killion comes from an old line. One in particular that was distressing to me. Colton is from the same lineage as the Were who mated with your great-great-grandmother, Rosalind. He's from the same family. How's that for the long-range designs of fate? After generations, by jumping a wall in a city where you were only visiting for a couple of days and supposedly behaving yourself, you met up with someone out of your rising spirit's goddamn past."

He shook his hand, still raised, as if cursing the fate he'd just spoken about. "It was fantastical. Far-fetched. Who could have believed it? How could I have trusted my instincts on the matter? I knew only that you had locked onto this Were with an uncanny adherence that seemed absurd, given that you hadn't even really met him. You'd only seen him once, out there, beyond these walls. Isn't that the truth?"

Rosalind frowned, not really understanding this at all. "Yes," she said. "That's true. I saw him for the first time in the park."

"It likely was the spirit in you that recognized him, and it didn't take much. I don't begin to claim to comprehend how that can happen, or if it actually did. You asked for what I believe to be the truth, and this is it."

Her father's theory was an astonishing one, and probably an idea that no one, including herself, would have taken seriously, had he mentioned it in this house while Colton had been hurt and healing. He had been right about that.

She was different now.

"How can a spirit identify someone they'd never seen before?" she asked. "It would have to mean that whatever kind of life that spirit manifests actually continues on. Not just instincts and urges, but actually able to recognize something beyond itself."

She was feeling strange, and went on in a rush. "Wouldn't that theory suggest that not only is a Banshee inside me, it's possessing me? Driving me toward what it wants?"

Her father countered, "Would you otherwise believe in love at first sight? A love so strong that you'd be willing to give up your life for a stranger ten minutes after laying eyes on him?"

"I don't believe this," Rosalind stated firmly.

"I can't blame you," her father said. "It is, however, the only explanation I have. And after accepting it as a possibility, however remote, and aside from the dangers now presenting themselves like a bad case of déjà-vu over what happened to your mother and I…I see no better way to explain what you so desperately want to understand."

Rosalind's stomach was churning. Although she wanted to discount her father's explanation, she was, at that moment, aware of Colton's thoughts. He was going to come in after her. She'd been away from him for too long.

The explanation her father had given her suddenly seemed viable. She felt as though a ray of moonlight had reached down inside her to help lighten the load, but it was actually the sensation of sudden enlightenment.

Inside her, in the dark space where the unknown hovered, some of her fear began dissipate. A small portion of it, anyway. For whatever reason, she had found her soul mate. The real one. The only one. And who cared, after all, how she had found Colton?

It was a game of sacrifice and give-and-take and spirits merging. That's what this larger-than-life love was.

Had her mother known about any of this? Foreseen it? Her mother had sacrificed herself for her family, with hopes that when the spirit rose within her daughter, if indeed it did, Rosalind would have the time to find her true love and explore her options.

Her father had other ideas.

A Banshee was probably the closest thing to real darkness on the planet. A monster magnet. Her father had maintained the hope that the creatures seeking a resting place for their black-hearted leader might never find it, and that his daughter might break the link of the Banshee spirit, who had changed the fates of so many, by being protected from all that.

By never meeting a mate.

By never setting foot outside their gates. Nothing like her mother's wishes.

But how tricky fate could be. Landau had invited them here. She had escaped her father's net. And in doing so, she had found Colton…setting the entire scenario into action.

Colton, a member of the same family as the Lycan male who had mated with the woman the Banshee had saved all those generations ago.

God help them.

Serendipity? Fate? She had found Colton in the park, and two families had been reunited by the spirit rising within her. The spirit who had recognized Colton from afar.

"Colton," Rosalind said as her knees finally began to give way.

He was there in a flash of taut, tense muscle, with a face strained paler than hers. His facial welts gave him an edgy, hungry look. She had never really seen him in the light.

But Colton Killion had always been dangerous.

What would have happened if the vampires hadn't attacked? If the bloodsuckers hadn't killed his family that night?

Would she have found Colton eventually, anyway? Would fate have taken care of the details, ensuring she would, and that the two families would again be joined together?

A date with destiny?

"We have to kill them all," she said to Colton. "All who know about me, and about you."

Colton glanced past her, to her father, who stood up as if he were well enough to ready for the next necessary fight.

"We have to stop them from making me one of them, completely. We can't let them put a black heart inside my chest."

"How do we do that?" he asked.

Rosalind started for the door, pausing when she

reached it. "I call them," she said with absolute certainty. "And hope they all show up."

The intensity of their bond made Rosalind look longingly at him one last time from the doorway. She wasn't seeking permission to do what she had said she would; she was letting him see her feelings.

There were plenty of questions still unasked and unanswered, Colton thought, and yet he had to go on trust here. Trust his gut. Trust her. Rosalind had unselfishly, and at great risk, led the demon away from him and the Landau pack that very night. Her motives had been pure. Thoughts of a black heart inside her chest, and what that might mean, were unthinkable.

More than any of them, Rosalind wanted to give a shout to all of the monsters in the area, sensing that culling monsters with a taste for blood was the only way to have any kind of peace, if only for a while.

If the creatures in this area that knew about them were removed from the equation, maybe no others would take up the scent.

He followed Rosalind outside. She walked to where the judge stood with the rest of his family and his pack.

"It's my problem," she said, and Colton knew how much effort it took for her to face them and to speak. "I'm sorry to have brought this sad doom to your doorstep. I know now that they won't go away or back off for any length of time. Though I'm not certain why they want us so much, or the actual specifics of that kind of lust, Colton and I have to face them."

She paused only to draw a breath. "I have no right to ask you to help us. You've been told what I am, and can see what Colton has become because of the vampires.

It's against my better judgment to ask for your aid, but I just don't know what else to do."

"We're in." Dylan Landau spoke up first, with a giant step forward.

Judge Landau looked to his son.

"We cleaned up the park a year ago. Now look at it," Dylan said. "Monsters think it's their personal playground and that they can come out whenever they want to."

"We don't know what to expect," the elder Landau cautioned.

"Vampires," Rosalind said. "And demons. Definitely more than one of each. Supernatural creatures out of nightmares. But then, so are we, really, when it comes right down to it."

Colton noticed Dana Delmonico's brief grin. Delmonico would know about those nightmares firsthand, since she likely hadn't known about werewolves until she was bitten by one.

His gaze moved to the others present. Every single one of those Weres nodded to him, in accord.

A small twitch in his chest made him bow his head.

"We're sure as hell not going to let you face them alone," Matt Wilson seconded, with the auburn-haired female by his side.

"It seems that my pack has made up their minds," Judge Landau observed. "But this night's almost over."

"Has it only been one?" Colton muttered, because it already felt like years since he'd last stood in this yard.

"Tomorrow," Rosalind said. "I'll call them then. I can't presume to see what will happen, but it's the only option open that I can see."

Jared Kirk had followed them into the yard. He said,

"The approaching sunrise will keep them down and give us time to prepare."

Judge Landau turned to his pack. "Tomorrow is Saturday. No one who counts will miss us at the day job." He turned back. "Jared?"

"I plan on being better by then," Rosalind's father said.

Landau looked at his son. "You understand how dangerous it's going to be."

"And how dangerous it'll be across the board if we don't take care of this new pest problem," Dana Delmonico added.

Colton almost smiled. Dana Delmonico was a tough cop and a tough Were. Not Lycan, but a perfect match for Dylan, all the same.

Again, facing this pack, he realized how much he had missed in the past by being a loner.

"We'll need police presence," Matt Wilson advised. "So others don't come wandering in."

"Adam Scott can arrange a perimeter," Dylan said. "With the help of a neighboring pack."

"There are other Weres on the force, outside the city?" Colton asked.

"Several good ones," Dylan replied.

"We can't take this fight to the park here," another Were said. "Besides being too close to home, outside police presence would be noted."

Colton looked more closely at the large brown-haired young man who added, "It's way too risky."

"Then we can bring them to the hospital grounds," the auburn-haired female who was Wilson's mate suggested. "No one hangs around a psychiatric ward, especially after dark."

"Good one, Jenna," Dylan said to the female before

turning back to Rosalind. "Does this work for you, Rosalind? Will you be able to bring them anywhere you choose?"

Like the Pied Piper? Colton thought.

"I'm not sure if I can bring them anywhere," she replied with a tired, sober face.

She continued to shake, part of that no doubt from being so close to this many others. But she continued to maintain her stance.

Although no one allowed their gazes to linger on her long, Colton read in their faces how uneasy they felt in her presence. They were equally as uneasy with him.

He didn't blame them. Two strange Lycans needed their help. They didn't have to go out of their way to oblige, but this was their territory, and Weres were nothing if not protective of their space.

If all went well, and that was a big *if*, what would happen afterward? They'd all return to their respective packs and homes and mates, and he and Rosalind, with or without her father, would be left to themselves.

The location of Rosalind's home had been compromised. He couldn't take her back to his apartment, and the thought of reclaiming his city life made his muscles quiver in distaste. Also, and the biggest what-if of all, any future depended on the premise that he and Rosalind would survive the next night.

"Thank you," he said to Landau and his pack; two simple words denoting a gratitude that couldn't actually be expressed to the proper degree.

"I'll stand guard until dawn," he announced, afraid to go back into the house with Rosalind bunking inside it, and especially afraid to go anywhere near her if this was to be his last night. His and hers.

Not the way to think, he chastised sternly. *That last-night business.* There might just as well be more nights. Someday he and Rosalind would be able to meet again, flesh to flesh, with no clothes to get in the way, and not a black heart between them. They would take up where they had left off.

He'd confess how much she meant to him as he entered her blistering heat, feeling her arms wrapped around him and hearing her murmur of approval. She'd be his, and he hers, their bodies and their souls finally free to fully explore an almost mystical union unfettered by the chains of DNA that had tangled things up.

Believing in that future seemed to be the only way for him to get through the next twenty-four hours.

Rosalind's eyes met his. Gray eyes that were bottomless and seductive. The pull of that seduction was like a soft tug on his wounded soul.

Meet me, her eyes invited. *Find me.*

And in that instant, Colton's heart, mind, body and soul, despite all the arguments to the contrary, and with the full backing of his beast, agreed that he would.

Rosalind rubbed at her ankle, free now of the chain, thanks to the Landaus. The livid red ring of burned skin had already faded in the past hour, though the spot still stung.

The bruises on her shins were a dark blue, and gave her the speckled appearance of a leopard, rather than a wolf. She'd forgotten about the pain already.

Filled with barely contained energy, she circled the rug on the floor in the room the Landaus had given her. Colton hadn't come inside. He was supposed to be standing guard, but other Weres were sharing that job, setting up a physical wall of muscle and bone and grit around her.

Colton's restlessness beat at her, adding fuel to her own anxiety. "Come on," she whispered to the window, insanely expecting the white wulf to reply.

She tore at her borrowed clothes, stripped to naked skin and tossed the discards in a corner, needing to be free and to breathe. The sun would soon rise. She guessed there was less than an hour of darkness left in what felt like an endless night. She dreaded the coming of daylight. She had never seen Colton in the sun. Both of them were somehow tied to darkness.

Would he still love her when that darkness had fled?

"Colton. Where are you?"

Close to the windowsill, and with the memory of what use she had made of a window the last time she had been a guest in this house, Rosalind peered out. She stayed there until her shoulders complained and her head began to throb.

"White wulf, do you hear me?"

Would the monsters ignore her, if Colton could? If she didn't have the ability to call a lover, what chance did she have against the rest of the world?

Something like anger stirred in her stomach. Her beast, maybe. Possibly it was the Death-caller she imagined to be like a beast and taking up space.

Scared of what that might mean, Rosalind clamped her teeth together so that the fangs would have no room to expand. Anger was the providence of vampires. She wasn't one of them.

Again, there was movement inside her, and she swore out loud. If the Death-caller was trying to tell her something, she didn't want to listen. If she knew ahead of time how this would turn out, and how many good Weres might lose their lives, she might not follow through.

The skin on the nape of her neck prickled and chilled up. Balmy Miami breezes exerted an unusually weighty pressure that made her nerve endings burn.

She blinked slowly as her heart began to rev.

Her muscles went rigid.

And she knew instinctively, as her legs finally crumpled beneath her, that Colton had come.

Chapter 28

Her white-haired lover appeared on the sill, looking like a real ghost; a fierce, feral werewolf in man form. The look in his eyes told her of his desire to swallow her whole.

He had somehow reached the third-floor window and wasn't breathing hard from the effort. He was half in and half out of the window, crouched in the space he crammed his generous bulk into. They stared at each other in silence. The tension building between them made Rosalind sway.

"I hoped you would come," she finally said in a husky tone.

He didn't move.

"You have doubts," she said, having to put that out there to get things he might be feeling that they'd never actually faced into the open.

"Yes," he said. "Doubts."

"You're not sure about the vampire traits I've adopted, or that have adopted me. Is that it? Fangs like mine hurt your loved ones."

He leaned into the room, closer to her.

"Because I have fangs and can perceive monsters with similar ones doesn't mean I can read their thoughts," she explained. "If they even have thoughts."

He waited for her to go on, probably sensing she would.

"I've been a rebel in most ways because of an energy too boundless to contain. It's there now, pushing me, encouraging me. Beast or spirit, that energy tells me that I must be near you."

She watched a muscle in Colton's right cheek twitch.

"It could be that the monsters simply sense my attraction to you and want you out of the way, as my father suggested. And it also might be that you were their target all along by belonging to an old Were family, and I'm the one in the way. Since we can't ask the monsters about their objectives, there's only one way to find out what their agenda is."

"By going after them," he said.

"Yes. I'm not really like them. You know that. But I can't have this hanging over me, and over us. I hate it all. Don't you imagine I'd like to be normal, like the rest of the Weres out there?"

Her confession moved him, and also possibly hurt him in some way. Her ghost unfolded himself and stepped into the room with an understanding light in his pale eyes. In spite of his formidable size and the fact that he now bore signs of the same strength and power she had first noticed in that blasted park before his injuries, his expression softened. When he looked at her lovingly, a groan of relief escaped through her lips.

"If I didn't care so much," he said, "none of this would matter. Can it be fate that brought us together? Some sort of metaphysical trick that we aren't even aware of? Something in me has found something in you that I've been searching for, and vice versa, that runs as deep as our DNA? Hell, I'd like to think of it like that. Who wouldn't want to believe that spirits continue on in the ones we love, and that true love can find us in a world this large?"

Although Colton hadn't touched her, Rosalind felt the heat of his gaze. Warmth had never seemed so close, while at the same time unattainable. If they were to physically meet tonight and she were to become more like him than she already was, her unique connection to the monsters might lessen or be lost altogether. If she couldn't key in to the bloodsuckers' location, everyone here would be at a loss.

As she saw it, she stood at the edge of a cliff with her toes hanging over, wanting Colton desperately and knowing how desperately he wanted her in return. The short distance separating them hummed with the frantic energy of withholding themselves from having what they needed most. Physical contact, and the signal to go ahead and take what they could, while they could.

"Can't you sleep?" he asked gently, looking to the bed.

"I'm afraid to shut my eyes," she confessed.

"What if I'm here beside you?"

"Won't that be the ruin of us both?"

"I'm your guard dog, Rosalind. Tomorrow will test our strength. You need some rest before tomorrow arrives."

"I have never been stronger," she whispered. *Another confession, and something you might not know.*

She went on before he could address her remark. "I'm attempting to contain the power surges that rise and fall inside me without my permission. I'm not sure where these surges are coming from or where their origins lie. Maybe all the different parts of me—all those monstrous traits—are vying for dominance. I have a war going on inside me, Colton, and can't take much more. Moving eases the urge to throw myself out of that window."

"Then I will have to distract you," he said.

She replied earnestly, "I wish you could." *But you can't. You won't. You're honorable, even now.*

Breath had become the thing uniting them lately; his warm breath on her face that shouted to her of how close he was. Her slow, exhaled sigh mingled sensuously with his in the open, and without their mouths having to meet.

As she faced him, the moment seemed suspended in time. Both of them wanted to give in to the urges. Just one move would crash the barrier they had erected, whether by accident or on purpose.

"Rationalization versus needs," he said. "We can't even console each other properly. But we're here, together. We're alive and surrounded by allies, and tomorrow might be a turning point. That will have to do for now."

He didn't believe this. His eyes told her that. They were wide, shining and surrounded by dark circles that were remnants of a pain that would never fully leave him. She had become a part of that pain.

Yet she looked deeply into Colton's eyes, tilting her head back to do so. "That's the difference between us," she said. "I've always been greedy, and have required more than what my life had to offer me."

Howl to howl. That's what had brought them together

and sealed the deal, Rosalind thought. *Spirit calling to spirit*. Those spirits were wresting the willpower from them both right here. Right now.

The dark thing in her soul did a slow turn, bringing up the image of an ancient memory she couldn't quite see. Was it this Were's image, and what lay inside him? Is that what the spirit in her was trying to tell her? That it was all right to give in, and that neither of them had to be strong all the time?

"It won't let up," she said, breaking off eye contact and hanging her head. "If you stay, it won't be in that window. Not for long."

His lips were inches from hers. She knew the feel of their fullness and the moistness within; knew she shouldn't do what her heart told her to do, and that there might be consequences. But the dark thing nestled inside her urged her to rebel this one last time. When joined with the wishes of her own spirit, that urge was too great to ignore.

She stood, and rose onto tiptoe.

Reaching up, taking hold of Colton's soft white hair with both of her hands, she pulled his lips to hers.

Chapter 29

Rosalind was liquid fire, blazing flames, raging desire in the shape of a woman. How could he stand against that?

The animal in Colton wanted more. The spirit in Rosalind demanded it. Through her tantalizing lips Colton felt the core of heat that awaited him. He had never experienced anything like this, not even with her, and was willing to accept the damage that might result.

It was absolutely necessary to reach that heat.

He closed his eyes, giving in to the shape and texture of her with all of his senses. Below his waist, he was already erect and aching. His beast was excitedly calling to hers. *All due to a kiss. This kiss. The culmination of so many withheld feelings.*

Their hands met near his thighs. Her fingers brushed over his. As she slid her tongue between his lips, her hand moved between their bodies to the hardness pressing against her. The murmur of her pleasure turned him on, drove him on, made him realize that he loved her with a fury that bordered on obscene.

She was already naked. Sensuously, seductively naked.

As the kiss deepened, Rosalind's sharp nails tore at his shirt, scratching his chest, leaving a sting. As if his partial bareness wasn't enough to satisfy her, her hands then sought the waistband of his pants. He heard the buttons pop.

Riled up and unable to wait much longer for what was going to happen, and what was inevitable, Colton pushed her hot hands aside and lifted her up. He'd always had this same compulsion to hold her.

Their bodies, locked together, crashed to the carpet. He rolled her over onto her back, reveling in the slender angles so sharp beneath him.

Her sinewy arms wrapped around his rippling back, hugging him close, assuring he wouldn't change his mind.

Never in a million years would he have changed it.

She gasped once, and growled low in her throat as if she needed air, but he didn't want to let up or let her go.

He took his mouth from hers for a span of seconds to allow her that breath, and looked into her eyes when she took it. White lashes made the gray irises seem lighter. Masses of tangled white hair framed her face. Long white strands spilled across the floor like rays of moonlight. These were ghostly signs. Symptoms of their intimacy.

They were his fault.

He came back to her when she flashed a smile, but he couldn't smile back. And when Rosalind ran her tongue across his chin in a slick downward slide that ended at his neck, then lightly bit into his flesh with her little white fangs, waves of surprised pleasure shot through both man and beast that made thoughts about promises and honor useless.

"Is that all you've got?" he asked as he stoked the curve of Rosalind's bare thigh with his fingers, inching them toward the heavenly place he would soon lose himself in if anything in the world would allow it; thinking that if he didn't get there soon, he might lose his mind.

"Not all I've got," she whispered with her head thrown back. "Not nearly everything."

Her voice was thick and incomparably sexy. Colton spread her legs with his. *For good or ill, we have jumped that boundary.* Whatever happened next, they were both equally to blame.

Her thighs were inferno-hot. He reached her soft, feminine folds without taking his gaze from hers. Dipping one finger inside her to test her readiness was nearly his undoing.

Just as it was hers.

Rosalind arched her back, lifting her breasts precariously close to his mouth. Her smooth skin was luminous in the darkened room and as pale as the meager light slanting through the window.

Soon, Colton thought fleetingly as he ran his tongue over the valley between her breasts, the moon would hand the sky over to her golden competitor. Sunrise was fast approaching.

They had so little time left. Not enough for taking one delicate pink bud of her nipple into his mouth, or removing his pants. "I'm sorry about that," he said.

Rosalind's eyes widened when he unleashed himself and settled between her legs. She opened her mouth as if she'd cry out when he pierced her petal-soft folds and slipped his cock inside her. But she didn't make a sound.

She writhed beneath him, sending her hips upward, and he had to withdraw, wait, hold on. His muscles shook with the effort.

Rosalind held him tighter.

His slight retreat shook him to the marrow, and made him colder. This isn't what they wanted. *No retreat.*

"More," Rosalind whispered, as if she had read his mind.

Harder. Faster. Now, she was demanding.

He sank into her again, knowing he belonged there and that he was claiming her for his own. His next thrust shot through her with a burning intensity that robbed them both of breath. He pulsed inside her, feeling her rush of sweet, blistering heat rain down to meet him.

Again, he plunged into her soft, warm silk. And again after that, caressing Rosalind from the inside out, each stroke more potent than the one before.

Deeper he went, feeling impossibly hard and long, until all thoughts about time vanished—blown away by the way Rosalind openly and unconditionally accepted him and the smoldering power in this union.

She met the beating of his hips with thrusts of hers. The sound of their bodies meeting filled the room with dull slapping echoes. Her heated legs wrapped around him like a fleshy velvet vice, making it more difficult for him to pull back.

Her hands were again in his hair, and on his shoulders. Her fingernails, like claws, raked his upper back.

He felt their wulfs connect in that mystical union that took them down to another layer of being. The soul of the wulf and the soul of a man were together and meeting their match, their refuge, their sanctuary, in Rosalind. The sensation was overwhelmingly complex, and had to be even more unimaginable for her, since she housed not only two spirits, but also a third.

If he was lost, so was she.

She came back for a kiss, and sucked his lips between hers. Her canines pinched his tongue, so that he tasted blood.

Colton squeezed his muscles and plunged in and out of his lover with a demonic force. He had been seeking this all his life, and perhaps, if the whole spirit theory was true, even longer. They weren't just two bodies merging; they were starving souls bringing life back, full circle.

Their spirits were anchored by an intimacy beyond the imagination…in a place where hunger was everything. Theirs was a relationship that wove mind, body and spirit into a braided whole.

Too soon, he found that place in her he had desperately needed to reach. *So hot. So very tight.* With a final push backed by all of his need and condoned by his wulf, he hit Rosalind's molten core and burst, drowning that core with a heat of his own and feeling as if the night had swallowed them both.

Rosalind, her mouth still clamped to his, screamed. That scream went on and on as her climax hit and stretched, and as he held her there.

God, was Colton's final oath when he could breathe again. *I'm home.*

The room had grown quiet. No breeze stirred the curtains or ruffled his hair as Colton stood at the foot of the bed like some sort of angelic sentinel, observing Rosalind.

He had counted every ragged breath she took in, and noted each flutter of her eyelids, until her eyes finally stayed closed sometime after dawn.

He talked to her then, whispering tender endearments as he kept watch, and fighting the constant yearning to lie down beside her.

The room smelled of open windows, warm sheets and hot, spent bodies. It smelled of wulf, of sex, and hardly like anything human. Rosalind's heat still warmed his veins, though his muscles were stiff from standing.

He waited until the sun rose before finally flexing his shoulders. He crossed to the window to see if Weres still roamed in the yard, knowing that daylight hours would allow them an overdue rest in preparation for tonight's show of strength.

Eventually, he'd also have to sit down, eat something, shut his eyes. But he didn't see how he could do any of those things when Rosalind looked so small lying there. In sleep, it was difficult to see the brave, supernatural entity she had become in the outline of a young woman curled up in a fetal position.

She smelled like him, he thought as his lips hovered longingly above hers for what seemed like the millionth time. But with the rising sun came a warning protest from his beast.

It was time to leave her.

He looked at her again, wishing for just one more minute. Her face was healing with incredible speed. Only a smooth pink line hinted at where the shard of glass had penetrated her cheek.

"There's enough Lycan left in you to access our healing powers. You'll be glad to know that, my love," he crooned.

Rosalind's face and hands were the only naked parts of her visible. A blanket covered the rest. The heady allure of those small areas—the length of her slender fingers, the sculpted edge of her jaw—drove him crazy. That same madness brought his beast in and out of focus as all parts of him lusted for the woman on the bed.

"Oh, yes, there has to be a next time. We'll see to it."

For werewolves, sex wasn't taken lightly. But slowness, carefulness, tenderness required discipline that only real love necessitated. And he'd come to love Rosalind with every fiber of his being.

"There's no mistake about that."

He ignored the knock at the door that came a few hours after dawn, and murmured a stream of assurances to Rosalind to cover the sound. Twice, he layered her with more blankets to calm her shudders, unable to close the window that was his only means of escape.

In Miami, chills like the ones covering Rosalind, if she were human, would be an indication of illness. In her, it was a manifestation of her internal tug-of-war.

"If I have hurt you, I'm sorry," he said.

She moved a leg, and made a troubled sound. Time, for Rosalind, was speeding toward what lay ahead.

When her father called out from the hallway, Colton glanced up from his place at Rosalind's side, surprised to find that the sun had again set, and that he had somehow missed an entire day.

"Open the door," Kirk said.

It was almost time. How many Weres would fall, in their honor, a few hours from now? he wondered.

The jangle of keys in the hallway made Colton wince. "Rosalind," he murmured.

Whatever spirit forced her to open her eyes gazed up

at him with deep black pupils. The intensity of her dark-eyed scrutiny caused his internal pressure to expand and his wulf to utter a growl through his too-human throat.

"Go now," she said, moving bloodless lips.

Rosalind was now whiter than white. He saw that clearly now, where he hadn't before. She'd become an albino, like him. Their lovemaking session had drained all remaining color from her. Every last bit.

He swore again, though he couldn't allow himself to feel guilty. The night had been necessary on so many levels for them both. They had both known there might be consequences.

"Eat something," he said, wanting to keep this news from her, and fighting the necessity of a parting. He wished more than anything to see her smile, and hear her laugh. "Eat for strength," he said. "And I don't mean little children."

He took the fact that her lips upturned as a good omen, sure it would be a terrible thing for them all if Banshees didn't have a sense of humor.

With a last lingering look at her, a heartfelt glance, he cleared his throat and said in a gravelly tone, "I'll be close." Then he headed for the window and passed through it, to the night beyond.

Colton landed on the grass in a crouch, both hands and one knee on the ground, and waited to hear the sound of bones breaking. When that didn't happen, he stood up.

Daylight had indeed passed. The light at the front of Landau's house hurt his sensitive eyes when he rounded the corner.

Someone was on the porch. He was glad to see that it was a female, and not Landau or Rosalind's father. Matt Wilson's mate got to her feet. "Jenna James, in case you missed my name last night," she said, holding up a plate covered by a dishcloth. "I saved this for you."

Colton glanced to the door.

"Some of them are inside, and some are on the walls," Jenna explained. "Landau can't leave the place unmanned when we go."

"We?" he said.

"You can read wulf minds a little, right?" she countered.

"What would make you assume that I can?"

"I'm a doctor trained to read facial expression and body language. I'm also a Were, and a female. We're better at knowing these things."

He took the plate gratefully and sat on the step, not sure he'd be able to keep anything down, but aware of the fact that he needed sustenance.

"I can't read minds," he said. "Sometimes I hear thoughts if they're loud enough. The more I heal, the more I hear, if I try."

"Then you probably know they're waiting inside to speak to you."

"Loud and clear," he said.

The door opened behind him with a crack of its metal bolts. He didn't whirl or greet the newcomer.

"She's gone," Jared Kirk announced angrily. "Rosalind is gone."

The crash of the plate hitting the step was the only other thing Colton heard as he faced Rosalind's father.

Chapter 30

Wildness had encompassed her. A violent impulse to surrender to the darkness rose in Rosalind's chest, throat and mouth. *Give up*, those impulses commanded. *Give in.*

She was pure spirit, but also a mixture of several things. At the moment, she felt like a creature of the air as she fled the need for food, for company and the ravenous desire to belong to Colton, body and soul. Once she had let go of those things, she became lighter, freer. As she walked, her feet barely touched the ground.

Without a trailing parade of Weres, she headed toward a foreign place. She veered far from the park and the Landaus, following the bits of information she had gleaned from the mind of one of the she-wulfs present on the lawn the night before.

"Fairview." That's what the place was called. It was an odd name for a building that housed mental anomalies, but that's where she'd call the creatures that had been seeking Colton or herself. That's where she'd make a stand, and find out what was behind everything that had happened so far.

She hadn't showered or dressed. The bloodsuckers would smell her lover on her bare skin. Would they come flying out of the shadows? Spring up from hidden fissures underground? Would several more of them mean that hordes of vampires were heading to the city every day, drawn by whatever ruled their nasty appetites?

"Tonight, Death calls to only a few."

Rosalind hesitated when those words came out, surprised. The thought hadn't been hers. The Death-caller had spoken through her.

She swallowed an oath and kept going, already feeling the attention of the monsters that likely sensed her just as easily as she had them. After experiencing Colton's beautiful warmth, the chill of vampires made her stomach turn over.

She flowed through the grounds of estate after estate, silencing hounds with a glare and evading security systems with no setting for spirits. She had outwitted the Weres and had gone off without them, leaving behind the men who were grounded by the heaviness of their beasts that had no full moon to free them.

Those Weres had been chained to the assumption that she'd wait for them because of their offer to help. None of them understood that it was for precisely that reason—their honor and the offer of aid—that she had left them behind.

On the sidelines, Weres did their best to help everyone. They fought secret battles so that humans and decent werewolves could walk openly almost anywhere they chose to. Landau and his pack were prime examples of those selfless few. Colton and Dana Delmonico, as police officers, were exemplary souls among them.

Colton...whose love gave her wings.

Yes, she sent to the monsters in the shadows grabbing hold of her trail. "Come to me," she beckoned. "Follow."

The building she had been searching for finally came into view. Fairview Hospital was a tall brick square emanating a faint odor of disinfectant. It sat in the middle of a large expanse of forested acreage, by itself, at the end of a long, winding road.

The building and its small courtyard looked to be immaculately cared for, and was surrounded by a six-foot chain-link fence. Frosted lights on posts near the entrance and farther down the driveway were the only sources of illumination, other than the moon.

There was no doubt about Fairview's strangeness and the necessity of it being removed from the city proper. Spirits inside the building wanted to answer her calls for monsters to follow. Though most of the beings inside were human, their minds temporarily expanded by trancelike states, a very small percentage were only humanlike, and bothered by demons of their own. And in there somewhere a Were male watched over them all, tending to lost souls with the calmness of a guardian angel.

Fairview wasn't a bad place, in spite of the pain inside it. Too bad that didn't make her feel any better.

Rosalind stopped with a hand on the fence to listen before moving on. She took in great gulps of air, processing its components.

Gone now was the salty smell of the ocean, so prevalent at Landau's house. A musty green odor of uncut grass

and old trees took the place of swaying palms and mani-
cured parkland. Aside from those things, and removed
from the hospital's smells, she detected an undercurrent
of stale blood.

The vampires had arrived.

Moving clear of the fence, Rosalind turned her face
into the sour bloodsucker scent. Her claws and fangs
sprung simultaneously as she tossed off a shudder of
distaste.

She walked toward the trees, not half as scared as she
supposed she should have been when whatever happened
here would determine the fate of so many.

The vampires' closeness rolled over her until her teeth
began to chatter. Her heart amped up its rhythm, thun-
dered; that beat as loud as if it were planted inside an
echo chamber.

She stopped with a hand on her chest, startled by what
felt like a new dual beat, and spun in place, searching
the dark for the cause of this phenomenon. She zeroed
in on a stretch of grass near the gnarled trees lining an
unused dirt road.

No. She shook her head as an intimately familiar scent
reached her.

"No!" she shouted, her body quaking as if something
inside her was trying to break loose. "Not you!"

There was no time to focus on who else was heading her way. The surface of her skin began to chill. Her
throat felt full. It was an all-too-familiar reaction, telling her that the beast and the other thing inside her also
recognized the scent.

It was the fragrance of wulf.

The dark thing inside her moved. It wanted to become

lost in that scent as much as she did, and began to heave its way upward, its darkness seeping out of her pores.

Rosalind growled and clenched her teeth. She shook her head to ward off this aggressive spirit's rise. But it was too late. Darkness had colored her white skin a deep, glossy black.

A cry escaped her, and there was no withholding what she had in the past so forcefully tamped down. The spirit she housed sought freedom, needing that freedom to proceed with whatever it had in mind.

The Banshee, the Death-caller, took her over with a terrible swiftness, forcing Rosalind to open her mouth wide. The sound she made filled the night—an awful wail that was both hers and the Death-caller's flung outward in unison. That shrill cry went on and on, creating waves in the air that shook the leaves on the trees.

It was a prediction. The Death-caller, long dormant, had come forth to do what it had been created to do... and that was to announce the coming of Death.

Trembling, Rosalind turned in time to watch the first batch of bloodsuckers reach the field. Their gaunt, corpse-pale faces shone like dry bones under a moon that wasn't theirs to blaspheme.

The walking dead rushed toward her, attracted to the darkness of her freed spirit, ignorant that the call had been an invitation to their final repose by an entity that knew this for a fact.

Rosalind whirled and tried to focus, but her attention was shattered by an intensifying acknowledgment of a wulf closing in.

From beneath the overhanging branches of the nearby trees, a white blur raced toward her, moving so fast, Rosalind couldn't track it. She knew what it was.

Ghost.

Half wolf, half man, Colton came on in all his silver-white werewolf glory, fully muscled up and growling fiercely.

"I would have saved you from this," she whispered to him.

He looked like fury personified, and moved like liquid motion—as fluid as mist, and raging silently with an incredible power that made his fur stand up. Like a battering ram, the ghost wulf plowed into the ragged line of oncoming vampires, snapping his teeth, cutting them down.

He kept running as the bloodsuckers he met disappeared in storms of black blood and ash. The sound of his heartbeat filled Rosalind's ears. His rage burned in her breast. She wasn't alone. Colton had come here, not because she needed saving, but to stand by her side.

Again, she became buoyant. A rush of heat replaced the ungodly chill. Her bones realigned in one smooth wave. Sinew snapped a new shape into existence. Her skin began to melt away, leaving fur in its place. White fur. And then she was running with a rhythm in her legs that kept pace with the hum of fast-approaching cars.

The white werewolf hit vampire after vampire with incredible force. Cries of rage went up as the vampires were scattered, now aware of the ghost whose presence was like a swinging hammer among them.

Shouts answered their cries, along with the awful sounds of bodies hitting bodies that made Rosalind hesitate in the middle of a vamp-killing strike. The Weres had come, had found her, and were taking up her fight.

Landau's pack had jumped from their cars, ready to rumble, but she sensed the curiosity that made them turn their eyes to her and to Colton—two white werewolves who had changed without the help of a full moon; ghostly beings, lethal, and weaving through the vampires as if they had been born for fighting.

Rosalind felt the brush of a hand at her throat. That slight touch made her melt again into another shape. A human shape with a fanged mouth, her skin blackened by the Banshee's second rise as a dominant force.

It was a new bit of insight that the Death-caller inside her wanted no part of the wulf.

She bit at the vampire next to her, ripping the hand from its arm, and moved in time to duck a deadly blow. There was fighting all around her. Without a full moon, the Weres stuck in human form were slashing at vampires with knives and loosing arrows from crossbows that took the place of wooden stakes.

Strike after strike hit home. Vampires went down. But it didn't matter to her what they did around her. The spirit inside her didn't see the deaths of those Weres tonight.

Only her own.

Stunned by this realization, Rosalind paused in the center of a vortex of fighting. She felt Colton's heartbeat tune to hers, then noticed that he'd also stopped moving. He lowered his claws. In slow motion, he turned to face her.

Chapter 31

Rosalind was looking at him with large unblinking eyes, Colton realized. Her outline wavered between wulf, vampire and human, failing to settle on any one thing.

She was confused.

He knew the feeling.

But Rosalind seemed to be lit from within, as if going through so many changes at once had created an energy flux that manifested as electricity. Blue sparks hugged her body in a sparkling aura. Against the darkness surrounding her, Rosalind looked like some sort of supernatural light show.

The only feature that didn't morph was her face. That face was damp and strained by exertion, and more beautiful than anything he had ever seen. So damn beautiful, he wanted to fall on his knees before her.

She opened her mouth. From her throat came a sound

that was low-pitched, unearthly, and it made Colton turn
from her. She had wailed moments ago and the vampires
had come for her. Now, he realized, she was announcing a newcomer.

A mixture of tastes hit him. As if he'd taken a bite
of something nasty, dirt, ash and the fire of what might
have been mythical brimstone stuck in this throat; a terrible, poisonous concoction that had no place on earth.

Rustling sounds on the grass beat at his nerve endings. The Weres who had made good headway against
the vampires had also noticed the newcomers and were
gearing up for a second battle.

But demons had to be infinitely harder to get rid of
than a nest of vampires on the rampage, Colton thought.
And demons were up next.

"Rosalind," he said.

She heard him. When he looked, her body was swaying from side to side. Her long hair, reaching to her waist,
blew in an unnatural wind caused by the fury of all those
sparks she was giving off.

One lone, dark strand, however, had survived the color
change to white. Crossing her pale features from her
forehead to her chin, the darkness accentuated the line
between her wulf's will and the lure of her other spirit.

She looked strong and courageous, angry and demented. But it wasn't Rosalind who looked at him with
big black eyes.

"Who are you?" Colton asked without closing the distance that lay between them. "What did you do with Rosalind?"

The entity turned her head to glance past him. It…
she…closed her eyes, shook her head and shifted shape
into the blackest thing he could have imagined. His

enemy, and Rosalind's. The kind of monster that had changed them both in the short span of one bleak night. *Vampire*.

She didn't attack, or run. She raised her face to search the night sky. From her fanged mouth came an ear-shattering sound that sent her blue sparks outward, and hurt Colton's ears.

Only peripherally aware of what was going on around them, Colton noticed that the fighting had slowed. There were less than a handful of vampires left, and all of the Weres who had ventured to stand against them remained. He saw none of the demons he knew slid through the shadows in the periphery. For some reason, they were keeping well back.

The vampires stopped fighting suddenly and without warning. Had Rosalind called them off with the awful sound she'd made?

Would they run to her, if they could? Would they run away, recognizing the hammer about to fall?

In their confused hesitation, those bloodsuckers were felled by the Weres, down to the last bloody fang. Without registering the carnage around her, Rosalind shape-shifted again. In place of the vampire hybrid stood a creature Colton had seen only once before, in his parents' backyard. *Demon*.

It felt to him as though there were only two of them in the field—he and Rosalind in her current incarnation—when in actuality they had an audience. Colton sensed the Weres warily gathering around them. Ragged and bloodstained, they were waiting to see if any other devilish creatures would turn up, and holding their breath.

Rosalind was a sight, and as scary as anything else that hell had spewed up tonight. She looked like one of the absent demonic brood, with skin that was yellow, withered and cracked. A ribbon of blood, black against the sallow face, ran down her chin. Her eyes were bloodred.

"Where are they?" Colton asked, knowing the demons had to be close. Rosalind's effervescent sparks had turned crimson.

Everyone readied for a new onslaught, though no one actually moved. And then Rosalind did. She lifted an arm in a gesture that invited the demons to join her, and they obeyed, pouring in from every direction at once.

But there were only six scaly, two-legged nightmares. A meager showing. They appeared to be part human, part reptile, and several things that Colton didn't care to think about. The ugly bastards had no eyes, and seemed to be bound together by the evil purpose they served.

The demons flocked to Rosalind like rats to the Piper, attracted by the voice, the sight of her, and her dark scent. Unable to resist such darkness, and seemingly mindless in their bedazzled state, they were extremely vulnerable. They were fools.

The Weres attacked with a force that filled the silence. Shots were fired; so many gunshots that Colton couldn't keep count. The demons hadn't been prepared for sabotage, when evil was their master. They had to have believed that Rosalind was one of them.

Muffled vibrations of leathery flesh being rent in the dark produced the rumble of an oncoming storm system. Colton could not watch. He had eyes for only one entity, and wanted Rosalind back.

Rosalind's demon spirit's eyeless gaze rose to meet his. Brilliant scarlet sparks reflected on the surface of skin that again began to morph.

He felt the tension and anxiousness of the Weres sidling closer. There was no time to tell them about the information they didn't have. He knew better than to expect another round of creatures this night. Rosalind had been visited by two species of monsters lately, and she had used two shapes to call them to their deaths. Two species. Only those. The spirit inside her had accomplished what she had come here to do. She had rid the area of harmful creatures, and in doing so, had seen to it that Rosalind was safe.

Maybe, Colton rationalized, this Banshee wasn't an evil spirit at all. And maybe this Death-caller didn't want to harm the Lycans.

If Jared Kirk's story had been true, this spirit had saved the woman she had been slated to call to her death so that that woman could mate with a Were.

What did that mean for Rosalind now?

He had to use every brain cell to work that information to his advantage.

"I believe you have one more in there," Colton said, facing Rosalind and nearly breathless, his arms raising in an open invitation. "And if truth be told, I prefer no colorful, sparkling auras at all, other than the ones created by what I'd like to do to you, and with you, in the near future."

He wanted to shout when the sparks wafted away and Rosalind's outline returned as if she had simply faded back into existence.

Colton wanted to close his eyes and give thanks for this brief sight of his lovely, wounded lover. But this wasn't over yet.

She was separated from him by less than ten feet. None of the Weres who had fought by her side, and for her, dared to go near her or get any closer, now that the night had again grown quiet and their enemies had been vanquished.

Rosalind continued to stare at him soundlessly.

"Also," he went on gently, "I have a soft spot for fur. Any color might do, really, though my favorite lately has been black. A deep, true, midnight black that's silky and exotic to the touch, and quite rare. Do you know anyone that description might fit?"

"Not anymore," she whispered.

Colton's heart stirred in his chest. They had made contact. It was a good sign.

"Second to that, I like werewolves with white fur," he said. "I could easily make do with someone who looks like that, as long as she had large, expressive green eyes. But mark my words, Rosalind, it has to be a Were. My mate has to be a she-wulf, and not any other kind of creature. We have to be a perfect fit, you see."

"That's a long list," Rosalind said tonelessly.

"Yes, well, I have looked Death in the eye on a couple of occasions, and want the time I have left to be special until I have to face it again. I want that time to be shared with someone special. That person is you. Who else would have me, like this?"

Fearing to move toward her, Colton opened his arms. *Rosalind*, he silent called. *Please come.*

He saw that she couldn't, and felt what was holding her back. The black presence that had wailed and called to the freaks who wished her harm still sat within Rosalind, on guard and carefully watching him.

"Can I speak to the Death-caller?" he asked, dropping his hands to his sides. Without waiting for a reply, he said, "I'm told that you know me, spirit."

Rosalind lowered her gaze. Her cheeks were hollow, her face haunted.

His eyes fixed on her. "We have you to thank for the warnings, Death-caller. We've heard your story and have seen what you can do. But it's time to let Rosalind go. It's time for her to live her own life."

The black eyes again looked up.

"Rosalind is flesh and blood," he said. "Though you might have loved her family, and might love her, you must see that she needs to be with her own kind. If she isn't allowed to be what she is meant to be, what's left for her?"

The spirit was listening, and hopefully understanding. Colton watched with fascination as a single tear slid down her pale cheek.

His heart stirred restlessly as he continued, groping for the right words to express himself. "I'm sorry. I don't know if you can leave her. I have no idea what leaving Rosalind would mean for you as a spirit. But I'll help if I can, and if that's possible. I love her, too, and will do whatever it takes to care for her. You know my feelings are true because you also recognize the blood that runs through my veins. Isn't that right? We supposed that's why Rosalind and I found each other—because you made sure that we did."

Rosalind's head shook. It was her voice that said, "Yes. She knows you. But she can't leave me. Being tucked inside my family's bloodline is her penance for disturbing the natural flow of life and death. She will pass through my line for an eternity."

"Then I don't care who is in there if you, Rosalind, are with me. I'll take all of you. Every last part."

She shook her head again. "I can't touch you like this."

Sadness rang in her remark. "What sort of life would we have?"

"Try," Colton suggested. "Reach out to me and see what happens."

"If I do, I might see things I don't want to see. I might know the time and place of your death. I have already seen mine."

"Yours?" he repeated. "What do you mean?"

"I die tonight. I've seen this."

Colton processed that, refusing to allow the confession to make sense. A streak of pure agony nearly derailed the next idea that came to him. He was grasping at straws, with the odds stacked against him. But he could not lose Rosalind.

He had to try everything, and study every angle.

"Maybe," he began, moving toward her, "you only think you will die. Maybe what you think of as Rosalind will be gone, while the real Rosalind will continue to breathe. Couldn't the death you saw merely be a metamorphosis of some kind?" He added after a breath, "Like going from a potential Night Wulf to a...ghost of one?"

Though Rosalind hadn't lowered her gaze, he sensed another energy fluctuation going on inside her. She was considering what he'd suggested.

"You're already no longer in danger of becoming a real Night Wulf, even if you were destined to be such a thing," he said, gambling on that in order to hold her attention. "There's no chance of a black heart taking over your chest, not with the spirit's presence inside you."

Colton cleared his throat to rid himself of the lump making speech difficult. He was desperate to have his theory proved right. He had to remain calm.

"I'm not afraid of you, Rosalind, or of any information you might turn up."

Stepping closer to her, Colton searched for the trace of moistness that had tracked down her cheek, sure that former hint of sadness had come from the spirit, who had to understand exactly what was going on.

"I've already walked Death's line, Rosalind. I may be living on borrowed time. What I want is to be with you for a while longer without running and fighting and facing our demons."

Rosalind didn't advance or take him up on his offer to test what remained between them. She appeared to be frozen in place.

"Please," he said, addressing the Banshee still present in the color of Rosalind's eyes. "If you can't let Rosalind go, at least let her have the love she deserves. You have the power to do this. You have done it before."

Probably he hadn't been meant to be a ghost wulf, he reasoned, since it had taken trauma to make him what he now was. But he was growing stronger with each passing night, and no longer felt pain in the same way. The only real pain he felt came from the possibility of losing Rosalind.

What did he have left to go back to, without her?

His changes had been radical. Because of that, it wasn't likely that he would be able to go back to the city and his job. And after what had happened here, fighting crime might seem elementary and mundane.

Still, he saw the folly of his former thought patterns now, surrounded by other Weres who had witnessed the unveiling of his secrets and Rosalind's secrets, and had aided in this fight with no questions asked. Like true friends. Like family.

He allowed his attention to momentarily drift.

Dylan Landau was there, his clothing torn and his expression one of concern. His mate, Miami PD's Dana Delmonico, was beside Dylan and naked, preferring, he supposed, to give in to her animal nature now that she had stumbled upon it.

Detective Matt Wilson stood behind Rosalind with his hand on the shoulder of the auburn-haired female who had offered Colton a plate of food and the use of her field.

Farther back, away from the rest, a furred-up Lycan female's stunning red pelt glowed in the moonlight, patchy with the dark blood of the two monstrous species she had helped to take down. That she-wulf's eyes glowed with green fire.

He had to stare at that red wulf, who was in wulf form without the moon guiding her to it. He shouldn't have been surprised about he and Rosalind not being the only Lycans with this gift.

He couldn't think now about the many surprises that had rocked the night. What he was feeling, in that moment, came darn close to sudden enlightenment. He had learned something here: a big lesson about trust, honor and the need for friends. And he had learned that one terrible sorrow didn't necessarily have to piggyback on another.

He accepted the fact that he had, so far, made good on his vow as Rosalind's protector, and therefore might even be well on his way to redeeming himself. Surely that had to score him some points with whoever was watching this from above...or through Rosalind's eyes?

"Try, Rosalind," he repeated, taking another step in her direction, and hoping she would meet him halfway. "Trust me, my love. Touch me."

The will of all the others present aided his request. The night virtually hummed with their hopes for him, and for this. Beneath the fierceness, werewolves were romantics at heart.

When Rosalind took a step, the buzz of ideas and hopes in Colton's head ceased. His heart nearly stopped beating. Having her so close was both frightening and reassuring. His ravenous hunger for Rosalind hadn't lessened one bit.

Rosalind took a second wary step, her expression blank, her eyes downcast, as if she were afraid to look at him.

"Please," he said. "Do this for us. Take a chance. Prove me right."

Her heartbeat began to quicken, matching the swift rise in his. Their gazes reconnected, and through that meeting of their eyes, their thoughts melded together.

This was proof, Colton wanted to shout. The proof of a true connection. She had to feel it, as he did. She had to know what it meant.

"Rosalind," he whispered, barely moving his lips. "Please."

Chapter 32

Rosalind couldn't escape the heartfelt plea in Colton's voice. She couldn't avoid his expression of need.

Torn, she wanted to shout to all the people whose eyes were trained on her. *I'm torn by what you say, and what I fear.*

Yet there was a sudden calmness spreading inside her where there had been only darkness. Although she still felt sick, that sickness had become less of a burden. She had, she now realized, always experienced this same momentary lightness when Colton was around.

The monsters were gone, though she barely remembered what had transpired. She had killed a few, but this was still a fight for her life. She wondered if Colton's theory was correct, and she wasn't going to die. Not in the way she had thought.

He wanted to believe that. So did she. And since she

was still standing after the creatures that had come after her had been taken down, and the spirit she housed had faded to allow her the time to test a love that waited for her if she were able to grasp it, Rosalind accepted the rise of former strengths she hadn't dared to use.

She was Lycan above all. Colton had told her that. And Lycans, early on, had to learn to be masters of their own destinies. She was young in terms of Lycan years, and was part darkness as well as wulf. Learning to control the dark parts was going to be a lesson hard-won. Still, she had a reason to live with what she had been given. Love shone from the eyes across from her. Colton's love, strangely accrued from a series of misfortunes, was not false or feigned.

God, how she loved him back.

She had loved him from the start. At first sight.

The spirit inside her had made this happen. That spirit had wanted it to happen. Maybe, in light of that…she should be thankful. She'd be all right. She'd make this trio within her work out, with her own wishes coming out on top.

Colton held his breath as Rosalind ran the rest of the way and flung herself into his arms. Or maybe it had been the other way around and he had rushed to gather her to him. He couldn't be sure.

His trembling arms closed around her slender body, enfolding her, pulling her tight. As they met, chest to chest and thigh to thigh, he whispered to her with his mouth in her tousled white hair. "I love you, little ghost."

She didn't wail or writhe or violently shift into something else. She didn't fall to the ground in the kind of death she had wrongly foreseen. Yes, it could be said that the old Rosalind had died inch by inch in his arms, he supposed, and that this last embrace was the culmination of that. But if that was so, and the black wulf had ceased to exist, it was not really a death but a transition, a passing from one kind of life to another, and from being alone to having found a soul mate.

He had been right about her ability to survive the many transitions. Maybe the spirit of a Death-caller had bolstered her and then backed off to offer him a hand in gaining a bright, shiny new future. If that were the truth, there was no clear way to thank that spirit directly. And yet that spirit, deep inside Rosalind, would know everything he felt, he supposed, if it was part of her. That spirit would take part in whatever events their future had in store.

He claimed Rosalind's waiting mouth hungrily, greedily, endlessly. Their hands traded explorations that were only the starting point for burning needs finally about to be appeased without interference…at least for now.

The sleek white she-wulf who would always have another strange entity compressed inside her returned his ardor. Her full, pale, quivering mouth clung to his in the manner of a drowning person in need of a lifeline. Like a woman who had to have this one last thing in order to find true happiness. And as though the spirit within her was finally getting what it also deserved and wanted so badly: a shot at happiness.

Then again, maybe those were his own feelings he was projecting onto the she-wulf in his arms.

Gratefully, gladly, aggressively, Colton's hands stroked

Rosalind. They would be on the ground in a minute, or up against a tree, but right then he was content to devour her mouth, savor her taste, become lost in the familiar burn of a love that had spanned the ages.

Rosalind was, hands down, the bravest creature of them all. He vowed never to stop kissing her, ever.

He had no inkling of how much time passed before he rose from her prone body onto his hands and knees, covered with sweat and panting from exertion. Sometime during their wild lovemaking session, the Weres had gone and the night had again grown eerily calm. Not even a breeze stirred the silence. Above them, the moon shone with a silver gleam, but it wasn't full, and its lure came nowhere near to the powerful longing for what he held in his arms.

They were ghosts. Alike. And temporarily, at least, free from marauding monsters that might in the days or months or years ahead return for reasons no one had yet actually discovered—other than dark seeking dark wherever they could find it.

With the ease of a sigh, punctuated by a symphony of bones simultaneously cracking, he and Rosalind, with their limbs still entwined, flowed from one shape to another. With their coats glistening and their muzzles quirking, they leaped to their feet.

But they didn't run to shed the excess energy that made them twice as strong as their human counterparts. Because their wulfs knew what to do with that energy, and were ten times as needy.

Colton growled his pleasure. Rosalind howled once. Raising their faces in unison, they bayed at the moon like their ancestors had done once upon a time, long ago, as they backed into shadows they had once feared for round two…or was it round ten…and to make good on their dreams.

* * * * *

THE WORLD IS BETTER WITH

Romance

Harlequin has everything from contemporary, passionate and heartwarming to suspenseful and inspirational stories.

Whatever your mood, we have a romance just for you!

Love the Harlequin book you just read?

Your opinion matters.

Review this book on your favorite book site, review site, blog or your own social media properties and share your opinion with other readers!

Be sure to connect with us at:
Harlequin.com/Newsletters
Facebook.com/HarlequinBooks
Twitter.com/HarlequinBooks

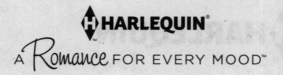

HARLEQUIN®

A *Romance* FOR EVERY MOOD™

Stay up-to-date on all your
romance-reading news with the
Harlequin Shopping Guide,
featuring bestselling authors, exciting new
miniseries, books to watch and more!

The newest issue will be delivered right to you
with our compliments! There are 4 each year.

Signing up is easy.

EMAIL

ShoppingGuide@Harlequin.ca

WRITE TO US

HARLEQUIN BOOKS
Attention: Customer Service Department
P.O. Box 9057, Buffalo, NY 14269-9057

OR PHONE

1-800-873-8635 in the United States
1-888-343-9777 in Canada

Please allow 4-6 weeks for delivery of the first issue by mail.